C000047773

The King's Engraver

A TALE OF ART, ESPIONAGE AND CRIME

CHRIS LETHBRIDGE

A TIME A PLACE A STORY

Copyright © Chris Lethbridge 2023

All rights reserved under International and Pan-American Copyright Conventions.

No part of this publication may be reproduced, distributed or transmitted in any form or by any means, including photocopying, recording, or other electronic or mechanical methods, without the prior written permission of the author or publisher, except in the case of brief quotations embodied in critical reviews.

For Grandfather Harry
He had a way with words

Anonymous preface to
'An impartial and Genuine History &c'
Published 1784.

To trace the various actions of human life
To their source, is beyond human reason;
Each mind has its own bias, and what
Motive is the cause of action, lies solely
In the breast of each individual.
Conjecture is but uncertainty, at the best;
We cannot see into the mind of man;
Therefore words and appearances are all
We have to go by, and by which
We are ever liable to be deceived.

Chapter 1

B reathless, and cradling a bundle wrapped in a shawl, the young
woman bangs at the door until she hears movement inside.

'I knows where Mr W is!' she shouts. 'I knows where e's 'idin!'

The door opens a few inches. An elderly manservant peers into the
early morning light, pushes up his *pince-nez*, adjusts his wig to conceal
his bald, reddening crown, and half-whispers 'Mr W?'

'Aye, Mr W. The gentleman what's in trouble with the Company.'
She lowers her voice to match his whisper and waves her package. 'I 'as
proof too, so I wants my reward. Three - 'undred - pound.'

The woman spells out the figure as if she can feel every single golden
guinea, running between her fingers. 'Like it said in the paper.'

'And exactly what "proof" do you have, Miss ...erm?'

'Mistress Freeman. Mistress Annie Freeman. A shoe, sir.'

'Ah, of course. Thank you and good day.'

The door closes again.

'A shoe with a W. Two Ws...'

Excited, she dances a jig on the doorstep, waving the packet high
above her head.

The manservant summons a maid from the scullery. He tells her to bring Annie to the servants' entrance and ask her to wait, quietly, until his master is ready to see her.

'Mistress Freeman, you have something for me I believe?'

Annie starts from her reverie.

'A shoe. Your Excellency. Mr W's shoe.'

'Show me.'

Annie's hands shake as she carefully unwraps the bundle and passes him a well-worn black shoe. His eyes narrow.

'This could belong to any gentleman.'

Annie snorts, seizes the shoe. Pulling back the strap, she shows him the letters stitched into the leather: Wm W R.

The Secretary of the East India Company focuses intently on Annie. 'Tell me. Where did you get this? How?'

Annie cannons through her explanation. A servant called Lawrence knocked at her door requesting rooms for his master, who seemed polite enough, even if he looked not quite a gentleman.

'I was a milliner's assistant.' Annie licks a fingertip and smooths her right eyebrow. 'I know what gentlefolk is like. Well, last night 'e asks my husband' – she is careful to pronounce the h – 'to mend this shoe. Mr Freeman, my husband. The best shoemaker in Stepney,' she adds.

'Knocked me sideways when I sees them Ws. I shows Mr F., and quick as a flash 'e says that's the one they bin looking for all over town. And about the three 'undred pound reward. Three *h*undred!'

The Secretary assures her that is the sum in question. 'First we must detain Mr Ryland.'

He makes Annie wait while he scribbles and seals a note and tells her to take it to Magistrate Sampson Wright at Bow Street. But Annie refuses to leave until he agrees to write and sign another note promising that, should Mr William Wynne Ryland be detained at her house, on the basis of her evidence, Mrs. Annie Freeman will be eligible to receive the three hundred pound reward.

It's not a purse of golden guineas, but it will have to do.

❖❖ · · ✦ · · ❖❖

The Whitehall Evening-Post   Sat. April 5th, 1783

A FORGERY

Whereas William Wynne Ryland stands charged before the Right Hon. The Lord Mayor on suspicion of feloniously and falsely making, forging and counterfeiting an Acceptance to two Bills of Exchange for Payment of 7114 pounds and for publishing the same as true, well knowing them to have been so falsely made and counterfeited, with intent to cheat and defraud the United East India Company.

Whoever will apprehend or cause the said William Wynne Ryland to be apprehended and delivered up to Justice, shall receive a Reward of 300 pounds, to be paid by Peter Mitchell, Esq, Secretary of the said Company immediately after his being apprehended and delivered up to the magistrate.

The said William Wynne Ryland is an Engraver. He has an house at Knightsbridge which he left on Tuesday the 1st of April Inst. was seen in London that Day about Eleven or Twelve O'Clock. He is about 50 years of Age, about 5 feet 9inches high, wears a wig, with a Club or Cue, and his own hair turned over in Front; a dark Complexion, thin Face, with strong Lines: his common Countenance very grave, but whilst he speaks rather smiling, and shews his Teeth, and has great, great Affability in his Manner.

William crumples the paper and tosses it into the corner of the room. "Great affability" - "A smiling villain". That he should be so condemned! How would Pa have taken that? God rest his soul. No, there must be an end to this misapprehension. When the hue and cry is over he will search for that fiend who has brought him to this distress. Till then, he must keep low in this cobbler's hovel and while away the time with his graver's burin and copper plate. It has always been his comfort. Now it is an escape from the malingering thought that perhaps the devil he is looking for lies within.

Some hours later, William is about his ablutions. Taking care not to splash the sketches and engraver's tools which are laid out beside a basin, he cups his hands and soaks his face in the chill water. The bells of St Dunstan ring out the hour. Already nine and he is not yet dressed. Where is that woman with his shoes?

A clatter of hooves and carriage wheels draws him to the window. Between the slats he sees a gathering by the churchyard opposite. Three burly fellows on horseback, conversing with a figure in a carriage. He can just make out an agitated arm, a shawl. Are these Stepney folk? It seems unlikely but his mind is so perturbed he would see thief-takers behind every tree. He watches for another breathless minute, till the group move on, around the back of the Church. They do not so much as glance at his refuge. He shrugs and turns back to his basin.

Moments later, there is a knock at the door. He grasps a scrap of towel, holds it tight against his face and waits, stock still. Can he ignore it? Surely it is just Freeman, returning his repair.

'Who is it?'

'A friend,' comes the reply.

He knows the voice, but why here, why now?

'Bailey?' he asks.

'Indeed, Master.'

'Are you alone?'

There is no reply, but he hears the handle turn. The door is pushed, but it will not open. He has locked it from the inside. William does not move. He hears footsteps descending the stairs and silence again. He edges back to the window, in time to see his old friend, Bailey, in consultation with a hulking giant of a man. There are orders, shouts and heavy tramping up the stairs. The door is rattled, heaved against its hinges.

He turns, seizes the first of his engraver's tools that comes to hand.

Chapter 2

Paris, 25 years earlier

A squall of rain beats out a rousing pattern on the tiles above William's head. Through a slit in the painted sheet that serves as a curtain, he can see the familiar slick-wet rooftops. Then the sun breaks through and the slick turns to a sheen. He smiles, watching the slates glisten and glow. His head is still dulled by a night of wine and eau-de-vie. Gabrielle lies asleep beside him, her breath lightly teasing his skin.

He is lying in a makeshift bed of quilts and cushions in the centre of a room hung all around with paper prints, drawings, chalk and pencil sketches, some complete, some barely begun. There are brushes, an easel, a palette half-cocked with colour - as if all caught in mid-stroke. On a table, a copper plate, etched with intricate design, awaits ink and paper to bring it to life. Alongside, an array of sharp-tipped burins, the engraver's tools. It has become an artist's cave, his apartment on the fourth floor in the Rue de la Huchette.

A ray of light sidles into this intimate space. For nearly a year he has been away in Rome, haunting the galleries of Old Masters and learning their secrets. Meantime, Gabrielle, a painter, has made these rooms her own and flourished in his absence. On his return, the previous night, there were tears and a ferocity of love. Now they lie together, entwined, but still distant from the months of separation.

As if she has followed his thoughts, Gabrielle lifts sleep-heavy lids, revealing the grey-flecked blue eyes he has drawn so many times. Again, they reach out for one another. No need for words. The question, *how could you have left me for so long?* shimmers in the body heat between them. It is just, and cannot be counter-said. There are no excuses, only opportunities seized, and choices made.

Two hours later, he slips away from her embrace. In silence, he dresses as best as he can, fingering with pride the fine stitching of his new black frock coat, purchased in Rome. Catching his image in the mirror he considers it not so severe as he once feared. True his nose is sharp but his mouth is mobile and twitches freely into a smile. He gathers his latest drawings into a much-battered leather portfolio and exits, leaving Gabrielle once again asleep.

On the streets below, the traders are in fine voice.

'Come buy my carp! Pork loins fresh from the abattoir. Crisp apples, sweet as you like, just picked this week in Norman orchards!'

At one of the market stalls, an elderly woman, well wrapped against the cold, recognises him and splits a grin across her wizened face. 'Bravo, le Gallois!' And to her daughter, 'See! *Tanton Guillaume est revenu.* Welcome back!'

A wrap of roasted chestnuts is tossed his way. He catches them with thanks, feels their warmth and bows. The day is starting well. A sharp breeze blows up from the river. After just over a year in the heat of Italy, he appreciates the bite in the air. Half-Welsh and bred in London, he is a northerner at heart and enjoys the chill. Another gust catches at his bulky portfolio, which threatens to fly off. Inside are the best samples of his work in Rome, chosen to show his Master, Jacques-Philippe Le Bas.

His workshop is not far. Clutching the precious sketches tight to his chest, William turns into Rue de la Harpe, and is forced to step swiftly aside as a cart full of timbers and rope lurches past him.

He stops before the entrance to a double fronted, three storey building on the east side of the street. Then a slap on the back nearly sends him sprawling, and he is enveloped in a bear hug and the rich smell of warm bread.

'Well, look who's back. Those Romans couldn't keep the Welshman for themselves, eh? Come, come, let's sup some coffee. We have catching up to do. Here, take these.'

Le Bas deftly exchanges a canvas-wrapped stack of bread and pastries for William's portfolio, and looks beneath the cover.

'Ha! You have been busy. So it was not all women and wine?'

William shrugs and smiles. He has learned from experience that secrets shared with Maître Le Bas do not remain secrets for long. But in all else he trusts him like a father. He is as solid as the walls of the Bastille. It is good to be back.

'Now, let me see, there is something different about you? A new frock coat. Quite the gentleman.' Then he spots a curl of black hair out of place. 'Your hair, tch-tch. Of course, down South, they know nothing. My father was a master-hairdresser and proud of it. Did I ever tell you that?' he says, with a wink.

'Once or twice, maître, once or twice.'

'Good, well that's clear then. In we go.'

Before they are through the door, two young men dash past with cries of 'Bonjour maître', 'Bonjour monsieur' and disappear inside.

Le Bas raises an eyebrow.

'My new apprentices. They'll be telling me they were up until the early hours finishing their plates, when I know they were out carousing. Were you as wicked in London?'

'Ravenet kept us in line.'

'I've said to Lizabeth many times we will visit him one day, but now with the war it is not so easy. How was the journey back from Italy?'

'Some grumbling at the border, but my sketchbooks posed little threat. And my French saw me through.'

'A word to the wise, this is Paris, we're not like the provinces. And war does strange things to weak minds. There are those who would find enemies behind every foreigner's door.'

'I shall be watchful.'

'Good, now come let's find Lizabeth, she'll be delighted you're back with us.'

He pushes open the door to the workshop. Six young men are sat at tables covered with prints and proofs, acid baths and tools. There are cries of: 'What kept you?' and, from the private rooms, off to the side, comes a woman's voice that William knows well.

'Is there bread at last? I am starving here and the coffee is cold.'

'Better than that,' Le Bas shouts back. 'I have found your lover loitering at the door again'

He winks at William and inclines his head, preparing for a reaction.

There's a harrumph, the sound of pots slammed down and a shrill 'What nonsense are you talking?' Madame Le Bas, wrapped in her bright green silk morning gown and her auburn hair pinned high on her head, emerges from the kitchen, ready to give her beloved husband a roasting. She sees William and stops for a moment to take stock, then beckons him over for a hug that is as all-embracing as her husband's. For over twenty-five years Elizabeth Le Bas has been the mother-hen for all the students who have come and gone through number 45 Rue de la Harpe. With no children of her own, she adopts everyone who comes into the house. She knows their whims, sees them through their moments of despair, and sings their praises when appropriate. But few dare to cross her.

'Ah, William we have missed you. Come, tell me all. You are a fortunate man. Gabrielle waited for you like an angel. Not that she was short of admirers,' she says, looking around at a couple of the apprentices, who swiftly avert their gaze, but cannot stop the blush rising up their necks.

Their discomfort does not escape William as he follows Madame Le Bas into the parlour. She is eager to find out his intentions after a year abroad. William reassures her that Paris is once again his home. It is an honest response. Though he has one ear open to the chatter in the workshop just beyond the door.

'... remind me about this branch, those leaves I will work on them ...Jean, he knows the mix for the *eau-forte*, learn from him before he's gone...'

He has missed it so much. For all his bluff exterior Le Bas knows how to play the Master's role. Some minutes later, he comes to rescue William from Madame's inquisition.

'Come my boy, it is time to show us your glories of the Eternal City.'

Madame gives way to her husband with a yawn. 'It is ever thus,' she says, 'work must come before love.' This prompts the required embrace from Le Bas, allowing William to slip back into the workshop. He hopes he has persuaded her that he is here to stay.

Before William can intervene, the precious sketches from his portfolio are spread across the tables. This is Le Bas' style: he has no secrets in his workshop.

'If we fail, we learn, we repair, we fail again, we learn again. That is how I am here'.

After some detailed comments, Le Bas draws him aside.

'Fine work, indeed. I have always said that the best draughtsmen make the best engravers. You know you have a place of work here whenever you desire.'

'I would be honoured.'

William takes his leave, assuring his friends that he will be back soon to share more stories. Le Bas accompanies him into the street. He wants a word out of earshot.

'You know Gabrielle has been here quite often while you were away. Lizabeth asked her in. I was cautious at first, but truth is, she has more talent in those slender hands than many of those rascals indoors. She draws like Fragonard and all the book publishers are now asking for her illustrations. She has many admirers.'

'So I hear. Perhaps I do not deserve her. '

'Well, that's for her to judge. She has waited for you, but she'll not wait for ever. Come, let's walk awhile.'

He takes William's portfolio under his arm and together they stroll down towards the south bank of the Seine. The bridge across to the Ile du Palais is blocked with carts. At the river's edge there are crowds waiting for a passage on the flimsy skiffs rowing back and forth, risking the rip currents around the tip of the island. They decide to stay on the bank and walk in the winter sun.

'Now, remind me, how old are you, my boy?'

'Nearly twenty-six.'

'And do you still receive the allowance from your godfather's estate?'

'For less than a year. Then I am on my own.'

'Indeed? High time for settling, I would say. High time. Now, did I ever tell you how I met Lizabeth?'

With a grin, William shakes his head though he must have heard this story half a dozen times.

'As you know, I am an impetuous man. Even more so when I was your age. So, one spring morning in '32, I am walking along the Rue de Buci, and I see this beauty laughing and singing with a friend, and oh her auburn hair, well you can imagine, I was looking with my father's eye and I could tell immediately this is a woman who looks after herself, who knows...what? Well, everything! Her mind, her body, men, women, art, light, shadow, fish, the price of bread, the meaning of the world. Yes, she is free as a bird. If she had sung to me, I could have died and joined the angels, but, fortunately for you, she just smiled.'

Le Bas stops and kneels down in front of William.

'So, I took her hand, right there, took her hand and knelt in the driest, least shit-trodden patch I could find and proposed. I asked her to spend her life with me. Now, of course, it didn't happen overnight, these matters have a way of meandering beyond necessary. But within a month, one short month, we were married in the eyes of God and, mark you, with the blessing of her papa, who was a good deal harder to please than the Almighty.'

'I am sure you were irresistible,' laughs William, dragging him to his feet. They walk on as Le Bas continues his tale.

'Yes, well that's as maybe, but the reason I am telling you this, and perhaps not for the first time, is that I had to learn how to be a man of business. To use my art, my skills to create an enterprise larger than myself. I set up the studio to pay our way, but you know Lizabeth soon saw where we were going and, when we were not blessed with children, she became a mother in her own way and slowly, with her help- ' His voice cracks with emotion. '- this son of a master-hairdresser became Jacques-Philippe Le Bas, master engraver of Rue de la Harpe.'

He pulls out a silk handkerchief to dab the moisture from his eyes.

'Ha, this wind, eh?'

They walk on in silence, while Le Bas collects his thoughts for the moral of his tale.

'So, now, I look at you. The favoured son of a London printer, who has dreams for you, just as my father did. You return from Rome full of grand ideas but you need a foundation. You need a calling card to seize the attention of the Court, the King's Mistress. My friend, Boucher, has another Pompadour on the easel this month. That makes eight portraits. Yes, old Bouche can do no wrong.'

Le Bas grasps William's elbow drawing him closer in.

'To my opinion, he is a touch too much in love with his cherubs and bare-arsed womenfolk but on my honour, he said you were the finest Welshman he had ever taught!'

'Ha, that is a compliment!' William chuckles. 'I did learn a good deal.'

'He's a graver too, he knows our business, knows what a line-man like you can do. I'll have a word with him, see if we can have you engrave one of his paintings.'

'Maitre, I am grateful as always.'

'*Eh bien*. It is in my interest. Another star rises from my school. Why not? And remember, in Gabrielle, you have a woman you love, who loves you, a woman of talent, an artist in her own right. What a pair you will be. It is time to make your mark, William. That is what we engravers do, in life, in love, 'tis all the same. Now my discourse is over and, today, I will not charge you.'

With a smile and a promise to speak on his behalf to "old Bouche", Le Bas departs.

William turns away from the river. They have walked as far as the Quai des Grands Augustins. Facing him is number 35, the home of another old friend, Johann Wille. Prussian by birth, Parisian by choice, Wille is a wealthy engraver and dealer in prints. He knows of every commission on offer. Fired up by Le Bas' lecture , William decides to pay Wille a visit. The door is opened by a maid, who regrets that the Master is not at home. William offers her his calling card.

'Please let maître Wille know that William Wynne Ryland is returned from Italy.'

Then he sets off for home. This bright December day has been full of promise. When a gaudy coach and four crosses his path, he bows and claps his hands together out of impulse, prompting smiles from a passing matron. Moments later he stops to watch the dying sunlight warm the stone walls of St Germain des Pres. How he loves this city! A joy after the stifling pretension of Rome's salons, thronged with spoiled boys rivalling each other in Grand Tour extravagance. What would he do if he had a quarter, an eighth of all their fathers' guineas? And why should he not, one day? He has more talent than any Duke's son in England or France. But first he has a mission, to regain Gabrielle's trust.

For the next two weeks, William and Gabrielle spend their nights four floors up on Rue de la Huchette. It is a time of rediscovery, free from constraint and the frustrations of distance. One moment she is all charm, a laughing raven-haired coquette, the next she is cursing him for his Italian venture.

'Take me as you find me, Guillaume. It is you who must earn my love again! I owe you nothing. You abandoned me.'

He recalls Le Bas' comment after first meeting Gabrielle.

'Raise a fence before her and she will take it in one leap, without a backward glance.'

In those early days, neither he nor Gabrielle felt obliged by other's expectations, by those who would see them wed. But now, perhaps, it is time to consider a more certain future. In the calm hours while she is asleep, he looks around their shared rooms. Her exuberant designs for the King's Players at Versailles hang beside her rainbow creations for the milliners of Rue St Honoré. Gabrielle's fire has in no way diminished in his absence. But there are signs of more formal work, bright, detailed illustrations for books of every type, from Greek mythology to the latest discovery in the natural world. Are these sure signs that she is open to a more settled life?

This question flickers through William's mind as he strolls each morning to Rue de la Harpe. If he is to live in Paris and commit to Gabrielle, he must make his fortune in this world of print and paper. It was always his father's dream. His obsession even. That William, the most talented of his sons should be the most accomplished. And William was not averse. As a boy, in Pa's London workshop, he would haul on the spokes of the heavy printer's wheel to make it turn. Each time it felt like a trick of magic, to conjure black lines and words out of the inked and polished plates.

Now he is at home In Le Bas' studio. Framed panels of waxed paper hang at angles from the windows, softening the light falling on each of the desks. William takes his place beside the masters of line, the engravers. He pushes the sharp, v-shaped tip of his burin just below the surface of the copper, gouging smooth curves by gently turning his plate on a hard leather cushion.

He is a maker of marks, of flicks and parallels, of subtle or bold cross-hatching. Each combination of lines like a painter's brush-strokes, creates the illusion of space, of distance, of light, joy, tenderness, anger, or Divine justice. He copies an artist's depiction of storm-driven clouds, flashes of lightning across Italian rocky hills or muscular Greek gods at play. But this is never slavish duplication. He has been taught to embellish, to use his draughtsman's skills to bring out details only hinted at in oils. He wants everyone to marvel at the intricacy, to ask "how did he do that?"

Chapter 3

L e Bas is true to his word. Within a week, a painting by Boucher arrives at Rue de la Harpe. It has been sent by one of his aristocratic patrons.

'Ha! You see William, the Gods are with you. The mighty Zeus, and old Bouche of course, sends you a challenge for your burin. Leda and the Swan.'

He pulls away the cloth covering the painting to reveal two naked women reclining on blue, gold and green brocade at the edge of a lake. One, her right arm upraised, shoos away a male swan. Its neck is arched as if poised to attack. These voluptuous figures are bathed in moonlight, with a rich dark green foliage behind them of bushes, reeds and overhanging trees.

William raises an eyebrow. He was hoping for something more grand, more noble for his calling card.

At least he leaves a little more to the imagination than others I have seen.'

William knows the story well. Zeus, King of the Gods, takes the form of a swan to seduce, some say to violate, the mortal Leda. From their coupling, a daughter is born, Helen of Troy.

Le Bas shrugs. 'What can I say? You know, for Bouche, this is his stock in trade. Sit with it awhile. We can discuss what is most appropriate...drypoint, etching... once you have come to know her.'

Some days later, William's impromptu visit to the door of number 35, Quai des Grands Augustins bears fruit. An invitation arrives for an afternoon gathering at the home of Johann Georg Wille. His elegant suite of rooms overlooking the Seine is a trusted haven for collectors, who come to consult, to admire and to purchase. One word from Johann, be it recommendation or critique, can launch or limit a career. At a more convivial level, he and his adored wife cater to an endless stream of compatriots, eager to know Paris yet hungry for home. It is said that a print purchased from the house of Wille can be identified by the lingering odour of sauerkraut, absorbed during even the shortest stay.

Over the years, Johann's gatherings have become famous for The Secret Sketch. The rules are always the same. A visit is arranged to an outdoor location; Johann believes in working from Nature. Each guest without exception is required to submit a drawing. It must be unsigned. Once back at Number 35, sauerkraut and Rhenish wines are served while Herr Wille makes his assessment.

On the day of the event, there is a wintry chill in the wind blowing up the Seine. Gabrielle steps down from the carriage and pulls her heavy turquoise shawl tight around her. 'Dear God, I hope we are not to be run up some hillside in this gale.'

'The Roman Baths perhaps? They're close and sheltered', William says.

'Perfect, ideal for this circus.'

'Oh, come now, we are among friends.'

Gabrielle stretches her back and walks ahead of him into the house. William follows and is not surprised to see her melt into a host of warm embraces as soon as she is inside.

He is relieved to discover the Baths are indeed their destination.

At first the guests wander among the ruins, looking for vantage points. Gabrielle walks off alone. She insists she will find her own view. William takes out his sketch book and enjoys the moment. He is back in his old world. Wille is everywhere, lightly cajoling, gleaning useful information about current projects, planned commitments, the daily chatter of the community.

Some hours later, they all return to the house on the Quai. The guests gather for the announcements. Wille whittles the list down to three, and then finally to the winner: an image of a raven strutting on ancient masonry - with fine detail, a questioning expression, looking directly at the viewer. He invites the artist responsible to step forward. William feels a sharp squeeze in his hand, as Gabrielle leaves his side to claim her prize, with a bow, and an endearing smile directed first to Wille and then to William. He feels a sting of jealousy but manages to return the smile. A collection of fruit tarts then emerges from the kitchen followed by Madame Wille, who presents them with an embrace to Gabrielle. Their distribution among her rivals softens the blow but some of the green-eyed men congratulate William, without much discretion.

'No, he protests, it is all her own I assure you. She is most talented. A true artist.'

When they return to Rue de la Huchette, William lights a candle in the stairwell. Their ascent is slow and unsteady. The fine Rhenish wine is partially to blame but Gabrielle is distracted, distant. She tries to open the door. He reaches past her to help.

'At least I am good at drawing birds,' she says, 'Birds on stone walls.'

Inside the room is cold. He starts to rekindle the fire. She falls back onto the divan, staring up at the ceiling.

'You won the competition,' he says.

'Only because he did not know it was by me, by a woman.'

He shakes his head. In the grate, the embers begin to glow. A flicker of flame.

'I saw Jacques congratulate you,' she says.

'I told him-'

'What, that I am a good pupil?

'That is not fair. It was your bird, adored by everyone.'

With the fire now ablaze, he sits beside her. They are close but not intimate. He reaches for his portfolio. 'Well, I too have a bird to deliver. Perhaps you can help me?'

And he pulls out one of the preliminary sketches he has made from the Boucher. The Zeus Swan with its arched neck.

She lifts it up to see better in the candlelight. She is quiet for just a moment, then it is as if he has set her on fire.

'*Non, Guillaume*. Tell me it is not true.'

She is up now, tearing another sketch from his hands, then seizing another and another, tossing them all around her, until they are covering the floor. There are swans everywhere.

'You have just spent a year in Rome, with the greatest Masters of all time and now, you are to glorify this... this fantasy for old lechers! Why don't you just show the truth. It would at least be honest.'

And before he can stop her, she seizes one of her brushes still loaded with paint and adds a crimson member of divine dimension to one of William's sketches.

'Ha! That's more like it. Or is this better?'

She draws a flaccid cock on another sketch.

'See, Zeus after the event. Or this...'

A green and ochre phallus emerges from her brush strokes, as if suffering some vile disease.

'He deserves it, this God who believes he can put it about wherever he likes.'

'Stop, Gabrielle. Stop this nonsense. Whatever the subject...these... Enough, Gabrielle!'

She refuses. So, he slaps the nearest cushion across her arm, sending her paint brush flying.

Cheeks flushed, she seizes a heavy pillow and lifts it above her head, narrowly missing the night-candle. As she brings the pillow crashing down on his back, it bursts along its seam, sending a flurry of feathers into the air. Like two blind boxers they swing at each other. Cushions and bolsters fly back and forth. With every blow, the feather cloud grows denser and more turbulent.

Soon they are panting, sweating with the exertion. Then, in a moment, just as it arose, the anger turns. They fall upon each other, ripping clothes out of their way, to find a release beneath an avalanche of white and grey feathers. As they drift off exhausted, it covers their spent bodies, their eyes, their ears, their hair.

Next morning, William wakes late to find that Gabrielle has left for a drawing class she gives to young girls in the district. The room reeks of oil of turpentine. He is summoning up the will to clean up the mess of paint and feathers, when there is a knock on the door. A boy from the local post house has a letter for Monsieur.

It is a double sheet folded over twice, then sealed and stamped in red wax. He recognises the Unicorn motif. It is the sign above the door of Boydell's, the most popular printshop in London. For a moment, he is back in Cheapside - a young apprentice pushing through the crowd gathered at the windows, eager to see whose works are on display.

William picks away at the wax. This is not the first time the seal has been broken. It is not uncommon, since England and France are now at war. But who should wish to read such letters?

He is more surprised that Boydell has taken the time to write. Pa says he does not even indulge in snuff, for fear of wasting precious minutes in a day.

William,

In the hope that this instrument finds you amenable, I have a request that is of the utmost import for yourself and our King-in-waiting.

In the autumn of the current Monarch's reign, there are those who are preparing for the next, the Grandson, to be George III. They desire he should become better known among the public, official and domestic. To this end the honourable Lord Bute, much spoken of as future First Minister, commissions Allan Ramsay, to paint a full-size Prince of Wales and likewise one of his good self. His intention is to have these images engraved. To multiply the benefit. The demand for them and later Coronation works will be very high indeed. His Excellency approached me, to discover a graver with French expertise. Now, you have this in abundance. We have long been awaiting your return, this chance of Royal patronage must surely expedite it.

Note that the work was offered first to the Scot, Robert Strange. But he has refused, alleging a prior visit to Rome. It is known he was a Stuart man, a damned Jacobite in '45. Perchance he could not stomach a commission for the future King George. No matter, the field is now open and you are currently at its head. You may be sure that I shall inform your father. I am obliged if you would inform me of your intentions post-haste.

Send my greetings to Messieurs Le Bas, Wille and Basan. For the latter, seeing trade is somewhat disturbed by war, I enclose a list of prints for you to negotiate on my behalf. I shall purchase only at a reasonable rate.

I bid you farewell in the certainty that we shall soon celebrate your addition to the Royal pensions list.

Au Revoir (I am learning myself French, that I may do business direct with these rascals. I attend a Huguenot church each Sunday. No rest for the wicked.)

John Boydell, Printseller

Cheapside, London

William creases the letter tight, fold over fold, as if he would make it disappear. The pulse at his temple drums a ragged beat. He brings the paper to his nose to savour any lingering reminder of a London that seemed so distant and now so close. He imagines himself emerging from a visit to the Royal court-in-waiting at Leicester House. He sports a topcoat trimmed with blue satin and a silk embroidered waistcoat. He is at last delivering on the promise his godfather, God rest his soul, once saw in him. He will not have spent his guineas on a wasted enterprise.

With one bound this letter can win him a Royal patron but far away from all that he loves in Paris, the life that is just beginning here. Gabrielle will never leave France. She would not even visit him in Rome. Unlike him, she has no lust to wander.

Pressure builds behind his eyes, as if he has spent too long scraping at his copper plate. Spots and flares dance across his vision and he lets his head roll back, eyes closed. He is the same man he was just minutes before but somehow everything is changed. Why did this not come earlier? Even when he was in Rome. At least Gabrielle was then hardened to his absence. But now? They are just retrieving the threads of a shared life together.

Other London memories break through. The fear of debt hanging like a chain about Pa's neck; the reek of brandy on Pa's breath at their final farewell. His brothers standing silent and morose, as if to say William's absence will lessen their lives, not caring whether it will enrich his. The almond scent of Ma, the desperation in her grip, steeling herself to send him off hopeful, when he knows how wretched she is feeling.

With these thoughts churning back and forth, William drifts off. He is woken at noon by a peal of bells, rippling across the narrow channel which separates Notre Dame from the Seine's southern bank. Nothing halts the daily rituals of worship and he too has calls to make. That afternoon he is to visit Johann Georg Wille. Could he discreetly ask his counsel? Before he sets out, he takes care to hide Boydell's letter beneath the mattress. Nothing is as yet decided.

At 35, Quai des Grands Augustins, his distracted knocking is answered by Mme Wille herself.

'Oh William, our guests decided to leave early for the sights of Paris and Johann agreed to accompany them to their first destination. He will not be long.'

She beckons him in and goes to slide a window closed.

'Forgive me, we are airing the rooms. Even we cannot endure the smell of sauerkraut every day.'

She releases a trill of laughter and guides William into her husband's library. Tea is served in porcelain cups. She enquires about his plans in Paris. She has spent sufficient time around her husband's acquaintances to know that they talk most freely about themselves. But William is unforthcoming. Not knowing of his recent discovery, she puts this down to an artistic attitude and excuses herself.

'I have a tradesman arriving on the hour. I am sure Johann will be home soon. He does so detest to be late.'

William surveys the room with an engraver's eye. Several of Wille's own works are hanging on the wall. They are skilful, but the real source of his wealth is piled up high on the wide mahogany desk. William cannot resist the temptation to pry. There are bills of trade from printsellers in London, Prague, Saxony, Madrid...Wille's trading web is legendary. Here is the proof of it.

Beside the papers, he observes the marks of daily habit: dark rings in the leather, wax stains from nocturnal shifts, and beneath the desk, scuffed parquet where Wille's heels have rubbed. This is a world forever demanding attention, opinion and advice. Could he, William Wynne Ryland, one day, be at the heart of such an exchange? He smiles for the first time today. Perhaps he is already half- way to London.

The sound of a door closing below breaks his reverie and he regains his seat. A whistled tune approaches. Maître Johann Wille enters, still wrapped up against the bitter wind. Broad in face and chest, he fills the room with a cheery disposition.

'Ah - ha My very best friend Mr William. So, now we have time alone, my compatriots were not patient, so eager to see Paris. They send their apologies and look forward to meeting another day. Unless this spiteful weather sends you back to Rome before.'

'Well-'

'- No of course not, you are back with your dear Gabrielle. Such a prodigious talent, she must be nurtured. '

William attends to an itch on his right ear lobe.

'I do what I can.'

'I'm sure you do... and I look forward to seeing your plate of Boucher's Leda.'

'Word travels fast.'

'This is Paris. Tongues wag, I listen. It is my profession.'

'Indeed'

Wille removes his coat. His eyes remain fixed on William.

'Monsieur Wille...'

'Johann'

'Thank you... Johann. I find myself in a dilemma and I would be grateful for your advice.

'Of course.' Wille pulls a chair closer to William and sits.

'This morning I received a letter from London, from John Boydell. I believe you know-'

'-the old rogue... yes.' He gestures to the pile of paper on his desk. 'There must be four or five orders from Boydell this past year alone. He complains, but he buys. Vernet is his favourite. He tells me one day soon we will be buying English prints from him. So, what is now on his mind?'

William holds nothing back: the offer, the royal commission, the link to the Court in waiting, the opportunity for patronage. In the telling, he feels again the fear and the thrill which the letter first stirred in him.

Wille is a mirror to his own deliberations. Indeed, his response is so swift, William is convinced he was already informed of the commission. If so, he covers it well.

'I will say to you what I would say to my own son. Whatever trepidation you feel now is as nothing to the disappointment you would feel if you do not seize the venture. Though this is no easy upheaval.'

'There you have the dilemma.'

'She would not travel with you?'

Unable to hold Wille's gaze, he looks beyond his shoulder, into the sky above Paris.

'Some ten years past, her father took her on a journey to Rome. Just months before, her mother had passed away, in childbirth. But within a week of reaching Venice, he caught an ague, which became a fever, which raged for three days of sweats and tore him from her on the morning of the fourth. An uncle fetched her back to Paris. She has never left, nor intends to.'

The air hangs heavy with the implications of Gabrielle's story. Then the sharp chime of a mantel clock, determined to mark the hour, ruptures the silence. Wille is freed to speak.

'I do not envy you your decision. I am fortunate, my dear Claudia would have carried me all the way from Prussia to Paris. Even now, London would not be out of the question. Though I am not throwing my hat into your ring.'

The smile is brief. He looks across at a small, framed engraving on the table beside him. A stern, moustachioed officer stares back.

'I will only say this. My father, God rest his soul, would bark at me that in life one should be like a climber of trees: "*Always make sure the next branch is firm before you shift your veight upwards*." Ah, but I have learned that is not always possible, sometimes you have to trust, to rise on your own belief in yourself. Perhaps the only way to free Gabrielle from her own fears is to show that you do not have any. Do you imagine Boydell would hesitate, if he was in your shoes?'

William risks a grin.

'I would dearly love to out-do Boydell.'

'And well you may. All I know is, if you desire to make a fortune, your balls are not always the best guide. There, in my country language, I have spoken.'

William, blushing, stammers his thanks and rises to take his leave. He turns right along the rain-soaked Quai. In the distance, behind the Cathedral, the clouds are stacked high, bruised purple-black with the threat of thunder. He picks up his pace, head down, feet slipping and

sliding beneath him. Clerks and messenger-boys weave past, wrapped
in their own thoughts. This is not a time for light exchanges of good
will. The storm is close and all would be safely under cover. The next
deluge strikes well before he reaches his street, so he finds a tavern and
sits out the worst of it. He orders an *eau-de-vie*. Thoughts of the Royal
offer still chew at his innards.

Next morning, he wakes early. One line in the letter is running circles
in his mind. Why did his rival engraver, Robert Strange, refuse so
prestigious an offer? Perhaps Boydell is right. No Jacobite would wish
to glorify the family they condemn as thieves, usurpers of the British
crown, stolen from the Stuarts. Indeed, William's own godfather,
whose legacy has paid his travel and study for many years, was wont to
damn King George without much asking. Long dead now, he would
shudder in his grave if he knew what his godson was considering. But
William tells himself this is the portrait of a King-to-be, born and bred
an Englishman.

What lies heavier on his heart is Gabrielle, but he cannot bring
himself to reveal the offer. She is still angry at the Boucher plate. She
will not have it in their rooms, so he continues to sketch its first outline
in Le Bas' studio. And time slips by, while Boydell and the future King
of England await his response.

Then one morning, while Gabrielle is at the market, another letter
arrives. It is from Pa.

*Forgive me, my dear William. It has been so long since we see you. I
only hope that you are not sick or in debt? The twin banes of my life. If
neither those, then may you be in sweet, good spirit. I send you greetings
from your mother, brothers, sister all in health.*

You may well divine the purpose for this writing. Mr Boydell has just this day made me aware of a golden opportunity for you, here, in London. Golden.

Please consider it most careful, it has so much to recommend, seeing how the king is often times sick and the young George appears not disagreeable. The Bute faction is placed to take the advantage. You will be among the first in the land to grave the image of a new King. Beware of jealous folk. Do not delay and see another take your place. I know no man with less patience than Boydell.

May God guide you in your decision. If not the God on high, then the God of Mammon.

I am your loving father. My sins are my own and I do not blame you for them.

He is so engrossed in reading that he only hears Gabrielle's footsteps as she reaches the door. He thrusts the open letter beneath a cushion on the bed.

'We meet at last,' he jokes.

'It is you who have been absent these past few days. I trust it is art not flesh that keeps us apart.'

He pulls her towards him and they embrace. The intimacy is a relief. Though, without warning, a flush of London memories flood his mind. Truth will out, he thinks, no matter how one tries to keep it hidden.

In playful mood, she bites his earlobe. He pulls back, exaggerates the hurt, to disengage.

'A mere nip,' she laughs, 'what man are you? I love the taste of blood. Yours, in particular.'

She tries to corner him between the door and the armoire. He slips aside, and escapes into the hallway, seizing his coat and portfolio as he goes.

'Tonight,' he calls out. 'I will forage up a feast for you.'

'Promise or I will slice your gizzard with your own burin.'

'I will be there, I promise. *À dieu, mon amour.*'
With that, he disappears down the stairs.

On his way home that evening, William searches out the apples, the *chaource* cheese and the Basque ham he knows Gabrielle loves best. They have wine aplenty, in the casks brought in from the country where Gabrielle's aunt has vines.

His friend, the chestnut-seller huddles over her fire. William picks up a bag. A few more are tossed in for her regular customer. It is dark now. The lamplighters call out the hour and the last bouquinistes are packing up their stalls. He walks along the Quai, past St Michel, along Rue de la Huchette, past the shuttered windows of the candle-lit cabarets and cafes. He stops for a moment to take in the sight of Notre Dame's facade. It flickers a soft reddish ochre as a parade of monks, carrying torches, chant their way into the Cathedral. He sees the gold symbol of the crucifixion held high. Though no longer a believer, he makes the sign of the cross. If there is a force that drives the world, he would rather it was Pan or Aphrodite or one of the Muses than this sacrificial lamb. With that thought he finds a spring in his step as he winds his way up and up to their shared rooms. It is a fine evening for love, he thinks to himself as he lifts the latch and loudly announces his return.

There is no response. The room is almost bare. The walls have been stripped of Gabrielle's artworks. The bed sheet and cushions are strewn across the floor. All her dresses, her shawls, her hats, all gone. For a second he thinks he has entered his neighbour's rooms. But there is his clock, his sketches, pencils, brushes. His possessions remain but hers have been erased entirely, as if painted over.

He has no voice but there is one crying out, trapped within his throat. All seemed so well just hours earlier. Then he sees his father's letter, crumpled into an angry ball on his desk. Beside it lies another sheet of paper. Blank. Though it has blotches, still damp, as if she sat crying here, intent on a response but no words came. Like a bolting horse she has run from him.

He sits, breathless, stunned. Eyes closed he sees her, desperate to say something of her pain but unwilling, unable.

In his confusion he reaches again for his father's letter, re-reads it over and over but only waves of anger surface. Even as he rips it apart, he knows he cannot blame his father's naive remembrances and pleas. This was his to hide or destroy just eight hours earlier and he did not do so.

In her pain she has dealt him as sharp a cut as she can deliver. To absent herself with no words. The wilder side of him is unleashed across the streets of Paris. He raps on the door of every mutual friend, shouts out her name from the top of the Tour St Jacques. There is no news, so sighting, no trace to give him hope. His bitter exuberance is washed away in the torrent of a passing storm. He dares not approach the one person who may know the truth, his master's wife, Elizabeth Le Bas. She would be sworn to secrecy and how can he approach their studio, when he must soon reject them too. It feels as if his frame cannot contain the loss, the guilt, the fear of upturning all that was certain in his life. He pours himself a mug of brandy and eventually falls into a fitful sleep.

It is morning when he wakes, trembling with cold. The window has been open all night. Where is Gabrielle now? What is she feeling? Can nothing be changed, reversed? For several days he sleeps, eats. No more than this. The ham is soon gone, the bread, the fruit, also, until he is scrambling around to find crumbs, stale remnants. He begins to drink his way through the wine. He is aware of knocking on the door which he ignores in silence or greets with a bellow to 'be gone!'. He has no intention of re-joining life.

Finally on the fourth day, there is a knocking so loud, so persistent he cannot refuse it. Grumbling curses, he staggers from his bed and opens the door. It is Le Bas. William collapses on to him. Le Bas' embrace is unusually stiff.

'Clean yourself up, my boy. When you are ready, we will talk.'

He turns and leaves with not even a farewell.

It is the shock William requires. By the next morning he still feels bilious at the consequences of his decision. But he can no longer hide. He sets off for a walk to clear his head. It is time to plan for his departure.

Chapter 4

William sets off into the maze of narrow streets south of the Seine, not paying much heed to his direction. After some minutes, he finds himself near the turning into Rue de la Harpe, but he is not yet ready to engage with Le Bas. So he walks on, to the street behind the studio. A cart and horse stand outside the rear door, piled high with slim wooden boxes, some wrapped in sacking, some held tight with leather straps and cord. The loading is being managed by a man in his late thirties. William recognises him as Alphonse Bailleu, who runs errands between artists' studios and their clients. Stocky, bearded, in leather cap and jerkin, he steadies the hefty Percheron mare, while his cautious assistants carry more boxes out of the building.

William stands back, observing. He will need a man he can trust, if he is to make it safely to Calais with Boydell's prints. When the assistants disappear inside, William greets Alphonse and enquires his destination.

'To Versailles, the Palace' is the brusque reply, confirming William's first impression. As another carefully wrapped box emerges, they agree to meet again.

William returns to the Rue de la Harpe the following day. Le Bas himself greets him at the door and suggests it might be best that they take a drink together, away from the studio. He guides William to a quiet corner of their favourite refuge, the Cafe Procope, giving his order to a passing waiter as they go.

'A cognac for myself and a tea for the Gallois, you know how he likes his hot water. *Merci. Merci.*'

Le Bas settles his large frame in to a round backed chair angled into the room, leaving William to face the window as the light fades outside.

'So. You are at least presentable today.'

'I must apologise.'

With a brusque wave, Le Bas dismisses his excuses.

'I have seen far worse, though 'tis true it was in the Regiment, for which I was entirely unsuited. An experience that taught me I should have listened to my hairdresser papa. He always said the art of war is highly overrated.'

'And I to my father, whose advice I have ignored for some years now'.

'He invites you to return?'

'Yes. I assume you know the rest?'

'I am not alone in that. The word is out. You are offered a golden commission in London on behalf of the future King, your fortune awaits you and you are leaving us and your amour Gabrielle. Did I miss anything?'

Sidestepping the enquiry, as his tea arrives, William demands what is most pressing to himself.

'Do you know where she is?'

'I have had no contact myself but Lizabeth, yes, she has spoken to her.'

'She is with her aunt in the country?'

'I am sworn to secrecy, but it is a reasonable assumption. She is adamant she does not want to see you... Ever, I believe was the word.'

'You know, I have not yet answered Boydell.'

'Then you are a fool. Accept and post-haste. The damage is done, the decision is made. Of course, we are sorry to see you go but Gabrielle is like a daughter to Lizabeth. We will do whatever we can for her.'

'You mean it would be easier for everyone if I was no longer here.'

Le Bas is distracted by raucous laughter in the main room.

He turns back to William and reaches out, as he was accustomed, to tap William on the knee, a paternal gesture, but his hand hangs in the air, uncertain and is then withdrawn. 'You are going are you not?'

William holds his Master's gaze. 'Yes...Yes I am.' He feels a surge within, as if somehow he is unleashed. 'I am leaving proud in all that I have learned from you and Ravenet and old Bouche. Proud and confident'.

'You are right to be so. You cannot deny fate.' And this time Le Bas does rest his hand on William's knee. It is as close to a blessing as he will receive. 'A Royal Portrait brings a rich pension.'

'Boydell will know the going rate. I am so long out of London. He owes me a favour if I fetch him the prints he craves.' Seeing his master's eyebrow lift, William explains. 'He has a deal with Basan.'

'Ahh, yes. The dealer on the rise. So, when do you leave?'

'As soon as the prints are ready.'

'Do not forget we are at war. You will need all your paperwork in order.' With that final advice, Le Bas, rises to his feet, tosses a handful of *sous* on to the table and bids William farewell. 'God Speed William, I wish it were in happier circumstances, but you go with our love.

Perhaps once you have made your fortune you will return, in peace time?'

'I hope.'

They embrace, this time with warmth.

His decision made, William replies first to his father, giving few details. No need to create false hope. But the lack of precision is also for his own sake. He is not yet at ease with the prospect of returning home. He writes next to Boydell to confirm his application for the Engraver's role. He also commits to the purchase of the long list of French prints, reminding Boydell that French print sellers are refusing English credit. He will need to arrange a bill of trade. This will infuriate Boydell, but after all, we are at war! This triggers other anxieties. There will be dangers on the route to Calais that have not troubled him in the anonymity of city life.

The following day he arranges an appointment with Monsieur Basan. He must procure the prints for Boydell with the utmost urgency. William cannot risk a London rival stepping in to seize the Royal commission.

Jean Francois Basan, high forehead, Roman nose, swept-back cheekbones and the conceited manner of a cavalry officer, is one of a new breed of print sellers. The son of a wealthy Parisian merchant, he is no amateur dilettante. Commerce runs in his blood. He swaggers around his emporium, answering would-be buyers with mannered tolerance. He welcomes William with a theatrical sigh:

'At last, an artist come to rescue me from these heathens.'

For all his brash self-regard, Basan has always impressed William. He sees how he inspires trust. The money-men give him capital to build up stock, their only guarantee being Basan's individual taste and experience. He has acquired the trappings of a gentleman. His wife brought him both a dowry and a country villa. Is she the source of this Parisian's extravagant confidence and bearing. Musing thus, William follows Basan into an inner room in the establishment.

'So, Monsieur le Gallois, how goes it? I'm glad to see the temptations of Rome have not enthralled you. How can I be of service?'

William takes the much-creased letter from his inner pocket, unfolds one of the sheets and hands it to Basan, with a slight bow.

'This-'

'-from one of your countrymen?'

'Someone you know well, Mr. Boydell'

'Ah ha'

'You share a mutual appreciation I believe '

'We have had our dealings, some disagreements about the value of certain works, but these are now a pale bruise compared to the wounds endured in the conflict between our two nations. War has never been good for our business. If I was trading cannon and shot, I would be in a better place.'

Basan retrieves his pince-nez from a chest pocket with exaggerated frustration. He would prefer them to be an affectation but after years of staring at the minute marks of engravers, he is woefully short-sighted. 'And he has asked you to act as middleman, to ease the passage through enemy ports. Back to your homeland?'

William inclines his head.

'You, with Paris at your feet? You are leaving us as a mere courier? I had much higher expectations for you, Monsieur.'

'There are other incentives involved.'

'Indeed, I have heard rumours.' Basan's tone suggests a righteous pleasure in such chatter. 'How long will you be gone?'

William feels his cheeks flush, he cannot hold Basan's gaze.

'I see.' Basan smiles and returns to the detail of Boydell's list, occasionally glancing at William, who now sits, lips pursed, his fingers tapping out a nervous rhythm against the arm of his chair. 'He took sixty of Vernet's Shipwreck last year and now he's after the Storm... He knows my terms but says nothing about payment. No credit, no exchanges with English prints.'

William nods, 'Indeed, it will not come as a surprise, but he knows what sells in London.'

'Yes, I do admire him, from afar, but do not let him know. I enjoy the edge between us. Now, if you forgive me, I must attend to my own buyers.'

They head back out into the busy salesroom and just before they part Basan leans in close enough for William to smell his floral scent.

'Remember we are at war. They are watching the ports. You will need a *laissez-passer* to reach Calais. The trading papers, I can provide, but the *laissez-passer*...' he shrugs, eyebrows raised, 'leave it with me. I may know someone.'

He accompanies William to the door. 'When do you leave?'

'Within the fortnight if all is ready.'

'That soon? I will make haste. But then you will still be here for the start of the Fair. I am planning my annual masquerade. Will you come? We have the most exquisite building for the night. The Hotel de Serpente. It is close by. A farewell to Paris.'

'I'd be delighted. Oh, for the papers, I expect there will be two of us, someone to help with the transport.'

'Understood. *Au revoir*. Until the masquerade.'

The next morning William arranges to meet Alphonse, the carter, in a coffeehouse near St Michel. William arrives first and commandeers a table set back in the far corner of the room. For the first time in Paris, he is somehow more aware of being a foreigner. The street pamphlets are full of chatter about English spies. He hesitates before ordering his glass of burgundy. The soft lilt in his voice has always charmed his French friends but could it now betray him? Even now he sees two ageing clerks, scowling at their fellow drinkers. Are they watching him or just suspicious of a man alone?

The street door swings open again and Alphonse enters. Ruddy cheeked, he looks like a man who has enjoyed many a drink in the past but today he has a sober and serious manner about him.

He makes his way over, passing the two clerks, who turn back to their reading, with a glance which could be interpreted as disappointment.

'Alphonse Baillieu, at your service, Monsieur.'

'William Wynne Ryland. Delighted.'

We met at Monsieur Le Bas' studio before you left for Italy?'

'Indeed, Le Bas always speaks highly of you. Patient and capable, were the words he used.'

'He is correct,' Alphonse replies, without smiling, 'but then I suffer no fools. As you can imagine, these are not easy times, even for a carter.'

They both sit.

But now'days I find all my clients in the print world. From Kings to sons of wigmakers. Le Bas is one of the best and many of his students, too, including Ravenet, before he left for England. '

William lets out a breath.

'Simon Ravenet! I was his apprentice in Lambeth.'

'Now there's something, because I joined him in '54, married an English woman. In London, I am known as Bailey, not Bailleu. Keeps it simple. I'd have been there for life but, in '57, papa fell sick and war broke out just as I returned to France.'

He glances around the room and lowers his voice.

'I have been keeping my head down ever since, 'case they cart me off to the Army.'

Something about his attire, clean and cared for, makes William suspect that he is not living alone in Paris. He is a man who would see to it that he had company wherever he lay his head.

'You are not alone, I've been here five years and just as I plan to leave, I feel that I am not safe.'

William signals to the counter for a coffee then turns with a smile to brief Alphonse. He is looking for help, to prepare Boydell's prints and his own bags for transport then accompany him on a journey to the coast. Until now he had expected the arrangement to end in Calais, but Alphonse's London life prompts him to offer another option:

'Would you risk a run across the Channel? Are you free to do so?'

A momentary blush seems to confirm William's suspicions about Alphonse's domestic arrangements. But he accepts. He has strong views on how to travel with the prints to Calais.

'I'd rule out the public coach. It's too slow. It'd take us five days and I've seen too many bags disappear off the back of it. Soon as it's dark or foul weather. Safer to hire a smaller *post-chaise* ourselves. With a good run we c'd do it in three days or less.'

Together they work out a solution. They will take no frames with them, just canvases and prints, so Alphonse can re-work his wooden cases to fit inside the post-chaise itself. It will be cramped but safe.

'As for the permits, I'll not be leaving without them,' says Alphonse. 'I'd rather lie low here and risk a press-gang than be locked up in some god-forsaken hole 'twixt here and the coast.'

William assures him that he has connections. Even now, some traders, couriers, second-son adventurers still travel between Paris and London. But none are above suspicion. Only papers from the highest authority will keep them out of trouble.

So, William agrees the deal with Alphonse and both set off to begin their preparations.

Three days later, they meet again and Alphonse has bad news.

'Every carrier in Paris and all around is committed for the Fair.'

It is just ten days before the City's annual fair opens on February 3rd. Thousands of traders are already bringing in their goods, their cloth, their trinkets, sheepskins, leather saddles, barrels of wine and bottles of eau-de-vie, any item indeed from which they can make a tidy sum. All heading into the city and the vast covered market place, that sits alongside the Abbey walls at St Germain. Even the most ancient cart is commandeered, and those carriers that possess a post-chaise will not want it to be leaving for Calais just as the fair is starting.

'It's business. Bring the fat and wealthy into town for their debauchery then cart them safely home.'

Before William can consider this first challenge, Alphonse has another.

'Basan's men make good progress with the prints, but they won't all be ready the same day. We need to store and pack them meantime. I thought perhaps Le Bas might help, he has the space.'

William has no desire to risk a lecture from Madame Le Bas. There is still no news from Gabrielle and he will do what he can to keep that wound concealed.

'I'll not be troubling Le Bas on Boydell's business, but there's a cellar next door to mine, on Rue De La Huchette. I know the watchman. It's well away from the madness around the Abbey. Leave that to me.'

'So, there's still the matter of...'

'... the carriage. Yes.'

William sits back to consider. At that moment a tray of hot soup is carried steaming across the room to a nearby table. The air is rich and moist with the odour of cabbage and carrots. William smiles. 'I have a thought. Maître Wille, the dealer, down on the Quai des Grands Augustins, number thirty-five.'

' I know him.'

'Well, he has his own post-chaise. Let me see if I can persuade him to let us take it to Calais. We can argue that we are keeping it safe for him during the Fair. There will be travellers on the road back to Paris for its return. That way we keep our plans between friends.'

Alphonse approves. 'After all we are at war. Already, I am feeling like a foreigner in my own country. I too could be under suspicion.' He has started to lay false trails, suggesting that he is travelling to Amiens on business. No mention of Calais or England. The sooner they can be on their way the better. 'And the *laissez-passer*?'

William suppresses a bilious sensation in his gut. 'I have to trust Basan - '

'Connections.' Alphonse replies. 'It is how the world turns.'

They agree to meet again just before the night of the Masquerade to confirm that everything is in place. As soon as they have the *laissez-passer*, they can leave.

Night and day, Paris is alive with carts, converging on the area around the Abbey of St Germain. The creak and clatter of wood and iron on cobbles is accompanied by more exotic sounds. The screech of parakeets, growl of tigers, the roar of bears, all travelling in bright painted cages proclaim their arrival for the Fair. In the coffee-houses, drowsy Parisians remind each other of the rhinoceros, which was the star of the Fair some years earlier and made its owner a small fortune in the process.

Sweet-meats, cheeses of all varieties, silks, spices, hats and leather goods, chased-silver toys, every form of luxury and necessity are wheeled into the vast indoor hall, with its high timbered roof, alongside the Abbey. Exhausted traders pack their goods on to trestle-tables lining the nine paths which criss cross the market. They catch what rest they can in rickety lofts somehow perched above their stalls. Many forgo sleep altogether, making extra sous by renting out their mattresses to the *filles de joie*, who swarm the streets tempting trade from gawping apprentices to gentlemen of every inclination. Money changes hands. It is the Fair's be all and end all.

Out on the streets, the raffle shysters unfold their tables and draw in their victims.

'Double your money...'

They target those about to enter the Market, their purses are still heavy.

'Watch the numbers now, watch the numbers, here's a one, here's a three and who has the six?

An accomplice shouts out and pockets the money already wagered.

William skirts around the nightly gathering of the mob. It's just like the August madness of St Bart's back home. But he's grateful for the distraction. The city is in a fever of comings and goings. One more will not be noticed.

The afternoon of Basan's Masquerade finds William and Alphonse almost ready to escape. Wille's post-chaise is theirs for the taking. They have letters of trade and Boydell's prints. But the precious laissez-passer is still elusive. He must wait until the evening for more news. To while away the hours, William joins the crowd heading towards St Germain. They are in good voice, singing and chanting as they go. The Fair is a mixing barrel. Everyone is drawn in, from noble to impoverished apprentice, from princess to seamstress. And since they are at war, there are loud, rough-polished cadets about to march away. A roar goes up. One hapless pickpocket drops his latest catch. He is kicked black and blue, but he is soon forgotten by the urgent mob. It thickens and sways on as one heaving beast.

William lets himself be borne along, past stalls piled high with pastries, through a steam-cloud dense with the scent of coffee, pickled brews of every flavour, fruit-laden perfumes. Beside him a lady dotted with beauty spots peers from her chaise, carried by two servants, dripping with sweat. Unable to progress, she waits becalmed, a target for bawdy invitations. From behind her fan, she pretends offence but cannot ignore the attention. Smartly-dressed young innocents wonder at this street ribaldry and pull their parents' coat sleeves, asking questions which will never receive honest answers.

William is listening for the music of the players. He has a passion for these *forains*, these street comedians, the trickster Arlecchino, long-suffering Pulcinella and their companions. His random quest draws him from raucous puppet show to torch-carrying acrobats flipping and leaping in slick unison. He pauses to witness the sobering magic of a bearded monkey, who can count and a smug cat, who predicts the future by walking with intent across a spread of cards.

'This one for fortune, this for a fall and this for death by grim accident.'

William also has a purchase in mind. There's a stall he knows where exotic masks from Italy are sold. If Basan's masquerade is to be his last soirée in Paris, he intends to bow out in Southern style.

He accepts a swig of *eau-de-vie*, releasing a *sou* from the purse clenched in his fist for safety. There's a rat-a-tat-tat and a circle opens around the drummer.

'Gather round, gather round, my friends.'

'Aye and you'll be passing round your hat!' shouts one groundling.

'We have to live!' comes the reply. And with a breath, another minstrel sends a stream of fire into the air so close to the meddlesome youth to make him leap.

'I could do as well as you any day,' he shouts back.

'Not what your lady-friend told me.'

'Ha!' Screams the crowd. '*Cocu! Cocu!*'

The cocky lad shrinks into oblivion, to hide his shame at being bested and probably not for the first time.

As the hurdy-gurdy strikes up, William scours the nearby stalls, he knows the mask maker will be close. Another burst of flame strikes a silver glint off to his left and William finds his man.

This year he has crescent moons, white faced, high cheek bones swathed in silk; blood-red devils, crowned jesters, multi-coloured tricksters, playing cards stacked ten high in patterns, dancing leaves bursting from the mouth of a Green Man, the smooth threat of an Egyptian jackal's head... and a three-cornered hat above a dark, smooth-skinned half mask, the Rake's favourite. There are pearls and rubies inlaid on golden leather. A sharp-horned goat, a Capricorn. And among these hollow eyes and gaping mouths, the mask makers, Armando and his daughter Francesca, are stitching, gluing and gilding. They are geniuses of the night at play.

Armando greets William with an embrace.

'I missed you last year, Guglielmo!'

'Indeed yes, I was away in your fair country.'

'Ah *che bellezza*! See Francesca, I said we would see him again.'

She turns to grace William with a shy smile. In that instant, he is transported back to the streets of Rome. He is sketching the chestnut curls of a young woman singing songs from her southern village. Day after day he would look for her in the shade where she slept away the hot afternoons.

'Remember, last time he took our Capricorn. La bella Gabrielle. She is not here tonight?'

Just the mention of her name drops ice in Willliam's blood. He feels himself shrink back.

'Ah, no, well - no matter - perhaps it is time for another mask, Guglielmo, to take you to a different world?'

William tries several, finally settling for a Harlequin in flaming crimson and deep turquoise. Though the expression on it's face is more melancholic than mischievous.

'I am returning soon to England but one day, one day I will be back.'

'*Arriverderci, Guglielmo, Arriverderci* '

By now the life-force pulsing through the Fair is even more intense and playful but it no longer has the power to lift him. Indeed, the opposite. William pushes a sad path home through the crowds. He will sleep for a few hours until it is time to dress for the Masquerade at l'Hotel de Serpente.

Later that evening, he is leaning over his narrow metal tub, pouring cold water over his head and shoulders. The shock revives him. It never fails. But it does let loose a flood of memories. Ma, pail in hand as he, still a boy, half- shrieks, half- laughs beneath her icy shower. "*It closes up the pores,*" she assures him, "*It will save you from all manner of diseases.*" Then, to a French summer's day, by a millstream. He stands uncertain, fearful, while Gabrielle, happy as a seal, calls him in. A city boy, he has never been full body under water. How will he not drown? But her jibes are spur enough and in a moment, he is with her, riding the swift current together, with kicks and splashes, until they reach a bend with overhanging trees. They dangle, arms entwined about the branches, embracing as the water rushes by.

He blinks a tear, and the memory is washed away.

William has worn black cloth since reaching an age when the decision became his own. It suits the colouring he received at birth, black hair, black eyebrows, black eyes. It is his mark, just as the black engravers ink is his life. Yet, in Paris, he has seen how black can be a foil to set off a layering of bright colour, a turquoise cravat or scarlet cloak.

Sadly, as he fingers through the more flamboyant items in his half-packed case, he finds each one is a gift from Gabrielle, each one a moment shared. At least he has his choice of mask. He unwraps the brooding harlequin and tries it on before the mirror. It is disturbing how it speaks to him of loss. A swig of brandy is the only solution to enliven his spirit, before he sets off for the encounter with the beau monde of Paris, most of whom know him as Gabrielle's amour.

Steeling himself for their looks and whispers, he crosses the Place St Michel and turns up towards the junction with Rue de la Serpente. Behind the heavy double gates, the elegant strain of a viola and harpsichord confirms the soirée is in play. He steps into the courtyard, already a bustle of glittering gowns, as masks greet masks with elaborate courtesy.

The theme is Winter Fire and Basan has not shirked on candles and torches. Every aspect of the ivy-clad facade appears aflame and in the windows, three floors of flickering light beckon the revellers inwards and upwards. Already, there is dancing in the ballroom, country style. The joyful music loosens the limbs and William finds himself at ease again. In the spirit of Pan, there is coquetry and flattery abounding. He catches sight of a reflection in a mirror, a shoulder wrapped in muslin, he thinks he recognises her dark tresses, the arch in her neck... He rushes to see but the shape is gone, swirling on among the gods and goddesses of the night. Was it Gabrielle in the soft flicker of candle-light? But she is surely far from Paris. Then Boucher, the painter, parts the crowds, making his entrance extravagantly masked. Everyone knows it his him and his wife and muse, Marie-Therese.

William thinks he sees Elizabeth Le Bas incline her discreet disguise to Madame Boucher. He has no desire for an encounter with these two devoted friends of Gabrielle. He slips through a doorway, along another corridor, beside the kitchen, steals a couple of pastries passing by and walks towards the sound of a soprano. Instead he finds the gaming room, with sober players at every table. He sits in one corner, to calm the blood. He has sworn to himself he will not play. He has too much at hazard already with his departure imminent.

He is engaged by the rival displays of extravagance, when he feels a firm hand on his shoulder. 'Good evening, monsieur le Gallois.'

He recognises the voice of his host, Basan.

'I am disappointed, I had more faith in my disguise.'

'Ah you men in black, you are more distinct than you suspect, in this sea of colour. If you know who you are looking for.'

'You were looking for me?

'There is someone who would like to meet you. I believe it will be of mutual advantage. But keep your wits about you.'

He guides William through two twists in the corridor and up a narrow backstairs to a large room, which is surprisingly quiet. A man is standing with his back to them, warming his hands at the fire. He is slight, of average build and height. When he turns he does so with a measured confidence. He wears no mask though indulges in a slight adjusting of his court wig, while Basan introduces William.

The stranger is in his middle years, somewhat worn about the eyes. His voice is soft, seductive in tone.

'I consider this a neutral zone, monsieur. Your anonymity is guaranteed.'

At once embarrassed, William removes his mask and places it on a side table.

Basan makes the introduction:

'Comte Charles- Francois de Broglie,' he announces and then retires, leaving them alone.

As the door closes, the sudden draft causes the candle-flames to dance and cast disturbing shadows on the wall. William remains standing, awkward and in shock at the sudden twist the evening has taken. He has only heard of one de Broglie and assumes this stranger is the Marshal.

'No, the battlefield is my brother Victor's domain.'

William sees he is irked by the confusion.

'I am the King's **personal** Chargé d'Affaires. We all play our part in the game. Sometimes for higher stakes than a cavalryman.'

William inclines his head. 'Delighted'.

He has been in France long enough to know the game of airs and graces. He may not be a gambler but there is a hand being dealt here. Play it well and who knows where it might lead.

De Broglie invites William to sit, pours them both a glass of cognac and joins him. 'Our mutual friend Basan speaks highly of you.'

'He is a good friend and has exquisite taste.'

One side of De Broglie's narrow mouth twitches into a brief smile. 'And France's greatest painter...' The tonic is ironic, as if he has issue with the accolade. '... Boucher himself has taken you under his wing.'

'Yes, he and Paris have been good to me.'

'For a man making his way in the world, these are friends to treasure, and yet I hear you are planning to leave us...'

William gathers his thoughts. The Count makes no effort to draw back. His gaze is unflinching. There is little point in denial. 'I am considering an offer ...'

'Monsieur, how long have you been away from England?'

'It is nearly five years.'

'A long time in a young man's career. And in that time our two countries find ourselves once more at war. And yet you have remained with us, on enemy territory so to speak.'

'For artistic reasons.'

'Indeed, but not that alone'

Again, William looks away. He is not surprised that this man, with his connections, knows more about his circumstances than he would like. But why he is now the subject of interest.

'The charms of Paris are legendary. I believe you have found a muse to inspire your work?'

Again, ice chills William's blood. His reply is just above a whisper. 'Gabrielle de la Roche - an accomplished artist in her own right.'

'You share more than a palette, Monsieur. And yet you wish to leave her and all of this.'

'I have my reasons.'

'Personal or Patriotic?'

'Personal'

Footsteps approach in the corridor, whispers and laughter, a dress brushes against the wall, the door creaks open, a masked Arlecchino peers around, looking for a quiet spot for an assignation, then sees them and retreats, closing the door. De Broglie is not distracted by the intruders. He shifts in his seat and continues. 'To separate the personal from the patriotic is in my experience, impossible. You are Gallois, I believe, William Wynne Ryland?'

'My father is from Wales. Yes. My mother English.'

'And the Wynne?'

'From my Godfather, William Watkins-Wynne.'

'Ah yes the generous benefactor'.

Again, William is startled by de Broglie's knowledge. 'Indeed, since I was a boy, my Godfather has paid for my apprenticeships.'

'And still does?'

'He passed away in '49 and left me annual funds for ten years.'

'So, you will be in need of money soon.'

'I will ... I am already earning my way, Monsieur.'

'Mmm...' Again, the smile flickers and fades away. 'So, let us take stock. We have a young man in Paris with a beautiful French lover, a commission from the leading artist in France, a year of study in Rome, on the threshold of glowing acclaim... and yet **still** you intend to return to England. It must be something very powerful pulling you back. You have never been close to your brothers ...'

At the mention of his family, William feels the familiar beating at his temples. 'Sir it is a private matter. And I resent ...'

'Monsieur William Wynne Ryland, you are here as a guest of the French nation. You are a citizen of a foreign power with whom we are at war. My compatriots and your compatriots are presently slaughtering each other from the Prussian plains to the forests of Canada. May I remind you that you are not in a position to resent anything.'

De Broglie sits back, a slight adjustment to his silken cuffs and the smile returns. The point is made. 'But there is no need for rancour. It is my duty to... connect with those who may wish to be of service to France.'

'Of service?'

'Indeed. My master appreciates fine craftsmanship. Your talents have not gone unnoticed.'

'I am honoured.'

'There is always a place for those who would use their particular, God-given gifts in his service.'

'I have heard that he is a generous benefactor.'

'To his friends he is most generous.' De Broglie's fingers, long and slender, smooth out a crease on his topcoat. 'Monsieur, how closely do you follow events in London?'

'I read the bulletins when they reach us here. Pa... my father writes infrequently.'

'He has a fair hand, though his grammar is wanting.' De Broglie's smile is infuriating. William cannot control the flush in his cheeks. He is being sorely tested.

'A necessary precaution.' The Frenchman assures him.

'I have nothing to hide. As you have no doubt discovered. My father's ramblings about the price of printer's ink are hardly a national secret. The war will not be won or lost because of it. '

'Monsieur. It is not what you have done which interests us, it is what you may do for us in the future. Are you aware of your godfather's loyalties?

The question leaps out of nowhere, trapping the air in William's chest. He murmurs, 'I know he was no friend of the current King of England.'

'Let me add a little to your knowledge. Your godfather was the leader of the Jacobites in Wales. He wanted to be rid of your King George and put a Stuart in his place. In '45, Charles Stuart raised his standard in Scotland and marched south. Your godfather was standing by to raise every rebel in Wales in his cause.'

'He...he was not accused of any crime, after the defeat.'

'Perhaps, but he was willing to bring others into the field on his behalf.'

'Who?'

'My master, Louis.' De Broglie pauses for effect. '...in '44 your beloved godfather made a secret journey to our Royal court at Versailles. His mission, to request our participation in the Stuart uprising. We were to invade England at his invitation. I have seen the letters myself. His code was a simple 'W'. But I can assure you it was him.'

William is silent. If his godfather was truly a traitor... De Broglie is one step ahead. 'I wonder how your godfather would have judged your plans to glorify the image of the next King, the young George.'

So, he has seen Boydell's letter too. 'I am no traitor to England, no soldier either. I am an artist and would earn my living by my graver and the sharp point of a needle ... no other weapons interest me.'

'Indeed?'

The gaze remains. William is aware his feet are twisted tightly one across the other. It is a habit. When engaged intently on his graving, his feet are always locked beneath him. He releases them gently and breathes.

'Let me be plain.' De Broglie says. 'We have, how shall I put it? A vacancy in London for a man with your artistic talents. You have heard perhaps of Dr Hensey.'

'The French spy?'

'I prefer to call him a friend of France. He was most diligent in forwarding information to us.'

'And you wish me to take the place of a man condemned to death, awaiting execution. What makes you think I would even consider this ?'

'That is for you to decide. You have talent and we know you have ambition, but do you have connections?' This last word was more caressed than spoken. 'A man from your background is always in need of friends. In fact, the vacancy is not the one left by the unfortunate Dr Hensey. He was merely the postmaster, the dispatcher of information. Your talents would be wasted in that role. We are in need of maps.'

'Maps?'

'Yes, the details of your coastline, its forts, its harbours, its defences. All of this would be of great interest to the King and my colleague the Secretary of State for War, as they prepare to invade England.'

'That is a traitor's role, sir.' William's blood is now racing.

'I prefer to look at it as a Royal Commission, no more nor less than the one which I believe you are considering. Come Monsieur, there is really no need for pretence, we know all that has been exchanged. We also understand you are intending to return to England with some merchandise for Monsieur Boydell.'

William stares at him. 'I cannot deny that.'

'As we are at war, that may prove difficult, first to transport it safely to Calais and then embark for England.'

'It is a legitimate cargo. Not contraband.'

'True, you and I know that but not everyone might see it that way.

With this the Count rises and walks across to the double window. He peers through the shutters. Then turns back to William. 'We train our men to be diligent, sometimes they overstep the mark, thinking to please us.'

He allows time for the threat to register, then pulls a document from his inside pocket. 'As a gesture of goodwill, I have here a letter of safe transit. Let us call this the first sign of my master's generosity, to the new W.'

William also rises. He takes the letter with a slight bow. 'I am indebted my Lord.'

'Indeed Monsieur, indeed you are.'

The Comte retrieves his mask from a side table. It is a magnificent pattern of sun's rays. He slides it on to his head and, with a bow, disappears into the pulsating crowd which fills the rooms and corridors of Hotel de Serpente.

Chapter 5

Dawn. Two Days Later

William and Alphonse are already half-way to Calais. The borrowed post-chaise, loaded with boxes of prints, rattles and leaps from one deep rut to another. The winter rains have left some stretches of road so deep in mud they have to make frequent diversions. Fortunately, the riders know the route so well that they still cover some fifty miles between breakfast and supper. So far Comte de Broglie's laissez-passer has mightily impressed both Alphonse and every inquisitive official along the way.

'How they look at you! Someone close to God must be on our side.'

At first, William merely inclines his head. But as they are waved through a third time, he does confess: 'Perhaps I did have words with the Almighty's manservant.'

'Well, as long as you did not have to sell your soul.'

William hides his fear with a forced smile. He is still not sure what price de Broglie will demand. But he has had the time to calculate the risks. If he can make it back to England, the rich prize of a King's commission must surely outweigh a threat from foreign spies. He can deny any accusations of complicity as a French fancy, borne out of churlish pique that their golden boy has turned his back on Paris. He is returning to his roots, to make Pa as proud of him as he once was.

When they reach the coast the following day, their papers again secure an easy passage, all the way through town to the harbour. Alphonse cannot contain his joy. 'Monsieur, that was the lightest encounter with the authorities of this Kingdom that I have ever enjoyed. Either they began their *eau-de-vie* early today or you have indeed bargained with the devil.'

William laughs. 'I'd put your money on the brandy, too early for Lucifer.'

And with this they set about transferring their cargo of French prints on to the shifting deck of a waiting packet.

Soon they are under sail and heading for the White Cliffs, some twenty miles ahead of them. The two tired travellers are lulled by the rhythmic slapping of grey-green water against the side. But the wind picks up and the boat begins to pitch and roll, Alphonse is soon awake. William, still half-dozing, watches as he takes a knife and block from his bag and starts to whittle at the wood. He is fashioning a fine handle for an engraver's burin. But some minutes later he slips the handle into his bag and discreetly draws out strips of pocket cloth, some dyed blood red. He begins to tie them together.

'What's this, Alphonse? Another device to secure our prints?'

Alphonse shakes his head and ignores him, until he has the knots complete. 'First, Monsieur, please remember, I am no longer Alphonse, well at least in public.'

He looks around to see if the captain or any of his men are in earshot. 'I am Bailey. *Tout court*. Bailey from London town.'

'*Entendu*', says William but Bailey glares back at him until he concedes 'Understood, Bailey from London Town. And the cloth?'

'*Eh bien*, you see. Bailey with the tooth-ache-' He begins to loop the cloth loosely under his jaw and over his head. '- cannot speak easy.' He tightens the cloth. and can now only mumble. '*Voila!*'

'Ha! says William. 'I have it. A man with the devil's own toothache cannot speak, ergo he cannot betray himself to be a dangerous French Spy; Ingenious. As a loyal citizen, I shall report him to the authorities as soon as we reach Dover.'

For this, he receives a sharp elbow in the ribs.

And so it is that an exhausted half-Welsh art dealer from Paris and his feverish assistant, mighty sick with infected gums, are waved through the port of Dover, with no papers checked other than the bills of trade from Monsieur Basan's print shop. Soon they are heading out in a hired post-chaise, up past the towering fortifications, stippled with cannon. Then they are once again on the open road, direction north-west, towards London. The overnight halt passes without incident. On the second day their rough slumber is broken in the final two miles, when the stench of cattle dung, pigs' guts, human waste and every manner of refuse combines with the acrid smoke from several thousand hearths and wafts its way into their dreams. They are back in the Great Metropolis.

Before long they are rattling up Ludgate Hill, a stone's throw from William's family home in Ave Maria Lane. Bailey has made a miraculous recovery from his toothache. But just before the turning into the Lane, they come to a halt behind a jumble of carts. William can hear Pa's dogs barking fit to burst. Something or someone has riled them. And now there are raised voices.

'Tell 'im, we'll be back! You tell 'im.'

'Aye, to take him to the Sponging house.'

Bailiffs! William leaps out and runs around the corner. A large cart is disappearing off in the direction of Smithfield, carrying a haul of cabinets and clothes. A pair of knuckleheads are still yelling insults over their shoulders, with a wary eye on Rufus and Revel scampering beside the cartwheels, teeth bared.

'Here boy! Here girl!' William shouts.

They stop still for a moment, torn between their duty and a distant memory. They were just over a year old when they last heard that voice.'Ruuufffurrrsss! Reeeevvvvelll!'

In seconds, they come leaping and squealing to greet William, sniffing at his mud-bespattered hose and breeches. Their joy is welcome relief after the encounter. Pa's letters always said money was scarce, but not to this degree. William looks up at the brick-fronted house where he was raised. The paintwork around the windows is a little worn, some pointing is missing, but at least the roof-tiles seem all in place.

By now the carriage has made it into the Lane. William unstraps his bags.'Now don't tarry, Bailey of London Town. You have a fine surprise there for Mr Boydell.'

'Until the morrow then.'

'My thanks for your company and all you have done.'

Bailey grins and passes over the wooden burin handle he fashioned on the boat. 'At your service, Master. Welcome home.'

And with a quizzical look in the direction of the disappearing bailiffs, Bailey leaps back on board and sets off to complete his journey.

William hears the scrape of a window opening above him. Through the narrow gap, a familiar hand appears, waving, then a familiar voice:

'Come Revel! Come Rufus ! The devils have fled...Oh my ! Oh my! There's... there's... It's William!'

And a minute later, out of the open door comes Ma, petite, white-haired Ma, in her blue kerchief and apron. There are hugs and tears and more hugs. Warm words are shared, health enquired after and confirmed, cheeks patted, amid much questioning of the details of his journey. Eventually the torrent of welcome subsides. William enters the old house, taking in the smells, the light, the smoke from the fire. It is all so little changed that for some moments he closes his eyes and feels as if his five years away perhaps never happened. Ma - Mary Ryland - has changed though, just as spirited but somehow ill at ease, as if between the questions about his welfare, something lies waiting to be discussed. But first she will feed him and bring him fresh hunks of bread and dripping and a mug of small beer and sit with him and repeat over and over how he has been missed and how they never thought he would be coming back. His most recent letter had only arrived three days past.

'Pa was not certain which day you would...Still here you are and that is all that matters.'

'Ma. The bailiffs?'

'Ah, yes, those leeches.'

She throws a wrap of paper into the fire. It flares for a moment and dies.

'Grandfather's cabinet?'

'Ay. It was all I could do to make 'em leave. They were after Joseph not his clothes.'

'Where is he?'

'Skulking round the corner in St Martins, with Pa. Do not concern yourself, they'll be back betimes.'

'Nay, I've come this far, I'll go fetch them.'

St Martin's Church on Ludgate Hill has been the Ryland family's refuge since he was a lad. It offered calm and solitude, when sibling rages were boiling over. For William, it was the place where he discovered his love of drawing. Saint's faces, priest's hands, visitors at prayer. All of them made shapes and lines for his pencil to discover. Lost in this exercise, he forgot the daily struggles back home. Though there were some days when all the family came to Church. He and his younger brothers were baptised here. Once a year his father, with a voice too loud for his children, would join in the celebrations of the nearby Stationers Company. These memories run rings inside his head as he walks with a soft tread into the nave.

He finds Pa first, asleep on one of the wooden pews. Joseph is lying next to him playing jacks, killing time like a bored child. Though he is only four years younger than William. He tosses the bones high into the air and catches them on the back of his hand. Pa sits up with a jolt, and Joseph whips round, eyes wide with fear. He has a knife in his hand.

'Whoahh there.'

William's hands are up, palms forward, calming his brother as he might an edgy stallion. And not for the first time.

'Easy there, Jo-boy.'

Joseph is still suspicious, but Pa instantly sees a familiar face.

'No! Is it truly you...?'

'Yes, Pa it is me. Not a ghost, not a bailiff neither.' He says, with a sly glance to Joseph who scowls back.

'Well met, well met, my boy! Come.'

He reaches out for him and they fumble an embrace, with the odour of street spirit enveloping William as they do so.

Pa releases him, scolding Joseph for his chill reception

'Is this a way to greet your long-lost brother? Indeed, any man after five year apart? When he left, you were spinning tops ... And still are,' he winks at William.

With a sullen grunt, Joseph edges forward to give him a peremptory clasp.

'So, this is where you spend your days?' William asks with a smile.

'We had visitors.'

'I know, I saw them. You never said you were in such trouble. Not a word'.

Pa rubs the back of his head as if that is all the response he has in him.

'How much do you owe? And to who?'

Pa glances at Joseph but says nothing.

'Well, for now, the danger is over. Come on, Ma says she'll cook up a fine supper.'

They return in an uneasy silence. Joseph, who has grown in bulk, since William last saw him, wheezes along beside them. His jealousy is dark and palpable.

That evening, just as they are finishing their suet pudding, there is a knock at the heavily-barred front door. It sets Rufus and Revel into another frenzy.

'Hush now!' shouts Pa.

Joseph makes for the side room. William runs to an upstairs window. He is just in time to see a young lad disappearing off down the Lane.

'No need to worry, Pa!' He shouts down.

William finds the familiar double-folded note.

'From John Boydell.'

'Just like him to waste no time.' says Pa.

Taking a candle from the table, William sits by the hearth, to read.

'He thanks for the prints delivered safely by Bailey. And I am invited to visit his shop on Cheapside at my earliest convenience.'

With Ma and Pa relieved, William reads on for himself. Boydell advises him to act as soon as possible on the Royal project. The painter, Allan Ramsay's studio is on the west side of the King's Square in Soho. He is expecting William. The two portraits to be engraved are not yet complete but near enough to gauge the work required. Any contract of engagement should be negotiated directly with the Earl of Bute, who has commissioned the portraits.

William blows out his cheeks and sits back.

'Boydell. The man should be a maker of clocks, he's that precise'

He hands the note to Pa, who has been pouring them both a tot of brandy.

'Perhaps, but that's why he'll soon be the wealthiest print seller in London,' says Pa.

'Well, then, he sets me a good example to follow. I'll be off to see Ramsay's portraits in the morning.'

And with that declaration of intent, William is aware of a profound exhaustion. He downs the brandy and stays awake just long enough to shake out his better clothes for next day's visit.

Chapter 6

William heads west along Fleet Street towards his meeting with Allan Ramsay, the artist. He has no portfolio with him. He will not present himself as another jobbing newcomer from Boydell's stable. No, he has had *un succès fou* in France. It is strange how their language comes to him first as he searches for a phrase. Is he now a man of the world? The very notion makes him smile. So runs the rhythm of his inner thoughts as he crosses streets that are both familiar and seen as if for the first time. While his fellow citizens scurry by, he registers the blackened chimney of his favourite bakehouse on Tavistock Street; the worn-down carvings on Jacques the apothecary's door. Pa always said they were signs of alchemy, vessels for turning lead into gold. He runs his fingers over them for good fortune.

As he passes through Covent Garden, he feels a tightening in his guts. The King's Square in Soho is moments away. Suddenly his choosing to quit Paris lies heavy within him. What is to be expected of him? And what of this Earl of Bute, this Scotsman, manoeuvring into the Prince's favour? There's been no time to test the opinion of the coffee-houses, to sample the latest gossip. Is he right to align himself with the new Court-in-waiting?

He turns left into Long Acre, just by the Carriage Manufactory. A family of painters are adding final touches to their latest six-wheeler. If he continues west, he can go by Leicester Fields and see for himself the Prince's residence.

Outside grand Leicester House, William stops for a moment. He imagines the young George, the future king, peering out at him from its half-shuttered windows. "Who is this ambitious Welshman?" He'd surely be the only one. It is the Scots who rise by favour of the Earl. And these are new men from the North. Not Jacobites. They swear loyalty to Bute and his protégé, the Prince.

William strolls on towards Soho and into the Square. At the centre of the ornate garden is the century-old statue of the merry monarch, King Charles. How does one turn frail human flesh into the regal figure of a King? With a bow to His Majesty in stone, he crosses the Square and announces his arrival at the ground floor of Allan Ramsay's studio.

'Mr Ramsay is in a sitting but will be finished shortly.' The assistant invites him to step up one floor, to wait in the family's private room, where tea is served. The walls of the drawing room are hung with red chalk studies, many of them of sights William recognises from his own journeys in and around Rome: the Arch of Constantine, the Coliseum, the Villa d'Este at Tivoli. The dates are recent. Ramsay has only returned to London in the past year.

Though charmed by these echos of Italy, it is the oil painting above the fireplace that catches William's attention. The portrait of a young woman is signed by Ramsay. She wears a fine lace shawl over a burgundy gown and sits beside a vase of cut flowers. But in her left hand what is that she is holding? A white rose, the symbol of the Jacobites in '45, when they tried to seize the British Crown. Yet Ramsay has chosen to show the rose dangled face down. A sign of grief for a lost cause?

Some might say it is treachery, from an artist commissioned to paint the future King of England, the arch-enemy of the Jacobites. Whatever the intention, William is on his guard, after his encounter with de Broglie, the French spy chief.

The door swings open and the room is instantly full of a gracious energy that dispels his fear. 'Ha! *Buon giorno,* Master Ryland. *Come sta?*' With his swarthy complexion and deep, brown eyes, this Scot could easily be mistaken for a citizen of Rome. 'Allan Ramsay, at your service.'

'*Molto Bene! Grazie*'. William replies with a slight bow.

'See, even on a chill February morning, we can share some southern warmth. I believe you were in Italy last year-?'

William begins a reply but Ramsay continues, '-our journeys must have crossed. My wife and I were on an extended stay. As you no doubt know, we were obliged to leave Scotland in somewhat of a hurry. It is a strange wee word, "elope" but I can thoroughly recommend it.'

'I can see it has served you well.' William turns to the chalk sketches. 'These are the fruits of your visit?'

'Yes, ancient sites, Old Masters... and a wee daughter too. Such times!'

They walk around the room, sharing experiences. By the time they reach the portrait over the fireplace, William feels emboldened to enquire: 'And this is ...?'

'My wife, Margaret.'

'Exquisite, and a lover of fine fabric. Such lacework. Many Parisian *demoiselles* would die for this.'

'Indeed, a blessing.'

'... and the white rose?'

'Aye, I thought that might catch your eye.'

William nods. 'A Jacobite rose, from the Painter of the future King's Portrait ...?'

'It was Margaret's choice, though more in sorrow than in anger. This portrait is not for public display. But with your background I thought you might appreciate it.'

William feigns ignorance.

'Your Godfather?'

So, the word is out. 'You are the second person who has spoken of his Jacobite leanings.' William says with some caution.

'The leader of the secret Cycle of the White Rose? They were more than leanings. He led the Society in Wales.'

'It is still fresh news to me.' William feels like he is at sea, watching clouds to see if a storm is coming.

'There is much talk of a French invasion, of barges being built in secret along their northern coast.' says Ramsay.

'I saw nothing. We reached Calais late in the day and left early in the morning. But we are at war. Rumours spread.'

'Aye, well, perhaps my little rose-'

'-is your insurance?' William suggests. 'It is well to be cautious.'

'Aye, given what you and I are undertaking.'

'Indeed, and how does the Earl view all this?'

Ramsay invites William into an adjoining room. A long oak table is covered with preparatory sketches for the two portraits. William takes in the soft features of the young Prince George, not yet twenty years of age. There are pieces of ermine and brocade, references for texture. In the far corner of the room two tall easels are draped in green baize.

Ramsay picks up a red chalk sketch of the Earl and passes it to William.'See. Our man. He believes he has the finest legs in Christendom.'

'You do him proud. I am sure.' William says, returning the sketch with a smile.

'Aye, well, here's Bute's game. His Lordship is looking forwards. Now, he knows I once painted for the Jacobites. More than a few of them. But see, says he, they are bygones. You know he's all for making peace with the French.'

'So we must make his profile public.'

Ramsay makes a mock salute. 'Him and his protégé. The Young Prince, bred in England.'

He steps aside and pulls the green cloth off the easels to reveal two full-length portraits in oil, one of the young George, the other of the Earl. 'One is born to rule, the other aspires to govern.'

Neither canvas is yet finished but William explores the strokes, the detail in the Crown and garments. To do these paintings justice, his engraving will take at least two years. Ramsay agrees. William must return soon to examine the portraits at his leisure. 'Once you have agreed terms with the Earl, of course. He is most often at his house out at Kew. There he is more at ease. Though, a word of warning.' Ramsay rests a hand on William's shoulder, 'he is a vain, bombastic man, you'll see as much for yourself -'

They are interrupted by the sound of a carriage coming to a halt, dogs barking and loud voices, then a weighty knock on the door downstairs. Ramsay is not expecting another client. His assistant comes running in, flustered and out of breath, urging Ramsay into the room next door for a whispered message. He returns, moments later, somewhat pleased. 'It appears dear William, that your meeting with the Earl is to take place a degree earlier than expected. Would you care to join me?'

William is now furious with himself for bringing no examples of his work. Entering the bright reception room, he bows to the Earl of Bute and the five or six members of his entourage, though he finds it hard not to look longer than he should at Bute's shapely calves. Truly they are magnificent and set off to some effect by the manner of his standing, one leg forward, just slightly bent at the knee. Pure chance or mere affectation? Now is not the time to judge. The Earl is in full flow.

'Here we are, here we are! Now then. You...you are all acquainted I believe.' Bute indicates a heavy-set, florid faced gentleman beside him. 'Perhaps not? William Chambers, architect, savant, all things good. A Scot on a fine day, with some Chinese and Swedish thrown into the mix, eh, a Chinese Viking, I say. He lived out East, among them, for years. Ha! so, there we have him and of course, Mr Ramsay.'

Allan Ramsay makes a gracious bow, as Bute continues. 'Artist *extraordinaire* and with so much to commend him, now he has renounced his rebel days... Not least his ability to steal one of the most handsome women in Scotland. And here now, I assume... Come, Come.' Bute beckons William forward. 'We have young William Wynne Ryland Esquire, fresh from the charms of Paris and eager to glorify the future King. Correct? All present? Good, well met, fine gentlemen because there are changes afoot and we must proceed in concord. This is not entirely an artistic endeavour, much though that has to recommend it. We are all here, why? Because there is a new locus of power, new men are rising and we must celebrate them... the future King, and I. We must be more widely known. And the sooner we begin the better. Who knows the ways of the Good Lord? Though it is indeed likely that some day fast approaching we shall be called upon.'

There is a shuffling of feet, a sharing of glances to demonstrate approval. 'Now good Mr Ramsay has already been at work. His canvases are not flashes of vanity, to gather dust in some royal corridor, they are to be the progenitors, if you will, of many versions that will emerge both from the team of Mr Ramsay and as engravings under the hand of good Mr Ryland. Should he prove willing to join our band.'

Bute's glance towards William, is one of expectation. This is a demand not a request. 'As patron, I may say, I am not without taste. If I meddle it is in my nature. Though I bow to superior knowledge when needs must.' Again, he pauses for no more than a second. 'Some claim I am lacking in humility. Tis true!' He slaps his gloved hand on the table. 'I will make no apology for that. Who became a leader in this world without a degree of arrogance? Did the Greeks value Alexander for his meekness or do we praise Voltaire for a line that fails to rattle the walls of conceited princes. No! So we too must do some rattling. You shall clothe our will and our strength in ermine, display on your canvases, your copper plates, the full majesty of the Crown that shall sit one day on the head of a new George, a new King. And in that glory stands our strength. I hope that I can count on your support.'

A chorus of 'Milord' is graced by the arrival of wine. 'A toast gentlemen? To George our present King and his successor, Prince George'

'To George ...!'

William has scarcely a moment to empty his glass, when Bute approaches and ushers him to a corner of the room, out of earshot of the others. 'So, Mr Ryland. You have been much feted in Paris, land of our enemies. And now you have returned to ply your scraper at home. I assume you intend to remain with the victors in this tiresome war!'

'Milord, one must search out masters wherever they reside. In Art just as in Politics.'

'Quite so. Quite so. You are aware you are not the first to be asked. Robbie Strange was not available.'

'So I understand.' William lowers his voice. 'A prior appointment in Rome, I hear.'

'So he alleges. He will learn he is not a man of our future.' Bute summons an acolyte to fill their glasses. 'And you, Mr Ryland, are you a man of our future? Five years amongst the French might make a wise Earl wonder.'

'I wield a graver not a sword, Milord.'

'Well, you make a good choice to keep it so. Deliver on this commission and your skills will be much in demand.

'England's star is rising, Milord. Under your leadership, we could rival the French in more than canon.'

Bute nods with some vigour. 'So our mutual friend, Mr Boydell, insists. He claims we have the artists to challenge them. Ha! Let's hope they do not invade before we can prove that eh?'

William senses a blush rising. He feigns a coughing fit. Just days before he was facing de Broglie and learning of just such an invasion plan. Fortunately, the Earl has already veered off on another tack.

'Now, apropos, I understand that the price of engraving is on the up. Would you have me deal with Boydell or shall we make our own arrangements?'

'I am my own man, milord.'

'It is the path to fortune. This does of course depend on the will and disposition of his future Majesty.'

'I trust you have that matter in your power, Milord.' He is a monkey to flattery this Scottish Laird.

'Well, let us say I have been granted some freedom, some funds. Now you have seen Ramsay's work, how long do you consider it will take to see them engraved?'

William knows he must be strong. No client of Le Bas' ever believed the time it takes to line-engrave a portrait. 'It is a complex work.'

'How long, sir, how long?'

'Two years at a minimum.'

'Two years!' Bute shakes his head as if he has misheard.

William attempts a smile. 'It is in the nature of the craft, Milord. One cannot hasten it. No-one who knows the skill will tell you any different.'

'Aye well. I have heard as much from other sources. Mezzotint would be more swift, they say.'

Again William nods and smiles. 'But my copper plates are best suited to deliver the many prints you require.'

'Quite so, quite so. I have heard that too. I will endeavour to engage with the future King on your behalf, for a sum of a hundred guineas per annum. We will see if more is needed until the job is done but I will stay close sir. I will be at your shoulder often enough.'

William suppresses his excitement and pushes further. 'And the rights Milord, to the finished plate and printing?'

'Well, as I understand it, you have Hogarth and his law of copyright to thank for that. With the King's blessing they would be yours.' With that the Earl of Bute, and his shapely calves, exits the building, followed closely by his eager architect, William Chambers.

'They are off to build more cottages in Kew,' laughs Ramsay, as they watch the Earl's carriage depart. But William is too engrossed in his own thoughts to register the jibe. It seems within a day of his arrival in London, he is well on his way to becoming *Calcographus Regis Britanniae*... The King's Engraver.

William says his farewells and heads towards St Martin's Lane, past his former drawing school. Outside Old Slaughters Coffeehouse he looks up at the first floor window to see if Hogarth is at his favourite seat, watching the world pass by. But today the wicked and the impoverished are safe from his keen eyes. The thought puts William in mind of his own beginnings. The deal with Bute bodes well but there is no certainty when the Royal guineas will start to flow his way. So, he sets off for the Strand, to the banking house of Messrs Pemberton, Touché and Grave, who control his Welsh Godfather's estate. For nearly a decade, it has been the source of a modest but constant stream of funds. Now there is less than a year left before the legacy dries up. He informs the clerk on duty of his return to England and obtains a small advance to see him through the coming month.

Back home in Ave Maria Lane, Pa and Joseph are in the studio, working a short print run for bookplates. Ma ladles out some pea soup and sits down beside him. In her soft, weary voice, she reveals more about their troubles. They stem as much from Joseph's gaming losses as from Pa's drinking habits. William offers her some coins from his advance. He swears her to silence. Joseph would call it charity and erupt.

That evening there's another message.

My dear Boy.

William smiles. When Boydell sees advantage, he is all oil and charm.

I am so pleased you have already made the acquaintance of Ramsay and the Earl.

A fine pair ... Do come to see me tomorrow.

The champion of English print sellers holds court beneath the sign of the Unicorn, on the corner of Queen Street and Cheapside. It is here that John Boydell reigns over an enterprise of paper and ink. He has always cast a weathered eye to the main chance. When he first walked to London from his native Flintshire, he was minded to make his fortune with the East India Company. But the vicious manner of the Company men did not appeal. Instead, he found himself attracted to the art of engraving. He became an apprentice by day and a student of drawing at night, attending the life classes at Hogarth's St Martins Lane Academy. Though he soon discovered he could make a better living from trading prints than making them.

Discipline and order are the watchwords which govern every aspect of his life. His morning begins at five o'clock with a cold splash under the pump in Ironmonger Lane. For the rest of the day, no time nor money is wasted. Even his marriage to his beloved Elizabeth was trimmed to the bone: "Our mutual happiness was not interrupted by visitors or feasting; not one farthing spent, not so much as a glass of wine or any addition of clothes."

Queen Street, Cheapside, is where shoppers come in search of novelty and tradition in equal measure. Boydell has a nose for what sells well. He caters for all tastes: the landscapes of Claude Lorrain, the storm scenes of Vernet, Hunter's gravid uterus or Mr Milton's curious set of geometrical prints.

As William enters, there's a barely perceptible upwards nod from his host. He should wait for him in the private room. Here the privileged visitor can view his Hogarth prints, a portrait by Sir Joshua Reynolds, or fresh landscapes by Poussin, newly arrived from Paris. William takes the stairs to the inner sanctum. Its odour of leather, polish and paper dust never changes. He settles himself into a broad-backed armchair and dreams that one day he will have his own establishment to rival Boydell.

Suddenly an inner door behind him swings wide open. A shock of blond hair wrapped in a blanket hurtles into the room. It stops abruptly when it realises the chair is occupied. 'Oh my!... Oh dear! ' comes a young girl's voice from within the blanket.

William has little time to react before John Boydell himself walks in. 'Mary you little ragamuffin! Whaaaattt are you doing in my office?'

A smiling face emerges. 'Sorry Uncle, Jos and I were playin' and I thought he were hidin' in here, so I came runnin' in and ... Oh dear!'

Amused, William observes the infamous Boydell carapace soften and melt away. 'Well, you should learn to knock before you enter. What would my brother have said! Now go out and come back nicely.'

'I don't know nicely,' says the voice.

'Ha! Run along, until you do. Go find Josiah, he will teach you.'

The blond-haired bundle disappears.

'Apologies; Mary, my niece. She's a handful but a bright one. I wager one day she and her brother will be running this printshop. With no children of our own, it will be a comfort.'

He strides to the window, to keep an eye on the flow of customers. With his back to William, he comes straight to the point. 'You did a fine job relieving the French of such excellent prints. Bailey has been with us, sorting through the lists and all is good. I am astonished they let you go so freely...'

He turns. His left eyebrow adds a question mark to the observation. William will not be drawn. 'You must have done something to please them. I hear you beat them at their own game.'

William fingers his cravat.

'Everything in Paris is driven by fashion or money., When I won the Rome Prize it was assumed that guineas must have been exchanged.

'And were they?'

'Nay, I won. Fair and square. We live and die by our gravers do we not Mr Boydell?'

'Indeed, history, portraits, pastoral. Mark my words, we'll soon be leading the French. That time is nigh. Apart from your good self, there are some excellent burinistes coming through, Woollett and ...But I digress, we have some guineas to exchange ourselves, I believe.'

The fingers on William's right hand seem to tingle at the thought. Amused, he stretches them one by as if he is counting out a price. 'Ten per cent of the value. As we agreed.'

'Hmm, I have to sell them first. Though to be sure, they'll fly off without a care. An advance would be acceptable?'

Boydell takes a bill already prepared, adds his brief, efficient signature and hands over the paper, with just a degree of reluctance. He sits himself in a chair close to William. 'I am obliged to you for one matter. Your man, Bailey, fine worker, careful hands. I am minded to offer him work in my shop. What say ye?'

William allows one eyebrow to twitch upwards. 'He was highly thought of by Basan and Le Bas, and I have no hold on him.'

'Well, the 'Bailey' doesn't fool me, he's a French man through and through, but no mind he can help me with my correspondence. So long as he's no spy!'

'Oh, I can vouch for Bailey.' William replies, pulling himself swiftly out of the deep armchair, to hide the colour rising to his cheeks. He is sure his awkwardness does not go unnoticed. They walk together down into the main print room. A set of anatomical works, engraved by his former tutor, Ravenet, catches William's eye. 'Le Bas was asking after him. Said he was one of his best pupils'.

'Well, we've done well to keep him over here. He's my quiet genius. I hear that he and Hogarth are about to collaborate again.'

'Still in Lambeth?' William asks.

'Yes, he is at home among the orchards.'

With that, they take polite leave of each other. A new relationship has begun. Both share ambition but William will be his own man.

'It is agreed.' William declares a week later, at dinner with Ma and Pa. 'I shall shortly be starting the engraving of Ramsay's Prince George.'

He is also tempted to share his work on Leda and the Swan. But he holds back. The copper plate has lain untouched in his bags since he returned from Paris. His memory of Gabrielle is too raw, too recent.

The next morning he is woken by the tolling of St Sepulchre's bells. It is so close and so loud the window panes threaten to leap from their frames. There is no more mournful sound in London. It will be an Execution Day. In Newgate Gaol, just a street away, a huddle of prisoners in the condemned cell will be waking to their last day. Soon they will be bound and loaded on to carts, while the Ordinary makes his rounds exhorting them to pray for their tarnished souls. And then they will be off, rumbling along the Oxford Road to the hanging tree at Tyburn.

To blank out such thoughts, he rises from his bed to unwrap his drawings for Boucher's Leda and the copper plate, with its first marks incised in a Paris which already seems so far away. The foliage is in outline, as is the swan's arched neck and wings but still no detail, no identity in the two young women. He pulls out more sketches and finds some of Gabrielle, her profile, sleeping and laughing. Each one a self-inflicted wound.

And still the bells toll and horses neigh in the streets below. More carts will be arriving to transport other wretches westward. As on every Execution Day, Ma will be on her knees, mouthing prayers, in the alcove by the fire which has long- served as her private chapel; Pa, crossing himself and mumbling his own incantation, practices for the moment he too will meet his Maker. He is adamant, there is no destiny that we do not make ourselves.

Gabrielle's eyes look up at William in accusation. Between the sketches he finds some white feathers, which must have fallen into his portfolio during that wild night. They make her absence, his loss, more brutal. He feels a sudden urge to escape. He will cross the river to Lambeth Marsh. To look for his old master, the Frenchman Simon Ravenet. He too once made the journey from Paris, to fashion a new life for himself as Hogarth's Engraver.

Chapter 7

As a young apprentice his daily journey to Ravenet's Lambeth studio took him east, then south, but today he has a mind to see the new Westminster Bridge. His portfolio is heavy on his shoulder. It bulges with his Paris prints and the Leda plate. In another leather pouch he carries the set of sharp-tipped burins, which Ravenet gifted him just before he set off for Paris, some five years past. There have been times when he felt he could lose everything except them and still be happy. But now, as he strides into the sharp wind whipping up the Strand, he has grander ambitions in play.

After half an hour of vigorous walking, sidestepping chaises and carriages, he passes through Whitehall. And there is the bold, new Bridge. Fifteen arches of brick, Portland and Purbeck stone. Half-way across he stops to rest in one of the alcoves. On the left bank, he can see the dome of St Paul's Cathedral and the smoking city bundled around it. It has always been home but now it bristles with possibilities, with Royal prospects. And on the opposite side of the silvered Thames, a more sedate prospect stretches back into the distance. A pattern of orchards is lined with ditches and sharp poplars. Here fruit bushes and vegetable plots thrive in the lush fields reclaimed from marshland.

Though, even now, along the curving bank, he can see how the new bridge is bringing change to this gentle terrain. Like pockmarks, a scattering of swiftly built hovels, stands out along the edges of the river. How long before these harbingers of industry spread across the open ground? He presses on and soon sees smoke idling up from the chimneys alongside the L-shaped cottage and former stable block, where he was apprenticed. He remembers the excitement when he first came here to learn from Hogarth's favourite collaborator. In those days there were always two or three preparing the inks, or the acid baths. But when he knocks on the familiar oak door, he is greeted by Jackson, the elderly housekeeper. There are no apprentices, and the master is not at home.

'He left early to take the copper plates to Battersea, the Enamel works, a mile down river. He'll be back by noon.'

William decides to walk on, beside the river. In the distance he can see the flint and stone tower of St Mary's Church, standing high above the Archbishop's Palace. He follows the ancient pilgrim's path, a route he often took as an apprentice. The South door still opens to a gentle push. There is a lingering trace of incense from the morning's Mass. Now all is quiet inside. Sunlight strikes bright patterns on the whitewashed walls. Although he is now a grown man and has every right to visit, he finds himself treading lightly, as if he is trespassing on God's property.

To the left of the baptism stone font, he finds the low arched opening to the Tower. Ducking his head, he slips through to the base of narrow circling stairs. He offloads his heavy portfolio and pouch. There are one hundred and thirty-three steps to the top.

Winding his way up and round and round again, he is soon breathing hard. He loses count at around fifty. He is grateful for a brief rest, holding on to a rope dangling down the central column. The odour of cold stone has not changed. He passes the wooden doors to the belfry, with its eight squat iron bells. He was once caught in the tower on a ringing day and he was deaf to all sound for a week.

At last, he reaches the half-sized door through which he can clamber outside, on to the square wooden platform. Whether it is from relief or emotion, his eyes well with tears as he finds himself once again in a place he first discovered at fifteen. Behind the door, there are still the faint traces of his initials, *W. W. R.*, scratched with his burin. It earned him a slap from his master when he heard him boasting to his fellow-apprentices. But there it is, one of his first marks with the tool that is now going to earn him a Royal Pension.

The view lifts him as high as it did on that first day. The morning's air is so clear he can see the shadowed hills of Hampstead and Highgate in the far distance. Below them the familiar lines of his city reminds him of Pa's prize possession, a map of London engraved by Wenceslaus Hollar. William is convinced the Dutchman must have climbed this tower himself and seen London as it was in his time, some hundred years earlier.

He lies flat on his back on the wooden platform. He feels again the thrill of this secret space. He would come here in all weathers, sheltering in the stairwell from a spring downpour or huddling against the stone parapet to watch lightning crash over London.

And he was not always alone. Here too are memories of first love, of promises, long-broken and left far behind when he set off for Paris.

Closing his eyes he can see Mary Brown at her fruit stall, where he first meets her outside the gates of the Archbishop's Palace. Her father keeps his Grace's orchards. She is fourteen years old, with the spirit of a young girl but the cares of a woman much older. She is still shifting through grief for her mother, dead from a wasting sickness, six months before. With her twin brother already away at sea, she is now the carer for the family. Her days are broken by moments of a tormented grief. It leaves her craving solace and reassurance.

So, William, the apprentice from the city, with his shock of black hair, and ready smile is an exotic creature to her. He shakes her world. She in her turn is a comfort to him. He is welcomed into her family. St Mary's is their Church though she has never been up the Tower.

For many months she will not join him. But she is curious about his work. She visits him at Ravenet's studio and soon she starts to help with the preparations of ink. She watches William, entranced by the ease with which he marks his plates . She starts to learn the trade. She is soon of great assistance to Ravenet.

But then one day she hears William in whispered conversations. There are plans afoot that he will not share. There is a chill between them.

Then comes the morning when he announces that he will be leaving for Paris - in a matter of days.

'How long will you be gone?'

William will not answer. At first she wrote but after the first year he had heard nothing more from her .

William wakes from his reverie when the sun is almost overhead. He rushes down the steps, takes up his portfolio and heads outside. Surely Ravenet must be returned from Battersea by now.

Just as he leaves the church, he sees a young woman. Wrapped against the bitter wind, in muffler and heavy coat. He is certain she is familiar. Something about the way she walks, somehow rolling on the balls of her feet. It is surely her. He walks at a brisker pace. Just as she is about to cross the road he calls out.

'Mary! Mary Brown.'

The bob of brown hair turns into the sun, towards him. He squints to see.

'Sir, you are mistaken. I am not Mary. I am Sarah.'

Confused, he stammers an apology and heads back along the pilgrim path.

William finds Ravenet in the studio. He glances up from a book of medical illustrations. He has never been an ebullient soul and the passing years have further softened his beard and his manner.

'Ahhhh... *Cher Guillaume*. I am honoured by your visit.'

He puts the book down gently and rises.

'I heard tell you were home, but I rarely venture across the River these days.'

They embrace. William feels a loss of bulk in the old master's frame, a fragility beneath his thick woollen coat. 'You are wise. Frenchmen are not always met with favour.'

Ravenet sighs. 'Yes. There are many that must keep their loyalties to themselves but at least Boydell stands by me and Hogarth too.'

He gestures to the array of prints hanging all around the walls. Scenes from Hogarth's *Marriage à la Mode*, designs for the Battersea enamels, and anatomical works for Dr Hunter. He picks up a sheet depicting the arteries of the heart and thrusts it into William's hands. Ravenet has never been one for light discourse.

'Look, see here. I ask myself, is it God's or Nature's work? How could any power conceive of this, prior to creating it? It is said the good Lord counts even the hairs of our head, but how? It is truly beyond our understanding. I sit here, my burin gouging line by line. Am I alone? Or somehow a hireling of the Creator, copying his work. Is that how you see it too?'

William is aware of Ravenet's kind though probing attention. He is being read, as thoroughly as any anatomical work.

'Sometimes, when I am pushing across the plate, I do wonder who or what is guiding my hand.'

It is enough to earn a nod from Ravenet.

'Forgive me, these are weighty thoughts and you just returned from Paris. A cause for celebration. I have something for the moment.'

Ravenet disappears into the cellar and re-emerges with a dusty bottle.

'Apple brandy. You will share with me and tell me of your plans?'

The spirit loosens William's tongue and he describes all the events leading up to his Royal commission. The fee of 100 guineas is just the beginning. He hopes soon to double that, though even then he could scarcely call himself a gentleman. He wants 500 a year or more. That is his current aspiration.

'Patience and courage, William. I have every confidence in you. Now tell me what of your own work?'

William shares his early designs for Boucher's Leda.

'How faithful will you be to old Bouche's women - Leda and her friend? Is there a muse to guide you?'

William's smile is tight.

Ravenet walks across the studio and begins to rummage in a pile of papers. After some frustrated mumbling he pulls out a sheaf of sketches and passes them to William.

They are all of a young woman, though not naked as in Boucher's work. It is the face that catches William's attention.

'Mary? That is Mary is it not?'

Ravenet has the smile of a fisherman. 'Ahh, you see the likeness. I have not lost my draughtsman's skills.'

He beckons William to sit again. 'About a month after you left for Paris, Mary came to visit. She was desperate to know when you would return.'

'I did write...' William offers, his cheeks flushing.

'Yes, but when one year becomes another ...tis hard to still believe. So, I found her work in the studio. Soon she was helping everywhere, ordering the ink, the *eau-forte*... and in exchange she asked me to teach her French. And she did speak it passably... with a Lambeth edge.'

'Then?'

'Well then her father sickened and with her brother still at sea, she had little time to herself, what with the orchard and-'

'-When did you last see her?' asks William, attempting nonchalance.

'Ahh, last week, I do believe.'

'Last week!'

'Yes, her cider vinegar is my saviour. On Fridays, she still has the stall by the Church.'

William glances down and brushes specks of chalk from his sleeve.

Ravenet shifts the conversation, aware how much Mary has suffered these past years. But when William is gathering up his prints to return home, he still has Mary on his mind. 'She is perhaps a mother herself now. With young mouths to feed?'

Ravenet merely shakes his head. He has seen enough of life to let things unfold as they will. If it is to be, so be it. Though he does invite William to return, to use the studio as a refuge where he can work on his Leda.

They part with a warm embrace. William sets off towards Westminster Bridge in a far less jangled state of mind than he had endured that morning.

The visit to Ravenet is not the only event to settle William's spirits. His contribution of much-needed guineas has kept the bailiffs at bay. The house on Ave Maria Lane is calmer now. Though that is also in part because his brother Joseph has not been seen for several days.

'He has never been one to bear your doing well,' Ma says. She keeps her eyes on her embroidery.

William shrugs. If Jo is off on another of his jaunts, he'll be back when he needs money. 'He'll end up in gaol, one day. Pa knows it too.'

Ma blinks and passes him a needle to thread.

That night William decides he will work at his father's studio on Bute's Royal commission. Then one day a week he will go to Lambeth and grave the Leda plate under Ravenet's guidance. He smiles to himself. And why should that not be on a Friday?

Ravenet greets him with a tease.

'Ah William, I was expecting you.'

William avoids his gaze. 'Yes, well, it seemed appropriate.'

'Indeed! Your good father is in need of some Lambeth apples. Or vinegar perhaps? I have heard it highly commended for ailments of the heart.'

William scowls. He has never been able to hide his thoughts from this dear man.

'Now to work.'

William lays out his burins, settles the copper plate on his leather cushion and begins to cut lines for the swan's wings. But his mind is distracted by thoughts of Mary. How will he find her? How should he greet her? How will she respond? He is soon making mistakes and falls to cursing at his clumsiness. Finally, Ravenet picks up a hessian bag and throws it at him.

'Go, now, before your agitation drives me to my brandy aforenoon!'

William arrives breathless beside the wall of St Mary's churchyard where he stops to gather his wits. He is surprised by his excitement. After all he is not the callow youth of five years past. He has lived in Paris, encountered Counts and Dukes, studied with the greatest painters in France. He has loved and lost Gabrielle, a woman so different to any he has known before. Even now he is engaged on a Royal commission. And yet in this moment he feels as skittish as a sand-fly.

He looks out over the headstones. The grave of Mary's mother is not far, just out of sight on the other side of the Church. He remembers sitting beside Mary as she replaced the flowers.

He walks towards the South door. The stall is just ahead of him. But its canvas awning is still roped up. She is not there yet. Feeling somewhat foolish, he thinks he will escape up into the Tower.

At that instant, he hears a snatch of song coming from a distance.

'I gave my love a cherry that has no stone,
I gave my love a chicken that has no bone'

He presses himself into the doorway. To hide and to listen.

'I told my love a story that has no end
I gave my love a baby with no crying'

It is a girl's voice, a young child's voice. Too young to be Mary.

But then from a little closer, accompanied by the sound of a cart being wheeled across paving slabs, the next verse floats through the trees around the graveyard to find him.

'How can there be a cherry that has no stone?
How can there be a chicken that has no bone?'

His neck is prickling. That warm lilt, he would recognise it anywhere...

'How can there be a story that has no end?
How can there be a baby with no crying?'

He cannot help himself. He knows he has no voice to match, but shakily at first and then, with more confidence, the words come ...
'A cherry when it blossoms it has no stone. A chicken when its pipping it has no bone'

There is a stillness in the trees. The girls and the cart have stopped.

Then, giggling, they join in with the final responses: *'The story that I love you it has no end. A baby when it's sleeping has no crying...'*

The rumble squeak of the cart starts up again and it is moving faster, and very close. He hears Mary now, laughing to her companion. 'I know no other voice so rough it could curdle milk in the churn!'

'Oh my!' she exclaims as they come around the corner. 'Oh my! William!'

She stands rock-still as if she has seen a spectre. As if one of the gargoyles has dropped from the tower to stand before her. 'It is you, William?'

Then she is running towards him. There are tears flowing everywhere at first, hugs and kisses and then decorum, then separation. She stands back, dabbing at her eyes with a pretty emerald green kerchief. Still shaking, she introduces Margaret her younger sister who is all abuzz. She wants to show William everything they have brought with them for the stall. 'See we have daffodils, cured hams and vinegar for all ailments.'

Though William is trying to pay heed to young Margaret, he glances away often to where Mary is standing, watching him. Those warm brown, chestnut, eyes. His chest tightens. Her fingers reach for her bonnet. Now Mary is not vain, but perhaps she is thinking about the dress she might have worn if she had known. The ribbon she would have chosen. Pure fancy of his mind's making... but in that moment all his feelings for her flood back.

He turns again to congratulate her sister on her produce.

The next hours pass in reminiscence. Mary tells him of her fear for Sam, her twin brother, now at sea, fighting the French. 'If he were here he'd bloody your face for being a traitor. I heard him say as much. You were gone so long he swore blind you were now become a Frenchman.'

'Well, he was never approving...'

She looks at him askance. 'But you are not French?'

He laughs. 'No, no, still half a Welshman with Ma's blood of Feltham coursing through. Though I do speak French.'

'And you are not alone in that, *Monsieur*!'

'So I hear.'

'*Ouais, je paarle Franzais...*'

'Ha ha, we are well matched.'

Mary's eyebrows arch. 'Indeed? There is a small matter of five years absence. I do not call that a match, *Monsieur*.'

'*Touché.*'

He bows. 'There is much to address but let us be friends again.'

And so begins the new pattern to his London life, divided between his father's studio and the Friday visits to Lambeth. Mary is wary but she has no artifice. She makes it plain that she has little aspiration for the position in Society he craves. For her the Court, the noble and the royal charade is so distant as to be another world. Her comfort lies closer to home. When they are alone, he is still the apprentice who shared his dreams with her.

Chapter 8

Mary is not alone in her fears for a brother fighting in the King's Navy. In the City coffeehouses, William finds all the talk is of war. Some have friends or cousins fighting alongside Frederick of Prussia against the Russians and the Austrians. Others wait for despatches from the Americas where the French and Spanish challenge for their share of Empire.

It seems as if the known world is a-flame. Grub Street's daily news is full of wild calculations, of distances from the south coast to London. How long would Dover hold out? Could a mounted force land in Ireland? Could the French be stopped?

Rumours spread of traitors at work, spies despatching secrets of the country's defences, across the water to the enemy. One man becomes the focus of this fear: Dr Florence Hensey, an Irishman by birth, a Roman Catholic by upbringing and faith. Since his arrest, the previous summer, he has been pacing out his days in Newgate Gaol. His guilt is widely assumed. He was seized returning from a Catholic mass. In itself that is no crime but it is coupled with the discovery of foreign correspondence.

William is drawn towards the clamour surrounding Dr Hensey. Just months before, in Paris, the Comte de Broglie described him as a postmaster, a forwarder of letters. It seems that he was much more than that. Now the French King's agents will be looking for a replacement. It seems that even in his homeland William may not be safe.

Though his first Royal commission is now secured, William still struggles with such thoughts. As he makes his marks, as his burin scrapes back and forth across the copper plate, he replays in his head the encounter with the Comte. How long will it be before he calls in William's debt for the precious *laissez-passer*?

June arrives, hot as ever, but with a frequent, drenching rain. The city steams and perspires. None more so than Dr Hensey, who is due before Lord Chief Justice Mansfield, on Monday the Twelfth. On the eve, William convinces himself that it is always wise to *Know thy Enemy*. He tells no-one of his intention.

As Monday dawns, he takes care to dress in his customary black. He wears no insignia or colouring that might be seen as favouring a foreign nation. Then, through the waking streets, he makes his way to Westminster Hall. He has with him a pocket sketch book and a set of pencils. These place him as an observer, present for no other reason than to capture the moment, for art, not politics. On the Green, a loud and belligerent crowd is already cheering. He enquires the reason.

'Lord Mansfield's carriage.'

'... just arrived!'

'A hanging judge,' the red-eyed patriot declares.

William skirts the surging throng, looking for a side entrance. He finds one for advocates. There seem to be many arriving, be-wigged and also in black. He slips in among them, waving his sketch book to indicate an official capacity. But there are no questions. He soon finds himself inside the Hall and the Court of the King's Bench. The tiered stalls set up for onlookers are already heaving in anticipation.

The gentlemen of the jury mouth their solemn oaths.

'Good men and true!' declares William's neighbour swaying into him. 'I hear scores were turned away.' His breath is stale with beer.

Lord Mansfield enters to another cheer and the case is underway. Much of the judicial exchange washes over William. His interest is in the details of discovery. A letter-carrier, James Newman, florid and inflated with self-importance, takes the stand. He explains how he came to suspect Dr Hensey.

We letter-carriers or postmen, have great opportunities to know the characters and dispositions of gentlemen in the several neighbourhoods of this part of the town, from their servants, connexions and correspondents; but to be plain, if I once learn that a person who lives a genteel life, is a Roman Catholic, I immediately look on him as one who by education and principle is an inveterate enemy to my king, my country and the Protestant Religion:

This bitter hatred of all that is foreign comes as no surprise to William. But there are lessons here for his own safety. The trial moves on to Hensey's modus operandi. He gathers information from the coffee-houses. In Valentine's, where parliamentarians chatter, he absorbs the rumours of the day; in Lloyd's, weary shipping clerks announce the latest arrivals. In Will's, opposite the Admiralty, naval officers discuss the month's manoeuvres for the Fleet. Then, at night, he composes innocent letters to friends abroad. But between each line, he inserts his treasonous reports, dipping his quill into lemon juice, which instantly disappears. It can only be seen again when the paper is warmed above a candle. In one such message, the prosecutor says, he exhorts the French to invade.: "Public credit is almost totally destroyed and the finances quite exhausted. Now in my opinion is the time to strike the final blow."

The evidence is overwhelming. The verdict never in doubt. A great cheer greets Lord Mansfield's condemnation. 'Hang him! Hang him!' is the cry. Amidst the jubilation, William seeks some distance from the crowd and sets off towards Soho. He needs to think through what he has just witnessed. Dr Hensey's secret world is somehow enticing. All is never quite what it seems. It is a shadow play that ordinary folk can only guess at. A web of deceit far more intricate than even his most complex engraving. But there are those in charge who master its complexity. His own encounter with the Comte de Broglie... now there is someone who was born to pull the strings that make mere mortals leap.

William is just stepping into Berwick Street, when his reverie is shattered by a coarse bellow:

'Whoaahh !

There is a clatter of horses' hooves, the squeal of metal on wood. He feels a hand grasp his shoulder and haul him backwards with such force he goes sprawling.

Momentarily befuddled he hears more shouts.

'Whoahh! Now! Whoahh!... Damn your eyes!.... Whoahh... Steady now! Steady.'

He looks up in time to see a coach and four, swaying back and forth just a few feet from him. The driver, a brute of a man, jumps down, flaring with indignation. He is still shouting. 'Next time I'll run 'ee down, no question asked.'

A small crowd is already gathering. Their presence emboldens the fellow.

'Sleep walking 'e was.'

'Aye, Damn fool.'

'You was in the right.'

William struggles to rise. He glances across and sees a towering figure step forward, hands raised.

'Peace now. Peace, gentlemen.' The stranger's accent is Italian, soft, from the south.

Now the driver's blood is up. He pulls a cudgel from his belt.

'Damned ... who are you to tell ?'

William hears just a whisper of sliding steel, but in that moment the stranger has drawn his rapier and whipped its point to within an inch of the driver's chest. Again, he calls for peace. He waits, arm outstretched, one eyebrow raised, as if to enquire of the driver what his next move will be. The man's anger drains from his face. Ashen, he looks around. Some in the crowd already back away. He turns and clambers back on to his carriage. From the safety of his seat, he spits a defiant gob towards William and cracks his whip. The wheels grip and roll away.

William brushes himself down and offers a hand of thanks to his protector. 'I am indebted to you sir!'

The stranger bows. 'Domenico Angelo Malevotti Tremamondo at your service. You may call me Angelo. Expert in all the arts of defence.'

'Indeed, and of offence too.'

'Sometimes it is necessary.' He looks around at some of the crowd who are still watching them with suspicion.

'Come. It is perhaps best to move along. Where are you headed?'

'Towards Soho.'

'Excellent. We are well met.' He presents his card to William, who reads it out aloud as they make their way up Berwick Street.

'Riding and Fencing academy, King's Square ... Ha, I was fortunate indeed'

'Fortune favours the brave. My motto, sir. I have been proven correct many times.'

'Perhaps I need some of your education.'

'Gentlemen are always welcome. I am proud to say the young Prince of Wales has graced us with his presence.'

When William proffers his own card, Angelo laughs out loud. 'Forgive me. It amuses me, how life turns and turns and always surprises.'

'How so?'

'You are an engraver.'

'Yes, recently returned from France and just-'

'Well, there you see. We have it. Fortune smiles on both of us. I am just in mind to assemble a book of instruction, a veritable '*Ecole d'Armes*' it is to be, with noble combatants, myself included, demonstrating every pose and stance of swordmanship.'

'And I-'

'-you, sir, may be just the person to assist.' At that moment Angelo realises they have reached the Square. 'But forgive me, we must continue this anon. I must turn an idle youth into a warrior. Come by, at your leisure. You must meet my illustrator, a fine draughtsman. He is there most days.'

Two days later, William returns to the Square. He passes a row of carriages, each with a growing pile of fresh droppings before it. A huddle of drivers and footmen is gathered near the gates of Angelo's Academy. From within, he can hear Angelo's booming voice. 'You may soon be lord of all the Indies but here you are in my domain. Do not sit upon a horse as if it is a bag of turnips, or some kitchen maid you have a mind to tup. No sir ! I want straight back, knees tight, loose wrists...'

William makes his way towards a group of boys awaiting a tongue-lashing.

'We will make a cavalier out of you yet, young sir ... round you go... round again ... excellent and Next!'

Angelo spots William in the shadows and ushers him forward. 'Ah, Signor Ryland. A moment. If you would make yourself at home. Young Frederick here will show you to the fencing school.'

Young Frederick is much relieved to escape his turn. They pass through a warren of brick-lined corridors into a bright, whitewashed hall. Here, the atmosphere is much calmer. In the centre, two fencers are poised, epées in hand. Another man, with his back to William, is guiding them from beside his easel. He moves back and forth from his sketching, as he directs their movements. William is loathe to interrupt a fellow artist at work. He has an enthusiasm about him that is somehow familiar. Finally, the sequence is complete. Frederick takes a flagon of wine over to the swordsmen and William approaches the illustrator. Just as he is about to speak, the man turns. He is heavy set, sharp nosed and... quite extraordinary... he is John Gwynn.

For a moment they both stand, stock-still, jaws dropped in utter surprise. It is Gwynn, as he likes to be known, who recovers first. 'William? William Wynne Ryland?'

'In the flesh, Mr Gwynn, in the flesh.'

'Come! Let me hold you, young man.'

Gwynn gathers him in for a crushing embrace. His strength has not diminished. He has the force of a carpenter, his first calling.

'Not so young as I was,' William croaks, as he disentangles himself.

'Well then, old friend. But you still have ten years on me.'

'It does not show. How goes the architect?'

Gwynn fails to hide a momentary tensing around the eyes. He picks up a fallen pencil. 'Well, you knew me as a dreamer of city-scapes...five years have flown by and here I am... in a nursery for the sons of nobility.'

'I for one am grateful.' William says. 'It reunites me with your wise head and warm heart.'

'We make do.'

William leafs through the sketches on the easel. 'Far more than that. One day, I wager, London will wake to your talents.'

'As Paris did to yours.'

'In a modest way.'

'Ha, There are few secrets at Slaughters, we downed a flagon or two when we heard you won the Prix de Rome.'

'Few secrets anywhere it seems.'

William pulls out another sketch, depicting both a graceful parry, and a lethal strike. 'Perhaps I should take some instruction.'

'Hmm, Angelo did tell me how he saved your life from over-eager patriots! He is hopefull that you may use your burin to recreate my sketches. Come, let me show you what we are about ...'

And the two men, their friendship instantly resumed, discuss the Italian's ambition for his *Ecole d'Armes*. It will require scores of engravings, showing every move and counter move in the noble art of fencing.

A little later they are joined by Angelo, flushed with the exertions of the morning's class. '*Mi scusa*, William. They are a sorry lot. They need some new blood in their ancient lines. Perhaps an opportunity for your good self, whose star is rising? Are you a marrying man?'

'Already spoken for.'

William's response is instant, instinctive. He is not the only one to be surprised. Gwynn eyes him closely. 'Really William? You are a dark horse. We must soon to the tavern, there is much to share I believe.'

William smiles and shifts the conversation back to the prints. The illustrations are quite simple, line drawings, they do not have the complexity of the Royal portrait. He agrees a sum for thirty plates to be engraved over two years. In the course of the negotiations, Angelo reveals his own love of Paris. At other times William would have taken this at face value, but these days he is suspicious of any association with France.

When Gwynn accompanies him to the gates, William shares his misgivings.

'Oh, rest easy on that score. I would vouch for Angelo with my life, there is not a greater British patriot. He married young Frances just three years past and they are settled here.'

'But he is ideally placed to discover all manner of comings and goings. Is it not a perfect cover for -?'

Gwynn clicks his tongue. 'Not you too! Spies in every shadow, invasion barges on their way. This is mere tittle-tattle!'

William frowns. 'Well we need some victories to wipe them away.'

'They'll come, they'll come... but meanwhile let us meet soon. I am eager to know the future Mrs Ryland. I assume she does exist?'

'Oh, she exists.'

'In Paris or London?'

'Very much home grown.'

'You have me intrigued. Tomorrow say, at Slaughter's? At three?'

'Until the morrow.'

'Stay safe. We have need of you and your burin!'

When they meet the following day, William shares more than a flagon of Rhenish. For the first time since leaving Paris, he feels able to talk about the future, without regret. It is as much about the re-awakening of his affections for Mary as it is about his ambition to become a gentleman of means. Gwynn is a good sounding board but above all he is a practical man.

'There are many in your position who seek an easier route.'

'Such as?'

'Angelo's solution... an heiress or a wealthy widow.'

William pours himself another glass. 'Believe me, that has never been far from my mind ...' He takes a slow sip. '... there is something in me... Almost like a promise I have made myself... That insists I must succeed by my hand alone.'

'No-one doubts your promise, but would not a few thousand a year help to make it real.'

'What Mary lacks in guineas she has in-' he hesitates.

'-in what? In love, in joy, in humour, in body? How can she sustain you? You say she has no interest in wealth, in society? What kind of partner could she be in your journey, your dreams?'

William looks him in the eye, though he doesn't see his old friend. He has in mind an image of the old Tower at St Mary's, where he and Mary have been courting. He replies in a voice that is both warm and distant. 'Oh, all of the above and more she has, and my best interest too.'

Gwynn knows William well enough to recognise when his heart is set. It was the same when he resolved to leave for Paris. So it is, now that he is returned. 'Well, in that case, I am the first to wish you well. But I will hold you to your promise. I will see you rich as Croesus, a rival to Boydell.'

'I'll drink to that.' They raise their glasses in salute.

'And to that end, I offer you space in my studio in Green Court.'

'To Leicester Fields, then. A toast, with thanks '

'To your very good fortune.'

Chapter 9

As a wet June gives way to a parched July, William's thoughts are all of breezy Lambeth. Once Friday's work on the Leda plate is done, he bids farewell to Ravenet and heads down the pilgrim path to the Church. He has left word for Mary to join him at the tower. He places a smooth blue pebble in the corner of the second step, to show that he is already there. He begins to walk up, the sweat chilling on the back of his neck. There is a sudden flutter of wings. A pigeon beats past his head and disappears above him. Unable to find an escape, it comes fluttering all the way back, hits the wooden door of the belfry and drops down, stunned. William gathers it up and rushes on to the top of the tower. He places the bird in the centre of the platform, and sits beside it, willing it back to life. After a minute or two, a pair of beady eyes flick open, startled. Then they close again. It is still too dazed to move.

William lies back, looks up at the blue sky and falls asleep. A short while later, he is woken by the sound of footsteps and then silence. He knows it is Mary because she always pauses at the top step.

'Oh My ... Dear Lord... I do not know that I will ever be used... so many... what's this?'

Mary takes the pigeon in her lap. There is no struggle.

William reaches out for her. She leans back, avoiding his grasp.

'This is no time to be a-fondling. I have a charge.' She smiles. 'He will be well soon though.'

She asks William for news from the City. 'Have there been battles at sea?'

All she knows of her brother Sam is that he is on some Admiral's flagship. But there is little to reassure her. Though rumour has it that a confrontation is coming. 'Many say next year it will come to a head. It shall not be over swiftly.'

She sighs and moves the talking on to them. William shades his eyes to look at her. She takes a breath to settle herself as if she is trying to remember all the words she has been intending to say.

'I am loving you again, William. I did try not to. I didn't do well at that though. Because it don't make no sense, not to. So, then I says to myself, what is it that I want? And the truth is that I wants to be with you. But I want nothing of your grand friends. That is not my world and never shall be.'

William raises himself on to one elbow. He stretches out a hand to reassure her, but then let's it drop. He is not sure what is about to come.

'So what I needs to know is what is the future for us? Do you have an eye to that or are you come here just to play with my heart and leave it. Again?'

The questions come as no surprise. Ever since the encounter with Gwynn, William has been rehearsing his answers.

And so that evening, with a grateful pigeon as witness, there is an agreement reached. It mirrors their view from the Tower, where the Thames both joins and divides their two very different worlds. The plan is for a betrothal, then marriage. William will take lodgings with Gwynn in the City. Mary will continue to look after her father and sister in Lambeth. On Friday, Saturday and Sunday, William will join her. Both are surprised by the ease with which their plan emerges. That is not to say there will not be conflict in the practice. For now, they have a map, to guide their future.

It is sealed, under the stars, though it is not to be consummated until the day set for the wedding. The only contrary issue is that Pa is not content. He saw a much more advantageous match. 'More in keeping with your ambitions,' he says, unable to look him in the eye.

But William will not be deflected. To keep matters discreet, he applies for a wedding license, rather than the proclamation of the Parish banns. So it is, when August 15th comes around, neither Ma nor Pa, nor even his youngest brother John, attend the ceremony. It is his old Master Ravenet and Mary's papa, both Lambeth residents, who sign the certificate. The wedding is a subdued affair, though no less loving for all that.

The following year of the Lord, 1759, is well marked as Annus Mirabilis. The French are on the retreat by land and sea. From the backwoods of Canada to the banks of the Ohio and the rich coast of Bengal, Britain is on the ascendant. And closer to home, William and Mary have cause to celebrate with the birth of a healthy first child, Mary Charlotte on 17th May. But William's path to wealth is not progressing as swiftly as Britain's bloody route to Empire.

On the morning of April 21st, 1760, a large crowd is gathering outside the Great Hall of the Society of Arts, Manufactures and Commerce in Little Denmark Street, just off the Strand. London's first exhibition of living artists is about to open. Admission is free. A Catalogue may be purchased for sixpence.

William and Gwynn are on their way from their shared studio just
off Leicester Fields. They are both in a dark temper. William is furious
with himself. Both the Leda plate and the portrait of the future King
George are still months from completion. After two years in London,
he has nothing ready to exhibit. It is not as if he had not been warned.
Gwynn was at the Turks Head in Soho back in November, when two
dozen artists and engravers decided on this exhibition. But still William
missed the deadline.

He is entirely at fault. He has allowed himself to be distracted. The
birth of his first born, the many plates required for Angelo's fencing
book, and his own search for perfection in the Royal portrait. Heaven
knows what Bute will say, if the old King dies before it is ready.

William's bout of the black dog is matched by his companion.
Gwynn spent months on his designs for the new Bridge to cross the
Thames at Blackfriars only to see his plans rejected by the committee.
So, neither men are in the best of heads when they reach Little Denmark
Street. A horde of would-be visitors are already spilling across the
narrow road. Fortunately, William's old master, Ravenet, is among
them.

To lighten their mood, he guides them via the backstairs, into the
Grand Hall and over to the painting which is already judged to be the
triumph of the Exhibition: Richard Wilson's latest landscape from
Italy.

The view of lofty mountain peaks is romantic but this is a grim tale
of hubris. Niobe has seven beloved sons and seven beautiful daughters.
She brags about them to the Gods, who become jealous. The divine
twins, Apollo and Artemis, decide to slaughter Niobe's children. Every
one of them. In her grief, she turns to rock. The waterfalls are her tears,
flowing for eternity.

'This is not a tale for Mary,' William says. 'She is heavy with our
second even now. To lose even one would be pain enough.'

They are distracted by an approaching hubbub. William turns to see Boydell the print seller among the first visitors. He is in conversation with a shortish, rounded young man, in his middle twenties. William remembers him from his days at the St Martin's Lane Academy. William Woollett, nicknamed Woll, for his owlish appearance and tendency to blink when in company. He has become one of Boydell's favourite engravers. William's brief bow of recognition betrays his jealousy.

Boydell is as brusque as ever, though not without grace. He compliments Ravenet for his exhibits on show, then commiserates with Gwynn for his Blackfriars project, 'Judges do not always make choices for the right reasons.' To William, he is sharp. 'How go the Royal and the Bute portrait? No doubt there is much work in our Lord's calves? We know he is as proud of them as a Highland dancing master.'

William takes this amiss, a pointed jibe about the time he's taking on his plates. How he wishes he had his Leda and the Swan complete, so he could silence Boydell with his finest work.

His humour is not improved when Boydell introduces Woll as the up-and-coming British engraver of landscapes. 'We will soon be vying with the French.'

'Indeed.'

William still thinks of Woollett as the country lad, the son of a Kentish publican, with passable talent but lacking in technique. It seems he has been making progress.

The summer is spent in the shade of the Lambeth orchards, which soon ring to the cries of another healthy child, Mary-Anne. But Bute's plates are still not ready, and the autumn brings unwelcome news.

Early in the morning of the 25th October, the half-blind old king, George II collapses between his close stool and his writing desk. Within hours he has breathed his last. Behind the shuttered windows of Kensington Palace, his twenty-two-year-old grandson pays his respects. After the funeral, there must be a Marriage, a Coronation. Though young George will do nothing without the Earl of Bute's say-so. And Bute's preparations must now deliver. Next day William is summoned to Ramsay's studio in Soho Square.

The windowpanes rattle to the sound of the Earl's displeasure. 'Six months, Sir! Six months? What have you been doing these past two years ? Idling in the stews, I'll be bound.'

William offers up the latest proof. 'A print of the Royal Portrait, as it is stands, milord.'

'Just the Prince?' Bute is turning quite puce. Behind him Allan Ramsay shakes his head, cautioning William not to add more to the disaster. 'And when pray, do you intend to deliver the engraving of myself? Another two years?'

'No milord, I have been working at them both, but you said to favour the Prince , I mean his Majesty... so perhaps another year of work is needed for yourself.'

'Damn you, sir.'

Ramsay attempts to step in. 'Milord, there is rich detail-'

'-And yet you deliver your paintings within six months or less.'

Ramsay nods. 'It is in the nature of the technique Milord. A very different technique.'

'Well. Well.' Bute absorbs the point. He breathes in, deep to the belly. And out.

'You understand, gentlemen. I, er, We, must control... there will be many attempts to rush out some bastard works, to profit from the public craving. Do you have no assistants, to speed the process?'

'Engraving is by its nature solo work, the size of the plate does not allow-'

'Quite so, quite so. Well, in that case we must increase your canvas copies, Mr Ramsay. Bring in more people, make haste and prepare yourself. Within the year we intend to have his Majesty wed and crowned. We will need another portrait, full length, in coronation robes, the full ermine, I believe. And then there'll be the Queen, whoever she may be. And Master Ryland. Six months you say?'

'Six months.'

'I will hold you to that, you may be sure. Good day to you... Gentlemen.'

The ringing sound of crystal cuts through the silence. Margaret arrives, bearing a tray of comfort. 'I thought perhaps...'

'Most welcome.'

'Indeed,' Ramsay says. 'The Lord is out of sorts but William's plate is magnificent and will be magnificent. I can see already from the proofs. And the King will see it too.'

'Your very good health, Sir.'

Ramsay shows him to the door. As they step into the autumn sunlight, a grand carriage hurtles past. It circles around and comes to a halt in front of the large mansion on the far corner of Sutton Row. A footman steps out to greet a woman of middling age, clad in scarlet Turban and matching silk gown.

William raises an enquiring eyebrow.

'Ah yes. My new neighbour, Teresa Cornelys. From Venice. She has sung her way into the hearts and nether regions of countless gallants. Now she has plans to liven up our little Square, concerts by Bach and Abel, gaming tables... '

La Cornelys gives them an exuberant wave. At which they both smile and bow.

'I feel inclined to throw her a bouquet.'

'They say she has the voice of a Siren. You would do well to bind y'self to the mast or Mary will have a lonely Christmas!'

'My engraver's desk shall be my mast. If I am to deliver the Prince, I have six months hard graft ahead.'

'Aye, the masquerade at Carlisle House shall wait... but not forever.'

The setting sun is warm on William's back. He is in Gwynn's studio but his engraver's tools are put away. Instead of his burin and copper plate, he has a quill in hand and paper on the desk before him. He is preparing copy for the Daily Advertiser, one week hence.

27th May, 1761:

This day is publish'd, price One Guinea a whole length portrait of his present Majesty from an original Picture, painted by Mr Ramsay in the Possession of the Earl of Bute.

Oh, such relief to be at last able to write these words. He looks up at the easel opposite. There it is, the proof he has just showed the Earl. And soon it will have William's new title inscribed below: *Calcographus Regis Britanniae.* The King's Engraver. It is official, with more commissions promised. Ramsay's portrait for the Coronation will soon be complete and William is to engrave this too. So, the annual pension doubles to two hundred pounds. gentleman's income. And he has high hopes for the selling of the prints.

He takes up his quill again.

Engraved and sold by W.Ryland, at the Red Lamp in Litchfield-Street, near Newport Market, St Ann's Soho, R and J Dodley, in Pall-Mall, and by all the Booksellers and Printsellers in Town and Country.

It is a beginning. One day he will have his own establishment, to match Boydell's in London or Basan in Paris. For now, he must sell where he can.

The Royal portrait is not the only work that is complete. Beside it on the easel, William now has the final proof of Boucher's Leda and the Swan. His long-promised calling card is also a triumph. He had it ready to show at the Society of Artist's Exhibition in Spring Gardens. The reactions were more than favourable.

His old master Ravenet is delighted: 'I recognise Mary's features. Leda's face and figure, you have them to perfection'

He does not ask who inspired those of her companion. That is best kept as William's secret.

The following months are even more profitable than William could have dreamed. The time is propitious. King George's Marriage and Coronation are set fair for the autumn. As Bute predicted, Ramsay's portrait of the former Prince is the first official image. The prints are in high demand. Trade is so intense that William calls on his old friend Bailey. He assists with the frequent deliveries between printer and printsellers. One morning he delights William with a bold-faced confidence:

'My master Boydell is beside himself with jealousy.'

So, at last, William has the means to find a more fitting residence for a gentleman artist. When the young King purchases Buckingham House as an establishment for his new Queen Caroline, the area becomes most fashionable. William takes up a lease on a house hard by, 62 Stafford Row. He hopes it will soon entice Mary over from Lambeth.

To celebrate, that night he joins Ramsay at Madame Cornelys' newly opened establishment. Between the gaming tables and the flowing wine, he finds himself at dawn, flush out of money and staggering home alone through Leicester Fields.

Suddenly there is the sound of canon fire. It seems to come from the roof of one of the courts at the southern end of the Fields. William stumbles towards it, uncertain if this is a warning he should heed. Is it invasion? Perhaps a fire? As he approaches, he hears shouts and laughter. A rowdy chorus heralds another blast.

He is about to beat on one of the courtyard doors when it opens inwards. And out falls Woll or to be more precise, William Woollett Esq, Boydell's much prized engraver. His face is blackened with soot, split by a beaming gap-toothed smile. His eyes are blinking, as if he has been momentarily unsighted. There is a sharp stench of cordite about him. He is followed by three others, who William also knows, the printer Peter Hadrill and his assistants. They are all in high spirits. They push past him, without a hint of recognition.

'Oh my. Woll. You outdid yourself sir.'

'A mighty cannonade.'

'One of your best.'

'Lillibeth and the twins are not so pleased.'

'Best to the tavern, then.'

'To the Tavern. Yes. But it is dawn sir.'

'Ah then to Smithfield. Always drink a-plenty there.'

'To the Porters arms.'

'To my Niobe,' Woll shouts out. 'Complete at last.'

They disappear off in the direction of Smithfield.

It is a moment William will remember. Boydell's investment in Woll pays off handsomely. The *Niobe* is so well-received that he makes some 10,000 guineas from the subscription sales. Woll himself earns 2000 guineas, which mollifies his weary wife, Lillibet. For William, it is a sign. There is handsome money to be made.

Chapter 10

'So many poses, counter-poses...' William is in Angelo's Academy. He and Gwynn are sifting through the hundred proofs for his book on Fencing. 'If we were apt, we should be the best swordsmen in England.'

There is a clash of steel on steel behind them. They turn to watch the two fencers. One is compact, muscular but seems half the height of his opponent.

'An uneven match.' William observes.

'No. Watch, the little fellow.'

'He has the measure of Angelo?'

'More so. He struck three times without yielding a scratch. That ferocious devil is the Chevalier. Dragoon and diplomat, in that order.'

A Frenchman. That is of more concern to William, though he seeks to hide it with a yawn. 'Well, he has no need of instruction.'

'He would not take it. Though he is ready to model any pose for us.'

Some minutes later, their work is interrupted by Angelo's booming voice. 'Gentleman may I present our latest champion, the Chevalier d'Eon.' They stand to exchange greetings. The Dragoon is all smiles. He likes to win. 'William here is almost a Frenchie.'

William glowers at Angelo but is polite. '*Enchanté..*'

'*Enchanté.*' the Chevalier replies.

William gestures to the prints in front of him. 'I spent several years in Paris. Now I earn my living with my burin.'

'He is modest.' Angelo insists. 'My book is a mere distraction. William is the King's Engraver.'

The Chevalier locks eyes with William, who has the disturbing impression that the Frenchman already knows exactly who he is.

'And what brings you to London?' William asks.

'I am here to negotiate the Peace.'

This catches Gwynn's attention. 'If you argue as well as you fight, dear Bute will be at a loss.'

'We must work within the possible. Of course, both sides believe they are mistreated.' The Chevalier's tone is smooth, delicate even, contrasting with the vigour of his blade-work.

'You are here with the new Ambassador?' Gwynn asks.

'Yes. But in France...' he turns quite deliberately towards William, 'I work with the Kings' Private Secretary, the Comte de Broglie.'

William's face drains white. He had hoped never to hear this name again. The Chevalier d'Eon has made a palpable hit. Though neither Gwynn nor Angelo are aware. With a gracious bow the diplomat departs, leaving William wondering what his next move will be. Later that afternoon, he asks Gwynn for his opinion of d'Eon.

'Oh. No better than any of his ilk, a country noble on the make, I should say. A nimble fellow with a caustic tongue. Never trust a man who smiles so much.'

William nods. 'Some say there are guineas offered to those most pliable in Parliament.'

'France will do what it can to cut its losses.'

William cannot bring himself to take even his closest friend into his confidence. He makes no mention of his encounter with the Comte de Broglie. Instead, over the following weeks, he loses himself in a fever of work. With Peace at hand, he must complete Bute's portrait or be damned again by the Earl.

In January, the Earl of Bute's engraving has been four years in the making. Politics moves swifter than art. By the time the prints are on sale, the Earl's public image is already fading in value. Within months this Scottish cuckoo, who removed the war-hawks from their nest, will find himself out in the cold. At least his one aim, to deliver Peace, is achieved. The following month, William is again at Angelo's when Gwynn arrives breathless from Westminster. 'The preliminaries have been signed and despatched to France.'

'Thank the Lord.' sighs William.

'What is more, our half-sized hero with the foil-'

'The Chevalier?'

'The one and only. D'Eon is given the honour of taking the papers to Versailles to his illustrious Majesty.' This seems to amuse Gwynn but, for a moment, William is back in France. He imagines the scene, with de Broglie watching from the shadows, no doubt distraught that his grand scheme for the invasion of England is on hold. For now at least.

'I cannot say I will miss him.' William says. 'He had a swagger.'

Gwynn smiles. 'And I for one have never known a more delicious source of gossip. Though I would not trust him to keep his country's secrets, if he cannot keep his own.'

Peace with France brings the nation's heroes home. In April, Mary's brother Sam returns to Lambeth. He has grown into his father's frame, now a barrel of a young man, with scarred chin, blond hair in a sailor's queue and deep-set brown eyes which have seen much more than he will ever tell. Beneath the blossom of the apple trees, he softens day by day. He plays hide and seek with his young nieces, while Mary watches, pregnant with another child.

Sam still spars with William. He mocks his lengthy absence in Paris, "living with the enemy", but it is without malice. War has beaten the fight out of him. He sees that Mary is content and protected. This change of heart frees her to consider other options. One night, after the children are a-bed, she shares her thoughts with William. 'Sam says he's not for travelling no more. He's all for taking up the orchards. If Anne tends to father -'

'-then you are free to cross the river.'

'On one condition.'

'Ah-ha.'

'It is one you care for too.' She is sitting in her deep-cushioned chair beside the hearth. One hand resting on her belly. William is pacing. Tankard in hand. He likes to measure out the flagstones as he walks back and forth in his father-in-law's kitchen. 'We must settle the rift with your Pa. It pains me that he never wishes to see his grandchildren.'

William pauses. 'I... I cannot fathom it, myself. It is a blindness he has.'

'He sees well enough. But what he sees is "the Lambeth girl". Not a daughter, bearing young ones, his flesh and blood.'

William presses his lips together. It has been many months since he visited Ma and Pa. His brother Joseph fuels his father's bitterness. As if William's success was not enough for them. They hoped for more, and Mary is their scapegoat. 'We can but try.'

'I'm willing, if it is only for the girls and whoever is on the way.' She strokes a gentle circle around her middle.

So, one sweltering Saturday in August, William and Mary cross the river from Lambeth, to visit Ma and Pa. At the house off Ludgate Hill, there is little breeze in the courtyard garden. They all sit, sharing the shade of the lime tree, sipping his mother's elderflower cordial. William pulls out a pencil sketch he has brought with him. It shows his daughters and the latest addition to the family. A son, born just two weeks earlier. 'We would have brought the girls but these dog days are unbearable.'

'Too much for the new-born.' Mary adds, fanning herself with a rush fan. Ma nods.

Pa examines the sketch more closely. 'They are comely, most easy on the eye. What are you to call the young one?'

'William, after myself.'

His father grunts approval. Rufus, the setter, nuzzles at William's hand.

'You heard that Revell passed since you were last here.' Ma says, looking behind her as if she might still see him, sitting on his step by the door.

'Yes.' Mary smiles at her. Then turns the conversation back to where it belongs. 'We are to hold the baptism in Covent Garden. At St Paul's Church.'

'Very grand.' Says Pa. Then, to William. 'Must be setting you back a fair dole.'

'It is near the studio I am now renting... in Russell Street.'

'I am sure it is delightful.' Ma says.

'Your son is moving up in the world, Ma. Just so we all remember where we come from.'

The family gathering breaks up a little later, after a cold collation, suiting the mood and temperature of the day.

'Why do they hate me so?' Mary demands, as soon as they are on their way home.

'My mother was warm, I thought.' William says. 'But true, my father has fixations and delusions. I sometimes wish my Godfather never promised him so much. It set up such expectations.'

Mary's lips are pursed.

A week before the Christening day, William has an appointment with Gwynn, at Angelo's Academy in Soho Square. William is still not happy with the final proofs of the bookplates. 'See, here and here, those marks are not on my plate.' He hands Gwynn his loupe.

'A fault in the paper, perhaps?'

William shakes his head and looks for another example. He hears Angelo's voice raised in greeting and looks up to see a familiar face, across the other side of the fencing hall. It is the Chevalier d'Eon. He sports his Dragoon uniform, but even from distance William can see it carries a new medal. The Cross of St Louis gleams on his chest.

'Damnation.' William hisses. There is no time to retreat. If he had just seen him earlier. His hand holding the loupe is starting to shake.

'My Greetings, Messieurs.' The Frenchman is all smiles.

'Welcome. Monsieur d'Eon.' Gwynn teases him.

'Chevalier.' replies the Dragoon.

William nods towards the Chevalier's new medal. 'So your compatriots did not hang you after all?'

The comment emerges harsher than intended but its target is gracious.

'There are many who see Peace as a blessing.' D'Eon replies with some restraint.

Gwynn makes his excuses. He must continue to work through the proofs. D'Eon beckons William to join him. With a backwards scowl at Gwynn, he acquiesces. They walk through the corridors out to the *manège*. It is all quiet, the lessons are over for the day. In the distance the grooms are busy, washing down their charges.

D'Eon stops at the fence to watch. 'You know, this Peace... history will be the judge of what we have achieved.'

'No doubt, you did what you thought was right.' William replies, watching the grooms at work. 'I am more concerned with the future.'

'Ah yes. Angelo tells me you are again a proud father.'

William inclines his head. There is a prickling sensation starting at the base of his spine. A tightness. 'A brother for my two daughters.'

'And will they learn French? With a father so fluent in our language.'

The tightness is now pulling at William's neck. Something is awry. 'Well, my wife has been learning too, so we do speak some French with them.'

'Perhaps you should.' The perpetual smile leaves d'Eon's face. His voice steps down a tone. 'So that they may one day converse with their stepsister.'

William is sure he has misheard. 'Stepsister?'

'Ahh.. I thought as much.' The smile is back. 'We were not sure if you had been informed. Your former companion...' D'Eon hesitates. They both step back, to allow a groom to walk past guiding one of Angelo's ponies. William would have willingly leapt on its back to escape.

'Your former companion..' D'Eon continues.

'...Gabrielle, she is well?'

'Oh yes. We keep an eye on her. She is as well as a young mother and child can be...'

'A child!' William grips the wooden rail beside him. 'She never said.'

'Your departure was not a father's duty.'

'I did not know.'

'No? Well that is as maybe.' With this, the Chevalier steps aside, draws his foil and begins a series of rapid poses, thrusts and parries. He laughs. 'Be still my restless spirit.'

William's blood is up. 'Do you have no heart, d'Eon? No sense of what this does to me.'

D'Eon's smirk is cruel. But his foil is sheathed as quickly as it emerged. 'Loyalty. Duty. This is what concerns me.'

'I am an artist.' William declares. 'I have no-'

'-no loyalties? Not even to your family?'

At this moment, Gwynn comes around the corner. He needs William. A question about a detail he has found. D'Eon bows. The gracious smile is back. 'When all is finished, I look forward to my copy of the Book. Good day, to you both... Honoured Architect and King's Engraver. No doubt we will see each other soon.'

Returning to Russell Street, William's head is in a swirl. Gabrielle left him. For years these words softened his guilt. But this unknown child rips all comfort from him. It threatens his future. Exposure, for some trumped up collusion, a public trial and humiliation, a bloody execution even. True, the new King has pardoned Hensey, the French spy, as a gesture to the Peace, but there are no guarantees of clemency. Treason is treason even in peacetime. Is d'Eon lying, to torment him, to bend him to their will? The coffeehouses are full of warnings. The French will never suffer the loss of their territories. Comte de Broglie's plans to invade may yet have their day.

At three o'clock on Friday, 12th September, the bells of St Paul's ring out across Covent Garden. At the Church steps, William and Mary greet family and friends arriving for the Christening. Mary is in her favourite pink bodice and he has a new blue silk waistcoat. His father makes much of Mary's brother Sam in his naval uniform. Though he cannot resist a jibe at his own sons.

'Fought for God and Country in the coffee house and the tavern, eh boys?'

Mary grasps William's hand so tight it is slippery with sweat. Fortunately, Gwynn is at hand to lighten the mood. From behind his back, he reveals a high-scented bouquet. 'To the Mother of all Mothers, dear Mary.'

At the font, William passes over the wriggling bundle that is his son. The anxiety of the moment is not helped by thoughts churning William's belly, of another child, a baby that he never knew. The elderly Reverend struggles with young William, who shows no wish to enter Christ's Family in peace. He lets loose a scream, then a gurgle as the Holy water splashes across his forehead. The act is done. But William cannot rid himself of the image of Gabrielle, alone with their baby daughter. He never asked d'Eon for her name. Will she be an artist too? He has a sudden, wild notion of escaping to France. Though this soon subsides, as his guests gather around to speculate on the young lad's future.

William sees Bailey, hovering towards the back of the crowd. Now there is a man who would understand, with a family on both sides of the Channel. So, smiling all the while, William pushes his way out towards his old companion from Paris. 'I expect this is nothing new for you.'

'Oh, each time it is a wonder.' Bailey replies, pushing lank hair back off his forehead.

'You still find it so? I confess, I have begun to lose what faith I had.'

'I meant it is a wonder that we come together in hope. I am not one
for faith. But hope, yes.'

William has no answer. He turns to watch his girls. They are giggling
together, entranced by all the attention.

'I have a little present for your young ones.' From a deep pocket,
Bailey pulls out an exquisite wooden swan. The carving is so detailed,
every feather stands out. The neck is erect, its eyes watchful. 'I have been
working on it awhile. It was your engraving that inspired me ... '

William's hands tremble as he reaches out for it. 'It is beautiful,
thank you. I will, er, I will keep it safe for them, for when we return
home.'

His guts are so tight it hurts, but this is not the time to raise the
spectre of Gabrielle and her child. He thanks Bailey again and promises
to be in touch.

The last weeks of September are full of practical distractions. The
house at Stafford Row must be made ready for Mary and the children.
She is now ready to leave her beloved Lambeth and join William. In
turn he must make more of his studio in Russell Street. On
Gwynn's recommendation, he takes on an apprentice. Joseph Strutt
is a fourteen-year-old miller's son from Maidstone, with the fleshy
physique of his father's profession. He shows early signs of talent and
a passion for organisation that shames William every day. All this keeps
him so busy that William is not aware of a dangerous storm brewing at
the French Embassy.

The first William hears of it is in early October. He and Gwynn are
invited to Angelo's to celebrate the publication of his *Ecole des Armes*.
Surrounded by London's finest swordsmen, William notices there is

one man missing. The Chevalier. When he raises this with Gwynn, he receives a knowing look. They retreat to a quiet corner of the room. 'The French dragoon has had his handsome nose put well out of joint. After lording it around town, he's back to being a Resident. The new Ambassador, the Duc de Guerchy, is no *ami*. Different faction in Versailles.' Gwynn takes another sip of Rhenish. 'And it goes back a-ways too, some military escapade where Guerchy left him dangerously exposed.'

'That would upset our man.' William observes.

'Cannot stand to be under the same roof, I hear.'

'But why is he not here?'

'D'Eon is the proverbial bad penny. He'll turn up.'

Chapter 11

Two days later, in the small hours before dawn William is woken by a loud knocking at his door in Stafford Row. Mary and the children have not yet moved in. Only Joseph Strutt, the apprentice, is in the house. He reaches the door before William. There is a muffled exchange.

'Speak Strutt, who is it?' William demands.

'A messenger. Says he's from the Chevalier.'

William pushes Strutt aside and opens the door wide. A hunched figure is trying to cover his head from pelting rain. Seeing William he blurts out his message, 'My master begs you to return with me to Soho.'

William glances up the narrow street. A carriage horse is tossing its head in the downpour. 'Damn his eyes, what tomfoolery is this? At this ungodly hour?'

The figure hunches his head even deeper into his chest. William turns inside to find Strutt already busy lighting candles. 'Jo, I will go with this man. Stay here today, that Mary may find someone when she comes with the young'uns.'

Some ten minutes later, Strutt is helping William on with his boots. 'Trust me master, I will not move.'

Out of earshot of the messenger, William whispers, 'If I do not return by day's end, go find Fieldings men. Tell them who summoned me.'

'In faith, I will sir.'

'I trust in hope not faith sir. Remember that Master Strutt.'

It's a swift journey across the quiet city. Turning into Brewer Street, William sees several heavy-set figures pacing in the shadows. Four men in dragoon uniforms emerge from number 38, and hustle William into the house. They are carrying short swords and speaking French. Inside, a mess of timbers, rope and sacking forms a makeshift barricade. Similar structures block the corridors leading off both sides of the entrance hall. It is theatrical, dramatic. But the faint charcoal smell of blackpowder suggests this is no farce.

Upstairs, there are maps spread across the oak table. Sitting in a large wing back chair is a French officer. His face bears a striking resemblance to the Chevalier, who then emerges from the shadows. 'Ah. Monsieur Ryland. Welcome to Fort d'Eon. Forgive me, this masquerade, but matters have deteriorated somewhat, I had no -'

Suddenly furious, William finds his tongue. 'What in God's name? French soldiers! Barricades -'

'-Poisoning and Kidnap is happening, that is what!' D'Eon responds. 'Well... might have happened!'

'Of whom? The King ?'

'No, the King of England is safe. But I, Chevalier d'Eon, on the other hand, have narrowly escaped with my life. Just hours ago.'

His hand goes to his heart as if to calm himself. 'Come, an apple brandy perhaps?' He says, indicating a dark bottle on the table beside them.

William shakes his head. But d'Eon has already turned to pour three glasses without listening for a reply. 'From my cellar in Tonnerre. A taste of homeland.'

'Why did you ever leave?'

'I chose a life in service of my King, Louis.'

D'Eon's accomplice is quiet, but his eyes have not left William.

'Forgive me,' says the Chevalier. 'My cousin, a distant member of my family, the Marquis de la Roziere- like myself in the service of the King.'

William nods. 'You said kidnap?'

Weary after the initial excitement, William takes a seat for D'Eon's explanation.

'Just two nights ago, the Ambassador, Guerchy, invites me to a meal, a pretence of reconciliation. After dinner, drinking spirits in the English way, in the absence of the ladies, he offers me a special toast. Minutes later I am feeling ill, falling all about. I must find air. I am afraid, so I escape. Down into the basement and out through a side window and into the road. Then, I run to the house here in Brewer Street. Where cousin Roziere brings me in and hides me.'

'Hides you? From-'

'-Guerchy and his clique. From my loyal friends I hear there was a kidnap plot, boatmen waiting at the Thames steps, a ship standing by at Gravesend to leave for France with me on board.'

William empties his glass. This is such madness. If Gwynn were here, he'd damn it all as absurd poppycock. But d'Eon is adamant. 'Why would they do this, you may ask? My own people. Well, Versailles casts a long shadow.'

'But not over me. It has no hold over me!' William stands up to leave. Roziere is on his feet in an instant and moves to block his path. William steps back, palms out to indicate no harm intended. He tries a different tack. 'Chevalier, Marquis, I understand your compatriots are after you, but what am I in this... this game?'

Roziere glances to d'Eon, who nods and invites William to join them at the table. It is covered with maps.

He examines one of the line drawings. At each location there are details of fortifications, of heights of cliffs, depths of harbour water. 'These are maps for -'

'For invasion.' says Roziere with enthusiasm.

William turns on D'Eon. 'Yet you, you negotiated the Peace.'

D'Eon shrugs. 'You know our history. Every Peace is just a prelude to war.'

De Roziere clears his throat. 'So, we must be prepared. My maps for the King, begin at the Southern Foreland. I am working my way west to ... here...' He indicates the coastal town of Eastbourne.

William shakes his head. 'I still see no need for me. Your maps are excellent.'

D'Eon fingers his St Louis medal. 'There are those who do not appreciate my connection to the King. They want me gone. I know too much. I have papers, insurance let us call it, that they want. And these maps also.'

'We need copies.' De Roziere explains. 'Copies that cannot be discovered, that can be hidden. We thought with your skills you would-'

'Commit treason? Why would you expect...'

There is a screech outside. An owl perhaps. D'Eon opens the shutters an inch or two, but all is quiet in the street. 'I believe my master Comte de Broglie made you aware. Your Godfather... the Jacobite.'

'God rest his soul, he lived in different times. There were many Jacobites in his day.'

The corner of D'Eon's mouth twists into a smile. 'He worked against the Crown and left you funds to live in France. You were in liaison with Gabrielle, the daughter of a high ranking official-'

'-what?'

'Yes.' D'Eon continues. 'The daughter of a King's counsellor. Deceased. But still a detail she may have forgotten to tell you. Gabrielle is a rebel. An attractive quality, no doubt? And she is now the mother of your child.'

William leans back in his chair and closes his eyes. He can hear the guards downstairs murmuring and stamping their feet. Everyone here is on edge. To avoid betrayal, he must play his part. He blinks and nods to D'Eon. 'I would need materials.'

'Indeed.' William sees De Rozière smile for the first time. 'It would be best if they came from you. Less suspicious ... and we do not demand an instant response.'

'Then why this charade before dawn?' William asks.

'We are soldiers. It is in our instinct to act.' De Rozière's smile curls into a sneer. 'That is perhaps not an artist's response.'

William looks at d'Eon, who is more reassuring. 'Take your time. Decide how you can help us, and so help yourself.'

A carriage is summoned. Soon he is passing the Queen's Palace, looming out of the early morning fog. Then home to Stafford Row. His hand shakes as he reaches for the bell pull. Strutt is there in seconds, he must have fallen asleep in the corridor.

'Such an unnecessary journey.' William declares, brushing himself down.

'You are well?'

'Yes, yes, I need some rest. And you too! We have a busy day ahead of us. Now... nothing of this to my wife.'

At noon, the arrival of Mary, Pinney the housekeeper and the three children is a welcome distraction. Strutt has thought of every detail but they are all kept busy until the evening, laying out the rooms. It is only later that night, after Mary has retired, that William is once again alone.

He pours himself a brandy. If he is to engage with this French venture, there must be no chance of discovery.

For several nights, William expects a knock on his door at any moment but there's relief when d'Eon goes public. His dispute with the Ambassador is the talk of all the coffee houses. Weeks turn into months. William assumes the quarrel is settled. He hears nothing more, until the Spring of 1764.

Early one evening, he is working in the Russell Street studio. He and Strutt are looking at the latest proofs of the Coronation Portrait. A carriage comes to a halt outside. From the studio window, William sees he has guests, his youngest brother John and Henry Bryer, Pa's apprentice. They push open the door, before he has time to step out to greet them.

'Brother Joseph has been a fool,' says John.

'He is in jail.' Henry declares.

'A damn fool.' John continues. 'Pa wants you to know.'

'Whoah, now.' William says. 'Calm yourselves. Come, I'll clear some room.' He sets chairs for them by the open fire. He frowns an apology to Gwynn. 'A family matter.'

'I will take my lea- '

'-No, do stay. Wise counsel may be needed.'

Once all our settled, brother John relays what they have heard just this afternoon. 'Joseph was with his band of ne'er-do-wells out Richmond way. And being in a tavern late, and their purses emptied, they take it into their heads to go a-thieving.'

William's frown deepens. 'Hell's teeth. What were they thinking?'

'Thinking did not trouble them. They ride out on the highway and stop the first carriage they see.'

Bryer joins in. 'Two spinsters, scared witless, hand over purses, 20 guineas a piece,'

'They are not harmed?' Gwynn asks.

'No, that at least he spared us.' John says. 'But the numskulls then return to the tavern and boast to all and sundry what they have been about. Next day, still sleeping off their exploits, they are surprised by magistrate's men.'

'And now they are in Kingston lock up. Awaiting trial.' Bryer's tone is a touch too smug for William's liking.

Gwynn breaks the silence. 'A hanging offence. With clemency, perhaps some years in the hulks, if he survives.'

William is distracted. Why did Pa not come himself? He looks across at Bryer. Pa's apprentice is some years older than his own, Jo Strutt, and of different mettle. City born and bred, the son of a merchant, he has the confidence of his birth. But this now, this Joseph fiasco, is a family matter. William addresses John. 'Are you and Marie to marry?'

John flushes. 'No date is fixed but the betrothal is now approved.'

William nods, his bottom lip rising into a pout. 'A jeweller's daughter... so at least there is one match, one son, Pa may boast of...if Joseph does not shame us all.'

'William, it is not like that. Pa loves you and Mary and his grandchildren.'

'He has never said so. She will always be "the Lambeth Mary." '

John twists the brim of his hat back and forth between his fingers. William smiles. 'Pa's love is not today's concern. Joseph is our blood. It is just that-'

'-you do have the King's favour.' John insists.

'Aye, for now. But it is a card I had no wish to play...'

'Joseph may go hang, then?'

William's mind is already on the next steps. 'Where is he, you say?'

'Kingston.' Bryer replies. 'He is already condemned. We have a month at best to save him.'

William shakes his head, 'There are implications for me you know...'

That evening, Mary is adamant. 'If t'were my brother, who had been so foolish. I would move heaven and earth.'

William knows she is in the right, but she does not know what else is in play. She cannot know. At any time he could be betrayed by D'Eon.

'You must go to the King.' She insists. 'He is your patron. Use the influence you have. Ask the Queen.'

Three days pass before William gives way. Within hours, brother John is outside the house at Stafford Row in a post-chaise. 'Pa is not well, he cannot bear to make the journey.'

William's eyes betray his thoughts. More likely he cannot bear the shame. He sees a basket wedged between John's feet. Ma has sent a pie. Few words are spoken as they head west out of London and then south through Richmond. The roads are hard rutted, with no rain now for nearly a month. The Old Gaol, known locally as the Stockhouse, is half-way along Clarence Street, Kingston's principal thoroughfare. It is a mean, squat stone and flint building. Prisoners fester here before their appearance at the Assizes.

'Morning, gentlemen, and how are we?' The Governor is all smiles. There is money to be made from these City folk. Their brother is not one of his usual stock-in-trade. Since Joseph Ryland was first taken at a nearby tavern, there have been several visitors. Each must pay his price for care and comforts.

The stench of human filth is too strong. William retches and cannot enter. He urges John to go ahead while he takes some air. At the back of the gaol, he pisses against the outside wall. There is a barred, slit window above his head. He hears his brothers' voices.

'Ma sent pie to keep you well.' says John. 'She is so tired of crying-'.

Then comes Joseph's wheedling, plaintive tones. 'She knows. Done and done for I am. Chaplain says I'll be hanging from the tree before June is over.'

'We are doing what we can.' replies John.

The gaoler pushes against the heavy cell door. He beckons William forward. Joseph is curled up on his straw mattress, knees hugged to his chest. His cheeks are blotched a vivid red. It darkens his eyes.

The sight of William only stirs up more bitterness. 'Come to gloat now have 'ee?' He turns to the wall, letting out a sigh that seems to shrink him even further.

John has his kerchief up across his mouth and nose. His eyes implore William to respond. But he cannot at first. What is it in Nature that a mother can have children so different one from t'other? He keeps the thought to himself. 'You know, I am working for the King.'

Jo stays facing the wall. His finger traces dark lines in the grey-green mould. 'Five years you spent kissing the French. Now you're in cahoots with our King and Queen. What did I do wrong?'

William, mouth pinched, wants to remind Jo of his Judgement Day. But he remembers Mary's words. There are softer ways. 'I offer no guarantees. My credit with the King is still good. For now, my powder is dry.'

'And my revels may just strike a spark into your powder, brother William. Blow your royal pension sky high. I know why you are here.'

John now has his kerchief off. 'You are sentenced to die, Joseph. There's none that's brave with a rope around their neck.'

'Go hang yourselves. Both of you.'

On the journey home William swears he will do his utmost to seek a pardon. This madness does not deserve a hanging. T'was a drunken escapade, no more. It is dark when he arrives at Stafford Row. The children are already a-bed and he is grateful that Mary is too tired to talk. He reassures her that he has a plan.

He is at Ramsay's studio in Soho Square by ten in the morning. A swarm of assistants are preparing canvases and paint, copying details from one Royal Portrait to another and taking a stream of advice and instructions from Ramsay himself. William is invited to the private salon on the first floor. Its decoration has changed since his first visit. Many of the Italian sketches have been replaced by studies of the new Royal Family. William is amused to see they hang alongside the portrait of Ramsay's wife, still dangling her Jacobite rose. A few minutes later, the artist joins him. 'It is like having a roomful of clocks. I wind up my artists each morning and pray that they keep time, at least till luncheon. So, tell me. Why the urgency?'

William sets out the dilemma. He ends with a request for Ramsay's guidance. 'You know how to negotiate the whims of the Court far better than I.'

To his relief, Ramsay is instantly engaged. 'I shall work on the Queen's side. She has more compassion than our Farmer King. I know that she is taken by your likeness of her King, in the first engraving. She detests shoddy imitations.'

'What hope is there?'

Ramsay pauses for a moment. 'It is not without precedent. Even Hensey was pardoned.'

'My brother's life has no such weight. This can be no more than a favour.'

'It is all in the telling. I will paint it light, as summer froth, misjudged by a heavy-handed official. A case to be dismissed without a thought.' Ramsay claps him on the shoulder.

William bows. 'I am indebted to you sir.'

'There will be time to repay the favour. At the gaming tables of La Cornelys, perhaps? But first, I must deliver. The Lord Chancellor has the Queen's ear. I'll play upon his vanity. I have heard he is sitting for portraits all across town. Within a week, I'll have an answer. Either way... Noose or no noose.' With a friendly bow, Ramsay exits the room, to oversee his assistants.

While he waits for news, William turns to his own Royal commission, the Coronation Portrait. The copper plate has been neglected. Seeing Ramsay's copying team in full flow, shames him into action. He sends word to Mary, via Jo Strutt, that he will work late at the studio in Russell Street this week and may well stay overnight.

Gwynn accompanies him. He has a set of Christopher Wren's original designs from King Charles' day and plans to while away the evening, imagining such vistas for today's City. The inn next door has a passable kitchen and a fair Portuguese red. So, come dinnertime, they are settling in to eat a mutton pottage and a glass or two. They are both too tired for conversation and certainly not amused when there is an insistent rap on the door.

The messenger is not one of Ramsay's men.

'Monsieur Ryland?' It is one of d'Eon's dragoons.

'Yes.' William hisses.

'The Chevalier invites you to attend him at your earliest convenience.'

'Is he not aware it is already evening?'

He turns to see if Gwynn is listening, but his old friend is absorbed in Wren's drawings.

'He said it would be in your brother's interest.'

'Oh damn him. My brother...' William feels his guts leap. This is how d'Eon sets his trap. 'Bear with me. I...I must fetch materials. Tell your master, tell him I will make my own way to Brewer Street.'

The dragoon's face is as blank as any used to obeying commands. 'Well? Be gone sir!'

'I have instructions to wait, for your safety.'

'Well wait then, damn you.' And William slams the door shut. Turning back, he almost collides with Gwynn. The raised voices have drawn him from his plans. 'I pray you, do not ask.' William turns him around and pushes him with some force back to the table and the plans. 'It would be best. For now. As a friend.'

Gwynn raises his hands, as if to placate an animal at bay. He returns to his architectural drawings.

William gathers materials that he had hoped he would never need: several quills, paper, a couple of brushes and a large bottle.

At 38 Brewer Street, the internal barricades are still intact. The Chevalier d'Eon and de Rozière are alone in their Map Room on the first floor, playing chess. Neither rises when he enters with his weighty bag.

'So, Monsieur Ryland.' D'Eon says. 'How swiftly positions can change, *n'est-ce pas*? It seems you are intending to play the Queen.'

William stands, shocked into silence.

'And now you are here. You have come to play with us. Am I right?'

Still William has no answer.

'Come now, the news of your brother's escapade is the talk of the coffeehouses. Of course, a good family man like yourself would do whatever you can to... pull strings. If that is the expression?' He pauses. William's lips are pursed.

'Well, matters here are also in a state of flux. Our enemies are manoeuvring, they attack me, by attacking my dear cousin here. They are threatening to expose him as a spy.'

'Though he spies for France?' William feels himself being drawn into such a web of deceit.

D'Eon sighs. 'Indeed, surprising is it not? As I have often said, Versailles is a place of shadows and mirrors, not everything is as it seems. One is in, one is out. We must prepare for the worst.'

'I live in hope,' William says, raising a smile from d'Eon.

'As you must.'

William knows he must pay his debt. But can he cut the risk of discovery? 'I have a proposal.' He says, as he opens the heavy jute bag he has brought with him from the studio. He pulls out a large glass bottle. It is filled with a pale, yellow liquid.

D'Eon casts an amused glance to de Rozière.

'No, it is not piss!' William pulls out the cork stopper and waves it beneath d'Eon's nose. 'Lemons.'

'You have been studying Hensey's game. But these are detailed maps, not a few lines of correspondence.'

'Oh, you will have your maps. I have spent a lifetime learning how to copy from observation. I will apply the same principles. On one condition.'

'Name it,' says D'Eon.

'I have your word that if I make these copies I am quits. Free of my debt to you and your master, the Comte de Broglie.'

D'Eon pulls at his ear, glances again to Rozière, who shrugs. 'We cannot speak for the Comte but I will assure him you have more than acquitted yourself. That is the best I can do.'

William sets to work. He lays out one map sheet at a time. Alongside he sets a blank sheet and slowly transcribes every detail of the lines and text from Roziere's maps. At first, the French pair stand close, peering over his shoulder. They demand to see an example. William has to sacrifice an hour's work. He holds his first sheet above a candle flame, and they watch as his invisible marks gradually emerge across the paper. He has produced an exact copy. His brown line reveals the coast and all its features. Every word of the text is legible and in the correct place.

'Truly, we French have taught you well.' D'Eon quips.

They trust him to continue. The irony is not lost on William. For him it is an act of betrayal, in the service of the French King. For what? To save the neck of his brother and his own fortune.

He presses on, with sheet after sheet. Only the watchman calling the hours gives him a sense of passing time. Around dawn, William adds the final text to the last map. D'Eon has been asleep on the couch across the other side of the room. He stirs and stretches himself awake, watching William gather up the sheets, which he has spread out to dry, well away from the heat of the hearth and the chimney.

'Come. I will show you where they are to be stored.' Up on the third floor, d'Eon pushes the bed back from the wall. He prises up a floorboard, then another. In the cavity, there is already a wooden box, filled with papers.

'My insurance,' he says.

William raises an eyebrow.

'Correspondence. All my instructions from King Louis. Rozière's orders to map the coastline. I will only release them when I obtain justice from Guerchy and my debts are paid. Now let us add-'

'No, Chevalier. A moment, if I may.'

D'Eon rises, surprised by this late resistance, but William's voice is measured, reassuring. 'They... your enemies...rivals, whoever they may be, know you have this correspondence. They also know de Roziere will have his maps and information somewhere here or about his person?'

The Chevalier shrugs.

'But they do not know you have copies of these maps.'

'So, they...must not exist?'

'Exactly. At first glance, they are still blank sheets, only the heat of a candle can betray their secrets'.

'So, where do you suggest they should... not exist ?'

'Well, not here, not the first place they would look if they ever stormed past your barricades.'

'You will keep them safe?'

It is William's turn to shrug, with even a hint of a tired smile. 'I am already implicated.'

While d'Eon is replacing the floor boards, William looks around at the room. The candlelight is dim, but he is sure he can see a row of court gowns in an open wardrobe. D'Eon catches his glance, making sure to close the door as they leave. 'Life is a masquerade is it not William?'

In the Map room, d'Eon consults with Rozière. There is both wisdom and risk in William's plan. They demand a final piece of insurance. William must sign his own name, in the lemon ink, on one of Rozière's original map sheets. It gives them a weapon, should he fail to take care of their copies. He has no choice. In this double-dealing world, he is just as likely to have his throat cut, or his head caved in and bundled into the Thames.

So he returns that morning to Russell Street, carrying the same sheets of paper, his quills and brushes, though the bottle which contained the lemon ink is now empty. He is met at the door by an anxious Gwynn, who begs forbearance. 'I was copying some of Wren's drawings and fell asleep on them.'

William sees with irritation a pool of candle wax has run all over his desk. 'So, we have both endured a hard night.'

It is all that he can say before he collapses on to the day bed in the corner of the Studio.

When he wakes it is already dusk. The events of the previous night feel like a dream, but the papers beside him are proof to the contrary. He finds them a temporary hiding place among his old prints. With no news still about his brother's fate, he sets off for home at Stafford Row.

As he arrives, Pa and brother John are just emerging. They rush over to greet him, beaming smiles all around.

'He is free!'

'Pardoned!'

'A King's pardon!'

'Well done, my boy. I knew you would deliver! Did I not say so, John?'

John raises a patient smile. 'Oh yes, Pa. You did.'

William let's their excitement wash over him. All he can feel is relief, not joy. His brother is safe, he is safe. His Royal pension is safe. But for now, he just needs to rest and take stock. He walks inside, hugs Mary and the children and retires to bed.

Late the following morning, William sits at his desk to compose a heartfelt letter of thanks to Ramsay for his timely intervention at court. The response, by return, makes all the anxiety worthwhile.

Ryland, It was a pleasure to oblige. Your credit with the K & Q remains intact. Though they have a mercenary crew. Do not be surprised if favour required in turn. For now, rest easy. La signora Cornelys ci sta aspettando.

From one gentleman artist to another.

Yours, Allan R.

That summer of 1764 is one of the wettest for a decade. His growing girls and sickly young son do not tolerate well the humid days. Mary suggests they decamp back to Lambeth for August. It suits William too. The children adore his apprentice, Jo Strutt, so he comes along, as tutor and companion. He is full of stories. From him, William learns far more of England's history than he has ever been taught in school.

Summer drifts into autumn with the family enjoying life in the Lambeth Orchards. For William, it is a relief to escape the city's chatter. Though he is saddened to hear of Hogarth's passing. He and Ravenet spend a tearful day together reflecting on how one great man had raised the reputation of English engraving.

Just before Christmas, when he and the family are all back in London, William hears disturbing news from his old friend, Gwynn. 'The mysterious Marquis, d'Eon's *cousin*, has flown the coop.'

These are Gwynn's first words as he joins William at their favourite table in the bay window of Slaughters coffee house. William hushes him. But Gwynn is fired up. 'Fled through the night. They'll be in Dover by now.'

'They?'

'They, He. I know not who else.'

'D'Eon?'

'Oh, d'Eon's not rushing home to France. He still has scores to settle. Owes a fortune too.

'How did he travel, de Rozière?'

'I have no idea, horse, post-chaise. Why do you ask?'

'No matter. Just curious.'

William sips at his coffee. It is still too hot. Did de Rozière escape with the maps, with the one that bears William's signature? What if he is caught before he is across the Channel?

'The word is, Ambassador Guerchy's hacks were on to him. He was no more cousin to d'Eon than you or I. They say he was wandering up and down the coast making maps. It's every-'

'-Why would they betray their own?'

'Ah well, there you have me. Not to be trusted. Either side. If I were you, I would keep well away from our friend, the Chevalier.'

'It is my intention,' William sighs.

Chapter 12

1765

'In court circles it is an advantage to have a highwayman in the family.'

Boydell's *bon mot* makes William laugh. Though he is curious. He has been summoned to Cheapside, to the Sign of the Unicorn for a meeting. It is surely not to exchange pleasantries. That is not the way of London's most successful print seller.

William is sitting in the inner sanctum. He would love to explore its treasures, but his host is already pacing back and forth.

'Some seven years ago I wrote to a promising engraver in Paris with a commission from the future King.'

William inclines his head. 'For which I am eternally grateful.'

'It's put a shirt or two on your back. And now it seems that Royalty has need of you again.'

'A commission from the Queen?'

Boydell clicks his tongue. 'My understanding is she favours a portrait by Cotes not Ramsay.'

'You are as ever well informed.'

'Flattery, William. Never flattery. One cannot judge if ill-informed.'
,

He really should have been a schoolmaster. Perhaps a lawyer, not
a schoolmaster, he has such narrow certainties. What would he have
made of 38, Brewer Street with its treasonous maps and women's
gowns. William tries not to smirk as Boydell continues.

'Well, here's the matter. I have had word from Dalton, the Keeper
of the King's Pictures. Young George is amassing a sizeable collection.
Now he has a mind to enter the Paris print market. He has a lengthy
list.'

'You are well placed to help with that?'

Boydell stops pacing. The wind in his sails has dropped.
'No...indeed. He has asked, in person, for you to cross the Channel in
April, to purchase these prints. He trusts the brother of a highwayman,
more than a crusty curmudgeon like m'self.'

So that is it. No wonder Boydell is on edge.

'Someone has been speaking on your behalf. Though you do know
the city.'

William is already weighing the benefits - they are substantial - and
the risks: more intrigue with those planning to invade England. And
then there is Gabrielle and her... their child.

'Of course, you will be offered a commission.' Boydell pushes out the
words, as if he is passing an unwilling stool. But he retains his merchant
face. 'I also wish to entrust you with some trade. To sell Woll's Niobe
and his latest Wilson plate.'

William grins. 'We must all turn our Royal cards to profit, when we
can.'

For a man of paltry humour, Boydell does well. He forces a smile.
'So, you accept?'

'I am in no position to refuse a King's Commission. Though it sends
me in the opposite direction to five years past.'

Boydell is a step ahead. 'I believe it makes good sense to take Bailey with you.'

'To report back on how Paris prints are trading?'

'I wanted to speak to you first.'

At that, their meeting is over.

February is spent in a fever of accumulation. All the printsellers in London soon know of William's journey. There are recommendations, orders, favours offered in exchange for commercial connections. William engages a banker to advise him on credit, on loans to buy prints in London to sell in Paris and vice versa. He prepares a stack of his own prints for sale. It is as enticing as the gaming table, laying guineas on red or black.

Though one friend retains a healthy scepticism.

'You journey into the land of our eternal enemy. Just how well are Royal George portraits going to sell?' Gwynn asks from behind his Daily Advertiser.

'Oh, the French love us in spite of themselves. And do not forget the termite mound of ex-patriates, second-sons and merchants far from home. Wherever they settle, they long for a little England.'

Mary also has her reservations. She is still not accustomed to life in Stafford Row. Everything is new. 'There are masons, carpenters everywhere I walk. This street is a builder's yard.'

William's impending absence only deepens her concern. His promise of Parisian gifts falls on stony ground.

'I am not one for silk and baubles. You knows that. For all I care you may buy them for some French madame.'

But he sees she does care. Each day her fear twists into a heightened attention to their well-being. Pinney is instructed to keep the flagstones spotless.

Mary relies even more on Jo Strutt. He helps with the girls' schooling and cares for young William, who is often sickly. With these duties and all the prints to prepare he is soon in need of assistance. So William engages his father's apprentice, Henry Bryer. He comes highly recommended, not least by himself. Though he and Strutt, the self-effacing Maidstone boy, are very different. They tolerate each other but no more than that.

There is little respite as the day of departure approaches. Bailey is kept busy assembling all of Boydell's prints, among them Woll's Niobe and engravings of the best paintings in England.

'He declares it is time for an English invasion.' Bailey says.

On the 12th April, all is ready. Their heavily laden carriage cavorts out on to the Dover Road. William is at last able to reflect on just how different this return journey will be. He is on a mission requested by the King. He is a father, a married man, with a wife and three children he adores. And, in the eyes of those who matter to him, he is now a gentleman artist.

Bailey snores loudly in the corner seat. This time, when they cross the Channel, there will be no need for tooth-ache trickery. But the memory reminds him of Gabrielle and their child. His chest tightens. And while he is recalling hidden pain, there is also the other shadow world. Those who may find another opportunity to reel him into their designs.

These thoughts are all wiped clean when they arrive in Calais. A guard-troop of French dragoons greets them. They have been sent through the good graces of the British Ambassador, the Earl of Hertford. Everything is in hand to ensure that William's Royal mission is a success. By the following afternoon, they reach the outskirts to the city. It is more of a homecoming than he had expected. He is buoyed up by the smell of the bakers, the streetsellers' cries. It's as good as a trip back to the Fair. But he is not blind to signs that France is suffering. The years of war and their aftermath have left fields untended, houses and hostelries boarded up. As dusk falls, they enter Paris itself. Even here he senses a palpable unease. At every turn he sees broken beggars curled up in rags, on church steps, sheltering in doorways. But he keeps his own counsel. He is not here to stay and Bailey's growing excitement is hard to resist.

They have their first sight of the slender spire of the Sainte Chapelle, the Tour St Jacques, the twin towers of Notre Dame, the bridges across the Seine, the hectic babble of ferry boats, the print shops and bird cages lining the *quais*. The yellow-white stone of the Conciergerie. How could all this not lift one's spirits? It is where he spent the freedom of his youth, such days of laughter and wild roaming. Yes, his eyes are moist.

'The wind? Bailey asks.

'*Oui, le vent.*'

They both smile.

Despite the lengthy journey William is eager to venture out across the City. 'Tomorrow I dine with Wille and the dealers but tonight, just you and I, we feast.'

The Ambassador has arranged rooms for them in a sumptuous Hotel near his residence. Gone are the days of tramping up the backstairs, off Rue de la Huchette. That night William discovers an unexpected package in his old leather sling bag. There is a note attached, written in his daughter's hand: '*Papa, Bon voyage! Bon Retour! Marie Charlotte.*'

Wrapped in a green silk scarf is Bailey's wooden sculpture of the Swan, his Christening present for William's children. He drops back on to the bed. Once again, the tears flow, this time he makes no attempt to stop them.

The Ambassador, the Earl of Hertford, calls on him at mid-day. They sit in the terrace garden in the soft April sunshine that Paris does so well. A footman brings them sherbet. William fingers the worn black cloth of his English coat and vows to visit a tailor on the Rue St Honoré before the week is out.

'Sad to say, we are in the last months of our sojourn. Lady Hertford and I leave for England this summer. We adore this city. Even its people. As I believe you do.'

William smiles. This smooth-faced diplomat has an easy manner, but how much does he know?

'They do infuriate us at times. Perhaps because we are so alike. The Normans made sure of that.'

William feels his Welsh blood rising. 'There were more ancient Britons.'

'True, we are a mongrel race. It can lead to jealousy, rivalry even.'

His measured tone does not waver, but his eyes lock on to William's. 'A word of caution, Mr Ryland. There are many in France and England, who resent the...current arrangements. There may be Peace between our two great nations, but do not assume this will always be the case. We must tread gently. Avoid their corns, if you follow?'

'I will be circumspect, your Excellency. Strictly business.'

'Wonderful. Monsieur Wille is delighted that you will be dining with him tonight.'

William arrives outside number 35, Quai des Grands Augustins just as the sun is setting over the Seine. He stands for a moment at the river's edge, enjoying the warmth of its last rays on his face. It is good to be back.

Johann-Georges Wille, the doyen of Paris print collectors, is little changed. His hair is perhaps more silver, his belly a few inches more pronounced. A victim of fine living, the war has been kind to him. 'Bonsoir William! So delighted. You are our guest of honour this evening. I looked up what we ate on your farewell dinner and it seems it was -'

'-Sauerkraut?' William says.

'Precisely. I keep a record of everything. Details matter. I believe you have already met his Excellency...'

The gathering is another echo of his years abroad. Young English nobles compete for cultured *bon mots*, which they exchange with French and German artists he remembers vaguely, though their names escape him. Among the Parisians, there is Pierre-Francois Basan, the print seller, slimmer, even more aquiline than William recalls, his hair swept back, still showing off a fine forehead.

'He has the eyes of a hawk do you not think?' William whips around to find Maître Le Bas at his shoulder. They embrace, though both are hesitant, as they remember circumstances which have come between them. No mention is made of Gabrielle, but William asks after Madame Le Bas.

'She is as ever, mistress of all she surveys.'

William glances around the room.

'Ah, she is indisposed this evening ... and knowing how heavy the food can be... So, tell me. The past seven years...?'

When William wakes the following morning, he laughs out loud at the luxury of silk sheets and lilac scented pillows. The conversation with Le

Bas, if awkward, still renewed old ties. The invitation is open for him to pass by the studio to show his Leda and the Swan.

First, he must attend to Royal business with Basan. His new establishment is in the same mansion where he first encountered the Comte de Broglie during the night of Masquerade. In the daylight, the Hotel de Serpente has an entirely different aspect. Now it is a bright temple to trade. William is greeted as a valued customer.

There is also much talk of Boydell, of Woll's latest landscape prints and the new collection of English Masters. While William is at pains to act as honest broker, he makes sure that Basan knows he is a trader too. He has prints to sell and the credit to stock up on French works for the London market.

'So, William, when will you have your own establishment?' Basan asks at the end of their negotiations. 'A fine address to rival Boydell?'

'I am already in conversation.' The words escape him without prior thought. If Gwynn were here he would take him aside for an honest talk. But in front of Basan, his claim must gain some legs.

'Really?'

'Oh yes. You will soon see the address, on my next prints. I will trade beneath the sign of the King's Arms.'

'Indeed, then we should drink to future business between the King and the House of the Serpent.'

Two days later, all the deals are done. William chooses to visit Le Bas at his studio, in the afternoon. It is the time when Elizabeth goes to market. He finds Le Bas alone, fidgeting with his hair. He invites William into the back room.

'So, show me.' says Le Bas .

'The Leda?'

'Of course. That is why you are here, is it not?'

'Entirely.'

William pulls out the plate and several stages of proofs. His hands are trembling. Not from fear of criticism but because he remembers the moment, in this studio, that he placed the very first marks on the copper.

Le Bas settles into his chair. He asks about decisions made, the London printers, the advice of their mutual friend, Ravenet. Finally, he asks about the model for Leda's companion. 'It strikes me this may well be your charming wife, Mary.'

'Correct.'

'Just, as you described her to me.'

'And Leda?' William asks.

Le Bas hesitates, as if edging around hot coals.

'I would venture it is Gabrielle?'

'Of course it is Gabrielle. It has always been Gabrielle.'

'Before you left-'

'-Well, yes, it was never said, but I think you knew it would always be Gabrielle!'

William's anger is bubbling up. 'And there is much more that you knew... or know! Indeed, I am at a loss what anyone knows anymore. I am the last to know anything. Did you know that she was with child? *Maitre.*'

William spits out the title with such bitterness, Le Bas shrinks back. He twists the cord of his portfolio back and forth between his fingers. 'William. Gabrielle was, is, a friend. A dear friend. As of course you are. But she suffered alone. Brought a child into this world alone.'

'How quick you are to assume I would walk out on the mother of my child. She left me. I did not know.'

Le Bas looks away.

William feels a wave of heat surge up from the hollow of his back. 'What has Gabrielle been saying?'

'I think it is better that she speaks for herself.'

'She wants to speak?'

'Do you?'

'Oh, I ...' William collapses back into his chair. ' I don't know any more, what I want.'

He looks back at the copper plate, the two women, the swan, somehow even more pathetic now. This god become plaything, impotent and lustful. So many memories! He must settle it. 'Yes, I will speak with her.'

Le Bas blows out his cheeks and curls a lock of his hair.

'Please tell Lizabeth that I will meet with Gabrielle before I return to England. Within a week.'

He nods.

'And *Maitre*, please impress upon her. There are no more games to be played. Good day.'

William mutters a farewell to the apprentices and lets himself out on to the street. His guts are churning. He has one urge, to walk on without stopping. Some hours later, tiredness halts him, in an orchard, beyond the City walls.

He wanders between the cherry and apple trees. It is not long before their dancing blossom teases the dark humour out of him. There is a glass outhouse set against an old brick wall. The door is not locked. Inside, the fragrant skin of limes and lemons stands out among lush foliage. William drops his portfolio to the floor and stretches flat on his back along a stone bench. The sky is a blue blur through mottled panes. It may not match the view from the Lambeth tower but it is still a refuge. He shuts his eyes. The anger is long gone, leaving a tender place for loneliness to settle. His mind drifts and images slide by...the wooden Swan, the courtyard of the Hotel Serpent, prints hanging in Boydell's shop window. His last sensation is the sharp, musty scent of citrus.

It is dusk when he awakes, stiff from the long walk and the hard bench. But he has no desire to rise immediately. He is caught half-way out of a dream. There is a ship's deck, with hatches flung open, revealing dark recesses below. Lemons are being loaded and stored here. He is helping, stacking and counting, hiding them away. Nearby there are barrels of black powder. Though none of the spectral figures alongside him seem aware of any danger. Then water begins to gurgle up from beneath the fruit. It rises over his ankles, up his calves, to his knees. It is rank and relentless. When it reaches his waist, he is instantly alert, eyes open, aware that someone is close behind him.

'Monsieur?'

He swings around but in the half-light can see no-one at first.

'Monsieur?'

A young lad, not more than six or seven, his clothes just rags, steps out of the shadows. William leaps to his feet. The boy shrinks back in fear.

'Ah! Monsieur. I thought you were not well. You were crying out and tossing and tossing about.'

William lifts his hands to show he means no harm. 'I was just sleeping, a bad dream perhaps.'

The boy nods, with a look that belies his age. 'You are in my house.'

'You live here?'

He nods again. 'Papa used to work the gardens here. Since he died and the new man is come... I call this my house.'

'It is a fine house. You look after it well.'

The boy beams.

'What is your name?'

'Jean.'

'Well Jean thank you for your hospitality. Now I must be heading back to my house, in Paris.

'I do not know Paris, but I know the wagon to market travels that way.' He waves over his left shoulder.

'Thank you. And God be with you.'

'*Bon voyage, Monsieur!*'

When William regains the highway, he turns back to wave a final goodbye. But the boy is no longer watching. He is sitting head bowed, beneath a cherry tree. It is an image of such gentle sadness. William promises himself he will one day engrave it on copper plate.

The next three days pass in a blur of commercial dealings and final preparations for the journey back to London. He has secured every print and painting on the King's list. His own works have sold well and Woll's Niobe is exceptionally popular.

With their departure looming, William and Bailey walk the length of the Rue St Honoré. They browse through the shops to choose candied fruits, wooden toys and cloth for their children, for Mary and for Bailey's English wife.

But still there is no word from Le Bas, Elizabeth or Gabrielle.

After a farewell dinner at Wille's, William decides to take a nocturnal walk through the streets to his hotel. There are just two days left. He is content to meander. Perhaps after all it is best that he leaves this part of his life behind him... Gabrielle, the Comte, the secrets of the French. He should let them all drop away and make his fortune in London. That will be adventure enough. And no doubt easier on the heart.

For safety, he keeps to streets that are lit, though his wine-fuelled bravado soon seeps away in the chill night. He starts to up his pace. It would not be good to meet with some desperado alone at this hour.

Just as he turns a corner into the narrow Rue de L'Echaudé, he hears the clatter of hooves. Three horsemen are bearing down on him.

The leading rider, an officer, dismounts. He takes William's papers and without a word walks back into a pool of light beneath the nearest streetlamp.

'Monsieur Ryland?'

'Yes.'

'You must follow us.'

'But my papers? They are in order. From the British Ambassador.'

The officer shrugs and orders his men to take up position behind William, who is watchful, trying to stay calm.

The soldiers escort him at walking pace back across the Seine. They enter a narrow courtyard. The officer places a blindfold over William's eyes. He leads him by the elbow, not too brusquely, up a staircase that has the odour of freshly polished wood. At the next level, they walk along a corridor. A door opens. The cloth is removed. He is standing beside tall, ornately carved double doors at the entrance to a room with a ceiling that seems inordinately high. In the centre, with candles all around it, is a table some thirty feet long, covered with maps.

He recognises the Comte de Broglie, now bearded and a little fuller in the face, in conversation with an aide. The Comte looks up with a smile. 'Monsieur Ryland.'

William feels his chest tighten. 'Your Excellency.'

'My apologies for the mask tonight. Not as elegant but serves it purpose.'

'Royal Secrets?'

'Exactly.' He gestures to the array of maps. 'As you can see, De Rozière did well. We have all the information we need-'

'-For invasion?'

'When it is the will of the King.'

So, even de Broglie is not sure of Royal approval.

'His own citizens will not thank him.'

'We do not require a lesson on the costs of war, Monsieur.'

'Then perhaps you could explain my presence here. I am a British citizen, on Royal duty.'

De Broglie lifts a corner of one of the maps, and draws it towards the nearest candle-flame. 'Oh yes, you have a distinctive mark.'

He lets the map drop before the heat reveals William's signature. 'We all have our secrets, *n'est-ce pas, Monsieur*?'

William sits back in his chair. His breath is shallow. He will give nothing away.

'And now you intend to return again to England?'

'My business here is finished.'

'In London, will you see the Chevalier d'Eon?'

'We are not regular acquaintances, but it is possible.'

'A word of caution. He no longer has my King's favour.'

William brushes imaginary dust off his breeches. 'That is not my concern.'

'He is withholding certain documents...Correspondence.'

'I understood he had already made them public.'

'A selection. Only. To appeal to the mob and his coffee-house supporters. We believe he has others. And we will find them.'

William avoids de Broglie's gaze. A moth lands on the nearest map. He wishes it would quietly consume every one of them.

'We have no quarrel with you, Monsieur. But we may find further need for your assistance. I am sure you understand.'

William makes do with a grunt. Acknowledgement rather than acquiescence. The meeting is over. He is dismissed from the Comte's presence. A closed carriage takes him back to the Hotel.

When he reaches the Hotel, there is a message waiting. It is from Le Bas. Just an address and a time.

He rises early. After breaking his fast, he wakes Bailey and gives him the news.

'I need two or three hours no more.' Before Bailey can protest, he hands him the message. 'Come fetch me, here in St-Cloud at 1pm. That way you know I will not delay our plans to depart.'

Just before eleven, William's carriage takes a slight incline leading to a stone arched entrance. They clatter through, following a curving path which ends in front of a modest stone country house. The windows are all shuttered. It appears there is no-one at home. A gentle breeze carries the distant treble of a child's laughter. He is about to follow the sound when a maid steps out from a side door.

'*Bonjour, Monsieur. Vous êtes...?*'

'*Guillaume. Guillaume Wynne Ryland.*'

'*Ah. Très bien. La petite, elle est au jardin.*'

He follows her to a white painted side gate, partially covered by Spring growth. She opens it for him and invites him to follow the path into the garden.

'*Je peux?*' William asks.

'*Oui, oui, elle vous attend.*'

A slim, angular woman, in her middle years is pushing a young girl on a swing. They have their backs to him but he assumes the child must be Constance. She has her mother's black locks and high forehead. She is teasing a brown and white spaniel beside her, dangling a scarf just above his nose as she swings back and forth.

'*Viens Jacquot. Viens. Saute, Saute.*'

His barks and her laughter hide William's footsteps. So his arrival is a surprise to all of them.

Even Jacquot goes silent for a moment, then comes sniffing and wagging his tail in greeting. The young girl drops her feet to the ground, halting the swing. She whispers back to her companion. They both turn towards him. It is Constance who speaks first.

'Are you Guillaume?'

'Yes.'

'The friend of Maman?'

'Yes, I hope so. And you must be Constance?'

He steps forward to shake her hand, aware that the formality, though awkward, seems entirely appropriate. They are of the same blood but strangers.

'And this is Jacquot. He is naughty. And this is Amabelle, my governess...' she pulls at her companion's sleeve. 'who is never naughty.'

They all laugh. Amabelle, who has been stiff with shyness, nods a greeting. *'Bonjour, Monsieur.'*

'Come, please come. I want to show you my house.' Constance is already off and running. But not towards the mansion. She is away into the woods with Jacquot yapping at her heels.

Amabelle shrugs at William, *'Voilà, Constance.'*

He glances back to the mansion. The shutters are still closed. So they follow the sound of crackling footsteps until the wood opens up to a clearing where there is a low tree house. He can see Constance's shoes just visible at the entrance.

'Come in, Guillaume' she calls, 'but you must bend yourself. You cannot stand.'

He turns to Amabelle for permission. With a tolerant smile, she finds a bench where she can rest and watch.

William crawls inside. He pulls himself into a sitting position, his back to the timber frame. Constance is assembling an array of characters she has made out of leaves and twigs. Each one is introduced and placed with care around a box-wood table. They are all friends and teachers from her convent school. Whilst she is talking, William sees a piece of broken tile, near his foot. He picks it up and begins to scratch at it with his pocket knife. Slowly an image emerges. It is a feather, floating in mid-air. When there is a brief pause in her storytelling, he hands the slate to Constance.

'For your Maman.'

She rubs her finger lightly over the feather as if to confirm its reality. Then she places it gently among the leaf people.

Their shared time passes all too quickly. The garden's stillness is pierced by the sound of a carriage arriving and the boom of Bailey's voice. He calls again for William. They must be gone. The journey back to England cannot be delayed.

William says his goodbyes to Constance. She will not look him in the face or leave the tree house to say farewell. On his way back up the path, William asks Amabelle whether Gabrielle is nearby. She reddens. Her reply is rehearsed. 'Madame is not here today. She is grateful for your visit.'

On the road, William has time to reflect. He may never know why Gabrielle did not appear. But he feels no anger or resentment. Instead he sees her generosity in arranging this visit. It is a painter's gift, framed in time, with no other intent than for him to know Constance. Whatever comes of it, there is no expectation. Just as the young boy in the orchard, lonely as he was, had asked nothing of him.

Chapter 13

Two years later. April 21st, 1767

In Jonathan's coffee-house, down a narrow alley off Cornhill, William is sitting with a rotund, bewhiskered man of middling age. Mr Walchoe Junior.

'Well, I call's it my home. Our bookshop has been on Cornhill for over a hundred year. My father and his father afore him...'

William looks up from some yellowing papers he has been studying closely. This is not the first time he has heard these tales.

'... traders from every corner of the Exchange buys their books from Walchoes... we've despatched them, wrapped and franked as far as Muscovy and the Indies.'

Mr Welchoe Junior offers William a chip of Lisbon sugar for his coffee and continues on. 'It's all in them pages, you can see for yourself. We was 'ere at the bursting of the South Sea Bubble. My gramp saw an old boy throw himself off the Exchange. Landed on the cobbles at his feet. The more thoughtful ones found themselves a high branch on the Heath.'

William offers a sympathetic nod, though his patience is thinning.

'And then there was the fire of '48 when the wigmakers went up, and took all the coffee houses with it. Least Jonathan's back just like it always was-'

'Yes, well, let's hope-'

'- Could happen again. Not as bad, mind, but still, being so close and all that. Course we has insurance now.'

'Well, as I say, let's hope, that is all behind you. Off to the countryside, now, you say?'

'Indeed, a fine parcel of land.' Mr Walchoe Junior takes a moment to indulge in a pinch of his favourite Wilson's snuff. 'Prints is it? You would be selling?'

'Yes, not so different from your books.'

'Not so weighty, mind.'

'No, not so weighty.'

A whiff of stale menthol irritates William's nose. He gathers the sheath of papers in front of him and folds them back into some order. 'Now, Mr Walchoe.'

'Junior.'

'... Junior. I am sure you have business to attend to. So I will not be keeping you much longer.'

'I am all ears, Mr Ryland. I see you is mighty taken by the place.'

'Yes, you see, we are soon to publish the King's Coronation Portrait at the Spring Exhibition. We have high hopes, for it, high hopes.'

'It would make a fine draw, that would. Number 27 being a corner site and all.'

Over one more coffee William and Walchoe Junior come to a provisional agreement for the rental of No 27 Cornhill. Neither Mary, his apprentice Strutt nor even Ma and Pa are aware of how far his ambition has taken him. At £150 a year rental, this is no small engagement.

So there is much at stake on the morning of April 22nd, when William arrives at Spring Gardens, near Charing Cross. The Coronation Print of King George III is to be William's Golden Goose. All the signs are good that it will keep on giving.

His brother John is already there, sporting a fine new moustache. He strolls over, arm-in-arm with his young wife, Marie. Judging by her line, there's another Ryland on the way. Beside them is a smartly dressed, square-jawed man William has met once or twice already. James Triquet is Marie's brother. He shares her ability to make everyone feel welcome, without giving away too much of themselves.

'Greetings, all.'

As William nods through the social niceties, he strains to catch any reference to his Coronation print. Leaving John and Marie to wander at will, William takes James on a tour of the Exhibition. They both studied at the St Martin's Lane academy, so they know many of the artists on show. But James' interest is more speculative than professional. He has recently stepped sideways into his father's business. He now owns one of the most reputable Silversmiths in the Strand. William sees in him a shared ambition, a drive to move beyond the artisan circle that their parents inhabited. Perhaps he may be persuaded to invest some of his silver guineas in a new venture?

They find Gwynn studying a drawing in much detail. He is in ironic mood. 'Gentlemen. I hope you have found some worthy works. See here Sir William Chambers, the ubiquitous architect of Kew, the Keeper of the King's Ear-'

'-And your rival?' William jibes.

'Yes, he has that honour. But it seems he has no compulsion to impress.' He reads out the title of the drawing: '*A Plan of a fish market to be erected on the Great Canal of Gottenburg*. Forgive me but it is hardly a da Vinci.'

Moving on, they find something of more interest. A mezzotint of The Wild Boy. The engraver is one Valentine Green.

'I would be happy to sell his works in my establishment.' William is about to reveal his hopes for 27 Cornhill, when he remembers the venture is still not open knowledge. Fortunately, it seems that James has not registered the remark.

The morning after the Exhibition, Gwynn and Henry Bryer, William's apprentice, are sitting in a back room at the Virginia. They sip their sweetened coffee, beside a morose Royal Engraver.

'This is not a post-mortem, William. The portrait lives and flourishes as full-blooded as the King himself.'

The Print's reception was not as effusive as William had wished for.

'They were never going to set off a canon like Woll Woollett. The King was crowned five years past. But Ramsay is still making a fortune with his painted copies and you will do the same with your prints. They'll be flowing from Mr Hadrill's works within days. So spirits up and let's talk shop. Ha! Young Bryer, tell me about the Emporium !'

It was Bryer who had first discovered that Walchoe Junior was looking to rent out 27 Cornhill. For months he has been wheedling away at William. Now he is concerned his master's disappointment threatens his own long-cherished project. 'Well, it is in the most coveted position, opposite the Exchange, it has been a booksellers, ...

'Walchoes, I know it well', Gwynn interjects.

'...for generations and it has two sides one facing Cornhill, the other Change Alley... '

William's fingers stretch out the taut skin between his eyes. Gwynn is right. This is no time to sit, nursing wounded pride. He leaps to his feet. 'Come, you are correct as ever, Mr Gwynn. No more words, Mr Bryer. To the shop, our shop. I will show it to you myself. To the King's Arms !'

Flushed with excitement, William assures the ever-understanding Benson that he will honour his charge on his return and leads the way out of the Virginia coffee house. They rush along Cornhill and are soon standing in front of Number 27. Bryer tries the doors but they are locked. Then William pulls a large key out of his pocket. He grins at his astonished apprentice.

'Yes, well, I admit to having had some words with Mr Walchoe Junior myself...let us say... in anticipation. We have access to estimate the works. So what do you think? A site worthy of the King's portrait is it not?'

Gwynn looks around. He takes in the froth of merchants and traders simmering around the entrance to the Royal Exchange, the lawyers' clerks and notaries, laden with papers, squeezing past each other down Change Alley. 'Master William, you have arrived. Long live the King's Arms.'

They spend the morning investigating the two storied premises. Gwynn is instantly planning its conversion into a working space for the purchase and storage of prints. They discuss the demands of the clientele. They examine the condition of the timbers, the state of the paintwork, the window glass, the shelving. They agree on a location for the office, an area for wrapping and dispatch and a secure corner for the holy of holies, where the most precious works will reside. There is even room at the back for a printing press. At noon, they are joined by Bailey, who has been summoned from his work at Boydell's Cheapside shop to offer his advice.

'This is your world, William. Leave the pretensions of the Exhibition Halls to others. This is where you are at home.'

'Is there room for another Boydell?' Mary asks.

She is sitting with William in the garden at Stafford Row. Strutt is a few feet away, guiding their son's hand as he draws a cornflower.

It is a gentle Sunday afternoon in May, judged by William to be the moment to reveal his intentions to his wife. It is time for him to become a gentleman dealer.

'The market is rising, Mary. "An English wave", Boydell calls it and all honour to him for setting it in motion. But I have as much right to ride it. I have the Paris dealers behind me.'

She shifts in her seat. He cannot tell if that is a good sign or not. Since the winter she has been complaining of a tightness in her back. Perhaps it is returned. 'You have already made plans?' She asks.

'Forethought, yes. Ears to the ground. Young Bryer has found a shop. It is well placed. Opposite the Exchange. A perfect site.'

'Costly too,' Strutt says, over his shoulder.

William purses his lips. When Bryer is concerned, Strutt is always looking for a fault line. If he had his way, William would keep to his engraving, not sully his talent hunting after more guineas. But he's one of the family now. He must be coddled, persuaded, just like Mary.

'How much?' she asks, with one eye on Strutt's back.

'A hundred and fifty per annum... Plus charges ... Poor Law, lamp and pavement taxes, water and land tax.'

Mary winces. 'You would need to borrow?'

'Oh and stock'. William adds. 'But nothing ventured, nothing gained.' He rises to his feet. He has a trump card to play and now is the moment.

'Do you remember in the Exhibition, Cotes' portrait of the Queen, in pastels, with her newborn..?'

'Charlotte, just like our own, how could I forget?'

'Well, the Royal pair are so enamoured of it they have commissioned another in oils, and ...' He pauses for effect. 'They have called upon the Engraver to the King.'

Strutt drops his pencil and swivels around to face William.

'Yes, I am now a double pensioner! First the King. Now the Queen. Another £100 a year, Another portrait to be sold at the King's Arms.'

Mary is on her feet. Sore back forgotten. 'Oh William. That is the best of news.' She hugs him close. Strutt nods his congratulations and returns to tutoring. The Master will have his way.

William continues with the revelations. In for a penny in for a pound. 'There are those would willingly lend to a man who is on his way upwards, with Royal favour, as you say. James Triquet, for one. I was talking with him just last week, and he is eager to help.'

'He is family now,' Mary says, though her tone suggests this is both a comfort and a risk.

Unlike Strutt, William's more jovial companions see his latest commission as cause for celebration. And there is one establishment in London which offers just the entertainment they crave. Ramsay's neighbour in Soho, Teresa Cornelys, declared that she would set London society alight, and she has been true to her word. At Carlisle House she now presides over a fantastical palace of nocturnal pleasure, where some two thousand masqueraders at a time can indulge in revels.

So it is that one Friday night in June, as St Anne's tolls nine, William, Gwynn, Alan and Margaret Ramsay join the throng massing in the Square. A chain of carriages disgorges lords, ladies, ministers, clerics, East India Company Nabobs and Princes of State. They run the gauntlet of a surging mob who come to gawp. Though at times it is hard to distinguish the ton from the down at heel. Dukes become footmen for the night, Duchesses dress as they fancy milkmaids might, had they the wherewithal to purchase yards of muslin. There are so many generals and admirals that if every one were genuine, there would be no-one in the field to defend the Kingdom, should the French attack.

Once inside the door, everyone is equal and such freedom lets loose the spirit of Eros. It is as close to the Paris Fair as William has found. With music and wine to further stir their blood, these pampered souls wander through a suite of exotic spaces each one a stage for some form of excess. William is grateful that this is an indulgence which Mary, has no desire to share. The leaders of the nation are here. Well used to revelry and abuse, they still stand transfixed by a half-naked Boadicea. Posing with shield and spear, perhaps she has lessons in defiance to pass on. In the next room, there are elderly lords at play, running wrinkled hands over taut bodies of musketeers or caressing the rouged cheeks of a centurion. These are the men who lay claim to an Empire, matching that of Rome. Such weighty cares demand release. For this night alone, their dominions can go hang. For Alan, Margaret and many like-minded Scots, there is a Stuart haven. They down the heather-flavoured spirit of their ancestors and toast the King over the water with bravado.

Lords of the jungle are elsewhere present. A python slides across a sleeping Duchess. She feels a tightness about the chest and has to be extracted in a faint from such unwelcome attention. There are lion cubs tearing up Teresa's fine curtains. And everywhere there are giant plumes, of every hue. They could be the covering of live beasts, or just another cleric, an archbishop, in disguise, making his way discreetly to rooms where the more adventurous disappear into shadows. William shies away from these orgiastic retreats. Though later when the drink has taken him hard, he does lead a dancing line of revellers out into the Square. He finds dear Gwynn in drunken discourse with the statue of King Charles, remonstrating with him for his treatment of Nell the orange-seller. He claims she is his ancient relative.

Rough words from the mob soon send William and the masqueraders back inside. Is that his old adversary the Chevalier d'Eon, in full domino and hood, stepping his way proudly through a minuet? He turns away and spies a young woman in the company of Lady Wentworth. She is in pastoral attire, full-face-masked and surrounded by adoring company. Young Nathaniel Dance, a painter he remembers from Italy, is in attendance, as well as an assortment of Greek philosophers.

Seeing William approach, she feigns exhaustion, fan fluttering in the heat. 'Oh I am weary of this world.'

'And yet so young.'

'You sir, what is your disguise?'

'I am a recorder of histories, of deeds and cities founded by the great Alexander. And you madame?'

'I am a painter of faces.'

'As in Scottish Woad? In Cabbage-Blue?'

'*Scusi, signor?*'

'Where is your stall and brush? There are Jacobites abounding here, would cry to see themselves be-daubed. T'would bring out their ...'

'...history?'

'Indeed. How the world turns,' he murmurs, the room around him now revolving, for reasons not remotely philosophical. He is uncertain he can remain upright.

'I hold a mirror up to art,' he says.

'Perhaps you are already seeing double.' With that, this mistress of the classical world, moves on to other, more stable characters, leaving him to guess at her identity.

Some days later, William is once again at Ramsay's studio in Soho Square. Their conversation soon turns to the half-remembered events of that chaotic night. William is intrigued to discover the identity of the masked wit and scholar with whom he had his last remembered conversation. Ramsay divines the answer in a trice.

'I believe you have encountered the Swiss Angel, who has come among us. She sings as beautifully as she paints. She has conquered Rome, now she takes London by storm.'

'She has a name this apparition?' William asks.

'Kauffmann, Angelica Kauffmann.'

'Ahh!' William rocks forward head in hands. 'Of course, what a fool... the Painter of Faces ? I took her at her word.'

'You would not be alone, my friend. She has already made a mockery of many admirers. But there is truth in her claim. She entranced Reynolds himself with her portrait. First she captures his likeness then she adopts his fees. Twenty guineas a full-length.'

He leafs through a copy of the week's Advertiser and finds a marked page. 'Listen to this:

"Our hearts to beauty willing homage pay,
We praise, admire, and gaze our souls away."

William mock swoons. Ramsay shooshes him, 'There is more !'

"But then the likeness she has done of thee,
O Reynolds! with astonishment we see;
Forced to submit, with all our pride we own
Such strength, such harmony excelled by none,
And thou art rivalled by thyself alone!"

'Now, there is a match to be made.'

'Methinks, thine eyes flash green, William.'

'A trick of the light, Mr Ramsay. But I will follow her career with interest.'

The preparations for opening 27 Cornhill proceed apace. William's pocket book fills with lists of Engravers, of works complete and works in hand. He and Henry Bryer spend their days gathering intelligence, enlisting friends and family to visit rival dealers, to see what is selling, at what price. Meanwhile, Bailey continues to keep William abreast of Boydell's latest plans, his subscriptions and commissions.

There are now weekly gatherings at the Virginia. Its tireless proprietor, Benson, is always on hand to find a quiet space for their deliberations. He watches their ceaseless scribbling of figures, the counting and re-counting of guineas to be spent. He knows reliable new customers when he sees them. His sharp blue eyes flicker appreciation from beneath a ragged thatch of fair hair. It is the only unruly mark of a man who rarely reveals his thoughts. William appreciates his discretion and knows its origin. Once, late at night, they shared a fine claret and Benson recalled the inside of a debtor's jail. He has no desire to return.

As the number of prints and plates to be purchased grows ever longer, William and Henry realise the price of their ambition. They have some subscriptions to the Coronation portrait but to open with anything resembling a full stock they will have to borrow money. With less than two months before the planned September launch, William arranges to meet James Triquet. Again, Benson makes available his back room in the Virginia.

On the appointed day, William and Henry are running late. They have been at 27 Cornhill, discussing new print drawers with their carpenter and time has run away from them.

'Not a good beginning, Henry. Not good at all. If there is one thing James abhors it is disorder.'

Bryer mouths an apology though he knows this is William's doing.

'Let's hope Benson keeps him entertained.'

When they hurtle through the back door into the Virginia, they find Triquet alone. His pocket watch is placed in full view on the table. They order hastily. Coffees arrive, delivered by Benson with a frown. Then discussions begin. James knows the purpose. They are in need of guineas. He is by nature a cautious man. He has built on the success of his papa's silver trade. He counts Spanish Dukes and Polish monarchs among his customers. But to date his financial ventures have been within the world he knows.

'My capital, in modest ways, has helped fellow silversmiths, rivals even, purchase materials, precious metals, jewels from Antwerp and beyond. Short-term arrangements, offers of credit in return for a modest interest on the sum.'

'Much appreciated I am sure.' William must play on personal trust and family ties. It is the blood that binds the Huguenot world, which is James' inheritance. He rounds off his pitch with a proposal.

'Given that this is a new venture, a new trade for you, perhaps you would be more comfortable to stand at one remove from our borrowing.'

'How so?' Triquets says, bemused.

'As guarantor.' William explains. 'You would provide a bond for an agreed amount against which we could borrow from others.'

'From banks or individuals known to us,' Bryer clarifies. 'So you would only be liable if we fail to repay these loans.'

James Triquet looks from one to the other, then down at his pocket watch. It still ticks away, as reliable as the day his papa presented it, on the completion of his Guild master-piece.

'Well, I can only hope your sales are more reliable than your time-keeping.'

William is soon adept at this exchange of credit. He sets out rules to keep young Bryer in check. 'Begin with small sums, with friends, small traders, those we know keep a bag of guineas hidden from their spouses for just such ventures. Then follow Triquet's example. Repay on time, when we must, build a reputation for rectitude.'

'It is a long game, we are playing, Henry. Start it well and we will build ourselves a business fit to rival Boydell.'

Chapter 14

On the first of October, the London Gazette carries the good news. At Number 27 Cornhill, William Wynne Ryland, Engraver to the King and Henry Bryer his partner in the venture, are now players in the print market. The sign of the King's Arms, painted by William himself, is hoisted into position against the brick facade. Taking pride of place, in the grand front windows, is the full-length portrait of His Majesty, King George III, in Coronation Robes.

Gwynn and William look around at the gathering of family, friends and rivals.

'It will be a quiet day in St Martin's Lane.' William says. ' All of Old Slaughters' regulars are here.'

'It is about time they paid you the attention that is your due.'

Seeing the increasingly rotund Woll Woollett, Gwynn cannot resist a quip. 'He has become swollen on the proceeds of Wilson's Niobe!'

'2000 guineas is a substantial feast.' William says. 'Though I see that his Maecenas is not here today.'

'Ah dear Boydell. Must be a little green at the gills.'

In the bay window, Royal Architect William Chambers, full glass in hand and Richard Dalton, the Keeper of the King's Pictures, are sharing court gossip. Signor Bartolozzi, Engraver to the masses, makes lion eyes at any one whose gaze lingers just too long in his direction. Tall and stout Signor Angelo towers over a defiant Chevalier d'Eon. They recall their first meetings with William. After several glasses of rum punch, they set to practising sharp moves without epée in hand. Nearby stands an elegant Thomas Gainsborough. He is up from Bath and talks airily with Joshua Reynolds about his latest portrait. He, in turn, only has eyes for Angelica. Though anyone who cares to observe would see that La Kauffmann has a distracted manner about her. Distracted by whom? William wonders, but has no time to discover. She does appear to wish herself elsewhere. At her new studio in Golden Square, perhaps?

The celebrations last long into the night. William's closest acquaintances drift away one by one until only Allan Ramsay is left. The two friends sit among the debris of festivities. William remarks on his concerns for Angelica. 'Quite out of sorts, I feel. Not like her to be so morose.'

Ramsay stirs alive, as if his embers have received a blast from the bellows. 'The Angel has fallen,' he says, only serving to deepen the mystery and arouse William's curiosity. He insists on more details. For encouragement he pours them both another brandy.

'La Kauffmann has met with a mishap, it seems of the romantic sort.' Ramsay explains. 'There is all hell to pay. Her father a slow but well-meaning man is even now hard at work, endeavouring to repair the damage.'

'No wonder she was *distraite*.'

'Yes. All hangs in the balance and Society can be unkind.' Ramsay rises to his feet and begins to pace up and down, halting occasionally to give as much dramatic impact to his tale as it warrants. 'I have this on the highest authority... Well, one step removed at least... the priest at the Catholic chapel off Golden Square... It seems she is wed!'

William's eyebrows curve upwards. 'No!'

'Indeed yes and to a most exceptional character, by the name of Count van Horn, a Dutchman.'

'A noble Dutchman?'

'Well so he says, though, and here's the thing. They say he is no Count at all.'

'Poor Angel.'

'It is a dark tale.' Ramsay sighs. 'I had the rest of it from one of his servants.'

'Such intrigue... '

Ramsay takes another sip and sits down. 'I do have a nose for folly. I know where it can lead.'

'So this fellow?'

'His name is Brandt. His mother was the real Count's housemaid, let us imagine, mistress. The boy Brandt appears to have been the illegitimate son of this unequal pairing.'

'And so he seeks to assume his father's role. Ha! It's a plot worthy of a tuppenny novel.'

'But far from welcome, for an artist on her way.'

'He can be sued... Bought off?' William asks. 'There are ways of salvaging...'

'I do hope so. She has a talent for painting history and powerful friends. Perhaps a discreet withdrawal will be enough.'

'I will speak to Gwynn. He and Reynolds will look out for her.'

The Angel's travails are much on William's mind as he opens the door of 27 Cornhill for his first day of trading. The fragility of reputation, of Society's approval, the public consequences of a private miscalculation. These are lessons to consider, wherever art and money meet.

Bryer arrives, full of excitement to be launching their great venture. Together they fold back the shutters on the broad bowed window, which looks out on the Exchange across the street. It is quiet now. Only the flower sellers and window cleaners are about.

'I have walked past the 'Change since I was a boy.' William declares, 'and never thought I would one day be placed so close.'

One by one they string up the prints which they have chosen to fill the window. Six across, four down. He remembers Mary's words from the night before. "You must think like a flower. Attract the bees." She knows the game. She's spent many an hour racking up her stall of fruits and vegetables.

William guides Henry in the choice of prints. Portraits, associations, talking points, fashion. All this variety will bring them in, the bees with their guineas. 'This will be your task. Each day, each week, keep them coming, keep them guessing. We'll soon see who are the artists of the moment.'

William feels like his whole life has been a preparation for this enterprise. As sales rise, so do his ambitions. He needs more money to commission works, purchase plates, and print proofs.

Later, that October, Mary and the girls are in Lambeth picking apples in the sunshine. William and James Triquet sit to one side, discussing the future of the King's Arms.

'It puts a heavy charge at the start,' William explains, 'but every plate we have is an opportunity to print.'

Triquet is cautious. He is not keen to guarantee more debt on his own. He suggests a meeting with an old school friend, John Linnell. They both went on to study at Hogarth's Academy in St Martins Lane.

'He is like ourselves, the son of an artisan, who has made good of his inheritance. He keeps some fifty of his father's staff in the furniture trade, and adds new clients every month. Lord Scarsdale at Kelvesdon Hall is one among them. He has more than enough capital to act as guarantor.'

Invitations are despatched by Bryer for a meeting at the Virginia on the following Monday at 2pm. Benson is forewarned that they will be needing the back room for a couple of hours with a light repast.

At the appointed hour, William, Henry Bryer and James Triquet are gathered around a table at the Virginia but there is no sign of John. To soothe James' irritation, William opens up a book he has just received from France. 'This will amuse you. The *Dictionnaire des Graveurs*, compiled by my Parisian dealer, Basan.'

'I thought they only do such lists when you are dead.' Henry says with a smile.

'Thank you, Henry.'

William is just about to read out his own entry, when they hear the sound of a chaise arriving and raised voices outside on the street. He sees James shift in his seat and brush the back of his hand across a damp brow. 'It seems the fare is in dispute?' William says.

They all turn towards the open door. Striding through the lawyers and notaries crowded on to the coffeehouse benches is the imposing figure of John Linnell. William's immediate thought is that he is a silken fellow. His waistcoat is elaborately embroidered with ochre thread. His hose matches it in colour and fabric. Even his skin has a sheen to it. This is a man who sails through a life of his own choosing. In his wake, are two companions, neither of whom is typical of the Virginia clientele. A young woman dressed head to toe in the brightest of canary yellow, and a bald-headed, stocky cove, who looks like he might keep a stable of bare-knuckle boxers in the shadier parts of town. As they progress between the dealmakers and the ever-hopeful, they leave a trail of open mouths and paused conversations.

Linnell catches sight of James and lurches into the back room with a loud, 'Ah hah, so this is where you are hiding now !' Slapping his old school friend on the back he turns to chivvy his companions. 'Come, Come! We are expected.'

William and Bryer exchange brief glances of concern, before forcing on their business smiles.

'Allow me do the formalities.' says the newcomer. 'John Linnell, Albert Jones and Mary Perfect.'

'Polly to her friends,' squeaks Mary.

'Of which there are no doubt many,' William declares.

'Yes, Polly Perfect...' Another squeak. '...in every capacity.' And a giggle.

James looking as if he has just had chalk scratched across his dry brain, quickly introduces William and Henry.

Wine is served, an excellent Portuguese and the platters of cheese are met with approval. Relieved, James asks William to begin with an introduction to the trade of the Cornhill enterprise. The conversation moves into the realm of prints, plates, the price of copper and French exchange. However, this is not a world that interests young Polly at all. Within minutes, she launches into a series of dramatic yawns and nasal twitches. William is so distracted he wonders if she has a history in the theatre or is planning to audition.

Linnell attempts to placate her. 'It is money on the wall, my dear Polly, money on the wall that these good fellows are about.'

'Aye well, I prefer money in the hand or the pocket, if you catch my drift... Gentlemen.' She raises her glass and downs what remains in one. 'Come Albert, I believe there is a milliner just around the corner in need of my attention. *A dio*, my friends.'

With that brusque farewell, Polly leaves them to their discussions.

'Apologies,' says John. 'It is not my practice to mix business with pleasure. There are some that do not know the difference.'

The momentary silence suggests that none of the assembled company believes him.

'Oh, if all business could be so pleasurable', says William, aware that beneath Linnell's brash exterior there is something of the professional, the artisan that he respects. He is no fop or macaroni, that is for sure. Perhaps just a little too easily tempted on to the primrose path.

So, glasses are filled, emptied and refilled as William and Bryer explain the profits of print selling and their requirements for further borrowing to continue an upward spiral.

At the end of the allotted two hours, Benson is at the door. 'My apologies but I have traders from the Newfoundland Society impatient for their meeting. I am under some pressure to give them access.'

A brief glance at the fur-clad behemoths waiting behind Benson suggests that it is prudent to oblige. So, the farewells are made out on the street. Linnell is forthright. He declares that he sees mutual benefit and wishes to help but must first have a conversation with James to clarify their joint position. He gives his old schoolfriend a hearty slap. 'Come James we shall walk. It seems Polly has taken the carriage.' In a theatrical whisper, he adds, 'She'll be the death of me.'

William and Henry exchange smiles of relief. 'Now there is a man who needs to set his house in order,' William says, 'but I do like him.'

Bryer opens the door to Number 27. 'He's well known to the best banks in the city. Just the guarantor we need.'

'Let's hope he keeps his credit clean.' William says. 'I hazard a guess Miss Perfect's millinery bills are not slight.'

With guineas in hand, albeit borrowed guineas, William can now invest in new plates and build his stock of popular proofs. Indeed his business at the King's Arms occupies William to such an extent that year he has little time for another drama unfolding within the community of London's artists. At the Turks Head and other watering-holes for London's painters, architects and engravers there are heated discussions on how best to establish an Academy to rival those of the French and the Italians. Much of the argument is about Annual Exhibitions. Some insist they should be free to all comers while others claim a charge, however modest, would filter out the undesirables. William is in the former camp. To him it is a choice between public liberty and elitism. He relies on Gwynn to keep him informed of progress. By December, the jostling is over. Gwynn's old rival, William Chambers has the King's ear and delivers his approval for a Royal Academy. Joshua Reynolds is to be President, and his dear friend Angelica Kauffmann is brought into the fold. Her ill-starred marriage is in the past. She is one of only two women to join Gwynn and some thirty-three other men as Founder Members. But not all of the St Martin's mob are happy. Engravers and Printsellers are excluded. For now, William is sanguine about the result. He will find other ways to grow his enterprise.

Chapter 15

Early February, 1769

'Leadenhall? Why to Leadenhall Market?'

Henry Bryer, William's former apprentice and now partner in the Cornhill shop, is inviting him to a supper. 'It is but a short walk. And there are excellent pies at the Excalibur.'

'Since when did you worry about the quality of your pies?' William removes his new spectacles. They are a blessing but he is still not accustomed to them. He looks at Henry. The young man often walks a fine line twixt the right and the wrong. A delivery of paper appears by chance, with no history or origin. Some copper plate is offered at low cost but never arrives. So, if pies are the bait, what is the lad hoping to capture?

It is perhaps no coincidence that the invitation to pie supper comes at a time when Strutt, the voice of restraint, is absent. So, William must be his own guardian for now. Though he is relieved when Henry says that he has also invited John Gwynn. He has barely seen him since he became so entranced by the Academy's Exhibition.

Henry has reserved a table in the Excalibur's upper room. It sits in a bay window overlooking East India House. To William's surprise there is another guest already waiting for them. Henry's elder brother, Jack, rises to greet them. If he was a painting, William thinks, he would be unvarnished, not quite finished. Though not without energy, just needing refinement.

'So, a family affair.' William observes.

'Oh, forgive me,' Henry says. 'But I have long wished you and Jack to talk. He is full of excellent ideas.'

They order wine and the conversation slides into a discussion of the success of the Kings Arms. William knows flattery when he hears it. Whenever the flow of compliments subsides, he sees how the brothers exchange enquiring glances. If Henry is the dutiful hound, Jack is more feline, watchful, self-possessed. There is an unspoken tension about the pair. He is just about to pierce the bubble and demand that they tell him what this is all about when Gwynn arrives.

With apologies for tardiness, he steps into the bay window and surveys the headquarters of the East India Company. Its facade dominates the street below but gives no clue as to what happens inside. 'Ah the true seat of power. The Imperial Corporation. These jackals now run half of India.' Gwynn pulls out a chair and joins the table. 'So, is this the next venture? Today, Cornhill, tomorrow the world?'

They all laugh, though Jack seems relieved when the pies arrive. Once they are all served and the wine is flowing, he proposes a toast. 'To the success of the King's Arms.'

'The King's Arms... and all who sail in her.' Gwynn replies with a grin.

'Well,' Jack continues. 'You are a man of foresight. You may be wondering what brings us all here. Excellent as they are, it is not just the pies. As you know, my brother Henry and I are both of merchant stock. My father is no jackal, but he worked a passage to Bengal with the Company, as quartermaster. To Coast and Bay and back two times.'

'I meant no...'

'No need, Mr Gwynn. The fact is we have been putting our merchant minds to work. It is in our blood to do so.'

'And your thinking has led to here.' Gwynn gestures out of the window. 'To these tax collectors?'

'Yes...the gentlemen across the way-'

Gwynn hrrumphs but Jack stays calm. '-now manage the financial affairs of Bengal, twenty million natives. Two hundred and fifty clerks... many far from home, with guineas to spend.'

'So you agree, they have their snouts in the trough?' Gwynn's sharp response prompts a rebuke from William.

'Gwynn, you are in a most disruptive mood today.'

'You know my feelings.'

'Indeed, but you are not proposing to suck the blood of natives, am I right, Jack?'

'No, our interest lies in these Company Nabobs, adrift abroad, far from the Home Country.'

Now Henry finds his voice. 'Already they are buying all the necessities of life: glass, silverware, saddles... that they are not able to acquire in India.'

'So we are selling them a taste of home?' asks William

'I believe it was our friend, Mr Linnell-' Jack begins.

'Business associate,' Gwynn suggests.

'Friend and colleague,' William responds, encouraging Jack to continue.

'Well, Mr Linnell, I understand had the measure of it... *Money on the Wall* he said. That's what you sell, your prints. Now when these clerks step inside their walls in Fort St George, Madras or Kolkata, what do they want to see? Another tiger? No. They want the green fields and cool streams of childhood summers. The cries of St Bartholomew's Fair. Vauxhall Gardens. Elegant St James...'

Henry joins in again. '...Tis true, what Jack says. Already we had such folk in Cornhill. They want English heroes, Marlborough, Drake...'

The brothers' excitement is contagious. 'A slice of old England, a stag, a hunt. Roast Beef on their walls.'

The idea is born and the Bryers will not let it lie down.

'Set our prints free,' cries Henry, 'send them on ships across the Ocean, to the Bay where every man jack thinks himself a king.'

William swills a last drop of wine around and around in his glass. 'But how do we reach their walls? Do not these leeches at the Company, control such trade? Would we not just become their lackeys? We have no King's Arms in Kolkatta High Street... if there is such a one?

'Not yet, but why not, one day?' Henry says.

Gwynn is ever practical. 'So how does one trade with them, Jack ?'

'The Captain's your man...They have the right to Private Trade.'

'But do they know about art?' William asks. 'how it appeals, how it is sold?'

'Well, first, the Captains are like gods out there. A twenty-gun salute every time they reach Port. Their every need looked after: houses, gardens everything. Provided they deliver the Company's goods. That done, they can make their guineas as they wish. In-country and private trade...importing from England and then taking back what will sell here.

'You are well informed, Henry.'

'We was raised on father's stories. When he was quartermaster. I could smell the spices by the end of each tale.'

'So this Private trade, it is at the Captain's discretion?' Gwynn persists.

'Whatever makes them money. Securing a command does not come cheap.' At this Jack stands up, mopping the pie grease from his lips.

William reaches for his glass, thinking there is about to be another toast. But Jack's play is not yet over.

'I...we,' nodding to brother, Henry. 'We have something we'd like to show. Call it a private tour if you will. Come gentlemen.'

With a protracted belch, Gwynn rises unsteadily, adjusts his wig and leans into William. 'Come, let us see what further mischief is afoot.'

Jack and Henry lead their companions down the narrow stairs and out into the street. They make a couple of sharp turns, then enter a covered passageway and into the open again, finding themselves in Bessiter Street. On one side, the brick wall of a warehouse extends the entire length of the street. They walk past the gated carriage entrance to a low door. Jack knocks twice. There is an answering knock and the door opens.

Jack ushers them in. 'Welcome to the Emporium,' he exclaims.

'Are we about to meet the famed Rhinoceri?' Gwynn whispers to William

The sight that greets them is not of exotic animals but it is no less exciting. There are row upon row of scaffolds with boxes, piled high.

'Come,' says, Jack. 'We may wander where we will. But we'd best not be caught. There are thousands of pounds of goods here for the taking...'

'Twenty-five tons of private trade on every ship. Outward bound to India, it's leather saddles, boots, building materials, nails .. fine upholstered chairs ... all sell at a premium. Then they buys up the luxuries for home.'

Jack Bryer runs his hands along a mahogany ornament. 'Imagine your best prints out there. For those poor fellows, all boiled up in the sun, the sight of a mountain stream, an English meadow. It would be more like a blessing on the wall to them. And they will pay. Several times the tickets you have at the King's Arms.'

He shows William the intricate carving on an ivory pendant. 'So Master, your thoughts?'

'Is no-one already at work on this? Sending prints I mean. What about the French or Boydell?'

'I have made discreet enquiries via Bailey and so far it seems they are cautious. Also, our Nabobs would buy British stock rather than deal with the French'.

There is a loud clatter of metal on metal.

'That'll be the main gate. A delivery.' Henry says, glancing at his brother.

'Come I believe it is time to go.' At a fast pace, Jack steers them around a stack of cases, to the small door where they entered.

They reassemble outside. William's mind is already churning through the possibilities. 'So there is much to consider. You and Jack put the word out.. discreetly mind. See which Captains show interest. Is there a season we must meet?'

'Around February, March they leave the Downs.'

'A year, then,' William says, 'to assemble all the works.'

'And raise funds for that!' Gwynn reminds them. 'I am in preparations for the Academy Exhibition till the end of April, so please do not count on me till then.'

William smiles. 'Of course, Gwynn, we will not press you.'

Three weeks later, under a leaden March sky, William and the Bryer brothers are on board a lighter heading down-river. Their destination is Howland Great Dock, near Deptford.

'Captain Mears and his ship the Egmont are just returned from the Coast of Coromandel and the Bay of Bengal.' Jack says. 'They take a toll these EastIndiamen. Tropical waters, Atlantic storms.'

William sits in the bow, looking across the dark water. There is scarcely a ripple. He tries to imagine the Egmont's wild journey East but it is far beyond his experience. As the lighter rounds a long right-hand bend in the Thames he is overwhelmed by a stench of fish unlike any he has encountered. Worse than Billingsgate on a hot August day. Looking back he can see the crew now have kerchiefs tightly wrapped around their faces.

'Could have warned us, damn you,' Jack shouts through a hastily tied cloth.

They are soon edging closer to shore. Black-headed gulls wheel in and out of thick banks of smoke above the entrance to the Dock. Through the arch, William can just make out a line of giant three-legged cast iron pots. Each has a fire roaring beneath it. As they disembark, the lightermen explain with a grin.

'Blubber boilers, my lads.'

'Aye we call this Greenland Dock now. There be so many whales brought in.'

'You're in luck, though. You'll find the Egmont at the far end there.'

They are relieved to move upwind from the blubber-smoke. Though the first sight of the Egmont does not impress. Stripped of her fore and aft masts, and with all her sailcloth gone for repair, she is a paltry skeleton.

'How can this slip of a ship carry ninety-nine men and a boy?' William says to no one in particular. As they stand, mouths agape, a shout comes from deep inside the wooden hull. 'Gentlemen. Step lively now.'

Through eyes still running from the smoke, they see Captain Charles Mears emerge, with grizzled beard, hooded eyes and skin tanned as dark as teak. Though there is something of the village cleric in his bearing. William senses calculation in every move he makes, an economy of effort that comes from being master of such restricted space for so many months. As they step aboard, he offers them his left hand in greeting, his right arm being wrapped in an elegant sling of indigo cloth.

'Yes, my own repairs are underway. A spar split off and caught me as we came round the Horn. But I'll mend. Just like the young lady here. May not look much now but give her time. She'll be ripe for another journey East. Come, I still have my cabin'.

The reek of blubber is now joined by the tang of old rope, tar and polished timber.

'Now this is what Pa's ship smelt of.' Jack says, giving William a hand down the steps.

'Mind your heads.' Mears calls out. 'I have no means to brew, but can offer you a glass of madeira. It removes the stench of whale.'

'I was beginning to think nothing would,' William replies, taking his hand from his face for the first time.

'Aye. London folk needs their soap and oil, but why boil it here?' Mears shakes his head. 'This used to be the finest docks in the land. Now we have a blubber factory. Case of money over sense.'

The visitors watch in silence as the Captain fills their glasses. There are sparse furnishings in his minuscule cabin. The drop-leaf desk is piled high with folded charts. A leather-bound logbook lies open beside them. On the panelling above, William sees a small print, a mezzotint of Trinity College, Dublin.

'I see you have a picture of home.'

'You have done your studying, Mr -'

'William.'

'Yes. My father is... was a Trinity Man. My brother and I spent our youth there before we followed the call of the sea.'

'How did that accord with Reverend Mears?'

'His calling was of a different nature, though I confess many times I have hoped that we were still in his prayers.' He passes out the glasses on a round silver tray. 'But you did not come all the way to the dock to discuss my dear papa. Your good health, gentlemen.'

He looks each of them in the eye and sits down. 'Now. To business.'

Fortified by the sweet liquor, William and the Bryers set out their case for a new market, supplying prints to the noble administrators of his employers, the Honourable East India Company.

Just as they are in full flow, there's a shout from below deck. They all turn to the open door where a younger version of Captain Mears, a more rugged individual, appears with a scowl across his pox-scarred face. 'Ah. I forgot we had company.' He makes to go, but the Captain calls him back and makes the introductions.

'William Mears, my brother and first mate.'

There is no room in the cabin, so he accepts a glass and leans against the door to listen.

Captain Mears explains. 'Mr Bryer here was just telling me there's money to be made shipping fancy prints and paintings across the High Seas for the Gentlemen of the East India Company. Give them a taste of home. Is that the gist of what ye has to tell me?'

Before Henry can reply, the first mate chips in. 'Bread and beef and sausages more like. That's the taste of home they'd dearly favour. If we could only get it fresh to them. Eight months it is from the Downs to Bengal, with a favourable wind. This is no gander down the Thames, my masters.'

He steps back from the door and points out a distant church. 'You see that tower? You ever seen a wave as high as that?' The visitors shake their heads. 'No, well not a surprise, they don't make 'em like that around here, but off the Cape o' Good Hope, they are two a penny, sirs, two a penny. You need your wits about you or you'll end up flat out beneath them.'

The Captain intervenes. 'What my brother is saying is that whatever we take on a venture East must be worth its weight. It cost us £5000 pounds sterling to secure this ship's bottom. We're not sailing to put a smile on our faces. This is business.' William notes the repetition of the phrase. 'Take your leather saddle, I can sell those by the hundreds if I had room for 'em. Fine London fashions, ladies' garments, likewise.'

'If we could keep them from rotting in the heat.' His brother adds.

'Now this is not to say we don't see the merit in your proposal. If we can make the high prices you claim.'

William attempts an explanation. 'We believe we are the first to...'

'Now there's the thing, you see. You know why we all leave around the February time?'

'To catch the winds?' asks Henry.

'Aye to be around the Cape to take the monsoon up from the South-East. So, what happens? All the East Indiamen arrive in Bengal Bay around the same weeks. Now if one has a cargo of glassware, so do half a dozen other ships. If you're not first, you'll be selling at half the price to some thieving warehouse. They'll keep the glass until the next time there's a demand for it. So, you see, a risky business all round.'

Brother William, still leaning in the doorway, sneezes into his sleeve. 'And strange as it may seem, we are not friends of risk. My brother and I. Too much at stake.' With that he heads back below deck.

The conversation shifts to practical matters, the weight of frames, the timing of departure, the threat of paper mould in tropical climes. As a squall of rain beats down on the deck outside, Captain Mears draws discussions to a close.

'You'd best be heading home before this worsens. I'll give you no answer off the cuff. We will make enquiries and suggest you do the same.

Decide what you will look to sell, the weight, the cost, what you wish to make from it and we shall talk again. Remember though. We all need a favourable wind.' He reaches behind the cabin door and retrieves three large squares of rough cloth. The visitors look bemused. 'You've not forgotten already... the blubber?

'Oh yes. Much obliged. Good day to you, Captain Mears.'

A week later Gwynn and William are at their usual table in the back room at the Virginia. They have a steaming pot of Benson's best java between them. Their conversation flicks back and forth and around the Bengal trade.

'I trust Bailey with my life,' William declares. 'but this is a secret he must keep under the nose of Boydell.'

'So, let us consider. To carry this Indian venture to success, you need to assemble a cargo of prints and paintings; package them safe to survive an ocean voyage of some eight months; do all of this without raising the suspicions of every print seller in town... '

'And find the wherewithal to fund all of the above.'

'Putting that aside, I say Bailey's still your man. Working for Boydell he knows what sells as well as any man.'

William nods. 'Since Paris I would trust no-one else to pack the prints. Though a night in the Channel is nothing like to what they face in the tropics.'

'The risks are high. But Mears stands to make a fine fortune each time he runs those waves. Your aim must be to do the same. If you hanker after that Bloomsbury mansion as much as he?'

William has the grace to colour up. It is true this challenge is on a level that has nothing to do with art, with the expectations of his Masters. This is about wealth.

'So, let us assume that you have Bailey on-side. Then you set the Bryer brothers to work. They are terriers both. They have trading in the blood and will toil all hours the good lord sends to find you the goods. Hadrill will print ?'

'Yes,' William says. 'He is also bound to Boydell and Woll, but he is discreet. The story we tell is that we are building stock for No 27. They know that we are growing on the back of the King's portrait. The sales are good, approaching £800 per annum. But for our cargo we will need to borrow thousands more.'

'Your genial guarantors? Linnell and Triquet. They must be pleased to see the shop is on the up.'

'I have not approached them yet. Once I have a figure ... '

Over the following weeks, William sets the wheels in motion. Bailey is briefed. His loyalty is not in question. The Bryers make lists to suit the tastes of Nabobs and Company Clerks. But William soon encounters opposition close to home.

'The East India Company? Are sure you know what you are about ?' It is the last week of April. Mary is sewing a line of red and yellow bunting for the children's Mayday excursion to Lambeth. 'My brother Sam, could advise you. After all, he has spent more time at sea then anyone else we know. Though he is not an EastIndia Man.'

William laughs 'They are a breed apart, tis true.'

'At least he could cast a seaman's eye over the ship,'Mary says. 'Give you confidence she'll make it to India and back.'

'It is still not certain that we go.'

Mary sits back, shaking her shoulders. 'Is that why you have said nothing to me? Or were you hoping that I would not find out until a shipwreck ruins us all.'

'There will be no shipwreck.'

'No? That is not what dear Strutt thinks.'

'Strutt?'

'He at least is reasonable. Not like those Bryer boys.'

So, the venture has already sprung a leak. William lays his burin down beside the copper plate. His voice is tight. 'They are of trader stock. They know the risks and the rewards.'

'And you, what do you know? For our daughters, our son. Are you prepared to lay their future on the line for some mad-cap enterprise?'

'If it comes to pass, I shall put my faith in Captain Mears.'

'And your Pa, what does he say to these shenanigans?'

'He does not know.'

She turns, looks at him square on, then continues with her sewing.

He hesitates to pursue this game.

'I understand these are new waters for all of us. I ask you just this. Bear with me. Trust me while we explore the prospects. But if there is a chance to better ourselves. I hope you will be there beside me?'

Mary sniffs and shrugs but says no more.

Some weeks later, the India conspirators gather again, this time beneath the blossom of a Lambeth orchard. It is early evening on May Day. The remnants of the dawn celebrations lie all about them. Empty flagons of cider, tangles of bright-coloured bunting, baskets of sweetmeats trampled underfoot by eager children who are now sleeping in the shade some yards away. It is an unlikely setting for Gwynn and the Bryer brothers to be discussing finance with William. But now that the secret is out he feels Mary may be reassured by more open dealing.

William has seen a first list of prints to be acquired for sale in India. The costs are higher than expected. He will need to borrow thousands of pounds. But the Bryers claim to have a solution to this fractious issue of credit.

'It is as old as the Greeks and the Romans.'

'The Phoenicians even, the greatest traders in the ancient world.'

'Respondentia, you say?' Gwynn rolls out the word with some disdain.

'It sticks somewhat on the tongue.' William agrees.

Jack is taking another gulp of cider. He wipes the back of his sleeve across his lips and tries once more. 'Well,' he says, 'as I understand it...'

William smiles as Gwynn's brow creases even deeper. 'Let us hope you understand as well as the lawyers who no doubt swim in these waters.'

Bryer's eyes narrow but he continues. 'The Respondentia Bond is a loan against the value of goods aboard a ship. When the ship arrives at port, the goods are delivered and the money is paid back.'

'So we borrow money against the prints we load on to Mears' ship?'

'Yes. They lend you a sum, say five hundred, a thousand pounds, then they give you a bond for the rest plus interest, payable when the ship returns. Payable out of the profits.'

'And while the ship is on the high seas we can use that Bond to borrow more money, which we pay back when we get our profits.'

Gwynn pours himself a glass of mead. 'So, in summary, the Egmont must make it in one piece to the Bay of Bengal, the prints must sell at the highest possible rate, and some eighteen months after leaving England the dear Captain must deliver our money safely home. Is that your view on this?'

There is silence.

'Meanwhile we live in uncertainty and debt.' says William.

'And all of the above requires the approval of the blessed Linnell and Triquet, your guarantors.'

A nod from both the Bryers is finally forthcoming.

Chapter 16

Many times that summer William wakes in a sweat, plagued with the direst imaginings, only to find that it is still June, July or August. The ship has not yet left the Downs and the deal has not yet been made.

By the autumn, no agreement is in place, but they must borrow to invest in prints to be ready for a February departure. A credit here, a credit there. Every detail is recorded in Bryer's leather-bound portfolio, with the same precision he engraves his copper plates.

'Turning copper into gold. That's what we are about,' William tells him.

But they are running at a loss. The column listing income from the shop is never long enough to match the deficits. Still the purchases for India are made. Twenty plates with prints, then thirty, forty. There are mezzotints by Valentine Green, a Tessier from Paris, a Hogarth *Marriage a la mode*.

Bailey is engaged to create ingenious wraps and frames to protect the works. He promises to keep down the cost.

'I may even borrow materials from under Boydell's nose,' he says. Though William is by now so overwrought that he does not appreciate the joke.

'Oh come now. Master William. How much have you achieved since our moonlit flight from Paris? Twelve years past and you have the favour and the pension of the King and Queen. George himself sits above your Cornhill shop and you are about to open a new market in the East. Consider these first prints as sowing English acorns into the rich soil of the Nabobs.'

'There will be much sleep lost before we see them sprout.' William says, blinking in the late October sun.

Still, he is encouraged by Bailey's support and pushes on with the assembling of prints and proofs. Meanwhile the Captain and First Mate are playing a long game. They have the Egmont. It is in their power to decide what private trade she will carry. They will not commit to William until they know the weight, the price and the likely profit of their other goods.

In early November, William receives a message from the Mears. The Egmont is once again ship-shape, her timbers caulked, her masts restored. On the eleventh, they are to slip down river to moor alongside the King's Yard in Deptford. There they will take on board the first of the heavy Company cargo, the iron, lead and copper. They are due in Leadenhall Street the following week to meet with Mr Webber, the owner of the Egmont. If William is still willing, they invite him to dine at the tavern opposite.

William needs the backing of his guarantors. Without it he cannot press the Mears for a loan based on the value of the prints. But just before he meets with Triquet the goldsmith and Linnell the cabinetmaker, he discovers the latter is heading down a primrose path to scandal.

The news is spilled by William's old friend, Allan Ramsay. He has it on good authority from his drinking companions in Soho Square.

'So, the story goes that John Linnell's amorata, the young and comely Polly -'

'Polly Perfect?'

'Always an unlikely claim. Yes, the Perfect Polly has entered an arrangement with Lord Conyngham. The good Lord is in his sixtieth year, though it seems a soldier's heart still beats within. He has established Polly in her own fine apartment, with a monthly income to match. Provided, and here's the rub, she agrees to be his life companion hereon in.'

'And Linnell is aware of all this.'

'Oh more than aware! He is deep within the affair. You see, the monthly sum is paid into a capital fund, in the name of John Linnell himself.'

' Oh my...'

'There is worse. He is not content to play Cupid to the old Lord. He continues to visit his darling in said apartment.'

'The rogue.'

'Sometimes hiding in the wardrobe when the Lord returns without notice.'

'Oh if only Hogarth was still among us. He would nail these devils.'

'T'would not be in your best interest. It is not the behaviour of a trusty guarantor.'

'Let us hope he is more circumspect with his own money. I will consult with Triquet.'

As the meeting with the Mears brothers is fast approaching, William wastes no time in revealing Linnell's activities to his fellow-guarantor.

'Well. Indeed.' Triquet declares. His cheeks are flushing a shade of rose. Perhaps more at the thought of saucy Polly than at the implications. But he recovers well.

'I have known John since the day he first copied from my school book. He does, at times, sail close to, if not, against the wind. But he has never failed to meet his obligations.'

They both smile at the nuance. Though William is still anxious.

'Sound dealing is a fragile commodity,' he says. 'If just one of my creditors fears that I cannot account for myself. I am done for. And this whole venture too.'

'You have my word, as a guildsman. I will keep John under watch. You can rely on our guarantee.'

The following week, William, Gwynn and the Bryers arrive at the Excalibur Inn for their meeting with the Mears brothers. After ordering food and ale, the Captain offers to make his report. "We are all Company men now." William imagines the same words being uttered in more prestigious rooms across the street.

'First, the good news, the loading of iron and copper is well advanced. We should be dropping down to Gravesend in December. There we will take on the lighter goods, the vitals and our water.'

'And the private trade?' Jack Bryer asks.

'Well. We are still assessing our options and the balance of our cargo.' The Captain pulls at his cuff, then glances at his brother. William feels his chest tighten.

'We have had some news just today that raises the risks somewhat.'

'How so?' William asks.

The Captain clears his throat. He leans forward, resting his elbows on the table.

'The latest Company packet from Madras reached the Downs two weeks ago. Her Bengal despatch may be some six months out of date but it says the rains have failed again. The rice harvest is under threat.' He pauses to let them consider his words, then looking William in the eyes he continues.

'We may be sailing into a land in famine. Already there are reports of farmers selling their children at the highest price, so others can survive.'

There is silence. No one is eating pie. Gwynn pushes his chair back and wipes his mouth.

'Surely there must be provisions in hand. This is not novel, from my understanding.'

'Perhaps but not three years in a row.'

'And the Company?'

Captain Mears glances out of the window, as if to make sure he is out of earshot.

'The truth is, the Company is more interested in seeing its revenues safe and on the increase. So this is not yet public knowledge and may not become so. I am giving you fair warning. Our owner, Mr Webber's advice is to take only what we can trust to sell. We may be called on to transport supplies.'

William glances to Gwynn and knows their thinking is in tune. This is not about relief. This will be profiteering.

But to their surprise, it seems that all is not lost. Captain Mears takes a swig of ale. Again he engages William directly.

'Now to the business between us. As you know, the print trade is untried, uncertain territory for us. There are no maps, no indications, no previous voyages to show this is a profit making trade...'

William nods slowly.

'... But that all said we can see the benefit in goods that could command a high price among the British residents. To be pioneers in such trade is both risk and advantage.'

Jack is now beaming smiles at brother Henry. But the Captain has not finished.

'You will understand, we must minimise the risk. It is in the nature of our business. So to place all our cards in full view...We are content to proceed with the loan, the Respondentia Bond, with the guarantors you have put forward...' Captain looks at his brother, for assent, and turns back to William.

'...But we want a guarantee of profit.'

There are intakes of breath around the table. William feels a sharp kick on his ankle. He sees Gwynn is frowning fit to burst. Now is the time for calm. It is his turn to stare down the Captain.

'So, you would push all the risk on to ourselves. Even if you do not succeed in selling the prints, you would still make a profit?'

Neither of the Mears brothers utter a word. They sit as gamblers do at Madame Cornelys' Soho tables, giving nothing away.

'This is piracy...' Jack mutters beneath his breath.

The Captain's back stiffens.

'I would be wary, Mr Bryer. Such words are not welcome, not welcome at all. At sea, men hang for less.'

William feels a hot swelling tighten between his eyes. Pray God, it is not a sign of sickness.

'Let me make our position clear. We have a ship and a command, which cost us some five thousand pounds to obtain. You have something that we do not need and do not know for certain who else will. Though I do not deny that they could...' He holds up his hand to halt another interruption from Jack. 'We, my brother and I, believe it is only just, correct and proper that you should make us feel a little more... comfortable about the venture.'

He pulls a stub of pencil from his pocket and on a scrap of card scratches out a figure and some words. He passes it to William. He looks at it, then reads it out aloud.

'Fifty per cent profit. Even if no pictures are sold.'

'It is piracy,' Jack Bryer hisses, unable to restrain himself.

Mears slams his palm hard down on the table. It is as threatening as a falling anchor.

'I shall not warn you again. This is business, not an encounter on the high seas!'

'I tell it as it is, no more.' Jack replies, defiant.

Again, a brooding silence is the response.

'When do you depart the Downs?' William asks.

All bodes well for late January, perhaps early February.

'So, we have some time.'

'Not long but, yes, a month or so to consider, before the clerks must set to work.'

At this, both Mears brothers, rise and bid farewell.

William closes the inner door. He sits back at the table. No-one ventures a word. The pressure between his eyes persists. He pinches his forehead between index finger and thumb to induce some flow of rejuvenating blood.

'If they leave in February, when are they due to return?' He asks.

'A year and a half at the earliest...'

'So, late Summer next year?'

'Yes.' The Bryer brothers reply in unison.

'We must survive till then. The Bond is our only hope, it must be signed and soon.'

'So we agree with the profit guarantee?' Again it is the brothers Bryer. Gwynn is silent, watching William.

'We... Yes. But no word to Triquet and Linnell. If all goes well they may never need to know. If all goes ill we descend together into the inferno. And I must answer for that.'

In mid-December, a message reaches them at the studio. Henry Bryer reads it out to William and Gwynn.

"*On 12th we moored in Long Reach, Gravesend. The Bridgewater, Vansittart and Royal Captain, all EastIndiamen bound for Bengal are already here. We take on vitals and water. Other goods arrive by lighter. Your acceptance received. Private goods and final papers to be signed in January. Much obliged. Christmas greetings. Captain Mears.*"

The Indian misadventure, as Mary has come to call it, casts a heavy shadow over the Ryland household. She has no knowledge of the latest arrangements, but she knows they are dangerously in debt. William fears he will soon default on rental payments for the Cornhill shop. Only the continuing high sales of the Royal Portrait sustain them. Henry, always the weaker of the two Bryers, spends his Twelfth Night abed with an ague and a migraine. His brother Jack mocks him for his lack of backbone but even he is anxious.

In early January the lawyers and their clerks are set to work completing the terms of the Respondentia Bond. William decides to take the documents in person to John Linnell's house in Berkeley Square. He still fears that the shennanigans between Polly Perfect and Lord Conyngham may undermine Linnell's commitment as guarantor.

As he reaches the North side of the Square he sees the ebullient cabinet maker outside the family workshop. He is barking instructions to an overwrought master of works.

'Lord St John does not want mirrored, or lacquer, he wants red, red as you can, cherry red, yes cherry red and for the legs of his Lady's commode, I have left the drawings on my desk. On my return we will review her legs, shall we not?'

'Ah William how good to see you.'

'Mr Linnell. I ... '

'Not now, Napier. You see I am just on my way... such a state of affairs... never a moment's rest.'

He sees the documents beneath William's arm.

'Ah ha, those are for me?'

He takes the bundle and waves it above his head for Napier to run at a pace to fetch.

'More business, Napier, another affair. You see now why I cannot always be available, I swim in many seas.'

'Pray the Lord you stay afloat in all of them, Master'.

William notes that Napier has the measure of his man. They head east into town.

'I trust everything is moving smoothly to a grand départ? Our prints shall soon be Bengal bound?'

Before William can reply, John has moved on.

'You remember there was talk of raising more credit on that Bond.'

William nods. 'Once we have it.'

'Well, methinks I have the ideal first call. Nothing certain, mind, but I hears there is a new partner at Hoare's. Of the family too. The youngest. Fat and Jovial Henry they call him. Just married, just inherited a fortune and open to a little side lending of his own, so I'm told.'

'It would be well for us-.'

'-Respectability is all. Others will trust you, if you have a Hoare in hand.' Then, realising what he has said, he guffaws so loudly, a passing horse shies away in surprise.

'Ha! Perhaps better not follow that fox home! A name's a name that's all there is to it.'

'So, you are still with us for the Bond? The documents are all in draft in the bundle.'

'Yes, fear not. You have my good name behind you. For what it is worth, my boy.'

'Its weight in gold for us.'

'Well, that's as maybe. Now I must be away. Let me know when the date is set for the signing.'

By the night of the 23rd January, William has all the necessary papers lying on his desk before him. He rubs his finger over the lines of ink. A life is made or lost by such flimsy stuff as this. He is thinking now of the Laissez Passez that cleared his path from Paris to Calais, so many years back ... the maps that he was obliged to copy for the Frenchman d'Eon... the signature in lemon juice that could still one day implicate him in treachery.

He is due to leave at dawn for the final meeting with the Mears but he cannot sleep. To calm his mind he turns to his beloved burin and copper plate. He works through the night incising lines. It comforts him.

Eddies of morning mist skitter above the dark Thames. William, Gwynn, the two Bryers, and their guarantors Linnell and Triquet are packed tight together in the stern of a lighter. They are on their way down-river to Gravesend. A flagon of sweetened brandy is passed around. They greet it with weary grunts. For the first hour there is little conversation but as the clouds lift and part, their mood lightens. They are stirred by the vessels surging past in both directions. Goods for the East, goods from the East. The Bryers begin a competition to guess the contents of each boat. William stands to one side, watching the procession. It is comforting to see that others trust their livelihood to the oceans. Linnell passes him the flagon.

'You have not forgotten the young Hoare?'

William raises his eyes. It is too early for money matters. But he cannot ignore his guarantor. At least he has made his own enquiries.

'It seems I too may have an entrée.'

'How so?'

'I knew his wife.'

Linnell raises a theatrical eyebrow.

'Tell me more.'

'It is not what you think. She is... was a painter. An excellent one, in fact, from Bath. She exhibited at the Society before she married.'

'Well then we shall pursue them. They shall be the first to appreciate our Money on the Wall.'

'First let us secure the Bond.'

As they turn the slow bend to Gravesend, they can see the masts of some half a dozen EastIndiamen. All are in the final days of taking on provisions, hogsheads of wine, barrels of water. The Bryers are convinced they can see goods for private trade wherever they look.

'See those there. Fine leather saddles. I am sure of it.'

Every ship is abuzz with loading and making safe. The sail masters are checking every sheet. From all directions there is a constant hammering. The carpenters are at work fashioning separations to cater for last minute passengers in the Great Cabin. Gwynn, whose first trade was in working wood, is absorbed by all the activity. He puts his arm around William's shoulders.

'You are a traveller, to Italy and France, but you know I have never left our shores. I find it hard to believe these men are off on a voyage of some eighteen months... two years even.'

'May Neptune keep them safe.'

They are interrupted by another shout from the Bryers.

'Ship Ahoy. There she is. The Egmont.'

With all her masts stepped up and newly painted, she is a fine sight.

William turns round to look. He manages a smile but there are tears welling in his eyes. So much now rides on this assembly of oak and rope and canvas.

A few minutes later they are ashore. They make their way to a tavern several streets back, where an upper room has been prepared for their final meeting with the Mears. It is the first time the guarantors have met the Captain. His conversation is peppered with references to 'a favourable wind'. He trots out the phrase like a lucky talisman and compliments the quality of Bailey's work.

'My only complaint is they are so well wrapped we have none to hang on our cabin walls.'

He is delighted when William surprises him with a fine Italian landscape engraved by Woollett. Finally, the wordy document defining the Respondentia Bond is removed from its own protective covering. It is circulated for their multiple signatures. It contains no mention of the profit guarantee demanded by the Mears. But they have been forewarned. William notes the Captain's log open on the desk. He has a neat hand. Will it be so precise when the Egmont is tossing in an Atlantic storm?

With a final toast they down their madeira under the watchful eye of the First Mate. He is keen to have these fellows off his busy ship. With the Bond secured, William and the Bryer brothers accompany Linnell and Triquet to the quayside.

'So, our thanks as always, gentlemen.'

'You are not returning with us?'

'We must agree the inventory with the Quarter-Master. There must be no confusion when they tally up the sales they will be making.'

Well fortified with alcohol and in high spirits, Linnell leaps somewhat riskily on board the empty lighter.

'God speed the Egmont and all who sail in her.' He claps an arm around his old school friend Triquet, who is turning green, either at the thought of Linnell's company or the rough ride home.

The following morning in Gravesend is a more leisurely affair. Amongst the bustle of final preparations, the merchandise is checked and signed for. The Mears are more preoccupied now with the arrival of the last members of their crew. There are still a few stragglers to make up the ninety-nine men and a boy. So the joint signature of a separate legal bond guaranteeing them their profit is brief and functional. As are the farewells.

'You do understand, our concern. This is the first ...'

'We hope of many.'

'Indeed'.

'This guarantee will not lessen your desire to sell?'

'Fear not, once ashore we become the best of merchants. An eye for a bargain, for a jewel, for the Nabobs' trade. That's the way to a Bloomsbury mansion. For all of us, Master William. For us all.'

A week later a message arrives from John Linnell, inviting William, Henry Bryer and Gwynn to meet him the following morning at 21 High Holborn.

'That is William Hamley's shop is it not the -'

'-Noah's Ark.'

'So now we have our meetings in a toyshop?'

'Another of Linnell's affectations.'

'Assignations more like.'

But no-one ignores a guarantor who is covering them for several thousand pounds. So next day they find themselves peering through the wide bay windows of Mr Hamley's Toy Emporium.

'Look,' Jack says.' there's a whole army there and a fort and a ...'

Soon he and Gwynn are setting out a force of bright painted, lead soldiers... French, English, Hanoverians...

' A bugler, see...'

When Linnell arrives, he joins them at play before William reminds him there must be a reason for this gathering.

'Ah, forgive me. I must draw this battle to a close. There is a serious purpose. At noon, we are expected at Fleet Street, the business and residence of the Fat and Jovial Henry Hoare, no less. And his dear wife with whom Mr Ryland here claims to be on intimate terms,

'I did not ...'

'Well as intimate as he will admit.'

' Now the Hoare's have a boy, nearly three years old . I thought perhaps a gift from this Noah's Ark. Now what will it be? Some colouring pencils would appeal to the artistic mother perhaps, an abacus to count the father's profits?

Laden with elaborate packages they reach the headquarters of the Hoare Family bank and residence just before noon. As the door opens, they are greeted by the sound of Fat and Jovial Henry playing his flute.

'He is not without talent.' Linnell's whisper is intended to be heard.

Henry seems to revel in his corpulence. He welcomes his visitors with a warmth that bodes well. William steps into a world to which he aspires for his own children... a world of French teachers, dancing and riding masters, music classes. A world in which five hundred pounds is but one drop in a pool that increases by the day. Here, money hangs on every wall.

'So, my wife informs me that you are Engraver to the King and Linnell here says you are now embarked on a novel enterprise?'

'We are despatching the best of prints to our compatriots in Bengal.'

There are shrieks of delight from a nearby room. Young George is opening his gifts. It brings a grin to his father's plump cheeks. And smooths the progress to more formal discussions. Linnell leads the way. He shows a copy of the Mears bond.

'I am one guarantor. I believe you know the other. James Triquet. Master jeweller of the Strand. He counts the King of Poland as a customer... '

By the 9th of February, they have the first instalment of money drawn against Hoare's private account. The loan of five hundred pounds is a welcome balance to their mountain of debt. Some two weeks later, news comes that the Egmont has left the Downs. Her journey South and East has begun.

Chapter 17

Since William can do nothing to hasten the Egmont's return, he takes refuge in engraving. His Royal commission, the Queen and Daughter Portrait by Francis Cotes, has been too long neglected. The turn of a pearl necklace and the sheen of a brocade bodice are now a welcome diversion. Another pastime, of a different calibre, arrives by messenger.

Allan Ramsay sends word there is to be a Teresa Cornelys extravaganza, for eight hundred guests. He offers to pay for William's subscription to this Soho masquerade. Though he also warns about the City mob. They will be out to claim the streets from the wealthy and the well-to-do. So on the night of the twenty-sixth, William hides his trickster costume beneath a heavy coat. He disguises his Venetian mask in an old wig and enters Soho on foot. He has never seen it so chaotic. Already, as St Anne's strikes nine, there are a host of chairmen and carriages inside the Square. The mob's flaming torches cast so many wild shadows, it is hard to tell who is friend or foe. For now, they are still in some good humour, lubricated by quantities of spirit that Mistress Cornelys has thought wise to provide.

William finds Ramsay waiting at the door with Richard Cosway, a fellow artist. He is in full Highland kilt and hose. Together they follow the rich and elegant into Carlisle House. The entrance hall has been transformed into a lush garden of Eden. Beside the Tree of Knowledge, stands Adam, a muscular and nearly naked figure. His privates are discreetly covered. He seems more statue than human until Cosway attempts to adjust his fig leaf. A firm hand clamps tight around his wrist and a voice hisses.

'I am Captain Watson of the Guards. Be gone, foul Jacobite.'

The insult is delivered between white teeth and a beatific smile. Cosway, already merry from early whiskies, escapes the First Man's grasp with a glance downwards.

'Lucky Eve, Captain Watson.'

William wanders on past the busy gambling tables, the stifling ballroom lit with a thousand candles, the discreet supper booths. It is a human menagerie. A druid, bedecked with mistletoe, is in earnest conversation with a double man, half-miller, half Chimney sweep. The painter George James struts about in a golden Midas cloak. While the daughter of Lord Galway parades her Indian gown embroidered with precious stones worth thirty thousand guineas or more. Among these exotic types are more traditional masqueraders. The Duke of Devonshire is not at all in costume and His Royal Highness the Duke of Gloucester restricts himself to an old English riding habit.

William cannot help notice that there is one character who draws attention above all others. It is not that her attire is risqué. It is rather that her half mask and dress leave her identity exposed. She has been recognised. As she flutters her fan from room to room she leaves a trail of whispered intrigue. She is broad-shouldered, well-set about the torso despite the efforts of a hard-working corset. To dispel any further doubt, her blue eyes and the French medal on her chest reveal her to be none other than the Chevalier d'Eon. What is more this diplomat,

Royal Spy and keeper of William's youthful secrets seems to be taking a coy pleasure in the scandal. Though he is not the only man dressed in woman's finery, there are few who carry it off with a flair that suggests a practiced hand at work.

There is another difference too, which Ramsay reveals, as they observe the Chevalier smooth her robe after yet another dance.

'There is substantial money changing hands at White's.'

'On d'Eon's dress ?'

'On what lies beneath.'

'And that is worth their guineas?'

'It seems there are none can say for certain. And it is driving the price so high.'

'A d'Eon bubble?'

'Something like. For those in the know.' Here Ramsay looks William square on. 'There is a fortune to be made.'

'Oh, that is not my game. Not that at all. I have no wish to meddle in the affairs of the Chevalier. Far from it. I would rather we never cross paths again.'

Aware that his vehemence might invite suspicion, William shrugs it off and goes in search of wine. Though the encounter has left its mark and somehow tarnished the abandon of the night. Soon after, he retires, making his way through a side exit, to avoid the crowd. They are now gathering again in the Square, ready to barrack the Lords and Ladies in their carriages and chairs when they depart.

An east wind brings a chill start to March. William and Henry Bryer arrive early each day in the Cornhill shop. They rue the cost of their rush to purchase so many works. The first five hundred pounds from Fat Jovial Henry is soon swallowed up. Though the loan is a useful vote of confidence from a financier. Now they must use the Bond to tempt others.

'We need a list of traders, merchants, family acquaintances.' William sips his morning coffee. 'Men who have done well in their professions and could have spare guineas to invest.'

The temptation of future profit attracts a sugar baker, Robert Bulkeley; a Spitalfields weaver, James Walker; a merchant James Mowbray of Leadenhall Street, who has long wished to find a way to make his fortune with the Company. Each of them loans William another five hundred pounds. The list soon lengthens. On the 27th April, Benjamin Hopkins, a merchant shopkeeper signs for five hundred and thirty five pounds, five shillings and six pence. Every penny is welcome. In May that sum is matched by Benjamin Thornton, a wine merchant from The Minories.

William discovers he has a skill in raising funds. These men see him as one of their own. A man with a dream of making good. But at night he is still tortured by fear. It's true he is forcing no-one to part with their savings. They are all protected by the guarantors, Linnell and Triquet. But they in turn have no notion of his secret deal with the Mears brothers. Fifty percent profit to be paid even if they do not sell a print. William can only hope the Egmont will deliver.

Despite the flow of money coming in, William still cannot make the rental payments due in May. In desperation he turns again to James Triquet. Discretion is now a matter of life or death. Any hint of their financial woes becoming public could bring more creditors into the field. Seated at their corner table in the Virginia, William is aware that he is being scrutinised. Triquet reaches forward and places his hand on William's wrist. The touch is gentle, concerned.

'My father taught me that a man's state of mind can rightly be judged by the state and disposition of his hands. From the placing or curling of the palm and the extension of the digits...'

The more William attempts to relax, the more his hands have a life of their own. He holds up his palms in surrender. 'You have me. The truth is, yes. We are in the muck. Deep. Up to our necks and nearly over them.'

'Yet I heard you were borrowing from every man jack with a guinea to spare.'

'Would that it were enough.' William says. 'We are about to default on the rent. Our Paris creditors are threatening action. And the Egmont is still another year away.'

Triquet hesitates for a moment. 'So, you must sell as many stock plates as will bring in guineas.'

'They are our seed corn. Without them we cannot-'

'-With them you lose your shop... you need guineas now.'

William feels a tremor in the fingers of his right hand. He clenches his fist but he is already betrayed. 'No need to say more.'

'No.'

With that the two men bid each other farewell with just a nod.

That morning William sets Henry Bryer the distressing task. He must sort through all the engraved copper plates acquired over the past year. 'Choose those that will bring in the best price. Spread word that this is a private sale, to raise funds for new purchases. The trade must not think we are selling up. It is a game. Play it well.'

While Henry assembles plates into piles, William turns back to one plate that he cannot afford to sell. Early each morning, he traces out the patterns and cuts the marks that define the portrait of the Queen and her young daughter. The cross-hatching sends his eyes awry. He blinks, looks away and for a moment rests. Then he turns back to the task. This is no time to waver.

So it goes on, week in, week out, only interrupted by visits to his favourite printer, Hadrill. He is one of the few suppliers who is not beating at the door demanding payment. They decide together where there is need of more shading, less depth or a sharper definition.

With this dedication, William has the plate ready by July . A proof is made, submitted to the King and Queen and returned with effusive gratitude and appreciation. Now he has another Royal portrait to sell. William instructs Hadrill to print its publication address as *Stafford Row, nr the Queen's Palace*. His home is now more secure than the shop on Cornhill. But they still have an urgent need of two hundred pounds just to stay afloat.

He finds Mary sitting at the parlour table with the children. They are finishing supper. But the deep furrow between William's eyes is enough to warn her that all is not well. So she blesses the girls and their young brother and shoos them upstairs.

At first William tries to lighten the tone. He leans forward to lift a piece of plum jam from the side of her mouth. 'So Mary dearest.' She pushes his hand away. 'The Queen's Portrait....'

'Something terrible has happened ?'

'No. By no means no. It is finished.' He pulls out a proof from his leather satchel. Taking care to avoid the mess the children have left, he lays it across the table.

'Oh William, she is magnificent... and the young princess. All that detail in the brocade. No wonder you have been squinting.'

He turns away, his eyes moist, not in triumph but from the thought of what he has to say. 'Well, the Queen is of your opinion too and the King, so I am led to believe. There were many compliments at court'

'And now she shall have pride of place in your window.' She looks more closely at the lettering. 'But you have said the prints are available here at Stafford Row, not Cornhill. Surely that is wrong ?

'Well...Mary...'

'No... You are not... ?'

'It is not definitive, but I cannot deny... we are on the edge. It is only by the good grace of Triquet that we continue. He has lent us thousands on a new bond. But we must do more. We shall be selling many of our plates soon, many of our prints too. Crossley is setting up the sale. We are discreet, but it's possible the word is already out. You can imagine, Boydell's crew are crowing.'

'Oh William.' She sinks down into her chair. He shifts the proof to stop it being ruined by the tears now coursing down her cheeks. 'That it has come to this...' Then it dawns on her that he has not yet asked the question that he brought with him. 'It is worse is it not?

He will not let his eyes meet hers.

'The jewellery?'

He nods.

'Noooooo.' The cry is shrill, but it doesn't come from Mary. They both turn to see the shadow of young Charlotte's nightdress disappear upstairs. She continues shouting as she goes. 'You cannot... They are to be mine, Mary-Anne's and mine.'

The door above slams shut, shaking dust from the ceiling.

William is about to follow her up, to hold her tight, to beg her forgiveness, but Mary holds him back. 'Let her go... Only yesterday she was asking me to show her my pearl necklace. The one that Sam brought back for me on his first Ocean journey.' She sighs. 'I will explain to her by and by. We are not losing them for ever. It is a loan to tide us over. Is it not?'

'I hope so. I have found a good man, a friend of Bailey's. I trust him to hold them until we can find the money.' He reaches out to hold her but her fists are clenched and will not open.

The following morning, William gathers together several small packages. Each is wrapped in a silken sleeve. He checks them all. One ring he had bought for Mary with his first pension from the King.

In Soho, he finds the premises of a Monsieur Baissant and receives a bill of exchange for two hundred pounds. It is far from enough but will keep the bailiffs away.

By October, William and Henry's financial woes are common knowledge among the City's printsellers. Opinion is divided as to the wisdom of their Indian venture. It is still too early. At best, the Egmont will only just have reached the Bay of Bengal.

The strain of waiting for news weighs heavily on William. As the evenings grow longer, he finds himself turning back to Pa.

'It lifts his spirits when you come a-visiting,' Ma confides.

'It has been too long.'

In truth, these times are also an escape. In Stafford Row, he feels recrimination in the air. His son now prefers the company of Master Strutt and his antiquarian collections. His daughters share whispered conversations, which falter and die away when he enters the room. This only prompts a counter-show of abrupt good humour. But his declarations of *"fortune favours the brave"* fail to ease the fear they all share.

With winter even the short journey to Ma and Pa becomes a risky venture through icy streets. But William persists. There is something in Pa's manner that troubles him. He begins to drift away in the middle of a conversation. He lets loose sharp words towards his beloved Ma , which he has never done before. Even when his own shadow of debt hung over him.

One evening as they are sitting together beside the hearth, Ma confesses her own fears. 'Pa is slipping from us.' William sees her hands are shaking beneath her embroidery.

'I feel it too... I hope that my...'

She reaches forward to push back a lock of his black hair. 'No, your Indian venture makes him proud. Never more so, even when your godfather Watkins-Wynne, God rest his soul, swore to see you through your studies... Pa has always expected you to make good... '

Ma rests her hand on his knee. With a soft smile she turns to look for hope among the flames dancing before them.

That New Year there are scant celebrations in either household. It feels, to William, as if his family is holding a collective breath, waiting for a sign that all will be well. But when the Spring melt comes, it brings more ill tidings.

On the first Friday in March, there is a hammering on the door of William's studio in Russell Street. It is Jo Strutt and he brings news that Henry Bryer, William's partner in the India venture, has collapsed. 'He does not speak, his left arm dangles loose and his face is all askew, as if some giant had taken it up and twisted it across.'

'That does not promise well.' William says pulling on his coat. 'Where is he now?'

'Abed, with a doctor in attendance. Leaches and cupping.'

William and Mary spend much of the next week at Henry's bedside. They listen to his laboured breath, hanging on any sign that he may be recovering. His young wife, also Mary, is distraught.

'One moment he is there, laughing' Jack said. 'Laughing like he was a boy again. Then down he drops, with no sense about it.'

There is some respite when Henry regains his voice. He forces out his thanks between twisted lips. He will need constant care, the doctor says. Once again William turns to James Triquet. 'Henry's wife could help in the shop, if there is money spared to pay for a nurse.'

'My trade is flourishing. I shall help this time. But do not on any account approach John Linnell.'

'He is unwell?'

'He has the law on his back. This Polly Perfect charade! The Lord Conyngham now knows he benefited from the payments to Polly. So he is after John and she has fled the country. She now sits and howls in Ireland, blaming everyone but herself. One day John will learn not to push his stick into a wasp-nest.'

'Unhappy times,' William says.

'Unhappy times indeed.'

In May, hopes rise when a message reaches William. One of the East India ships which left the Downs in February last year has returned. Can this be the Egmont? William rushes to Lloyds coffee-house, but when he consults the list, he finds it is the Greenwich, just home from Bombay. A week later, the mood within the community of traders darkens further when the East India packet, the Lapwing arrives off the Downs. Word soon spreads that her captain has news of the famine in Bengal. It is far worse than previous accounts. Millions of natives are at death's door. There are those in the City that abhor the tragedy and there are others, the ship-owners and the private traders, who now sleep uneasy, behind their stuccoed facades in Bloomsbury.

Following hard on these latest knocks, a lawyer's letter arrives from Paris. The artist and dealer, Tessier, is causing havoc over money he is owed. He must be placated or future trade with Paris is doomed. William explains to Triquet that he is obliged to go. With Henry Bryer still too sick to work, their wives will tend the Cornhill shop.

Just before he sets off for France, William pays a farewell visit to Ave Maria Lane. Ma warns him that Pa is much changed. 'His eyes are failing. He says he must see you while he can.'

William finds him sitting in near darkness, almost smothered beneath a thick embroidered wrap. But his voice still has spirit in it. 'I remember when you first returned from Paris. I told Ma you would bring home a Frenchie for your wife.' His cackle sets off an outburst of coughing. 'But no, you came alone... then found your Lambeth girl.'

William clenches his teeth. This is not the time to remind him how unwelcome he made Mary. He senses a question hanging in the air between them. For the first time he shares the story of Gabrielle and how he lost her. '... But she would not join me. She is a Parisian, through and through.'

'She is still there then?'

'I have had scant news.'

'It is best that way. Do not forget yourself. You are a husband and a father now, with three young'uns to be proud of...'

William dares not add that he has another daughter too, somewhere in France. It would be too much for the old soul to take on. He reaches out to take his father's hands. They are just skin and bone. Once they were warm and strong, gripping that great iron printer's wheel.

'Godspeed, my son. When you return, bring news of that damned ship of yours. Ha?'

Chapter 18

I n early June, William is on his way to Dover, with letters of credit in his pouch. This is to be a swift visit to Paris, long enough to restore his business reputation and no longer. But even this short journey has set some tongues wagging. Is his business foundering? Sharp as ever, his old rival, John Boydell, sent a list of works he wishes to obtain and money for the purchases. If William could refuse he would have done but the commission is substantial. At least it means that Bailey will be on his way in a couple of days. They can work together, once again. This time for Boydell. Strange how that wheel of fortune turns.

Five nights later, the moon is up over the cathedral of Notre Dame when William's carriage finally rolls across the Pont St Michel. A mob of valets, urchins and anxious relatives surround the dusty travellers who emerge blinking in the torch light. William trudges off into the familiar streets. Within minutes he is outside the white stone facade of Le Bas' house and studio. The side entrance opens and there is the beaming face of his former mentor, guide and old friend.

'*Enfin, enfin*, Monsieur Ryland.'

'Better late than never, *Maître*.'

'Come, come.' He envelops William in his arms.

After years of English etiquette it is good to be back among the French.

'And *Madame* ?' William asks

'Ah, she is in the country...looking after a friend of the family.'

William is too tired to enquire further.

'Come. I have put you at the top with the view of Our Lady. She is still magnificent is she not? You have your St Paul, but give me Our Lady any day.'

He lets the challenge pass. This is not the time for a debate over national treasures.

'Now. Your message said you are immediately into your affairs in the morning?'

William nods.

'You are wise to come in person. Old Tessier has been pouring a ton of the worst manure on your reputation. Pay him off, smooth his feathers and you will be back to business.'

'He seems particularly vindictive.'

'Old age and lack of money. 'Tis no excuse though, we all suffer from the same ailments eh?'

The view of the Cathedral from his room evokes a host of memories. They tighten in his gut and he is soon overwhelmed by a desperate longing to remain. He has brought a plate with him. He rests it on his leather cushion. By the light of the candle, he calms himself, pushing the burin across the copper. Within a few minutes he finds his head drooping. He sets the plate down, strips to his undergarments and curls up into a ball on the bed.

He wakes to a battering on the bedroom door.

'*Coucourou*! My friend!'

It is Le Bas announcing a fine breakfast with warm bread and quince jam. 'Here, you just have time. We will catch up on your news tonight. First you must tend to your honour... and your debts.' He pushes open the shutters. 'Oh my boy, you are as pale as a winter mouse. Sun and fresh air. Does that not exist in London, surely it is not always fog?'

Dragging on his crumpled formal clothes, black as always, for simplicity, William becomes a man of business. By ten o'clock, he is at the lawyer's office. He is soon embroiled in lengthy discussions for which he has neither the head nor heart. His French returns in fits and starts, though he is never able to master the figures. He is reduced to writing them down when he becomes confused. Still, he soldiers on and by mid-afternoon it seems that all the points of contention are settled. He is ready to share a bottle or two with Le Bas at a quiet tavern on the banks of the Seine.

'Tell me my friend, how is Ravenet, my old student? I have had little news this past year.'

William is ashamed. He too has had little contact. 'I know he has finally moved from Lambeth across the River. It was at the Exhibition, I saw him last. '

'Ah the Academy. I hear they are not so respectful of Engravers?'

'No nor printsellers. We are shunned. But I have found a way across that. I will be submitting drawings of my future prints.'

'And the family?'

'Well, and yours?'

'All good. Lizabeth is a tower of strength as always...'

Beneath this *badinage*, there is a question unasked. William raises his hand. Le Bas stops in mid-stream.

'Gabrielle? You want to know more?'

William can only nod. His hand drops to his knee which is now a-tremble.

'I told you that Lizabeth was in the country. Well. She is in Lavranche.'

'The Chateau?'

'Yes.'

More a fortified country house than a grand castle, the Chateau de Lavranche is the former home of Gabrielle's father, lying some twenty leagues south-west of Paris. William recalls her description of two conical slate-roofed towers above an inner courtyard, where she used to play, in the shade of an ancient peach tree.

'That is where she is living now?'

'Her daughter, Constance, is at school nearby.'

'And they live.. alone?'

'There was a man, but he left some time back.'

Le Bas' faint smile irks William. 'You chastise me still!'

'No, another,'

'Oh.'

'But there was an argument. Many it seems. He curbed her freedom.'

Now it is William's turn to smile. 'She still paints then?'

'Oh yes, she has had success, with portraits then more recently with sculptures.'

'I can see her working clay. She was always asking me about Roubiliac.'

'It is one of the reasons she loves that Chateau. The red earth is particularly fine...' Lebas' voice catches in his throat. He plays with a curl of hair. 'Gabrielle is not well.'

'Ah.' William sits back.

'We do not know how unwell. It is why Lizabeth set off to see her. It seems she is troubled...'

'In her mind, her body, How so ?'

'It began with a fever, then a creeping lassitude. She found she could no longer throw her clay as she was used. Constance sent us word when

she returned from her convent school to discover that the local doctor
had been at work. All the usual horrors, bleeding and cupping. Her
mother's mind was spinning with it all.'

'This contagion, is it passed?'

'No, it seems it still has a hold. And now we hear that she is not alone,
there are many in the local town and villages that are suffering.'

'Your wife...'

'I am worried for her. For all of them.'

William feels a stiffness start in the small of his back. It is as if hot
coals sit beneath his skin, swelling it as tight as a stuffed fowl. He shifts
and stretches but cannot release it.

The two men are quiet. Both watch as a pair of swans emerge from
reeds beside the river bank not far from them. They slip back into the
fast-flowing water, serene and silent. More sure of the world about
them than their human observers.

The decision comes unbidden but no less certain for that.

'I must go to her.' William says. 'I have secured most of what I came
for today. I know I cannot leave her in that state, and your wife too, in
danger.'

'You would risk all for a woman you once wronged? My friend, you
are no longer even in the same worlds.'

But William has already leapt ahead. 'Does Wille still have his post
chaise?'

'I believe so. But at this hour ?'

'I will wait until dawn. But can I ask you this? Make up a story, an
urgent delivery to the provinces, a client who must be looked after... I
do not want Wille to know that I am involved.'

Without another word, Le Bas throws on his coat and disappears
towards the Quai des Augustins. Meanwhile William prepares himself
for this unexpected journey. He has little choice in clothes because his
visit was intended to be short. At least he has a stout pair of travelling

boots. Who knows how those country roads will have survived the winter.

As a ruby dawn breaks over the road leading out of Paris, William sits clenched tight on the hard bench seat inside Wille's post-chaise. At first a strong scent of the sea confuses him until he realises that his coat is still encrusted with salt from his Channel crossing just days before. Now he is once again en route, travelling into an adventure that belongs more to his youthful past than to the family man that he has become.

The post-chaise reaches the top of a sloping drive just off the principal road to Lavranche. At the crest of a small hill, the Chateau dominates the land for miles around. The tired horses are finally brought to rest. The jolt wakes William from his stiff repose. He steps down into a countryside that his friend Woll would have deftly engraved. Field after green field, criss-crossed by lines of thorn bushes and low stone banks. A persistent breeze sets everything in motion, from the wisps of cloud, to the jagged sheen on a distant lake. Even the taciturn driver is charmed. 'Twill be the freshest grass they've had for many a month.'

For William the vision all around him feels like the continuation of a gentler dream. Here there is nothing of debt and legal wrangling. Then his attention is caught by a movement to his right. A black-painted carriage drawn by a solitary and aged bay horse is swaying along the deeply rutted path leading away from the ancient gates of the Chateau. Just as it swings across on to the country road, William sees a young girl's face glancing back at him. She holds his attention just for a moment then turns back. Within a minute the carriage is out of sight.

William's pulse is beating hard. Was that his daughter, their daughter, Constance?

Past and present come together in an instant, but it is just a glimpse and she is gone.

Galvanised by this encounter, William seizes his travelling bag and strides down towards the entrance. There before him are the conical towers, the narrow drawbridge, hovering over a deep moat, thick with reeds and lilies. He knocks at the studded door. After a minute it opens with a creak that has been demanding oil for centuries. He braces himself to see Gabrielle for the first time for over a decade. But the face that appears, bedecked with an ochre turban, is that of Lizabeth, Le Bas' beloved wife. She is somewhat fuller in the face and a little pinched about the eyes. But still magnificent.

She stops, as surprised as he is. There is a moment, he believes, she considers hurling the door back on its hinges, obliterating his arrival. But he makes a deliberate move inward with his leading foot and the possibility of denial is gone. He embraces her on the cheek. Her touch is quite rigid, cold even. He senses the fear in her welcome. 'This is not a place to be ... but now you are here, I am grateful.'

She invites him into the grassy courtyard. The peach tree, which Gabrielle once described, is still there, its lower branches splayed out at sharp angles, propped up on iron y-shaped rods. 'Come you must be hungry.'

He shakes his head.

'Then sit a while.'

She fetches a pail of water He sluices it over his head. The cold water is both a relief and a sharp awakening.

'Gabrielle ?' He whispers.

Lizabeth puts a finger to her lips and beckons him over to the far side of the courtyard, to a set of shuttered windows. She eases back one of the shutters, and he peers through. There is little light, but gradually his eyes adjust. He can see into a large room, with whitewashed walls. There are a number of clay busts on pedestals... among them a face he recognises. The young girl who left just a few minutes before. In some poses she is laughing, in others more pensive, but always with the intensity he had witnessed earlier.

He feels a touch on his shoulder. Lizabeth's eyes are questioning. She has her palm flat against her inclined head. He nods. Though he has still not been able to make out where Gabrielle is sleeping in that darkened space.

He steps back and follows Lizabeth silently across the courtyard to the kitchens. She places a cup of hot water flavoured with lemon balm and honey before him. 'So?'

Never has he felt so short a word to carry such a weight of doubt, of anger, of sorrow. At first William has no answer. He clasps the cup in both hands, breathes in the aroma and wonders how to explain his presence and his past. 'I had to come.'

Her lips remain pursed, the question still remains.

Minutes pass again. 'How is she ?'

Lizabeth screws up her mouth, twisting it to one side. It's a gesture William remembers from the studio, when a clumsy apprentice has spilt the acid or left it too long on a plate.

She gestures to her temple with one outstretched finger then shakes her head slowly.

'And the sickness ?'

She shrugs. Just then there is a cry, as piercing as an owl's screech.

'Betha ! Betha!'

Lizabeth spins around and is through the door in an instant. '*J'arrive ma belle, j'arrive...* '

William follows her out into the courtyard. The door into Gabrielle's room is open but he does not want to intrude. Instead he leans against a branch of the peach tree and waits. The shutters swing open. And there is Gabrielle. She is a shadow of the woman he knew, wrapped in a green silk shawl and holding out a bowl.

At first she doesn't see him. Then, lifting up her eyes to take in the bright light of the yard, she lets out a loud shriek. The bowl drops to the ground, where it smashes into a pattern of red shards. The noise startles her as much as his presence. She calls out his name. 'Guillaume? William?'

'Gabrielle.'

He steps forward, but she takes fright, as if surprised by what she thought was just a dream. Her palms are outstretched, stopping him in his tracks. '*Non. Non. Je suis malade, malade, malade...*'

Her voice increases in pitch with every repetition. He keeps moving towards her but at the third warning, he falters. He feels a tug. Lizabeth is beside him, pulling him back, not without care but insistent.

'Give it time,' she says. 'We had no idea you were coming... Not here, not now, not after so long !'

Just as he is searching again for the words to explain why he is here, the air begins to hum around them. Then comes the sound of beating wings, many many wings, hundreds and hundreds of pairs beating... The sky above the courtyard is now full of a swirling mass of white and grey and purple and orange. Several hundred birds are dipping and diving and circling overhead. As if on cue, the chaos resolves into one mass, funnelling down towards him and then across into the entrance to the vast pigeon loft, in the far left corner of the courtyard. There is a clutter of wings as each bird finds its niche in the hollowed out dome of wood and plaster. Then the murmur fades away to a gently cooing and there is silence again.

William turns back towards Gabrielle and sees a smile break across her face. A cloud of ivory-grey feathers is floating down in the still air.

He feels a soft trickle of tears start first from one eye, then from both. The flow becomes a stream.

In that instant William is back in the room they shared in Paris, twelve years before, passionately, playfully, beating each other with cushions, before making love on a bed covered with scattered feathers.

William feels the gaze of the women on him. Just watching, not intruding. A bell is rung inside the kitchen. Time reasserts itself. Gabrielle withdraws into her room and Lizabeth sets up a trestle table beneath the tree. Platters of food emerge with knives and clay cups of cider.

They eat in silence. Fresh pears, figs, goats cheese and thick dark country bread. William gradually regains his strength, a sense of himself.

He asks again about Gabrielle's illness. This time Lizabeth offers more detail.

'The doctors say it as a contagion. It has affected many in the region.'

'You say her mind is stained too?'

'There are night fears, anxieties. Several times she said she feared the King's spies were watching her.'

William feels his cheeks redden.

'Does that mean something to you too?' Lizabeth asks.

'No... well, not recently, not for many years now.' He looks up into her eyes. This is no time for dishonesty.

'There was a time when I was leaving Paris. We were at war... they wanted me to help them... but I do not believe Gabrielle had any reason to be concerned.'

'Apart from the fact you left her...'

'That yes ...'

He lets the uneasy silence settle once again. It is broken minutes later by a gentle knocking, becoming more urgent. William remembers the post-chaise driver has been outside with the horses all this time.

No doubt he fell asleep in the sunshine and now wants to know his master's plans. William turns to Lizabeth, who understands his question immediately. 'You may stay, there are enough rooms here.'

He invites the driver in for food, but he refuses. He was only given permission by Wille to be away for a day, two at most. William gives him some coins and a message.

'Please send thanks to your master, from Monsieur Le Bas. He will understand.'

William and Lizabeth take turns to watch over the room where Gabrielle sleeps. They never cross the threshold. Gabrielle will not let them come close.

At first, after the initial shock of seeing him, she seems to have gained strength. But the following morning the heat returns. She dabs her forehead and temples with the towels and cool water they leave for her. She sits at times quite listless, throwing a lump of clay back and forth in her hands as if she would create something out of that dismay but her hands never settle long enough for it to emerge. To see her in this torment, in this distress is an experience unlike any other that William has witnessed. Compared to this, his father's illness has been a placid slow moving descent.

By the third day Gabrielle cannot lift herself from her bed. They receive a visit from Sister Josephine, from the nearby convent. She has known Gabrielle since she was a girl. She brings news of sickness spreading in villages nearby. People are dying in their homes once the fever takes hold.

'You must take care.'

She trusts in the protection of the Lord. Donning a hood, a mask and gauntlets she enters Gabrielle's room and cleans and tends to her. She is still there in the evening, her rosary slipping through her fingers as she prays for Divine mercy. William and Lizabeth bring food to her, leaving it on the wide window ledge. The steam rising into the darkness is lit from behind by the candle always burning by Gabrielle's bed.

The pigeons make one more sortie before dusk and are now roosting again, murmuring into the night air. They seem to be keeping their movements subdued, out of deference for the sick woman, their beloved, who hovers between night and even longer darkness. Drawn to them for company, William walks gently into their resting place. The flickering light of his candle is reflected in many hundred pairs of eyes, bobbing and shifting, on row upon row above him. They start to coo, though not out of fear. It is soothing, reassuring. Maybe they know the end is coming. In this hollow hive of theirs, they witness it all, from hatching, to first flight, pairing and conception. Then death, by accident, sickness or old age. One more passing within the confines of the Chateau is no more, no less, than everyday occurrence.

For William, it feels as if this experience has obliterated the years of obsession with finance, trade and the dread of failure. He is now at the barest of essentials. The death of a loved one. He longs to hold her one last time. Even in her dying days Gabrielle has sought to protect those she loves, to stop them from suffering. He leaves the pigeons to their slumber. In the courtyard he finds Lizabeth leaning back against the peach tree. He sits beside her, gently lifts her head so she may let it drop against his shoulder. He feels her frame trembling while he sits, no longer able to cry, waiting for the moment that they both sense must be coming soon.

As the moon rises above them, the chatter of cicadas fades away, to be replaced by the prayers of Sister Josephine. William looks up at the clear night sky and feels a certainty of love, that gives him strength and takes away so much that was unclear in his heart, so much that was sheltered from the world.

On Lizabeth's advice, he does not stay for the funeral. Constance, Gabrielle's daughter, his daughter, will return soon. 'It is best that she is allowed to mourn Gabrielle alone. Not in the presence of the man who once left her mother. There will be another time. I will speak with Jacques. We have no children of our own. I would like to offer her a home in Paris. When she is ready, old enough, she can decide what is to become of her.'

Sister Josephine and her community make ready for the obsequies. William prepares himself to leave. A local farmer is persuaded to take him to the nearest town. Such is the fear in the region he insists that William sits in the back of his cart. The next day he finds a coach bound for Paris.

That evening he is once again in the side room beside Le Bas' studio. His old master is in a confusion of grief for Gabrielle and relief that Lizabeth is untouched. William reassures him. 'Lizabeth was an angel, watching over Gabrielle, night after night, soothing her.'

'And you, William, I expect tears and bitter wringing of hands, yet you are quite calm.'

William describes the passage of Gabrielle's last days. 'She was at peace, even in the heat of it. I could but attend and witness.'

'That is her last gift to you. Do not let it go to waste. And Constance?'

'Lizabeth says that you would take care of her?'

'It will be an honour for us.' Lebas' smile is gentle and loving. He offers William a glass of brandy. 'Come let us drink then to them both. To our beloved friend Gabrielle and our blessings on your daughter.'

'To Constance. May she blossom and grow in your care.'

Chapter 19

The closer William approaches Calais, the more the harsh countenance of his other life swells up like a storm cloud that cannot be ignored. It's true that his intended business, the placation of Tessier, has been a success. But there is still so much debt. His stomach aches at the thought of it. Everything still rides on this damned Indian venture.

When he reaches London, a fine June sky mocks his fear. Surely all cannot be lost on such a pure blue summer's day? But he soon discovers he has every reason to be anxious. Henry Bryer is still sick, struggling to walk or even write. And Pa is sliding deeper into a mute and pain-wracked state, that cannot last long. With staring eyes, he listens to William's whispered description of Gabrielle's passing. A gob of spittle hangs off Pa's lip, above a matt of white stubble. At the end of the account, his eyes are moist. He reaches out for William's hand and mouths a prayer. 'May the Lord have mercy...'

They sit in silence together. In the past it was always shared duties, obligations and money fears that bound them. But for this brief moment all that drops away. Leaving what? A tenderness, a warmth, a smile of understanding. The abrasive chatter of a magpie perched at the windowsill breaks the stillness. Pa tries to speak, though barely a few words emerge. 'What news? The Egmont..?'

William is tempted to lie, to conjure up a promising tale of pictures and prints sold at outrageous prices, of Nabobs desperate to buy. But Pa would have seen the truth in his eyes. 'Still not arrived. I am sure she will not tarry.'

Pa nods. His grip is faint and fading but it is enough to say he still has trust and hope. If only William could believe the same.

The two funeral carriages setting off from the quayside below Hammersmith are sturdy, well used to the rigours of the westward journey. The same cannot be said for their passengers. It has been many years since Ma saw her home village of Feltham, on the far side of Hounslow Heath. The country road is rutted, ridged and unforgiving. Ma grasps William's arm, and prays hard at every bend. He sits braced against the corner of the seat, wrapped in a black cloak, already covered in dust. He is surrounded by the Mary's in his life, his mother, his wife, and his two daughters. The Virgin is well represented. Though he lacks faith in Her ability to intercede, he prays that She keep his father's coffin safe. Strapped to the back of the carriage, it now rattles and winces against the ropes, as if Pa is determined to slip free from this earthly parade. At every rise and hollow, William expects to see him sliding off into the undergrowth. The pock-marked undertaker, as morose as his role demands, assures him that this has never happened in half a century of dedicated service.

When the coaches come to a brief rest, William can hear his brothers arguing in the other carriage. Joseph, the pardoned highwayman is still surly and at odds with life. He lambasts John, his more congenial younger sibling, with a tirade against their elder brother. 'Will only saved my life to look good before his royal patrons.'

William grins quietly to himself. No doubt he is doubly wicked in Joseph's green eyes, because he was so close to Pa, in his final days.

As they pass through Turnham Green, the bells of St Nicholas, Chiswick's village church, toll across the meadows. Just seven years earlier his childhood hero, William Hogarth, the little champion of engravers, was buried in the churchyard beside the willows and the river. His name lives on, honoured by Garrick as the 'great painter of mankind'. William reflects on what he will one day leave behind. That fortune, that dream of a Bloomsbury mansion. Is it approaching even now in the coffers of Captain Mears aboard the Egmont?

A huddle of friends and family have gathered in Feltham. Some have not seen Ma since her wedding. She and her sons are greeted with a bustle of reminiscence and condolence. William slips away from the mourners to supervise the unloading of the coffin, then enters St Dunstan's before the others. He slides into one of the pews at the back, hoping for a minute to reflect in peace. But the heavy scent of lilies, adorning every column, triggers memories that he had thought to have put behind him. Sharp pain sears the inside of his chest and down into the well of his stomach. He is still breathing hard when Pa's coffin is borne in, followed by his family. His daughters glance across to him, both frowning, before they walk the length of the nave to the front pew. As they settle he watches Ma turn to his eldest, to reassure her.

Looking around at the other mourners, William sees that even here he cannot escape his Indian venture. In the third row, sits a man of florid complexion. Johnnie Bryan is the family's greengrocer. How many times William has run to his shop in Newgate street to fetch a pound of tatters or a punnet of berries. He has never seen him without a smile on his face, but today his brow is creased, his eyes dim. He has lent William £500 of his savings, against the Bond and the profitable return of the *Egmont*. For all concerned, news of the ship's arrival at the Downs cannot come soon enough.

Henry Bryer is still too frail to do more than watch and wait, but his brother Jack is up early every day scouring the coffee-houses for information. Each afternoon he reports to William at the Cornhill shop. Its windows are now only partially covered with prints, so many having been already sold. It has become a refuge for William's creditors, the weaver, the wine-merchant, the gentleman-trader, each of them desperate to know whether the risk they have taken with their capital has paid off.

In the second week of September, as the clock in the Exchange strikes 4 o'clock, Jack Bryer bursts through the double doors of 27 Cornhill. 'She's here! She's here! The Egmont, William, she's back...'

William is not one to bless the Lord God Almighty but he utters a heartfelt 'thank you' to Whoever might be listening. Jack is all for setting off down river. But William advises patience. 'They'll have to offload the saltpetre first on their way up to Gravesend.'

They agree to wait for news from Captain Mears himself. He must come to East India House soon to make his report. So Jack heads down to the wharves to find a lighterman willing to carry a message to Mears for a few coins.

William's nerves are not helped by the gaggle of creditors who now assail him, desperate to know more. At least Mary and the children are still in Lambeth. William will not trouble them. They will be gathering early apples and pears, climbing trees and running wild in a way they cannot in the streets around Kensington. If only he was with them.

It is another five days before a laconic reply arrives from Captain Mears:

Rest and recovery much needed but will be in Leadenhall Street within the week.

William rips the note in two. 'Not a word of sales? After eighteen months.'

He passes the paper to Jack, who checks first to make sure nothing has been missed, then tosses it into the grate. 'He is a Company man!'

'But it's private trade will pay for his Bloomsbury mansion.'

'Aye well let's hope then he's made a tidy profit from our prints.'

What is gnawing at them both is the knowledge that whatever was sold in Bengal, the Mears brothers are guaranteed a profit on the entire stock of prints. That agreement is still a secret. He can only pray that the sales went so well he will never need to reveal its existence.

William and Jack are at the customs house every day. By early October, the Egmont's saltpetre has come in, a heavy load of mahogany, some private goods but so far no news about the prints. Then one evening, before they have seen or heard from the Mears, Jack sees another lighter arrive. 'Look, there! Are not those Bailey's cases?'

'I trust your eyes better than mine, Jack.'

'Come, quick, let's meet them at the dock.'

They are running now, dodging between the lines of porters, pushing past the wharf men, who fling curses at their backs. Both are agitated by the thought that their wooden cases are on board. Surely, they would not return empty cases. Would they?

Reaching the barrier overlooking the jetty, they stop to catch their breath. Jack begins to count the cases. At first to himself, then aloud... twenty, twenty-one...

'Oh God's teeth. All bar two or three are there.'

William has no words. He cannot bear to look. He sinks down on to a piled coil of rope and let's his head drop. Jack's anger swirls around him. 'Where are the Mears! Why have they told us nothing?'

But William is no longer present. In that moment he remembers the young boy he met, sitting so alone by the roadside north of Paris. It is as if everything he once had has been taken from him. He feels Jack drop down beside him. The acrid smell of his sweat is sharp in William's nostrils. He cannot open his eyes. All he can whisper is, 'I fear the worst.'

They make their way back to the Cornhill shop. They close all the blinds and outdo each other with draughts of Portuguese until their wits are dulled into oblivion.

When William wakes the blinds are still down despite the clock striking noon. The last exchange that William can recall from that wine-soaked night is Jack declaring that he will go next day to Leadenhall Street, the headquarters of the Company. 'I will wait all day all night, if I must. But we will have the truth from these charlatans. Eighteen months of our lives and how much more they have stolen from us. My brother lies half- crippled with worry. They have much to answer for...'

Some hours later, Jack returns. He is barely in the door before he is pouring out a bilious tale. 'The devils are home at last. Brown as nuts and in fine spirits, though a sight thinner than when they left.'

'And?'

'We were right to worry when we saw those cases.'

'No reason? No excuses?' William asks.

'The famine, the damned famine that we knew of. Bodies floating in the Hoogly. Sickness, disease, farmers selling their children... A distraction, an obsession for every Company man. So they said. No-one would buy, no-one had time to look.'

'They were all out making a killing...' William rubs his forehead as if to erase the picture in his mind. Bryer's anger is exhausting.

'Shifting rice along the coast, they said. No-one wanted money on their walls, when they could make it elsewhere.'

'Or they feared for their lives.'

'And the Mears escape with their profit, scot-free.'

William is up now, pacing back and forth. 'It is our friends Linnell and Triquet who must bear the burden of this.'

'The shop is lost?'

'We still have the prints to sell. If they survived two journeys across the Ocean.'

'We will have Bailey to thank if so.' Jack turns and makes to leave.

'Your brother?' William calls after him.

'I will tell him when he wakes. Sick and a bankrupt. What life is that?'

Chapter 20

'Look, it is a trading mishap.' Gwynn says. 'You are unfortunate merchants. A deal has gone awry. You have every right, since the law of 1705, to declare yourselves bankrupt and, God willing, be discharged of all your debts.'

'You are sure that is so? I fear that we shall be shamed, for leaving our guarantors so exposed, while we run for cover.'

'Linnell and Triquet knew what they were about. They knew the risks as much as you.'

At this William reddens at the roots.

'I had intended- '

'- but it was always easier not to...'

Gwynn removes his piece-nez, holds them up to the light then rubs them clean with his kerchief. 'Fear not. I think that is just part of their concerns. It is all the borrowing you have done against their Bond, that will be where the pain lies.'

'We may still recoup some funds by selling plates and pictures. They are mostly untouched.

'So Bailey's crates may save your guarantors a small fortune.'

News is soon spreading of the Egmont's return. William and Jack Bryer agree to split the ordeal of confession between them. Jack will inform John Linnell while William will visit his family friend, James Triquet.

Next morning, he is outside the double-fronted silversmith's shop on the Strand. Triquet sees him through the window and comes out to greet him. 'From your attire and countenance, I would wager a funeral was in prospect, but then you always do dress dark.' He claps William on the shoulder with such good will that it makes him wince.

'What news?'

William shrugs. 'I fear it is worse than a passing, though there are no deaths to report.'

'Let us not bring bad news into the establishment. Bear with me, I must fetch a stick, my leg has been stiff as iron this past week.'

While Triquet limps back inside, William recalls a devilish device his old friend Angelo, the expert in arms, once showed him. An innocent cane that hid a lethal blade. Who knows what Triquet could do when he hears how he has been duped? And all this when he already has such a fine enterprise.

Moments later they are walking down towards the river.

'You know the Egmont is returned?' William asks.

'Yes that news is everywhere…and other rumours too.'

'That is why I am here. So you would hear first-'

'-our dreams are not to be?'

This *sang-froid* is disturbing. William feels an unexpected anger stir in him, or is it jealousy? That Triquet should remain so calm. True he has not thrown all that he owns, all that he has created, into the abyss. There is a rock on which he stands which William has never possessed. Generations before have built up the Triquet funds, allowing him to take risks but not so great as to be undone. He will not go bankrupt into the night.

So when it comes to the moment when William must reveal the secret deal, it is almost done with relish. The outcome is again disturbing. There is no anger at the betrayal but a cold distancing that shames and cuts more deeply. How could William behave this way when he had done so much to aid him?

'The Captain and his brother were adamant. We felt-'

'- the risk was not yours to take. I would not expect that of you.' Triquet ups his pace, despite his painful leg, obliging William to follow behind like some scolded student.

'I think it best that in the future it is our lawyers who debate the figures. I assume you will apply for bankruptcy. No doubt we shall accept because it is in our interest to do so. But from now on, Bankrupt William, you must be open and honest. You understand there will be a claim on your household goods...'

'Of course.'

'Does John know?'

'Jack is on his way to Berkeley Square as we speak.'

Triquet grunts. 'That will be a pretty burst of fireworks. It could not happen at a darker time for him. The Conyngham case goes against him. John must repay all that he and the trollop Polly obtained by fraud. But that is his own affair. The primrose path is littered with men like him.'

'I hope he will be as understanding as you, James.'

'That is more than you deserve. Fortune favours the brave, some say, but she appears to have passed us by on this occasion. Good day, William.'

Later that afternoon, Jack reports back to William and Gwynn on his encounter with Linnell. 'I found him alone and at first he is his usual blustering self, but when I tell him of the secret deal, he turns puce and paces up and down uttering the bloodiest oaths, swearing to have us clapped in the Marshalsea or hung on Tyburn tree for the scoundrels we are... He says that if he wished he could prove you acted fraudulent and you would hang for that... and... and then he hurls a china vase at me. Smashes into pieces inches from my head. "There," he says, "that's for all your talk of money on the wall." So I ducks and run, then. He is still shouting after me in the street. He wants the bailiffs out on us by dawn tomorrow...'

Gwynn searches out a bottle of brandy and pours young Jack a glass. 'Come now. For your ordeal... This vase attack is the price of your dishonesty. No more than that. No scoundrel likes to be bettered by another.'

He turns to William with a more gentle tone. 'You will both have to make your accounts and your houses open to review. No doubt you will be called upon by the bailiffs. They will take their share. But you will not end up in the Marshalsea. If you hold strong, you can still live to trade another day.'

William and Henry Bryer are declared bankrupt on the 10th December. A week later the assessors Crosley and Winchcomb attend their houses to value their goods to be sold to pay at least a portion of their guarantors' losses. There is just enough time for Mary to despatch some of her more treasured possessions into Ma's care in Ludgate Hill.

With just a few days before Christmas, what remains is the bitter task of cataloguing all the remaining stock for sale at the Cornhill shop. It is beyond William. In six months he has lost the anchors that once held in place both his past and his future. First Gabrielle, then Pa and now the Indian venture. There must be a way to restore some hope, some ambition. But not yet.

In his despair William turns to his old friend and apprentice Jo Strutt. He is still attending drawing classes at the Academy and indulging his passion for antiquarian collections. A little extra cataloguing is no hardship for him. When Strutt arrives at the shop he is fired up to lambast the Bryers for their malign influence on William. But on seeing his Master's state, he holds back. 'Leave this to me. It is best you were at home, taking care of Mary and the children.'

'Oh, I fear they look on me as if I should have a B for Bankrupt fixed to my chest and be placed in the stocks...'

'Come now, that is just their own fear that lurks. But, if you need some distance, why not send them here. I will have plenty to occupy them and Mary knows your stock as well as anyone.'

So for the next few days, the Kings Arms is alive with the laughter of three children. William junior, Mary-Charlotte and Mary-Anne ... Strutt knows how to draw them out of themselves. He has played with all three since they were knee-high. Soon he has bright red and yellow ribbons dangling from every door and turned the listing of prints into a game. And even Mary is drawn in. Though her eyes are rimmed red with tiredness and tears. Still, she sings her favourite carols when she is bidden.

On the eve of Christmas, the catalogue is complete, and the shop closed until after Twelfth night. When they reach home they find two chairmen outside the door. They are attempting to deliver a large package. But no-one has answered their knocks. The younger, darker more handsome of the two, winks at the children and addresses Mary with a smile. 'Ah now there's a pretty happenstance. You find us weary and wondering what we will be drinking this side of midnight mass...'

Mary is in better spirits now. She sends William junior down to the cellar to fetch a cider bottle for the men. She is intrigued who should be sending them such a package. Once she has it inside on a table in the scullery, she can smell the rich scent of cloves. Oh, here's a treat.

She pulls open the wrapping to find a huge ham, dotted with the dark spice heads. Inside there is both an open message: *To the Ryland family from their friend, John Gwynn, Oxford* and a folded note addressed to William.

Chapter 21

M ary finds William at his desk, slumped over a copper plate. She eases the burin out from under his palm and nudges him awake. Smiling through her tears she describes Gwynn's gift of the ham. 'And he has sent you a message too. Here shall I open it.'

'No, no, just leave it by me. My eyes are not so bad I cannot read my own letters.'

Her own eyes narrow, as if to say, *I do not deserve the rough edge of your tongue*, but he turns away from her with a shrug. He is far from his former self.

Once she has left the room he reaches for the note. It is from Oxford. Did Gwynn say he had won the contract for the new Magdalen Bridge? If so, it has slipped William's mind, like so many other details, submerged in the chaos of the bankruptcy.

Master Ryland, I do hope that you, Mary and your beloved family will enjoy the cloven ham. I shall not let my friends starve at Christmas tide, though I regret I cannot share in the feast. The old bridge here is half submerged beneath the winter floods. My work must contend with nature to succeed.

Still, I have escaped the buzzing of the London hive and extend an open invitation. Come visit, give your hands and mind a rest awhile. The bailiffs cannot reach you here and I can promise fine wine, fair food, perhaps even a day without this damned rain.

Your lodging is at my expense. (I have just received three month's advance). Join me and we will plot your path from bankrupt to phoenix. To rise again, even from these sodden meadows. Your devoted friend, Gwynn the Bridge Builder

The road west is a silver-grey ribbon leading from one waterlogged valley to another. After the downpours in November and December the countryside cannot bear any further influx of water. Progress is slow. In every hollow, a cloying mud sucks at the wheels of the Fleet Street to Oxford coach. Huddled into a corner seat, William sees weary villagers sweeping out the brackish flood or stacking salvaged bed frames, tables and cupboards on carts to move to higher ground.

A heron flies, sharp as an arrow, above the submerged fields. He imagines it searching for the landscape's lost signposts. He feels some kinship with the bird. Where are his own pots of gold to be found? What can he salvage for the future, amongst the confusion of debt and obligation? With a grim smile he catches himself about to declare aloud that Gwynn will find him a challenge. But the shuttered faces of his travelling companions, an apothecary just returned from purchasing supplies, a frowning vicar and his sleeping wife, do not invite any form of dialogue.

Late that night the coach clatters up the High Road, leaving a trail of mud behind it. At the market square a handful of porters await the exhausted travellers. It is a wintry scene. Gwynn is stomping back and forth to keep warm in his leather over-breeches and a heavy coat. 'Greetings, Master. Welcome to the land of Noah.'

'I trust your Ark is more watertight than this old coach...'

'I was a carpenter's apprentice.'

'So you say. Now where is this inn? I have a longing for a fire and a brandy.'

Within minutes of arriving at the George, William has deposited his bags and re-joined Gwynn in the snug.

'We are fortunate. The place is quiet. The students are away, eating their families out of house and home.'

A candle-lit table is found near the hearth, swiftly followed by tankards of warm spiced wine and a plate of thick sliced country ham. As the flames flicker between the two friends, an unspoken convention allows each of them time to unburden and reveal their current state of mind. Each asks for little in return, other than an understanding ear. It is well past midnight when they call a temporary truce in the unravelling of dilemmas. William staggers up to his bed while Gwynn sets off into a bitter wind, towards Magdalen College, where he has arranged rooms for the duration of his contract.

The rough bedding makes William's neck, feet and forearms itch like the devil. He looks for distraction in nocturnal sounds. A patter and scurry overhead suggests a squirrel or perhaps a rat on a scavenging run. Eventually he drifts off to sleep.

Rising late, despite the damnedest crowing of a cock, William pulls on his tallest pair of boots and country breeches and sets off to see his friend at his College rooms. The evening's excesses reduce their initial exchange to grunts. Gwynn guides William to the site where the old Bridge is just barely visible above the murky swirl of the Cherwell. It is a muddy, somewhat perilous walk, but they make their way across to a hostelry serving eggs and warm bread to break their fast. It is here, across a rickety wooden table that the events of the past chaotic months are dissected and reviewed by Gwynn's gentle but persistent questioning. 'The King's Arms, your shop, your stock of plates, is it all gone?'

'In the hands of the Bankruptcy Commissioners. Leeches all, they've already done their assessments. We'll know soon enough. I'm told we are to expect the bailiffs soon, perhaps next month.'

'Oh poor Mary...'

'Aye, strong as she is, this is her worst fear confirmed. I had no answer for her sore eyes.'

'And your guarantors?'

"A brutal deception" were James' words. Till then he was with us as a family man. I will spare you Linnell's curses, they'd make a boatman blush!'

A ray of sunshine breaks thought the gloom suggesting the clouds are lifting. William puts down the coffee cup he has been nursing. He is in no mood to continue this postmortem. 'I came here to leave this money poison behind. Come, show me more of your bridge.'

For the rest of the morning, William is relieved to find distraction in details of water flow, the impact of wind and current, the resistance of local stone versus imports. Gwynn has never had such an attentive colleague. They become so engrossed in their work that they continue through into the afternoon before realising they are sharp with hunger. They return to the inn for bread and cheese, washed down by tankards of small beer.

For the next three days, the two friends continue their collaboration. There is no space or time for thoughts of London, of debt and obligation. With each day of physical activity followed by a sound night's sleep, William is recovering a more positive spirit.

On Friday, as they enter the George for dinner, Gwynn stops to tap the barometer. 'Set fair, see, just like you my boy. It seems the weather marches in step with your better humour.'

William attempts a grateful smile.

'Perhaps you should extend your stay. Come I have something to share with you.'

Once settled at their favourite table, Gwynn pulls out a bound stack of correspondence from his coat pocket. 'See, even here I cannot entirely escape the Academy. We are still months from the Exhibition and already there is a storm brewing.'

William feigns a lack of interest. 'Since I am merely an Engraver, I am not privy to all your squabbles.'

'So, you have no interest in the latest *contretemps*?'

William accepts the tease with a grin.'Tell me.'

'So, the painting in preparation by Signor Zoffany to celebrate the Academy. a drawing session, from the life, with all the academicians...'

'A swollen-headed commission, if ever there was one.'

'The King himself approves of it.'

'Ahh.' William says. 'And does his Queen approve of the exclusion of the fair Angelica and Moser's daughter Mary, the Academy's only two female members?'

'So you did know about this already!

'Rumour finds her way, even into my dark world.'

'Well, I have had an incessant stream of notes upon the matter.' Gwynn taps his correspondence.

'What is the honourable conclusion?'

'The ladies will appear, but as portraits hanging on the wall.'

William sneers. 'They may watch but not in person ?'

'His intention was to spare the ladies any-'

'-Nakedness? And yet they can spend hours studying Herculean hulks in bronze and marble with nothing left to the imagination.'

'Well, *apropos*.' Gwynn says. 'I have had words from Angelica and her father. They were in Ireland until Christmas, so at some distance from events but she appoints me her eyes and ears. She is sensitive of her reputation after that fiasco of a marriage.' Gwynn takes a final mouthful of his pie and pushes his plate away from him. He stays silent for a moment longer than he might, provoking William to look his friend in the eye.

'You have more to tell me? Gwynn. I know that look. Come, out with it.' He reaches forward to seize some of the folded letters, before Gwynn can stop him.

'What's this? More *billets doux* from the fair Angelica?'

'She trusts me. Lord knows, there are some that would feed the scandal mongers with morsels every week.'

'"*We are arriving Saturday.*" What's this ?'

'Ah, well, yes. I said I had something to share.'

William goes to rise.

'Sit down, you fool. Let me explain.' He pulls William back into his chair. 'Despite appearances, I am not all consumed by mud and bricks and mortar. I have a head on my shoulders and while you were hung out to dry by your Company nabobs I have been doing some thinking on the case. And I can see an interesting match.'

'Match?'

'No, wrong word. A symmetry perhaps, an artistic collaboration.'

'She is an artist. I am an engraver... a publisher of engravings.'

'There. You have it one.' Gwynn takes a swig of cider. 'So, I have invited her, and her father to Oxford. They arrive tomorrow on the afternoon coach, provided the mud doesn't swallow them up.'

'I am inclined to make you its first victim. You damned rogue... We have nothing prepared for them, no rooms, no dinner... no introductions.'

'Calm yourself, William. They are not royalty, though they spend enough time in its company. And they **are** delightfully connected to the beau monde. As soon as I made the suggestion, her father replied, "We have a friend who teaches music at one of the colleges." They are all cared for. They will stay in college rooms as honoured guests, no doubt invitations to Chapel will follow, requests to paint the Warden's portrait et cetera. We shall visit them the day after they arrive. I thought otherwise they would be too exhausted. So, now you know.'

At five o'clock the following afternoon, the two friends are in New College Lane, approaching the porter's lodge. They have been invited to a reception in Angelica's honour. William has salvaged his smartest topcoat and clean breeches for the occasion. He brushes a trace of dried Cherwell mud off Gwynn's wig. 'A badge of honour?'

'As good as any... Now remember, I will look after Papa Johann, while you make your case to Angelica. Remember she is a lover of History Painting. History, history, history, that is your entrée.'

William nods, though his mind is not on the distant past. At dawn he was all but overwhelmed by another wave of grief that left him numbed, entirely without spirit. Yet here he is, in need of a performance. His future is at stake. Oh if only young Strutt was here. He could expound on the life of every King and Queen, Saxon, Norman, Tudor... He'd give her chapter and verse. But perhaps that is not what Angelica seeks. *Andromache weeping over the death of Hector, Penelope alone, fending off the suitors* ... these are more her style.

The sound of a quartet greets them as they are guided around the quadrangle, and up a staircase towards the Founders Library. Excitement is building among their fellow-guests. William listens to the babble.

'I believe she may sing for us tonight.'

'She is a painter, Eustace.'

'No, but I hear that she has a delightful soprano.'

'From Austria?'

'Swiss, I think.'

'Still, from the mountains?'.

'Indeed.'

To these dewy-eyed folk, Angelica is a lustrous comet passing through their world for a day or two. Her arrival has been foretold, just as her presence will be dissected and much discussed. After all she is one of London's most sought after society portrait artists and a founding member of the Royal Academy. But for William these accomplishments are more than talking points, they are markers of a shared ambition. He is still *Engraver to the King*, though he fears his recent bankruptcy may well have cast an irrevocable shadow.

As he moves up the reception line, he catches a glimpse of Angelica's auburn curls, and nut brown eyes, glittering with laughter. And there is Papa Johann, ever watchful beside his daughter. He is bearded, stiff-backed, protective but not proprietorial. William is grateful when dear Gwynn steps forward to engage Papa in conversation. Now it is his turn. He bows to Angelica, who inclines her head.

'William, how wonderful to see you here. Gwynn did tell me that you help him with his little bridge.'

'I have become closely acquainted with Oxford mud.'

She smiles and in the instant William knows why her fellow-painters, from Nath Horne to the illustrious Joshua Reynolds are smitten by her. She has perfected the art of making everyone feel they are the only person of consequence in the room. Both flattery and charm are on her social palette. 'We are the last six months in Ireland. Rain and wind we know them well. But I would travel across continents to see my friends.'

'Loyalty indeed.'

'It is the deepest bond, do you not agree, William? Friendship I mean.'

'True, there are others which may prove more fragile.'

Seeing her blush, he curses himself for the unintended jibe. 'Forgive me, I was referring to my own most difficult situation.'

'Oh, do not apologise, I am accustomed to wear my feelings... how do you say?'

'On your sleeve?' William says.

'Yes, I think of it often when I am painting.' She wafts her left hand gently in the air. 'Without feelings, how should we know the truth?

It is William's turn to colour up. She allows him a moment before offering some balm. 'My condolences for your father and your recent... difficulties. A double blow, so unkind.'

'More lessons in life.'

'You do well to spend your time with Gwynn. He is a master in such lessons.' They both glance across to see their mutual friend still in fluent conversation. 'He will make a bridge-builder of my father before the night is out.'

William laughs and moves along, to allow another guest her moment in Angelica's company. He spends the next hour engaging with wise clerics and town worthies, who are delighted to meet another artist with Royal connections. It is a relief to speak of matters other than the East India Company. By the time the Dean announces a tour of the Cloisters and the Chapel's fine medieval stained glass, William's spirits have been well fortified by mulled wine. He sees Angelica looking out at the ancient city wall. 'A worthy setting for a work of history perhaps?'

'Indeed,' she replies, 'it is all around us here. These stones have borne witness to so much.' She turns and holds his gaze. 'I have heard the Queen speaks highly of your work, the Cotes, the Coronation portrait.'

'I am indebted to them. They sold well.'

At this instant, Papa Johann approaches, carrying Angelica's fur lined wrap. He acknowledges William with a brief bow.

'Oh Papa, you go on. I believe I will stay awhile, in the warm. Besides you know we saw the glass the last time we were here.'

'As you wish, Angel.' With a nod to William, Papa sets off downstairs.

Angelica is all smiles. 'His Majesty has a passion for history. He has been most supportive of the Academy.'

'Provided such rascals as myself, the engravers and the print sellers are kept out.'

She raises an eyebrow. 'You have your shop. On Cornhill... Oh. I am sorry has that gone too?'

William switches tack. 'I find it remarkable that you, a Swiss, have delved so deeply into our old stories. I saw your painting of Rowena, the Saxon princess, seducing the King of the Britons. Is that another of life's lessons?'

'A trifle extreme, but a lover's motives are not always easy to discern. And yes, I do paint from some experience.' This time there is no flush in her cheeks, no flinching from his gaze. He offers his arm and they walk farther into the room, which runs the length of the College quadrangle. William searches for another historical approach. 'I had an apprentice once, Joseph Strutt...'

She laughs in recognition. 'The Antiquarian? Studying at the Academy?'

'The very man. He spends every waking hour searching for old coins, inscriptions, Viking runes, Saxon swords.'

'I adore that in him. He says we must not let the Greeks and Romans have all our attention. English heroes and heroines were not so very different in their lives and loves.'

'Such feelings are more easily conveyed through history ?' William asks.

'They are universal among us.'

'And our more recent champions? West's Death of General Wolfe?'

'Oh, I am all for it. Benjamin is entirely right to set it in modern dress. There are enough classical tales in gowns and togas. If history is being made today, we should celebrate it as such.'

In these first exchanges, the artist and the engraver test the ground between them. She is keen to know more about the stipple technique which William learned in Paris. Soon a plan emerges for collaboration. It is to begin in time for the Academy's Spring Exhibition. William's yearning for commercial success sits well with Angelica's desire to find a wider market, particularly for her history paintings.

When their fellow guests return and find them still deep in conversation, there are more than a few jealous glances and whispered comments.

'I must release you back to your admirers.' William says. Though I doubt they will ever forgive my monopolising your company.'

'Oh, I am just another butterfly in their garden. I will be forgotten as soon as another, more colourful, alights!'

'You are too modest. But it is only fair to relieve your father from Gwynn's lessons in masonry.' With that William bids her farewell and sets off to find his dear friend to tell him all.

The moon is full over Magdalen Tower as William escorts an inebriate and swaying Gwynn along the High Road. 'See how the Bridge has entirely disappeared beneath the flood.' Gwynn says. 'This will be the devil of a task.'

'And I thought you had exhausted your bridge talk this evening.'

Gwynn laughs. 'Signor Kauffmann? It was a pleasure. Whether he would say the same I cannot tell, but he is no buffoon and will be watching your every step. And his daughter?

'I followed your advice. History, history history... and it is most certainly her passion. She is keen for us to combine forces.'

Gwynn stops for a moment. 'Excellent. I thought as much. So where are you to begin ?'

'Two of her Saxon heroines. I will draw them first and show them at your Academy's Spring Exhibition. As a statement of intent, a promise of line engravings to come.'

'Ingenious.' Gwynn says reaching to his friend for support. The wine is still at work.

But William's energy is now up. 'And we are agreed to play the Royal card. Her '67 painting '*Queen Charlotte raising the genius of fine art.*'

'Wise flattery! Though be aware the Angel is much sought after. You are not alone. Her Papa mentioned Bartolozzi, Sandby...'

'Time is short, so it will be mezzotint. I shall engage Burke, the young Irishman, to deliver it. He is most suited to her work and knows there will be more to follow.'

'So... you see ... there is life after India.' Gwynn says. And the two friends continue up the High Road.

Chapter 22

'London is about to go Angelica-mad. And you, Thomas Burke, mezzotinter of Dublin, shall be in at the start of this.'

The Irishman in question is trying to stop his right leg tapping out of control beneath the studio table. He is by nature a discreet, serious individual with high cheek bones and furrowed forehead. But now he is all smiles. After all it is the King's Engraver who addresses him. And when needs must, William knows how to play to his reputation. He has already revealed that they will be sharing this space with two Fellows of the Royal Academy. His friend Gwynn, the architect and Samuel Wale, a draughtsman.

'I will work night and day if I must.' Thomas assures him.

'Well, you mezzos have half the work done for you. All you do is scrape to create your chiaroscuro...'

Young Thomas' brow hesitates on the edge of a frown, but William is quick with a compliment. 'I saw your portrait of the Chevalier... a fine piece. An excellent likeness.'

'You know him, the Chevalier d'Eon?'

'We have had dealings in the past. It is in all our interests that they remain so.'

'Is it true he dresses as a woman?'

William is momentarily set back. His laugh is awkward. 'Is that what they say in Dublin?'

'No... only since I am in London, I have heard. When I scraped Huquier's *Chevalier*, they said it would sell so well because of all the wagers on his sex.'

'Well. Rumour often misses her target. And does much damage in the attempt. Never more so than in London. I suggest you keep your mind on Angelica and this work in hand. We want no scandal here.'

At this, William reveals a sketch by Angelica. 'Now you must know I am not set against mezzo. When speed is of the essence, you have that advantage. And this mezzotint must be ready for The Exhibition. Go to Miss Angel's studio, in Golden Square, in two days' time. I will see to it that her '*Queen Charlotte*' is there for you. Once we are begun, I will teach you another technique. The stipple, I learned in Paris from Demarteau. The soft light and shade is a joy, just like chalk. Makes my cross hatching seem an exhaustion of time. But that is for the future. For now, do we have an agreement?'

'That we have.'

Burke's demands are not excessive but times have changed since ten years back when Woll won his £100 for graving the Niobe. Boydell made some 8000 guineas from that print, so of course the gravers now want their reward.

On St George's Day, 23rd April, William secures a copy of the Morning Post. He brings it back in triumph to show Mary and the children.

'See Mary. *The Queen raising the Genius of the Arts*, painted by the Royal Academician Angelica Kauffmann, engraved by Thomas Burke and printed by William Ryland, Engraver to the King is now on sale at all distinguished publishers ...'

'No longer at Cornhill, the shop?'

'In all but name the shop is gone...Triquet will not pay beyond May.... We must move on...'

'After five years...' Mary sighs and goes back to brushing Charlotte's hair, with a force that provokes her daughter's cries.

The following day he is at the Academy Exhibition. Old Samuel Wale, Gwynn's friend, is on the hanging committee this year. It has served William well. His drawings of Angelica's recent works are well placed to promote his planned engravings. But, as expected, the chief interest is in Zoffany's Portrait of an Academy Drawing Class. Miss Moser and dear Angelica remain as portraits on the wall looking down at the self-important gathering of male artists.

'At least Gwynn and Samuel have their moment...' William turns to find the Angel on his shoulder. She continues tersely. '...Though we are as ever on the outside looking in...'

To move on to less conflicted ground, William invites her to view Benjamin West's latest history painting. It features William Penn the founder of Pennsylvania...surrounded by natives.

'This time Ben has his father and half-brother in the frame but you know that he charges for inclusion?'

'I wonder what he took from the Indians?' Angelica is decidedly not in the best of humours.

'Even in the Wolfe, he did the same. Some of those soldiers were nowhere near him at his death.'

'So', she sighs, 'we must take such histories with a pinch of snuff.'

'They belong to the victors and the patrons.'

'It is all theatre is it not' She wanders off, leaving William uncertain whether to follow or allow her space to vent elsewhere.

Just then he is relieved to see Gwynn, back from Oxford for the opening. He is as ever irrepressible. 'Greetings, greetings. And rumours too my boy. It seems Boydell is close to an engraving deal with West and Woollett...'

'For the Penn?

'No, no, for *the Death of Wolfe*... but it is such a deal. Woll demands 500 guineas. To afford that, even Boydell needs more subscribers. Which is where you come in.'

William raises an eyebrow but Gwynn persists.

'Truth is you still have a clientele. Do a deal with Boydell and you will see the guineas come home by the thousand. Mark my words.'

'Said the impoverished bridge builder.'

Gwynn bows. 'At least, I am pleased to see the Kauffmann collaboration is under way.'

'Yes. He has done excellent work the Irish mezzo.'

John Boydell's fear of wasting a moment of his time has not improved with age. He would prefer to meet in his second floor office, so as not to disrupt his daily schedule. He is after all London's premier print seller. But William is equally determined to show that he is not coming cap in hand, for favours. They settle on a back room at the Coffee House near Boydell's shop in Cheapside. Given that they are to discuss the engraving of West's *Death of Wolfe*, William is expecting Woll to be there. But Boydell is alone. He is as brusque as ever. 'All hail the bankrupt engraver.'

In other circumstances William would have risen to the jibe. But needs must. His jaw tightens around the slightest of smiles. Not that Boydell really cares.

'Oh my boy. Tis a badge of honour. You are not the first and you will not be the last. The fact your guarantors agreed to the bankruptcy, speaks highly of your integrity'.

William bows sharply.

'Indeed I salute you,'

Boydell sits back down and gestures for William to do likewise. 'See, you were brave, you were right. The Indian market is just waiting to be born, it was unfortunate, the Famine, the squabbling nabobs, the .. the ..'

'The lack of a salesman.' William offers.

'Exactly my point. Mark my words we will make it happen.'

No doubt you will, William thinks.

'I see you have thrown in your hat with the fair Angelica.'

William nods. 'We have an agreement.'

'Excellent, but not exclusive?'

'A preference goes a long way, *n'est-ce pas*?' William is eager to move the subject along. 'How is your French, *Monsieur*?'

'While trade prospers, I have more occasion to use it. But now, sir, on to matters of mutual interest. The Death of *Wolfe*. Young Benjamin is eager and Woll is the man to grave it but after my success with the Niobe ...'

'8000 guineas is some success.' William says.

'Indeed, though Woll now demands a small fortune.'

'Rightly so. He puts his life and soul into every copper plate. Each one a torment to his wife.'

'You know she whelps only twins?' Boydell says, in an uncharacteristic diversion.

'I had heard yes.'

'Five sets of twins - this past decade. Sadly none have lived long... but I have done my best for them.'

William wonders how much of this is another ploy prior to negotiation. He comes to the point. 'So to accommodate Woll, how much do you intend to sell for? A guinea a print?'

'Yes and between us we must raise...'

'If I am in.'

Boydell's laugh is harsh. 'What choice do you have, your arse is barely out of the debtor's den?'

'For which I am eternally grateful to my guarantors...How long does Woll say he needs?'

'That's the worry. Three years. He will etch at first and only once he is content will he line engrave.'

'It is his style and very successful too. '

'So are you in, William ? I hide nothing from you. You will have a third of all takings. We need your subscribers. Your name, Your title.'

William purses his lips. To let his old rival wait a little longer is tempting but to what end? If he can make guineas on his former good name and contacts then so be it.

'You have it. Have it all, name, title, the willing buyers. And may the muses bring their blessings down on us.'

The lease ends on the Cornhill shop in late May. William cannot bring himself to see the empty windows or the discarded frames. But he does insist on the return of the sign of the King's Arms, hung high above the shop with such gaiety just five years earlier. It is Jo Strutt who delivers it to him in a crate. William greets him with a laugh.

'I am not one to mourn the head of a king! Though I still appreciate his pension. And today you find me in good spirits. I believe it is my birthday or thereabouts. Forty years on and still no gout!'

'Congratulations Master.'

They share a glass of wine as they contemplate the old sign. William's initial light-heartedness evaporates. 'We have sold so many of our plates and prints. And yet, you know, I still cannot repay my guarantors...'

'I am sure they understand.'

'Linnell thinks only of his gold, but James has been a mountain of strength.'

'You have my support at all times, Master.'

'Indeed, there is a specific, Jo, in which you could help. I believe the shop may not be the only casualty...'

William raises his eyes to the ceiling.

'Your house?' Strutt exclaims. 'Oh...Mary...'

'Yes. Mary. I must break the news gently to her. I am minded to move West, away from the noise and of course the cost...'

'To where?'

'My mind is not made up. There are many artists who enjoy the quieter pleasures along the river.'

Strutt's eyes widen. 'And there's a wealth of history that way too.'

'You are our instructor in all things antiquarian, I look forward to your visits but also ask your help in soothing Mary's concerns, if and when we are to move.'

'I am at your service.'

'Thank you. Now to celebrate these forty years.' He empties the bottle into Strutt's glass.

'The bailiffs did not discover my best Portuguese.'

If Genius fire the Reader, Stay

If Nature touch thee, drop a tear
If neither move thee, turn away
For Hogarth's honoured dust lies here.

The epitaph is freshly carved into a milky stone plaque, beneath two urns, now absorbing the warm light of a July evening. William stands before this tomb, this celebration of the engraver's engraver, William Hogarth. It is a moment of quiet, after a day spent further west among family and friends in Feltham, marking a year since his father's burial. He looks out over the Thames, past the Eyot covered in reeds to the city of London , now just a blur rising in the far distance. Behind him, Mary sits resting against the solid, stone walls of St Nicholas' Church. William gives voice to his thoughts.

'How he would have laughed at my arrogance, my ambition...the Indian Venture, Paris, Rome... His idea of the Grand Tour was to take a handful of comrades to the Isle of Sheppey and crawl from one drinking house to another. And why go to Italy indeed when one has the beauty here.'

Mary joins him at the tomb. She takes his hand.

'You know, Mary, I am jealous of Woll. I can trace the folds in skin and fabric, but he has the skills to take you to another place, to picture a landscape, such as this.'

She places her head on his shoulder. It is the reassurance he needs.

'Just to observe this scene, for me, is comfort enough.' she says. 'It reminds me of my beloved Lambeth.'

On their way home, they stop to change horses at the Bell and Anchor, by Hammersmith Turnpike. They have a good hour to wait, so they take their tankards and wander outside. The road heading west is lined by a straggle of houses and cottages. On the south side they can see down North End Road, bordered by fields running towards to the river. On the north side just beyond the tavern is the entrance to James Lee's Vineyard Nursery.

'Come let's explore,' Mary says.

There are acres of well-tended plants and glass houses. Mary finds one of the assistants and they are soon away, discussing the fruiting, flowering cycle of the exotic plants. She is in her element, until they are summoned back by the ostler's bad tempered hollering. But it does not destroy their mood. And in the carriage home it is Mary who raises the thought of a move west.

It takes another year, but by autumn in the year of our Lord, 1773, the deed is done. William finds a small house just to the south of the Turnpike, within walking distance of the Vineyard. The family are delighted. There are schools nearby with space for the children to run wild. They are happy. Friends come to visit. He has a studio built in the garden, which she fills with plants recommended by James Lee himself.

It is a new beginning. Though William cannot escape all ties with his creditors and those who ran with him into the Indian venture. In desperation, William commits to paying both his former guarantors £100 each a year, for the rest of his life. His hopes now rest on two sources of income. He has his share in Woll's *Death of General Wolfe*, whenever it is finished. And his collaboration with Angelica proceeds apace.

Chapter 23

October 1773

'William. Mary-Anne. Come in now, on the instant. It is time to go.'

Mary is standing at the door of the new house. There is no sign of her two youngest children and they are due to leave so soon. 'Oh my, what have I produced?'

She turns her back with a despairing shrug, watched by her eldest daughter Mary-Charlotte, who is fourteen, an age when the practice of restraint weighs heavily, the bitter price of being the eldest. 'They are never ready.'

At that moment young Will bursts through the door on all fours with a bloodthirsty roar. He is swiftly followed by Mary-Anne, who leaps on to his back with arms spread, like a bird of prey. 'Is it true,' he shouts, 'that Mr Hunter has lions in his garden...?

'and tigers and elephants?' adds Mary-Anne.

'Now please, you two, just because you are going to visit wild animals, does not mean you must behave as one.'

'That's what Josiah told me.' says Mary-Anne. 'And an eagle sits on his fence and pecks out your eyes if you don't feed him pieces of meat.'

'Oh my!' says Mary, not sure who to believe.

'Josiah told me that too and he knows everything...' says young Will.

Mary shakes her head and hands out their coats. 'Well, your friend Mr Strutt may know more than most but he also speaks a good deal of stuff and nonsense.'

There is a knock at the door.

'Ah, speaking of the devil.' Mary smiles.

'Good morning, children.'

'Good morning, Josiah.'

'Your expert on stuff and nonsense has arrived.'

Mary cannot help herself and she too creases up with a grin. 'Now you know Jo...'

'Fear not Madame Ryland. I will not corrupt your children's minds a moment longer. Strictly the facts today. But the truth is yes you must feed the Eagle.'

'Told you! told you!'

'But with fish.' Jo frowns. 'Please children the facts.'

At that Will and Mary-Anne flap their wings and descend on poor Charlotte who has been demoted to a fish. They chase her out of the room, avoiding her attempts to swipe at them with her book.

Minutes later William comes downstairs. Oblivious to all the commotion. He is dressed in black as is customary but today he has allowed himself the indulgence of a fine blue silk waistcoat. The choice is not lost on Mary. It is not new, it is a legacy of his days in Paris. Though she understands it is appropriate. They are invited to tea with gentlefolk. Angelica Kauffman and her friend Anne Hunter, who lives nearby.

'So, are we all set, ready and correct? We are to take the carriage at the Bell and Anchor by the Turnpike. Angelica has arranged it.'

'Oh, Angelica...'says one of the 'eagles' rushing back through the room swooping and whooping.

'Oh Angelica,' shouts another 'eagle'.

'Will she be there today Papa?'

'She is very beautiful, is she not Mama?'

'She is a lady, Mary-Charlotte. I suggest you behave yourself if you would like to become one too.'

'She speaks French and Italian and German, does she not Papa?'

Mary's glance to William is as sharp as ice. 'And English, else you and I would have little to say to her, my girl!'

'But Papa speaks Italian with her.'

William blushes and raises an eyebrow at his son. He sets off towards the gate. 'Now, tell me, where is this coach... ?'

On the short journey to Earl's Court, William and Mary keep their own counsel, while Jo Strutt continues to entertain the children.

'Our hostess Anne is married to the great surgeon, Dr Hunter. They say he can whip off a leg in just ten seconds.'

'Sliced and diced,' shouts young Will.

'Sliced and diced,' echos Mary-Anne.

Strutt puts his fingers to his lips. 'Hush children. Or you will end up in one of his displays. He is a great collector of bones, Dr Hunter. His brother taught us anatomy at the Academy.'

'Now then Mr Strutt.' Mary tut-tuts. 'A little less of the detail if you please.'

Strutt raises one eyebrow in the manner the children all adore. It is clear that he knows more than their dear mother.

Mary has the last word. 'As a Collector of ancient Bones I believe you and Dr Hunter will have much in common.'

Again the eyebrow is raised and the children giggle.

They are not disappointed at the large and imposing stone mansion just off Earl's Court Lane. As for the wild animals, they are not immediately apparent but there are suspicious grunts, which Mary-Anne and Will are convinced indicate sleeping tigers.

Angelica and Anne are there to greet them, with apologies from Dr Hunter who has been detained on some surgical business.

'Another cadaver perhaps,' whispers Strutt a little too loudly in young Will's ear.

' He assures me that the bear is safely housed,' Anne explains, 'if the children would like to explore.'

'If you are sure it is safe?' Mary replies with some alarm.

'Oh yes,' Anne says. 'Though our neighbours have only just descended from their roof, where they took refuge, last night.'

'Oh my...' Mary is now quite pale.

'My dear, I jest. He has not escaped yet and I have warned John, that he must never do so.'

'Quite right,' says Mary, glancing around her. Though the wildest beast she can see is a green parrot in a tree above her. 'We did not have such outlandish creatures in Lambeth...'

Leaving the children to explore under the watchful eye of Mr Strutt, the ladies of the house invite Mary and William into the beautifully appointed salon. Its walls are hung with mirrors and portraits of Anne's parents and John's father.

Anne is a gracious hostess. She is tall, elegant, soft spoken, observant. When she compliments Mary on her shawl, which is quite simple, it is done with genuine affection. Where Anne is strong and calm, Angelica is more brittle, but passionate and full of enthusiasms. In nature, William thinks, Anne could be a mountain lake, delightful in its surface ripples, masking hidden depths. While Angelica is a bustling stream of bright water, always catching the light.

Soon their conversation shifts from reminiscence to Anne's current concern: the crisis building in the American colonies. She speaks of the native people, the originals, she calls them. She recalls the dignity of one of their leaders who recently attended one of her salons.

'There were some who treated him as an exhibit, but his own observations put our shallow imaginations to shame. He had more expression in his eyes than anyone observing him. We must always challenge that which constricts, must we not?'

All present nod, perhaps not quite sure how they may achieve this, but the sentiment is shared. 'Come, let me show you our portion of the great outdoors... I know that you are an orchard girl, Mary..?'

As Mary and Anne disappear into the orchard, Angelica engages William. 'How goes your life in the country?'

'Ah, it suits me well. A part of me....'

'... The mezzos are selling?'

'They are...and Thomas does fine work -'

'- you know that Bartolozzi and Spilsbury have been knocking upon my door, requesting access to my paintings. They are pushing to work in stipple, but I say, there, you are the master.'

William bows. 'I was fortunate to learn from Demarteau.'

'Well I have a thought, very much of the moment...On my way here to see dear Anne, it came to me. You remember my Pensive Muse, in memory of General Stanwix' daughter. That poor family were much in my mind last year when I made the same crossing from Ireland. What you may not know is that my inspiration was Anne's own poem, inspired by their loss at sea.'

'So the woman with flowers, clasping the urn... it is Anne's profile, not yours...'

'She has a much finer nose, do you not think?' Angelica turns to reveal the line.

'I assure you, they are both fine but different.'

'You have spent too long in salons, Mr Ryland...but to the point. The story is now very much in the public news because the General's will has been challenged in the courts. I made an etching. Can you work from this to create your stipple?'

'You always have an eye to opportunity.'

'We artists must know our market.'

'Too true,' William smiles. 'It will distract my mind from Woll's endless delays with the *Death of Wolfe*. We have missed our promise to the subscribers.'

'He still has some months to go?'

'Years even. I now measure his progress in twins'

'How so?' Angelica asks.

'His poor wife has already had three pairs, of whom sadly only two girls survive.'

'Hush! You know that Anne and John lost their first borne.'

'Even the illustrious surgeon?'

'He is a physician not a worker of miracles.' She looks around to make sure she is not overheard. 'Anne tells me he keeps the most irregular hours and comes home with the most distressing of ailments.'

'She has the patience of a saint.'

'So, you will consider it, the stipple?'

'Your Pensive Muse is now mine.'

'Excellent I do believe this will lead to many great things for you William,' she touches his arm just briefly.

At that moment Anne and Mary return from the garden. Angelica withdraws her hand but it has been noticed.

That night when the children are dreaming of cockatoos and hedgehogs and bears, William attempts to explain to Mary. 'She has spent too long in Italy.'

'Then I should read nothing into it, when I see you pawed and fawned upon?'

'It was hardly fawning. I was being offered a new painting to grave. No more.'

Indeed, he is himself unsure of what is at play. If there is dalliance, he cannot quite grasp its consequence. His thoughts as ever are on the material. The luxury of a Bloomsbury mansion still looms large in his mind.

'Mary, we should count ourselves fortunate. That we can have such folk as friends. You and Anne are of the same mind I believe, a love of all that fruits and flowers?'

'Tis true, *she* has no airs and graces.'

Over the coming months, William spends his time in Hammersmith. He converts one room into a studio and applies himself to the stipple. He still has the tools which Demarteau gave him in France. Each afternoon he works at the plate, gouging out patterns of dots to produce the tone he is after. He installs Pa's heavy printer and experiments with coloured inks to evoke the emotion in Angelica's work.

On Thursdays he travels into Leicester Fields, where young Thomas Burke works alongside him on more of Angelica's history pieces. The young Irishman is a swift learner and soon he is also taking up the stipple technique. These visits are also an opportunity see his old friend Gwynn. He is a dogged follower of the story unfolding on the far side of the Atlantic.

'I am no friend of the East India Company. That they have lost a cargo of tea in Boston Harbour does not dampen my spirits but, mark my words, this is just the beginning, a much greater falling off will follow.'

'The French will meddle?'

'Like as not. They are still out for revenge from '63. Old King Louis must pass on soon, who knows what the new one has in mind.'

Gwynn disappears back behind his paper. To William, the fiasco of his own involvement with the secret plans for a French invasion, seems so distant as to belong to another world. The growing resistance by the American colonists could change all that.

'Do you still see the Chevalier d'Eon?' William asks, as casually as he can muster.

'Oh we cross paths,' Gwynn mutters, 'but I cannot abide his constant harping on about the dire treatment he suffers from his compatriots. He wishes to go home but refuses every opportunity to do so. It seems his people are still refusing to pay his debts. So there is a stalemate.'

The paper drops, as Gwynn continues. 'You know there are more rumours about the Chevalier.'

'Come now, Gwynn, if d'Eon decides that on occasion he is more at ease in a domino or gown, I will not be one to mock. He is a masquerader. I could say the same about half the Lords in London.'

'True,' Gwynn says. 'But remember, should you know more than you might, there are guineas to be won.'

'That is not my style. You should know that. All I will say to the matter is that the French... do things differently.'

'To coin a phrase.'

'*Exactement.*'

On his way home to Hammersmith, William fears he will never escape his past. Though it has been many years, he does still yearn for the freedom of his days in Paris. Since Gabrielle's death, he has lost touch with his old friends Jean-Jaques and Lizabeth Le Bas. There was a letter soon after his return, to reassure him that Gabrielle's daughter is safe, but no news since then of her health or reaction to her mother's death.

His own distractions and perhaps a need to shelter himself from his own grief have kept him from writing back.

In April, William takes his latest stipple proof to Angelica's studio in Golden Square. He has added the mournful lines of Anne Hunter's poem and a dedication: *In memory of General Stanwix daughter*. Papa Johann greets him at the door:

'Ah William, I hope you are the bearer of good news.'

'Bitter-sweet Herr Kauffmann, bitter-sweet.'

He pulls out the proof to show him.

'Ah yes, of course. Fine work, for such a sad tale.'

A peal of laughter reaches them from the studio room upstairs.

'My daughter!' Johann raises a thick grey eyebrow. 'Come, she will lighten your mood. There is not much that dampens her spirits. Particularly when she is with friends.'

They enter the studio. 'I believe you know, Mrs Anne Hunter?'

'Yes, of course.' William bows. 'We are country neighbours. I have become very well acquainted with her profile.'

'Quite so,' replies Johann, somewhat bemused. 'I will leave you to your discussions.'

There is another peal of laughter.

'Shh - he does not know,' says Angelica once the door is closed.

'That Anne is your muse.' William says.

'No. I mean, yes!'

It is William's turn to raise a darker, thinner eyebrow.

'So, Ladies. The cause of your hilarity? I had been expecting a solemn review of my funerary urn and instead I find myself in a burlesque.'

'Well, maestro. Anne, my dear friend and muse, is helping me choose the works I intend to submit for this month's Academy exhibition. See, here, I have *The nymph Calypso saying farewell to Ulysses.*'

'Exquisitely sad,' says Anne, her head tilted to one side.

'Perhaps not so sad for his wife?' Angelica adds

William laughs. 'True, but Calypso is releasing him.'

'And here we have the wicked pair,' Anne continues. 'Paris and Helen encouraging Cupid to shoot his darts at them. Oh what chaos that little urchin causes...'

'So, what say you, maestro? Angelica giggles. 'Cupid or Calypso?'

William pauses to consider, then delivers his verdict. 'Methinks, they should both enter the ring. You have there the beginning of love and its ending. A double appeal.'

Angelica snorts in disapproval. 'A commercial judgement, that.'

'I should not wish to see you starve, Angelica.'

'How kind.'

'And now, I must reveal the other side of love...' He pulls out the proof and sets it on the easel. '...when it is lost.'

'Oh William it is also exquisitely sad,'Anne sighs. 'I did not know I could be so!'

Angelica is delighted. 'The heart-strings will be, how you say, tugged, by this will they not?'

William sits down on the chaise-longue to observe his work. He is exhausted.

'Congratulations Master William.'

He acknowledges their approval with a nod. 'Well the inspiration is of course in the original, and the muse.'

'Now we shall share in the success shall we not?' Angelica is all abuzz with excitement. 'We need to decide where and when it will be sold. For now, I too have a little surprise.'

She points William towards another easel which is leaning back against the wall, draped in a cream cloth.

'A cloth?' he asks.

'William! Go. Look.'

He eases the cloth to one side. Underneath there is a narrow wooden frame. Pulling the covering back even further he finds an engraving of a London street scene. He reads out the inscription: '*Old Somerset House in the Strand. 1697*. It is sad the building is no longer in such good state.'

Angelica tosses her head. 'We have been using it as the Academy school for some time now. But we have plans, grand plans. A transformation. Look a little closer.'

William holds the print up to catch more light from the window. His attention is drawn to the row of buildings facing the Strand just to the east of Somerset House. On one elegant facade, just above the door, someone has painted a minuscule golden crown... a shop sign.

Angelica is now looking over his shoulder. 'See, Number 159 - A fine location, is it not?

'For what, exactly?

'For your new print shop.'

'Ha ha, it is excellent. But, for a bankrupt?'

William's half-smile betrays him.

Angelica is delighted. 'I thought you might be tempted. Come, let us go there.'

'Now?'

'*Si, subito*! Gwynn is already there.'

'You have had all this planned? Angelica, I ...'

'Enough. You English, sometimes... Let me be, how you say, your gift horse. Come Anne, you too.'

'Within half of an hour, the three of them are stepping down into the Strand, just opposite the new church of St Mary. The street is wide, lined on both sides by grand facades, some five storeys high. The area is popular with jewellers, booksellers and furniture makers. Number 159 sits to the east of the main entrance to Somerset House. The window frames are in need of some work but inside it is spacious, well decorated and inviting. William pushes back a rising fear of past disasters and permits himself to dream again.

Chapter 24

I t is a tumultuous month. William slips into a frenzy of activity, with assistance from those friends who have remained loyal: Bailey, Gwynn, Jo Strutt, Angelica of course and Anne Hunter. To crown it all, the Stanwix print is ready. The final proof declares it published by William Wynne Ryland at 159, Strand.

The weight of bankruptcy is lifting. For stock he has relied on the favours of fellow engravers. Even Woll, still slaving over the *Death of General Wolfe,* supplies copies of his most successful landscapes.

His family join in the celebrations. Mary still has no desire to be part of the *beau monde* but it is through her endeavours that the shop itself has been transformed, made welcoming. She now instructs William's favourite printer, Hadrill. Her absence from Hammersmith has also given the children more freedom. 'At their age' she tells him, 'I was already looking after father and my sister.'

In that first month of May, their sales of the Stanwix memorial stipple are more than encouraging. Angelica is delighted. 'You know William, I have learned much from dear papa, but what touches the heart and opens the purse, I think that is something I have taught myself.'

Buoyed by this success they plan the next subjects for William to commission. Thomas is now working on both stipples and mezzotints. But there is one print that William needs finished more than any other. It has now been over two years since Woll began work on *Death of General Wolfe*. It is high time that William saw some proofs.

The weather is inclement. William's heavy coat is sodden. At least the rain dampens the summer stench of vegetables on the turn, in Covent Garden. He pushes open the gate into Denmark Court. A puddle forms around him, while he waits for Peter Hadrill, master-printer, to answer his knock on the door to No 12. Just as William knocks a third time, the gate behind him swings open.

'Ah, the devil is about his business and will not be disturbed eh?' It is William Woollett, Woll to his friends. He is bundled up against the downpour, clutching a thin portfolio to his ample frame in a vain attempt to keep it from the elements.

'Well, suffer no more, I have been here so often I took the liberty of acquiring a key from the landlord, who happens to sup at the same hostelry as my good self'.

He turns his key in the lock and ushers William inside. 'Come, let us surprise the dear fellow.'

They tiptoe up the narrow curving stairs like two conspiring school fellows. They cannot resist a whispered conversation.

'So how goes the Wolfe?' William asks, gesturing towards Woll's portfolio.

'What Wolfe?'

'Come now, do not tell me- '

'- Ha! Indeed. My every waking hour is spent with the General and his mournful men. I am so engrossed in his dying, I have become quite morose. There are times I feel it would be a blessed curse to join him in eternity.'

William grunts in sympathy as they make yet another turn.

'Only my good wife's condition prevents me.' Woll sighs.

'How goes the lying in?'

'No worse than before. This pair seem healthy beasts. They kick like mules but it is early days. Here we are.'

Woll pushes William forward into the room.

'Enter stage right, followed by a ghost! '

'Godsblood!' The expletive originates from the room next door to the one they have entered so unexpectedly. 'Who goes there?

'It is I, er, we,' says Woll. 'It is us, dear Peter. Come to beard thee in thy papery lair.'

The response is a little softer in tone. 'Ah, gentlemen. I will be with you in a brief moment. I am giving birth to one more proof and I am almost done.'

William and Woll are entirely at home in a room cluttered with stacks of paper of all sizes and thickness, bottles of ink, black and red on the shelves, all lit by a skylight, now rattling under the constant battering of rain drops. They remove their dripping coats. Woll carries them into a side room. When he returns, he finds William already delving into his slim portfolio. 'Patience, master Ryland. The General is not to be rushed.'

'Ha! No that's true. What is it three years a-bed?'

'Nearly three years of toil, three years of ...

'... Wishing you were a mezzotinter ?' William says.

'Well, yes!'

'It is worth every stroke, I am sure. Come now, show us your latest...'

Woll removes his slither of copper plate from its wrapping and hands it to his old friend and fellow engraver. 'I can tell 'ee, old Boydell will have his money's worth.'

'And you and I stand to share a small fortune. Should this be the success it ought to be.'

Woll is silent, waiting for the response.

'Ah Woll, you are excelling yourself.' William smiles.

'Really?

'Really,' William says, handing back the plate. 'Provided you finish this decade.'

'Ah now that, is in the hands of the Gods, the Muses, and the good health of my dear wife.'

A few minutes later, Peter Hadrill, finally steps briskly into the room. He is of middling height and stature but his face is made so distinctive by high cheekbones, mutton chop whiskers and grey-blue eyes that these are the only features he needs to command attention. William has the sense that he is constantly sizing people up, wondering what their image might look like run under the heavy roller of his printing press.

Woll shows him the latest lines on the copper plate. Peter examines the details with his loupe, leans back and passes comment with a straight face. 'If I had not known it was you Woll, I would have declared a Master had been at work.'

Woll laughs. He turns to William and declares, 'I would not work with anyone else!'

All three know they have something most special emerging here. It is nearly dusk when the working session draws to a close. Woll takes his leave, but William tarries a few minutes longer.

'It is a master-work but really how much longer can we allow him? We are struggling with subscribers and still nothing to show.'

'He lives and breathes this plate.' Peter says, wiping traces of ink off his hands. 'Just last week we was in the Turks Head and half way through the evening, myself and my boys were laughing about the latest madness from the Colonists across the water... and Woll lifts his head and says "*what is all your merriment*?" And I says where have you been dear Woll and he says "*Oh I was wondering which direction I should grave the lines for the General's coat.*"

William laughs. 'Well, I for one will be grateful the day I hear him fire that cannon from his roof.'

'I wager it will be another year.'

'We could have lost an Empire, by then.'

'You think it will come to that, the Americas?' asks Peter.

'It is coming to a head.'

''Twas always thus.' Peter muses. 'Where there are fortunes to be made and lost.'

William shakes his head. 'I burned my fingers in the East. I will not be chasing guineas in the West.'

'General Wolfe will do you proud.' Peter assures him 'Another year. You will see.'

After William takes leave of Hadrill, he wanders across broad Southampton Street and among the market traders closing down their stalls in Covent Garden.

'Come buy, young man, come buy ... all has to go... all the goodness, half the price ... come ladies, for a ha'penny!'

But William is not thinking about buying, his mind is a-buzz with how he too can sell more. There is relief that the Wolfe engraving has all the makings of a success. Anxiety, too, because he needs funds to commission more works from his own menagerie of stipplers and mezzotinters. Again he needs money in hand to put money on the wall. Over the coming months he renews old acquaintances in the coffee-houses around the Exchange. These men would never dream of venturing around the Cape to India, to make their fortune. They are *habitués* of the smart salons, observers of the rising, newly-moneyed gentry. As he settles into their company and sees how their funds can fuel his ambition, William does wonder how they sleep at night. Sometimes when the conversation becomes saturated in figures and calculations, he daydreams of his new friends in Hammersmith, content with tending their gardens. He has no illusions about the world of paper money and its obsessions. But for now that is not his concern. He takes their investment and begins to re-build his portfolio of prints.

Chapter 25

1775

A meeting is called at Hadrill's printing works. When William arrives, he is met by Joseph, the printer's assistant, who warns him that his master's modest room is now cramped with the interested parties: John Boydell and Mary his niece, who now helps to run her uncle's Cheapside printshop and Woll the engraver. He has put on more weight. His cap sits not so jauntily on his mop of hair.

As senior partner in the group, Boydell calls them all to order. 'It has been four years that I am paying Woll's engraving fees. Our subscribers, those that have already put down a portion of their guineas, and even the painter himself, dear Benjamin, they are all running short of patience.'

His comments set off a coughing fit in Woll, that quite promises to carry the poor man away. His face is turning puce. Boydell, who fears contagion at the best of times, covers his face with a kerchief and waits for the fit to subside. Moments later, Woll attempts to explain the delay, between further bouts of coughing.

'... In a year, twas never possible ... we all knew it... staked my life and my health on this, as has my dear wife. Now I fear for her... three hearts a-beating in her belly. ...how many will make it into this world? .... A precious time, precious lives - so do not be saying that I sit at home with naught else on my mind than that Wolfe is dead... I shall not join him before I am ready. ...No, not for all the money in this hard world.'

William sees Mary Boydell has her shawl pulled up over her nose and mouth. He passes her a cotton kerchief, freshly washed, and raises his eyebrows, as if to say, this is not my doing. Even her uncle appears moved, though it is most likely due to fear of Woll's condition. The Alderman attempts to calm his man. 'Dear Woll. We all know this is remarkable work. Benjamin is more than delighted, it is just the question of time.'

'He must know how long it takes... he painted the damn thing did he not?'

The others concur with nods and murmurs, but Boydell wants a commitment. 'Come now, let us at least plan for an announcement. This side of Christmas? If you believe it's possible? Peter?'

'I think so, provided all goes smooth.'

'Well then, I suggest we inform our subscribers accordingly. Pray the Lord, the anticipation may tempt others in as well. The fear of missing out can be a great loosener of the purse strings, eh William?'

As they leave, Boydell invites Woll and William to join him for lunch. This is uncommon generosity and Boydell's awkward smile convinces William that something is awry.

Once inside the backroom of the Turks Head in Soho, Boydell is beaming. 'Come masters, let me insist on a hearty meal for your good selves. Eh Woll? You look like it would not go amiss.'

'Well, it is true that I do neglect myself in these times,' Woll says, with an eyebrow raised towards William.

'It must be hard with your wife abed…' Boydell, catching his niece's glance, hastily corrects himself … 'with child, I mean, of course…'

'Ah, indeed!' Woll replies with a smile. 'It is always thus, eh William? You are the same? The closer I reach to the final stroke, the more I wish to work my burin.' Seeing Boydell's deepening frown, Woll returns to a serious tone. 'Once the plate is with Hadrill, for the final proof, well that's an end to it. He has a touch, you know, that few have. Would trust my life with him. Not that it need go that far, eh?'

'Oh, yes, your printer. Now, I have something to-'

But before Boydell can ask his question, the server arrives. 'A pie for these young men and ales all round. Perhaps just some bread for me. My thanks. '

Their order taken, William still senses the unease in Boydell. Perhaps it is the lack of advance money. There are few subscribers so far, despite the popularity of Wolfe's story, the British hero, the soldier-martyr.

'So, now.' Boydell continues. 'I saw Mr Benjamin himself. Just yesterday.'

'Everything is still in accord?' asks Woll.

'Oh yes. We have his consent. He was accompanied by a good friend of his, of ours, the Italian, Signor Bartolozzi, a most accomplished graver.' Boydell pauses. 'Now, gentlemen, this is no easy matter for myself.'

Ah, William thinks, here it comes…Bartolozzi is a rival engraver, a man of undeniable talent already making his way in the stipple market with a factory of apprentices.

'Now it seems that Signor Bartolozzi is not quite of the same opinion as your good selves regarding Mr Hadrill.'

William raises his eyes at Woll. So, this smooth Italian is insinuating himself into their plans for the Wolfe. Boydell's confirmation is as curt as ever. 'Bartolozzi recommends replacing Hadrill with his most favoured printer, Mrs Hocquet, of Denmark Street.'

Woll's top lip trembles. 'I have seen five of my dear children pass away before me. Several have not lived on this earth as long as I have worked the Wolfe plate. So much time, so much love I have given it. I have worked it from every angle, and all for one final moment: the placing of the finished plate beneath the roller. It is an exchange of trust. Hadrill has worked with us for years. Bartolozzi knows nothing of what we do,' Woll stammers. 'Mrs Hocquet knows nothing of it neither. William, surely you cannot bear this too. Speak man, speak up.'

William is in shock. 'Hadrill is not the most tractable, but oh he is without doubt the best printer I have found in the fifteen years I have been back in England. With so much riding on such a prestigious print, one that is soon to be shown to the King, it is pure folly to hand it to Mrs Hocquet. However able, however highly recommended.'

But the Alderman holds fast. It is his money that is at stake. His choice of printer will therefore prevail.

By the time the dispute has simmered into a muted discomfort, their pies are cold, their appetite has gone and the lunch which began in such good spirits is soon at an end.

For many of their fellow Londoners the spring of 1775 is the point at which England's conflict with the American rebels turns bloody. For William and Woll, it marks the moment when they lost their own private battle. Despite their protestations, Alderman Boydell is adamant. 'Once Woll has the final version of the copper plate it will go to Mrs Hocquet's printing house.'

By the time that day dawns, Woll is so distraught he has become quite unwell. He can barely bring himself to hand the plate over to William. 'You know this is not right! To send the hero of Quebec, the man who drove out the French, to send this memory of his death to a French woman! I do not hold her origins against her, but surely it is not right? Damn Boydell, it is not right!'

William makes his way through the morning bustle of Covent Garden. He buys himself a sprig of blossom to lift his spirits. In Denmark Street, Madame Hoquet greets him with her young son beside her at the door. A woman of confident bearing and an easy manner, she invites him to attend but William cannot bear to be there a moment longer than is necessary. He gives her Woll's detailed instructions. He will pass the next day for a review.

'Fear not, Monsieur Ryland, you may trust me to deliver the finest proofs. The King himself will be proud.'

'We are in your hands, Madame. Goodbye, young man,' William says, in passing but the boy scowls back at him and disappears inside.

Madame Hocquet shakes her head. 'I am sorry, Monsieur. It is the age you know.'

'Indeed. Until the morrow then.' William bows as he turns to leave.

Now, there are many accounts of what happened that afternoon at the house of Madame Hocquet. There are some more reliable than others, but according to Joseph Matthews, apprentice to Mr Hadrill, who heard it from Woll himself, some days later, events transpired along the following lines.

Mrs Hocquet is preparing the plate for printing in the company of her son, who is accustomed to helping with the heavy rolling. Just as the plate is about to be laid into the printer bed, she is indisposed. Trusting her son to place the plate, she absents herself for some minutes. On her return she hears the most distressing sounds... a banging of metal against metal, amid the cries of her son "*So General Wolfe is dying ... and I'll be damned if I do not kill him quite...*" She rushes through the door to see her son wielding a hammer and bringing it down with mighty force on to the copper, on to the head of the already martyred General Wolfe...

'*Non! Non! Non! Mais tu es fou ! Jean qu'est ce que tu fais!!! Non! Vas-ton!*'

Seizing the hammer she threatens her own son with a blow, sending him howling back into the next room as she looks in horror at the catastrophe he has wrought on the precious engraving. She collapses on to the floor.

'Oh what am I to do! *Monstre*! What do you do! What ? They bash my head too for this, oh cruel boy... *méchant*!'

From the next room comes a sobbing in reply, but also in defiance. 'They kill the French, so I kill the General. It is just, just, Maman.'

And the two of them lie in their separate, desolate huddles, one in dismal confusion the other in desperation, while the dying General Wolfe, his most delicate features all but obliterated, suffers the ignominy of a second brutal annihilation at the hands of the old enemy.

William is the first to hear of the disaster. A package arrives. Bemused by the sight of Mrs Hocquet rushing away into the crowded street, he thinks at first that she wants to surprise him with the latest print.

On opening the package, his head jerks back in horror. His first thought is of Woll's reaction, his second is of the impact this could have on all their fortunes. How unjust is this turn of events. Coming just as he thought his luck was improving after the Indian fiasco. At least that he could foresee, make preparations to mitigate the losses, but this, this is a lightning strike out of a blue sky. Oh Woll! How is he going to take this? His child... now with a smashed head.

He looks again. The deceased General's features have quite disappeared. There is a dent but fortunately the hammer head seems to have fallen flat against the copper surface. So it has not dug too deep a groove. Perhaps this is retrievable. This thin sliver of detail on which his dreams, his family's fortunes and those of Woll and of Boydell, now depend.

In haste, William sends a short note to Boydell. He is not the priority. That dubious honour lies with Woll, who has spent these past years working at every detail and line, to create the best replica of West's painting.

William finds him in jovial mood.. His face is lighter, the bulbous, dark patches round his eyes are gone. William is distraught at what his news will do to him. Woll is in his studio room but instead of a graver he has a ladle in his hand. He is carefully packing black powder into a home-made cartridge. Beside him is his short stub of a brass cannon.

'If all goes well with Mrs Hocquet's prints I will fire my beauty tonight from the rooftops. The word is spreading, you will be there I hope. Remember the Niobe, that was a night. Well, this darling is double the strength.'

'But your dear wife ...' William's heart is pumping fit to burst.

'Oh she is used to it by now and the twins must prepare for life with a father of some eccentricity. They will meet me soon enough eh ?'

William takes hold of Woll's hands to stop him for a moment. His grip is severe, painful even.

'Eh what is it with you man, I could blow us both out of the door if you are not more careful.'

'My apologies,' William says. 'It is just that I need your attention for a matter which...'

'Which what, man? My, you are quite white. Are sure you are well? You are not bringing the ague into this house, with our babes not yet ...'

'No no it is not the ague, but I do have news about our dear child, well your dear child.' William can barely look him in the eye.

'How so?' Woll drops his powder ladle to the floor. 'What is it? Tell me, the proof is not good? You have seen it already?'

'It is worse than that.'

'What?' Woll demands. 'Sir, speak. I am now quite cold - all a shiver.'

William pulls out the copper plate. There is a moment of silence and then a screech that would not have been out of place in the Exeter Street menagerie.

'No! No! No! Damn Boydell for his shameful interference and damn Bartolozzi and all his friends. Damn, damn, damn the lot of them! They have undone me and all my years of work.'

William has no words to console him.

'Oh my!' says Woll, as he runs his finger over the battered head of his General. Then he bursts into another fit of wailing, as plaintive and piercing as if he had discovered one of his own children wounded in an alley.

There is a knock on the door and his startled wife appears.

'What is this William!'

By now Woll has sunk into a corner of the room. He is rocking back and forth, moaning. William guides Lizabeth back out to her bed. He feels her shoulders are shaking. He explains a little of the mishap. It is a printing issue, a set back, no more.

For Woll, there is nothing to be done until he has come through this first response. So William sets about the practical matter of making safe the black powder and the cannon wadding, which sits forlorn, unwanted in the middle of the room. Then he bids farewell to Woll, promising that he will return the following day. There is barely an acknowledgement from the disconsolate engraver. William must look elsewhere for a solution.

He heads for Hadrill's studio and finds the printer deep in discussion with Joseph his assistant. It seems that word has spread already. Small wonder. London's graving community is tight knit, there are few secrets kept for long. At least he knows it would not have been Willliam's decision to take the work elsewhere.

'Tapping out the hammer dents from the back side of the plate. That is our only hope.' Hadrill suggests. 'It will depend on how severe a blow that devil of a boy delivered. Provided the hammer head did not bite too deeply Woll may be able to repair it. In a month or two...'

'... or three or four !' William exclaims. 'We are in Woll's hands now.'

The next morning William finds Woll is rising to the challenge.

'I have spent years engraving the Death of the poor General, now I must resuscitate him like Lazarus. I feel the hand of the Lord upon me.'

William winces. 'It will need all of that and more time too.'

'We must not let out a word of this!'

'Too late.' William recounts his visit to Hadrill.

'Well, we must spread word then that the damage is not great, no more than a slip up in the printing.'

'Long live the General!' William declares.

'Aye, well, I would prefer him dying.' Woll's smile returns at last. 'Is Boydell aware?'

'I have sent word.'

With no certainty that the Wolfe is recoverable, William is forced to rely even more on his collaboration with Angelica. Pairs of prints are all the rage and her paintings make the ideal subjects. With the help of Thomas Burke, William plays on the heartstrings of his clientele. He commissions *Faith*, to hang alongside *Hope*. He looks for a print to partner with *A Lady in a Turkish dress* and finds her in the *Portrait of the Duchess of Richmond*.

On three days a week, Mary comes up from Hammersmith to join him at the shop. She proves herself a firm ally in negotiations. Many make the mistake of assuming that this quiet-spoken, humble woman is an easy target. No, she stands her ground and on many occasions emerges stronger for it.

While William and Mary struggle to balance their books, the coffee-houses are full of talk of much deeper conflicts. There are lines of resistance spreading out across the East coast of America. There are shots fired in anger in Lexington. There is talk of civil war, of a collapse in trade. Even the all-powerful East India Company is in turmoil. Its attempt to sell off surplus tea in the West is proving a disaster. It is a fragile time, the beginnings of a conflagration, which Gwynn had predicted many years earlier. For William, his greatest fear is of the French entering the ring, threatening invasion once again. It is hard to tell what is true and what is rumour. Official announcements lag behind the stories told in a thousand private letters, all claiming that the fever is rising and will not be easily assuaged. The Colonist rebels are adamant, they will not submit to a tax- collecting Monarch nor his red-coat army.

As winter approaches, William is relieved that his own commercial risks lie much closer to home. He ups the frequency of his visits to Woll's studio. Always reassuring, always appreciative, still he cannot hide his anxiety. Finally, in November, he is privy to a miracle. Woll reveals the copper plate. With infinite finesse, he has repaired the damage of the hammer blows. Wolfe's features are restored. As the woody smoke of the season's bonfires waft across the city, William and Woll are at last ready to produce the proofs. To their combined joy, word comes from the Palace, that the King himself requests to see a copy. Given the troubling outlook for England's Western colonies, perhaps it is no surprise he wishes to celebrate Wolfe's triumph at Quebec. At the formal presentation, the sovereign, always an enthusiastic promoter of history painting, is delighted. He appoints Woll, or William Woollett as he knows him, *Historical Engraver to the King*, with a royal pension.

That evening the streets of Leicester Fields are full of engravers and their apprentices. After celebrating in the Turks Head, they gather near Woll's Green Street residence to toast the hero of the hour. Even Boydell is present and most pleased. 'You made me my first 2,000 guineas - we shall make ten times that amount with Wolfe.'

Woll's Royal Seal of approval necessitates one final change to the plate, with the incorporation in the letters of his new title. They are finally ready to run off the first completed prints.

Chapter 26

Over the next months, William throws himself into the most pressing concern, making as much capital as he can out of the sales of the Wolfe print. There are orders coming in from all over England, Germany and even France.

'Which is surprising,' Gwynn remarks, as they sit surrounded by a stack of newspapers. 'Perhaps it is because our man, Wolfe, died in the process. They love a martyr do the French. Or is it perhaps to fuel their thirst for revenge.'

William nods in agreement but he is distracted by reports of the latest outrage in America. Now it seems they want their own independence, whatever that means. He hands the paper to Gwynn. 'See this, it may not be British for long, the way the mood is shifting.'

'Well I do not disagree with much of what they stand for. I just do not believe that the majority want to cut themselves off from the Mother Country. They need our trade and above all they need our silver.'

'They are not a mere handful and the French would dearly love to help.'

'Mmm. We shall see.'

With the Wolfe prints doing so well abroad, both William and Mary are always busy at the shop. Back in Hammersmith, their two daughters and young William are growing up fast. New arrangements will have to be made. With William's finances improving, Mary-Anne and Mary-Charlotte have been attending an Academy for young ladies in Chiswick Lane. It was recommended to them by Anne Hunter, as an excellent establishment, priding itself on the most progressive ideas. Even the French philosopher, Jean-Jacques Rousseau paid a visit during his recent stay in the village. His old friend, Dr William Rose runs the boys' school, Bradmore House, also in the Lane. Young Mary-Anne was even invited to walk with them along the Thames. But now she has reached the age of sixteen she has outgrown the school and has ambitions of her own.

'You know many of my friends are being sent to Paris to improve their French.' She explains to her Mama at supper one evening in Hammersmith.

'To France? But are we not nearly at war with them?'

'No Mama, we are not.'

'How many of your friends ?' Mary asks.

'Well there's Marie-Hélène.'

'Who is French...' The clarification from her sister is met with a scowl. She returns a beatific smile before returning to her book.

'True but Papa always says Paris is the most beautiful city in the world and I have never been. Why do I need to learn French if I am not permitted to use it. The Philosopher said I had a pretty accent.'

'I am sure he did.' Mama's response closes the conversation for now. Both Lambeth born and bred she cannot understand this desire to flee abroad. But she knows this is not the end of the campaign.

By September a decision can no longer be delayed. They are all gathered one Saturday morning beside the river. Mary-Anne declares that even John Wilkes' daughter was educated in a French convent.

'Well that may have taught her better manners than her father could,' William replies. 'I am not agin it, though if the Colonial war worsens, it could bring France against us.'

'And our darling Mary-Anne would be stranded...'

'... I could think of worse places to be ...' says Mary-Anne.

'... and the cost, we cannot forget.'

'There is another solution.' As soon as he utters these words William is aware that he is on uncertain ground. But he cannot take them back. 'We could bring France to you.'

The three Marys in his life look at him askance.

'Well, this Christmas-tide, Woll was home in Maidstone at his parents' inn. And he paid a visit to the paper maker, James Whatman. His mill is just outside the town. It seems that James, a widower, has daughters, who are not far off your age. And they have a governess, a French woman, a distant cousin I believe. Most delightful young lady.'

'Oh.' Mary says, now watching her husband with increased attention as he persists with his story. His eyes are fixed on the middle distance, where a shag is drying out its feathers on the far bank of the Thames.

'Well, as I understood it. Mr Whatman, when he marries his new wife, Susannah, believes there will be no place for Madeleine... Miss Calpet. He did even go so far as to ask Woll if he might know of any position in London... So, you see, perhaps if she was here she could continue your lessons in French and school you in other subjects as well.'

'Mmm... 'Neither Mama nor Mary-Anne is immediately enamoured of the idea. The one is somewhat concerned about a much younger woman, entering their home, the other sees her dreams of Paris fast disappearing.

'At least let me enquire if she is still looking for a position.' William says. 'We do not need to decide today.'

'There are practical considerations too.' Mary says. 'Where would she live? Our house is too small.'

'Well I am sure we can find a room for her nearby, in Hammersmith? Mr Lee at the Nurseries always says he has places to rent.'

Not long after, Mary's young William departs for an apprenticeship with Jo Strutt. And so, within a month, the Ryland household loses a son and gains a French governess. By the middle of September, Madeleine is installed in a small set of rooms on the ground floor of a cottage, within walking distance of the Hammersmith Turnpike.

Madeleine is a bright, brown-eyed spirit, with a liquid laugh and an instant success with the two girls. Even Mary is won over by her willingness to help in any way. But for William, there are other matters that month which distract his attention.

As William's costs rise, his dealings with the moneymen of Lombard Street increase apace. It is no longer a one-way supply of credit. He too can make a fine return. Every man-jack with guineas to spare is learning how to loan this paper money, these bills on London that circulate throughout the city, keeping its commerce afloat. Interest earned on discounted bills is the key to a gentleman's future. A few points in the hundred soon add up. But it is a fragile world, dependent on trust. His own guarantors, are still to be fully reimbursed. Every day there are cases before the courts of those that would subvert a deal.

'And who is this whispering nag,' asks Gwynn as they take a walk in St James Park.

'Edward Tooke. The credit clerk at Pell and Down's.'

'So they were caught napping?'

'It seems not.' William is eager to tell his tale. 'They spotted the knavery on the instant. 'twas back in July. Twelve noon on the twelfth.'

'Precise.'

'Indeed.' Williams stops for a moment to wipe perspiration from his brow. Wearing black is all very well, but would be tolerable in a lighter cloth. 'So, at that hour a certain Marmaduke Langley attends the bank of Pell and Down's with a note for payment to the sum of £21 pounds and seven shillings, to be drawn on Andrew Donaldson's account.'

'So, he is the victim?'

Willliam nods. 'Tooke takes one look at the note and says: "*That is not a Donaldson signature, sir.*" In fact, he told me it was plain to see. It was a wrapped hand, cramped and tight, not the free bold hand of Mr Donaldson.'

'Good man. So, they claps this Marmaduke in the ...'

'Ah no! That fellow was just the dupe - a trader in Leather Lane. The real culprit was a Henry Daniel. He gulled the Marmaduke into becoming messenger for the price of a drink or two.'

'And now they have this Daniel?'

'The court has passed judgement. Death by hanging.'

'Oh, what a lesson therein lies, William. If one is to commit forgery one had best be a master at it. Or off you trot to Tyburn.'

'It is harsh, he had many witnesses to his good character.'

That evening William sits alone in his room above the shop. He has recently taken to staying over several times a week. A glass of best Portuguese glows warm red in the candlelight. Among the pile of papers before him there is no doubt a bill for Archie Paxton, his ever-tolerant wine dealer, that should have been paid months earlier. On the credit side there is also now a stack of papers, bills of exchange each accruing interest over time. Each, with the appropriate signatures and acceptances, could buy a horse, a house or resuscitate a dream. They are cruel with potential, fragile paper records of trust, of hope, of sworn obligation.

He pulls out one of these bills and unfolds it on the desk before him, flattening its creases with his palm. He considers it for some time, then he dips his quill in the brass ink pot, and on a separate paper, begins to trace the line of a signature. It is a simple flowing gesture, matching what he senses as the original energy and angle of attack. He guesses the weight and feel of the fingers which made this mark.

This is still a challenge. Even for someone who has spent a lifetime copying the brush strokes of artistic genius, each with their own moments of pause and movement. He soon sees how the search for perfection could become obsessive. After all he knows what it means to spend many years on one print when he is line engraving.

It is nearly dawn before there is no variation between his version of each signature and that of the original. Although he is exhausted, stiff and sore in back and hands, there is a solitary satisfaction. No harm in it. Mere play. Like counting out clay coins or dreaming of a win on the City Lottery, it will go no further. Just as an alchemist, who discovers the secret to turning base metal into gold, declines to profit from it, fearing it would subvert the world outside his laboratory - and knowing that the practice carries with it the ultimate sanction.

Chapter 27

Winter, 1777

One chilly afternoon in January, William helps Mary into a post-chaise in the Strand. They settle into the back in silence. The interior smells most strongly of a recent assignation but William holds back the remark. A look from Mary is enough. She thinks the same.

'How many years is it?' He asks.

'My dear?'

'That we are together?'

'Twenty.' Mary shivers in the cold.

He smiles. 'A lifetime for some.'

'For our daughters yes.'

'And we are still content?'

'We are,' Mary says, laying a hand on his knee. William notices that she does not look at him. Her gaze is fixed on the passing business of the street. Relations between them have been cooler. Both blame the tiredness of the frequent travel and the business of the shop. It is the reason for their journey to Knightsbridge.

As a troop of Horseguards emerges from their barracks, William exclaims, 'This is the street!'

Mary raises her eyebrows at the line of terraced houses. Proximity is not always matched by intimacy with neighbours. At least they are on the edge of the Royal Park. For William, his concern is more that this is not the most fashionable part of Knightsbridge. But they are both of a mind to make a move. Within a fortnight the decision is made and soon the family are settling into 2, High Row.

In March, William and Thomas, his loyal Irish graver, are invited to Angelica's studio to discuss the works that she will exhibit this Spring. While gathering up their proofs, Thomas asks if Madeleine could accompany them. William pretends to be surprised but he has been aware for some time there has been a passion brewing. Thomas has found one too many excuses recently to spend some hours at the house. In truth, William is delighted. He also enjoys the company of his daughters' governess. Indeed, he cannot deny a *frisson* of jealousy. So it is the three of them who arrive in Golden Square to meet the Angel.

They find her in a sharp and agitated state of mind. She is now one of the most successful artists in London and in constant demand.

'Why, I have half of London, always at my door.!'

She greets Madeleine with a genteel courtesy which betrays an instant judgement. William takes a breath and searches out the works they have come to see.

'Oh why, Angelica, what is this ? Poor cupid chastised.'

'Some say it is a pleasure to be targeted.' She turns to Madeleine. 'And you Mademoiselle, with your eyes, no doubt you have tempted Cupid to un-sheath his arrows.'

'Me. No.' She blushes.

'Come now, you are among friends. Not one stray arrow to confess, Mademoiselle? In Paris perhaps?'

'Oh well yes, in Paris.'

'The imp is most active I believe. In Spring.'

'That is what we are told.'

William attempts to divert attention from Madeleine. 'No doubt one reason my daughter Mary is so keen to be despatched there for her studies.'

Angelica winces. 'To a convent I would hope.'

' Ha! That is not her expectation.'

'Meanwhile you have the delightful Madeleine to bring a taste of Paris into your life.'

William glances at Angelica. Where is this leading. 'It is a delight to practice the language yes.'

'The French tongue, so pretty is it not?' Angelica insists.

William nods and picks up another painting. 'And your other work? *Sterne's Poor Maria*. This is melancholy. Dear Angelica, I fear you are not showing yourself at your most cheerful.'

'I paint as I feel.'

'Are we to know the cause?' William is now roused to play the game. 'Seeing as we are in the mood for sharing.'

Angelica gives him a look that would shrivel a lion. 'It is a tedious affair, no more.'

But William will not be cowed. He knows Angelica's friend Joshua Reynolds blows hot and cold with her affections. 'Well if you will not share, let me indulge myself. Your painting reminds me of a boy.'

Angelica frowns. Her lips gather into a threatening pout. 'I have half the Academy telling me my women look too masculine, my men not enough...'

'No, no let me explain.'

And for some minutes, William holds them all enthralled with his description of the sad young boy he met so many years back, sitting all alone in his garden outside Paris.

His honesty touches Angelica. 'So, let this wretched youth be in your mind when you engrave *Poor Maria*.'

'You are sure?' William asks. 'Bartolozzi no doubt has an interest in it, not being an historical work.'

'Of course he does. But it is in my gift. Your lines will draw out such tears as I have shed in private.'

As if William didn't have enough to haunt his nights, his youthful dealings with the erratic Chevalier d'Eon return again to trouble him. The French spy and diplomat is still a thorn in the flesh of his compatriots in London. D'Eon is keen to return home to France but cannot agree terms with his new monarch, Louis XVI. The argument began over debts unpaid but there are other issues at stake. He has taken to appearing at several intimate soirées in a black silk gown, declaring himself to have acquired the habit in the service of his country. Of course, Gwynn has the full story.

'Those in the know say that he still has secret state papers that the French wish to secure, so Louis has called his bluff. He will neither confirm nor deny that the Chevalier once spied on the Russian court as a Madame. But he is so exasperated by d'Eon's antics he will only allow him to return if he sets aside his beloved Dragoon attire and wears women's garb from now on.'

'For good?'

'Yes. And those in the gambling game, who have now bet thousands upon the mystery of his sex, are desperate. They will have a conclusion before he, or she leaves the country. There is more sport in this for our sad nobles, than grieving for the loss of Empire. They are still seeking out any that know him or knew her, intimately.'

Gwynn leaves his last word lingering between them. William's ambitions for a life of ease and plenty are no secret. But he has never revealed the compromise that embroiled him in French plans for invasion.

'You know this easy money is rank temptation, but like Eve's apple, there is a danger lurking.' William holds the gaze of his old friend. 'Now, I cannot explain, one day perhaps. But please no more talk of d'Eon and his sex.'

'In that case, are you free later this month - the 27th - for a visit to my friends the Langdales?'

'The gin family?'

Gwynn nods. 'Indeed.'

'What is the occasion?'

'I have places reserved on their terrace. For the execution parade... Dr Dodds, the Macaroni Priest, the failed forger.'

Williams feels the skin on his neck begin to itch. 'Oh...I will stay for the passing by, along the Tyburn Road, but have no desire to watch the whole sad spectacle.'

As William leaves Knightsbridge early in the morning on the 27th, what weighs most heavily on his mind is the thought of this disgraced priest, Dr Dodds, copying an Earl's signature. Surely this must count as the most ludicrous way to extract money from a bank. The last cry of a drowning man? Even if the line was perfection itself, Dodds must have known that at any point the bank could approach the Earl, for approval. It was an invitation to the hangman.

With these morbid thoughts engaging him, William approaches Newgate Jail, so close to his childhood home. Ma is still in the old house. But she will be keeping to her room. She has always had a horror of Hanging Days. The bells toll on and on, as the wretched victims prepare for death.

Yet, in the streets, there is a high spirit of holiday among the thousands come to watch. As William walks up towards Langdales Gin Distillery in Holborn, the street sellers are already fleecing the crowd. Many are already worse for wear. The Langdales are good Catholics, strictly observant, always at Mass, they keep themselves on the right side of the law but they know these days are good for business. And they had best keep good relations with the London mob, who consider every papist a potential traitor.

'A sunny cup, William. Come it is a glorious day!' Gwynn is already on Langdale's terrace, surrounded by a host of his friends. There is Angelo, the master of arms; Samuel Whale the draughtsman and Moser from the Academy. The theatre folk are there too. A frail, though still animated Garrick, the nation's leading actor, with Sheridan the playwright and a young Frenchman with dark, inquisitive eyes, who William half recognises but cannot place. From the flush in all their cheeks, the gin is already flowing.

William is irked by their *bonhomie*. 'There are those below who will not see another day.'

'Oh, why so glum. You must have seen a hundred such parades.' Gwynn hands him a mug of gin punch.

'And each time I wonder why. But yes it is a spectacle.' William sees that the young Frenchman has a sheaf of drawing paper. Between swigs, he is sketching the crowds below them with a swift flowing hand. Now he remembers. They have met before at one of the Academy Exhibitions. This is De Loutherbourg, the artist Garrick brought over from Paris to create the most entrancing, illuminated scenes for his theatre at Drury Lane. No-one has seen the like in London. It is no wonder he is here, at this macabre performance. He would have revelled in the gory days of Rome, as the genius of their imperial festas.

Just then, the mob's cheers ring out. The prisoners' carts are emerging on to Holborn. They reserve the loudest shout for Dodd's carriage. His fate has somehow earned their sympathy. It is impossible to see the man from above, though he is so moved by the people's support he does lean out and wave. On the terrace, some join in the cheering. Others are more circumspect. William sees the elder Langdale has his hands clasped tightly around a bible. His lips move in constant recitation.

De Loutherbourg has now brought out a large stretcher of paper and his stub of charcoal flies back and forth, as the crowd surges up the road towards the hanging tree at Tyburn. Like hounds scenting blood, they must be in at the death. For the next two heaving miles, they will push and elbow their way forward to be as close as they can to the drop.

'Not I,' Gwynn says. 'It turns my stomach to see them dangle.'

'Nor I.' William sighs. 'And yet we are here. Again.'

'Well, better to be here than in his carriage.' And the two friends watch as the Langdale terrace empties and the mob's cries disappear into the distance.

That night, William stays late at the shop in the Strand. When he is alone, he pours himself a brandy. The day demands it. The bills of exchange with his practiced signatures lie close by but tonight he cannot bring himself to draw a line. Dodd's execution has left a bitter pall over them. Even as playful exercise, they carry a weight of consequence. They must remain his secret. One among many that he has accumulated. Do all men have such confidences? And women too? No doubt Mary does not bare all that twists within her. Does she sit in the dark and contemplate her own version of a perfect life? Just out of reach, always just out of reach.

In August, William is relieved to read in the Morning Post that the Chevalier d'Eon has finally set off for France, in a coach and four, in the full green splendour of his Dragoon uniform. But the threat from his countrymen is far from over, just as Gwynn predicted. After fighting near Saratoga, General Burgoyne and nearly six thousand British troops are surrounded and obliged to surrender. As the year turns, this humiliation brings France into the war, bound to support the American Patriots by a treaty of amity and commerce. Soon the Spanish will join them. The Catholic noose is tightening around Protestant Britain. It is once more an island fortress, anxious and on edge.

William's nights are now disturbed by dreams of a gilt-edged room in Versailles, where the Comte de Broglie holds sway, unrolling map after map of the coast of Britain and every one holds William's signature... in crisp brown lettering. Then, in shadow play, King Louis arrives with his Chief Minister Vergennes and a host of military staff, all laughing about the coming invasion and the champagne they will drink in the clubs of London. They raise a glass to toast the English King's Engraver.

William's private nightmares are soon matched by a public fear of invasion. On the street there is a rising antipathy to all things French. It has an unexpected effect on the harmony of the family. Madeleine announces that she has been offered a position in a school just outside Paris. She confesses that she no longer feels at ease.

'We are at war. I am better among my own people.'

Her announcement prompts another wave of demands from both Mary-Anne and Mary-Charlotte, who have never let up on their desire to visit Paris, to learn French. Mary is aghast at the very thought. 'What if Madeleine is herself a spy, come to take our daughters away.'

William, having lived in Paris through a previous war, is more relaxed. 'It is very much of the fashion, the schools in France are highly thought of.'

'But they could be thrown into jail. Are you out of your mind? I do wonder at times. Perhaps my brother was right about you, all along. A Frenchie, he always said you were.'

So, William finds himself harassed from both sides. His daughters are importunate. He cannot deny he has always lauded Paris and spoken with such love of the city since they were old enough to hear his stories. There are still packets plowing back and forth between Dover and the enemy's ports but how long this will be allowed is uncertain. Many say each vessel is full of spies and this cannot be tolerated for long. At first, William thinks of going with them but he fears being embroiled again with the French authorities, so soon after the Chevalier has finally departed. Instead he writes to his old friend and Master, Jean-Jacques Le Bas, to ask if he and Lizabeth will keep a watchful eye on his daughters if they venture into France. When he receives a favourable reply, he decides to risk Mary's wrath. Charlotte being now twenty will work as a teacher of English at Madeleine's school and Mary-Anne will attend as a pupil.

The talk of invasion grows wilder. News filters through the coffee houses ... the Spanish are to join the French campaign. William has never known Gwynn so anxious. 'It is '79. In twenty years we have gone from Annus Mirabilis to Horribilis. We have no Admiral Drake. Our Farmer George cannot match the Virgin Queen for a rousing speech. If their fleets do combine, our Navy is done for. We are at the mercy of their troops massing on the Brittany coast.'

Such conversations are a bitter trial for William. For all he knows the very maps he copied are even now spread out before Vergennes' war cabinet. If de Broglie's plans still hold sway, Plymouth, Portsmouth and the Isle of Wight are all in peril. Yet he can say nothing for fear of exposing his own misdeeds. Instead, all he can do is agree with Gwynn. 'We must pray for a Protestant wind, like the one that blew apart the Armada two hundred years ago.'

For once, William is prepared to seek divine intervention. When the enemy's combined fleet is sighted off Plymouth, fear in London reaches a crescendo. The sound of servants and apprentices practising their musket drills is heard in all the open land across the city.

By September, the enemy across the water has still not delivered the coup de grace. From private correspondence and overheard conversations, rumours are soon rife that England has once again escaped disaster. This time it is a combination of both sickness and wind that has saved the day. First, the Spanish and the French fleets are unable to strike early because of the adroit manoeuvring of England's reduced ships of the line. Then the enemy crews, who have been out at sea for several weeks run short of supplies and are stricken with a deadly bout of smallpox. The result is that their chance of landing on English soil is gone for good. William has not conspired in his nation's downfall. And now a fresh, new decade approaches.

Chapter 28

1780 January

Several carriages sweep into the courtyard of Somerset House. The Academicians have a council meeting to approve Angelica's paintings for the new Lecture Room. An hour or so later, she taps at the window of William's printshop. Her smile suggests her works have met with approval.

He helps her off with her heavy coat. 'Come warm yourself by the fire. I was expecting you earlier.'

'Oh William, you know how artists love to talk.'

'Some do, some just...'

'Count their money...'

'*Touché*. How is the fraternity? I hear the Italian is deciding who shall exhibit this year.'

Angelica frowns. 'If you refer to our mutual friend, Signor Bartolozzi, it is true he is to be one of three who choose.'

'*Associate Member* Bartolozzi,' William cannot hide a bitter note.

'Well you have never expressed an interest... and green eyes do not suit you.'

He mock-grimaces. 'No I have other plans.'

'That is no surprise.'

'Mmm.' He is distracted by the rattle of one of the last of the contractors' carts lumbering past his windows. It is a relief after so many years of work. 'Yes, I have decided, I shall have my **own** exhibition. This Spring. Well, May, to be precise.'

Angelica swings around on her seat beside the hearth. 'Your own?'

'Yes. All my works. A collection. It is time is it not? For anyone who cares to come see my wares. Not like your annual affair, no paying public. I will spare myself no blushes, there will be everything, from the early days...'

'Your Leda?'

'Why not my Leda and her swan? My portraits, every one of my scratchings.'

'The King, the Earl, the Queen ?' Angelica's enthusiasm is as charming as ever.

'Yes, a lifetime of works and then of course our collaboration, so all of Thomas' prints that I have published. I have in mind there must be well over a hundred I can assemble.'

'And where will this grand spectacle be held?'

'In Piccadilly. Pollard the printseller has rooms, bright spacious rooms, not so grand as you have created here in Somerset House, but grand enough for William Wynne.'

'And you will sell?' Her merchant mind is always alert.

'If I am blessed with good fortune.'

'Well, you deserve some grace.'

He bows and offers her a warming cup of spiced wine. 'And you? I hear that Cupid has an empty quiver.'

'Ah ha...' Her fingers brush against her cheek but fail to hide the rush of blood. 'That could imply he has missed his target.'

'Not this time, I am led to believe, by your maidenly blush. So becoming on one so ...'

'.. Old?' Her eyes narrow, beneath arched brows.

'I did not say it.'

'Oh William I shall miss your tenderness.'

'So you do have plans, to desert me, with your Signor Zucchi?'

'There is nothing certain.'

'Amen to that dear lady.'

And so, in Spring, the country is still at war but London's citizens no longer dream of French dragoons galloping down the Strand. Instead they flock to new Somerset House in their tens of thousands. The Academy's first exhibition there is a resounding success, though not without some scandal. The Morning Post publishes a letter complaining that certain classical statues (among them, the Farne Hercules and the Apollo Belvedere) are "... *in their present state of nudity, to the terror of every decent woman who enters the room ...*"

Angelica is bemused. 'So I am allowed to study such licentious objects and yet I am still not permitted to attend Life Drawing classes with male nudes. Such is the world.'

But William has no reason to complain. The hordes descending on the Exhibition also find their way to his print shop just a few doors away. Mary, Strutt and William Junior are all enlisted to cope with this surge of customers. William, himself, is busy in Piccadilly with preparations for his own exhibition. He has secured some days of Bailey's time. They work all hours. In total there are one hundred and forty-six works to hang.

'There you have it. Truly money on the wall, Monsieur Bailey.'

He will not admit that some of the earlier prints remind him too sharply of his failures. No-one else knows that he has still not repaid his two guarantors in full. Even though he now has guineas flowing his way, he cannot bring himself to part with them, for a lost cause. He has not even honoured the promised repayment of one hundred pounds a year. He shrugs and somehow pushes such thoughts back into the cross-hatched recesses of his mind.

At least his frail Ma is still alive to witness his achievements. She is part carried, part restrained as she struggles to examine every single work. Her comments are mostly complimentary. But the outing is her last. She slips away in her sleep, one night towards the end of May.

His exhibition closes the day after Ma's funeral. He has no time to grieve her passing. In the stifling early summer heat, William, Bailey and half a dozen assistants are busy, packing up all the prints and paintings. Some must be returned to their owners, others to the shop in the Strand. By early evening, they have the last work wrapped.

William waits for what seems like an eternity for Bailey to bring up their carts.

'It is like Saint Barth's Fair out there.'

They are both so tired, they think no more about it. As soon as the prints are loaded they set off through towards the Strand. William dozes off as they inch forward through boisterous crowds.

It is late when they reach the shop. Many friends and collaborators have already left. Mary, Angelica and Anne Hunter have been acting as hosts and judging from the empty bottles there has been a fine entertainment. Just as William and Bailey are settling into their own refreshment, there is a loud knocking at the door. Strutt rushes forward thinking that he has locked someone outside. 'Well now, this is a surprise.' He says, catching William's attention.

There in the entrance are Mary's sister and brother Sam. William cocks his head in welcome. These two rarely leave Lambeth. He ushers them in to the parlour, out of earshot, then offers them a glass of port from the bottle he is clutching to his chest.

'Na, this is no social call. There are enough drunkards on the streets. We are come with a warning. There is trouble starting, from South of the ...'

'...river.' William completes his sentence. It is a habit that has always infuriated Sam.

'St Georges Field. There are Protestant blue cockades everywhere, in the trees, the caps, the carts. And their rough chants of No...'

... Popery!'

'William. There are tens of thousands even now in Parliament Square. I am thinking you are not seeing the danger here.'

'Not yet, no. I am not.' William takes a heavy swig of port. 'Now, as I understand it, their target is the Act. The loosening of laws agin the old Faith. The Catholics. That is their concern. Not us everyday folk.'

'But we heard others...' Mary's sister's eyes are wide with fear. '...agitators.'

'There are soldiers?' William asks.

She nods. 'Though most seemed to favour the crowd. Surely they will not fire on their own people?'

'We shall see.'

Sam turns to leave. 'Well, we came to warn you...'

Just at that moment the door to the parlour falls open. Mary has also allowed herself a drink. It has been a long month and all seems to have gone so well.

'Brother!'

'Mary.' There is a brief moment of embrace.

'You will not tarry.'

'No there are others I must warn, that may heed my news with more diligence than your man.'

'What...what news?'

'Ask William, he knows it all. As always. Good night to you and fare thee well.'

By now, news of the riotous assembly before Parliament, has reached the few remaining guests. Angelica is caught in two minds. Should she remain in the city or make her way with Anne to her house in Earl's Court?

'Of course, come stay with us. My husband is still in surgery but these ruffians will not venture far out west. And should they do so, we now have the bears.' Anne's giggle suggests she too has had a glass. 'Ha, it is an occasion to let them loose. Though they would leave little on the bone for dear John to dissect.' Her infectious laugh sets Angelica off as well.

'Ladies. Please!' It is Strutt who speaks out. Perhaps more sober than the others. 'We need to see you all safe to your homes.'

Angelica hesitates. Her hand strays to the cross at her throat. Though much traveled, she has never seen a Protestant mob. 'No, Anne. I thank you but I cannot leave my father alone at Golden Square. The Bavarian Ambassador's Chapel is so close to us. It could draw the attention of the mob.'

'We could go fetch him hither?' Strutt suggests.

'The Count? I think the ambassador would ...'

'... No your father.'

Angelica pauses for a moment. 'Ah but then we leave our house unguarded. I think there is no alternative. I must return and soon, before matters worsen. Surely, the City militia, they will keep good order, no?'

'Let us hope, but these summer nights.' Strutt shrugs. 'Who knows what mischief is afoot.'

The party is swiftly ended. The warm satisfaction that came from the Exhibition is long gone.

'Why?' William muses to no one in particular. 'Why is it always thus. I cannot hold with hope for more than a day. It wings away from me as it would from a leper.' He is tempted to return to the port that had been such good company a moment earlier, but something tells him he will need all his wits this night.

They summon carriages. Anne heads west with Mary, Strutt and young William, who is excited by the prospect of bears on the loose.

Gwynn, William and Bailey accompany Angelica to Golden Square. It is a short carriage ride, even avoiding the main streets. But already they see groups of young bloods with blue cockades running through the streets.

'They are coming up from Parliament.' Gwynn observes. 'This is not good.'

The shutters of the Embassy at number 23 are closed. Though the flicker of candlelight suggests someone is about.

'Poor man.' Angelica says softly 'I would go to him.'

'Angelica, Your father.' Anne has her friend's hand tightly clasped.

'He can wait. I do believe Count Haslang needs our help.'

At this, she slips free and rushes off to knock at the door. The shutters above open an inch or two. She calls the others to her. 'We have little time. I have offered to store any of the valuables in my house.'

In an instant, Bailey takes charge. He despatches one of the Count's servants to watch for rioters coming down Warwick Street. Then he sets up a human chain from the Chapel to Angelica's door. He and two footmen seize whatever they can of the Altar plate. They pass it down the line to Gwynn, William and on to Angelica and her father who hasten with it inside. Though it seems like only minutes before they hear distant shouts and drumming. They are just bringing out the gilt ornaments when there is a warning cry from the look out.

'Take cover. Now!' Bailey shouts up to the Count, who is attempting to rip out the fastenings which hold the Altar Piece in place.

'Now Count, or they will be among us!'

'Lord have mercy on our souls... '

With that the Count and his men join Bailey, Gwynn and William seeking refuge in Angelica's house. The heavy bolts are slid across and they make their way upstairs in darkness. No-one dares to light a candle. They are only just in time. A host of flaming torches pours into the Square. The mob's blood is up. The Chapel is eviscerated. Its awnings, pews, balustrades are hauled out... anything that can be used as firewood is torn apart.

William peers between the shutter slats. He is transfixed by the destruction. They are tossing Mass books out on to the street. A flaming torch is held close and the pile is alight. Even the precious Altar Piece is broken up. Then they start on the Ambassador's residence. The Square is soon littered with drawers from his oak desk, his silk waistcoats and bottles stolen from his cellar. These hold no threat of Popery. This is brazen thieving. When one looter emerges with a pair of silver candlesticks, the mob fight among themselves.

Fortunately, Angelica does not witness the violence. Gwynn has taken her and Johann into the back rooms for safety. But Bailey is trembling beside William. He cannot tell whether it is from fear or anger.

'I never thought to see the like...' he whispers.

More and more books from the Chapel are thrown on to the fires. Burning flecks of paper float up into the night sky. A thick grey-black smoke comes through the shutters. They both have their kerchiefs out, held over nose and mouth to stifle any risk of a cough and discovery by the drunken mob.

Then as quickly as they appeared, the vandals are gone. Perhaps spooked by the distant sound of marching troops. Inside the house, Angelica finds space for her unexpected guests to rest and seek whatever comfort they can in sleep.

The next morning William and Bailey are up just after dawn.

'We need a storm,' William mutters. 'T'would clear the air and cool the streets.'

'Praise God it would cause less damage than these animals.'

They venture out, still wary. All is quiet on the Square. The jagged stack of broken furniture is still smoking. The books of Catholic worship are reduced to ashes. Inside the Chapel itself, there is nothing to be salvaged. It is a hollow shell, stinking of urine and incense.

When they return to the house, Angelica is awake. She stands at the door in her *peignoir*, her hair coiled up high. There are tears in her eyes. 'Such brutes. They have no understanding. Only hate.'

Bailey nods. 'And I fear we have not seen the last of it.'

At first, it seems that he may be proved wrong. By mid-day there are troops stationed in the Square, with several taking up positions inside the Chapel. Though there is little left to defend. And by the early afternoon, they are joined by curious citizens, come to see what damage has been done.

'Like crows, they come to pick at Catholic remains,' the Ambassador complains.

Gwynn's usual good humour has disappeared. 'Lord Gordon has poked up a nest of hornets, with his Protestant Association. He may be against the loosening of restrictions on Catholics but there are others with far deeper grievances. I fear he has given them a field in which to play.'

As dusk creeps in, more rumours start to fly. William overhears talk of further Catholic targets, among them the Gin merchants in Holborn. He finds a boy on Warwick Street who'll run across the city for a coin. William cannot bear the thought of Langdales torn apart. Gwynn's friends have always been the most courteous, the most discreet of hosts.

It is agreed that it would be wise to head West, to join Mary and Anne. So, under cover of darkness, they take the side roads to Earl's Court.

It is well they did. For the next five nights it is as if a vicious whirlwind blows through London. Just as Gwynn predicted, the mob move beyond attacks on Catholic premises. Their sights are set on the great bastions of suffering, the gaols and the sponging houses, where so many debtors and wretched prisoners have perished. They hunt down the Justices who have condemned their kin and drive them from their homes. Even the Bank of England comes under attack, though here the troops do stand and fight, with musket volleys and charges with fixed bayonets. When order is at last restored across the City, over two hundred rioters are dead and perhaps another hundred lie wounded in the hospitals. Some have died from drinking neat gin at Langdales, which they burned to the ground. William's warning had come too late.

When it is safe to return to Holborn, Gwynn finds no trace of his friends. He cannot bear to look at the smoking remains of the Distillery. He leans on William for support as they walk on through the battered streets to Lincoln's Inn Fields where the violence began. 'We have not seen destruction on this scale since the Great Fire. I have spent my life in awe of Wren, hoping to continue his vision in some small way. I have strived for all that is best in building anew... Adam's Adelphi...like Rome reborn. What does all that mean now? Does it stand for nothing if in a few nights of madness it can all be rent asunder?'

For William, it is the consequence of the riots rather than the immediate damage which is most devastating. Some weeks later he is invited back to Golden Square. The skin on his back prickles even as he enters the salon. Deep down, he has some inkling of what is to come. Angelica cannot bear to tell him alone, so the deed is to be done with both Papa Johann and Anne Hunter in attendance, discreet as always.

As soon as he is settled, Angelica begins, though she cannot look him in the eye. 'As you know I have been considering a journey south. Dear Papa is determined to see his Swiss homeland before he becomes too old to travel. And I...'

'The recent horrors drive you from us?' William's enquiry is flint-edged.

'I cannot say they are not an influence. There is a fierce resentment in this island race.'

'And yet we have a foreign king.'

'A most British foreign king.' Angelica laughs. 'What is more British than this gardener-King?'

William looks around at Papa Johann and Anne for support. 'Fear lies beneath the skin. Just months ago a Catholic army of revenge was almost at our throats. Now we are at the point of losing our America. 'Tis not surprising there is fear. But if you will run...'

'That is unjust. I am Swiss, not English. I owe no loyalty to such people.'

His bitterness distresses him. There has been so much which has not been said between them. And now, well, now it is too late. 'I saw you more a citizen of the world. This new world that is breaching forth?'

'Perhaps. As I once thought you were, William. Though you are sharp now, in your hurting. And I do believe you are not as observant as I had credited you.'

With a smile she raises her left hand to her cheek. A large gem catches the morning light. William feels his back prickle up yet again.

'Ah. So Cupid did find his mark.'

She laughs. 'Antonio, not Cupid.'

'You will marry here?'

'In Italy. We will spend some time in Venice.'

William glances across to Anne. She places her finger to her lips. William shrugs, sits back for a moment, not willing to press further. This is perhaps the last conversation he will have with Angelica. Then without a further thought he finds himself declaring, 'You should know that I too have considered leaving?'

'Indeed?'

'My girls are already in France. My son apprenticed to a man I trust. And my wife, well perhaps she would travel too. She has already come far from the Lambeth orchards where we met. Though I am not certain.'

'Where would you go?'

'I have never truly left Paris. An old friend, Brookshaw, has been there for years and now he graves for Queen Marie-Antoinette.' He looks up and attempts to hold her gaze. 'Though if I am honest, dear Angelica, it is your departure prompts this speculation. It renders me a sad and jealous fool.'

He thinks he sees a shadow of doubt pass across her face. But it does not linger. She is adamant. 'Even though I am not present, our collaboration can still continue.'

'Though others already come knocking. Bartolozzi...'

She waves a dismissive hand. 'Oh, he is importunate.'

'He has a crew about him, they will make you more money than I ever can.'

'Always your fortune, William? Is it so much in doubt?'

'It is a longing, I confess. I have no land, no trees, no fields to my name. No wealth secreted beneath my bed, no sacks of guineas to count alone at night. What I have is all on paper, whether my prints, or my bills of trade. All Paper. To Paper I am beholden.'

'Well beware, it is not the death of you.' With this she rises. The most formal of their encounters is over. 'Farewell, dear William. I do hope you find some comfort to soften that taut brow of yours.'

'Dear Angelica.' He makes a formal bow as if he needs to draw a line between them. 'Anne. Papa Johann.'

He turns to leave. As he does so, he is convinced he hears a sob. But he will not turn around. This is a mark that will not be smoothed away.

Chapter 29

Some months later William is at his desk in the shop. He is brooding late at night as has become his custom. He pours himself a glass of Archie's best Portuguese. A last drop he tells himself. Though since Angelica's departure there is always another bottle. He is irritated by the pile of papers which Mary has set out for him to review. His mind travels back to Paris, to his mentor Wille's gargantuan desk. Those stacks of bills had once so impressed him. Now he would be rid of them all. But as he flicks his fingers through them there is one that takes his eye. It is a lawyer's letter and it concerns a man he once knew in his Cornhill days. John Jordan was one of those raw-eyed Alley cats, who inhabit the lanes just off the Exchange. He always had a scheme, a trick, a combine as he called it, which would one day make his fortune. Though as the years passed they never seemed to deliver.

The letter begins with an account of Mr Jordan's demise back in the high summer of '74. Recently his last will and testament has come to light. William is one of the beneficiaries. Some twenty-two shares in the Liverpool Water Company are now his.

A smile breaks William's sullen mood. The letter brings back memories of John Jordan, fired up by a morning of coffee at Jonathan's in the Alley. 'Mark my words,' he would declare. 'Forget this City, much as it is dear to our hearts. Liverpool is where we'll find our pot of gold. It has doubled in size these past ten years and if it can, it will do, again and again. But soon the 'pool cannot grow no more. And you know for why? Because it is fresh out of water. Water fresh to drink that is. So, you ask. "What's that to me?" Well, it so happens that up the road in Bootle there is water. Abundant springs in Bootle and I, John Jordan, resident rat of Exchange Alley. I has the rights… see here.' At this point he would wave a smudged document above his head. 'I has the rights, see, to run conduits from said springs to Liverpool. Ha! Now tell me why I shall not make a fortune out of this ? Men, and women must drink. Ergo, he who supplies them water shall be a rich man.'

The next day, William makes discreet enquiries. It seems that at launch these shares were worth ten pounds each but have been quietly rising. Even after John Jordan's passing, the company still has the rights to Bootle's spring. *"A potential for growth"* are the words his informant uses. But there is investment needed.

William begins to spread the word, discreetly, without fuss or fanfare. He knows that the scent of money to be made will do the talking for him. Soon his shares are trading several hundred pounds above their face value.

William has good reason to be looking for new wells to tap. Though Angelica has been gone less than a year, already he has lost interest in his prints. He tried at first to rekindle his old passion for line-engraving. There is an historical plate under way. Its subject is King Alfred, a worthy hero for these days of war. But progress is slow. His eyesight is fading. He reminds himself he is not yet fifty. Surely he has more years in him. But in truth it is the will which is lacking. All around he sees so many competitors. Even in his domain, the coloured stipples of

Angelica's works, there are others now at work. Bartolozzi is making his own fortune.

It is Mary who keeps the shop afloat. She works with Strutt when he is free from his studies of antiquity and another printseller, who has his own premises nearby. Together they at least keep the bills paid and make the most of being on the doorstep of the Royal Academy.

So, in his desperation, William goes in search of men with money to spare. Those looking for a swift fortune among the brokers and traders of the Exchange. To puff up a Bubble, he needs an insider. Someone like Jordan, who knows the workings of this arcane world, where deals are done on a shake and a nod. Through good offices of the lawyer, Wellbelove, he is told of another beneficiary to Jordan's Will, a certain Ignatius Valley. One morning, he finds his man, asleep at a table in Benson's Virginia Coffeehouse. William leans forward until he is at ear-level. 'Ignatius?' He whispers.

This fellow of some forty years, with close cropped hair and no wig, groans and shrugs his shoulders. His eyes remain tightly closed. 'Who wishes to know?'

'A friend of John Jordan.'

'He is in hell, so you must be the devil. But my time is not yet up.'

William laughs. 'He must have been mistaken. He said you had a nose for an affair.'

'That's as maybe. Right now I sniff's nought but the rain on your coat and Benson's fearsome brew.'

With this Ignatius hauls himself upright. He takes in the elegant cut of William's topcoat and breaks into a smile that reveals not all his teeth are present. 'A gentleman devil. I am honoured.'

'Likewise,' William replies, sitting down on the bench opposite.

'And I am most partial to a brew myself. If you could oblige. My head is summat outa place.'

William orders a coffee and proceeds to interrogate his new acquaintance. The lawyer had provided scant information beyond his origins in St Helena.

'Aye, I am a Saint,' Ignatius confirms, 'and proud of it. Born and raised in Jamestown on that old rock in the Ocean. The son of slaves, though my Pa was a freedman on the Island. As soon as I was able I finds a passage out to England. Portsmouth first, then up to Liverpool. In the docks. A foreman within five years and then I has my own yard and crew.'

'So this is how you came to know Jordan?'

There is a brief pause when a cup of Benson's best arrives. Ignatius reaches into his waist pocket and pulls out a flask of rum. He offers William a tot then brings his coffee up to the brim. 'Made for each other they are... Now you was askin'? Yes, so Mr Jordan some ten years back comes to the 'Pool, making all manner of promises. Looking for men he was, to start a channel and lay the conduits out. To show it was a go. Impress the money folk.'

'So they did begin already?'

Ignatius takes a slug of coffee and eyes William before continuing. 'Well, there's the thing. Jordan was all talk and when the money stopped, so did the work. Scarce a few hundred yards I'd say.'

'But there's a business to be ...'

'Oh aye they cannot wash in rum and beer...'

'And you, like me, have shares in hand.' William brings out his paper certificates, prompting Ignatius to dig deep again in his pocket and bring out a matching set, though somewhat stained with rum. Now bonded over their shared inheritance, William and Ignatius set to plotting how they can raise more money for their venture. If they can just persuade some willing gulls to part with cash.

William proposes his banker, Henry Pell, as one source but Ignatius counsels against it. 'I am not for the banks m'self. I seen what happens when they goes down. Like dominoes it is and your guineas are overboard before you know it. No, what we need is slippery money. I mean by that money that can slide in and out unnoticed.'

'Private money?'

'Exactly!' Ignatius, suddenly alert, slams his hand hard on the table. 'Now I do know a man, a colonial, goes by the name of Lydius. I met him when he first came across. He's not young, some way past three score years and ten, though you'd not know it. Tall, hardy fellow. Claims to own land on the Eastern Seaboard, a trader with the Indians. You'd like him, he's another devil like you, dresses all in black. Though he says he's a man of God, son of a Calvinist. Never touches a drop. But I know he has plenty of guineas that he'd like to clean, if you get my drift.'

So William and his new found partner are now thick as thieves. Ignatius promises to find out the whereabouts of John Henry Lydius and arrange a meeting.

In the meantime, William takes his old friend, Gwynn, into his confidence. He is suffering from the gout but insists on walking, with the aid of a stout cane. They meander slowly around Leicester Fields. Gwynn has already heard tell of old Mr Lydius and the ripples he has set in motion.

'He is a dealer in land-rights that cannot be substantiated. He has a trail of cases against him in New York. Now he threatens to do the same here. He claims to be a man of God, but that God is Mammon, so beware.'

'So he is a charlatan?'

'Well I would not call him that to his face, unless you are handier with a pistol than I recall.'

'He has guineas though?'

Gwynn stops and prods the ground ahead of him with his cane. 'Here, help me over this, will you? He leans on William, who guides him around a muddy stream at the bottom of the Fields. 'Now that is worthy of an Oxford meadow... So, you were saying... yes he has guineas and more tall tales than guineas too, so all I say to you is keep your wits about you.'

Forewarned, William is prepared to mistrust the American when the invitation arrives from Ignatius. They are to sup with John-Henry and his friends in a Southwark tavern. There is no mistaking their man. He is indeed clad all in black, whiskered in grey, and furnished with deep-set blue eyes that have seen more than many care to dream. The tattoos on his forehead, neck and hands are not of a common sort. Instead of mermaids and anchors, there are swirling patterns of snakes and eyes, like a many-headed hydra. At first, he keeps his own counsel, allowing his friends to make the conversation. They are on a smaller scale than him, day-traders and hangers-on. William sees them as birds pecking insects off an ox's back. When John-Henry does speak, which is rare enough, he drawls out the words, spitting gobs of tobacco between the rough phrases. Then he dominates the room with his tales of trading furs, hunting in the northern forests with the natives. There is some mention of land rights but about that he is cautious. Above all he is eager for it to be known that he has wealth, significant wealth. Though to William's dismay he does not at first seem interested in the Liverpool venture. Still they part on good terms and agree to meet again.

After this first encounter William hears nothing more for several weeks. Then one Sunday morning, when he and Ignatius are sitting over coffee in the Virginian, they see the tall, slightly stooping figure of John-Henry peering through the bay window. He sees them, smiles and comes to join them. He removes his blackened leather cap and eases himself on to the bench.

'Gentlemen. I wish to explain.' Before he has the chance to do so. Benson arrives with a spittoon. He knows his man. 'Ah thank'ee kindly.' The spittoon resounds with a thud as the first plug of tobacco hits its mark. 'Now, as I was saying. It is not that I am agin your Liverpool venture. It has much promise in it and I am of a mind to invest. But I'm here to tell 'ee that I am off to Amsterdam within the week. There is some business to conclude. Land transactions, of that sort. There are many pioneers among the Dutch. Fine traders too.'

The explanation made, John-Henry digresses on to the merits and misdeeds of the Dutch, the French and the English in their treatment of the natives. This continues for the time it takes for a coffee or two to be drunk. And then as abruptly as he arrived, he rises to say his farewells. He has one last request to ask of William. 'Seeing as you and I are now friends, I would be obliged if I may use your address to forward my bills of exchange to London.'

William accepts without demur.

'Most grateful,' John-Henry offers him a bear of a hug. 'I have a colleague, a Mr Hagglestone. He may perhaps be in contact with you?'

William sees no harm in this. Though, as Ignatius says, after John-Henry's departure, it is not a name which inspires the greatest of trust.

That Christmas, both William and England are in a matching gloom. The army's humiliation and surrender at Yorktown has all but ended any hope of saving the American colonies. But peace with

France is still to be agreed, which means his daughters remain in enemy territory. They are at least in good health, which Mary puts down to her regular despatch of Lambeth cider vinegar. Though how it ever reaches them William has never understood.

Chapter 30

A letter arrives from William's old master and mentor Le Bas. In a
shaky hand he announces the recent death of his wife Lizabeth.
Before he too passes, he would dearly love to see William return to Paris,
at least one more time.

It is bitter news and the invitation leaves William troubled. The
American war is all but over and there has been talk of peace with
France. Though no-one can put a date to it. Such affairs of state can
drag on for months or years. He knows full well the risks of travelling
in time of war. The regular packets no longer run from Dover to Calais.
They were stopped for fear of information passing too readily into
enemy hands. He would need to find a captain willing to slip across at
night. Perhaps he could use Burke's latest print of the dying Elouise
as a pretext. The story of Abelard and Elouise must surely sell well in
France. If he can secure letters of transit as a trader then he is prepared
to run the gauntlet.

He writes back to Le Bas to say that he will do his best to see
him before the spring. Then he also pens a letter to Basan, the Paris
print seller who already deals in many of his works. He asks for help

in securing the trader's papers. Meanwhile, at home, he has Mary's blessing because the journey will allow him to visit their daughters in the village where they are now teaching.

'I fear I would be a hindrance, given that I am not of the travelling sort.'

By April 14th all is ready. William takes just a small bag and the portfolio of prints. Within five days he finds himself in a fast post-chaise bumping across the paving stones of St Michel. He is back in Paris.

Once in the streets, William is discreet. He does not try his French with the market traders. Indeed there are none now that he recognises. And there is an edge to the exchanges he hears around him. It is late afternoon, when many are queuing for the best deals of the day. Bruised apples that have not sold, cheeses just on the turn. No one wants to pay the asking price. At every corner, there are haggard veterans with missing or scorched limbs. They plead with distant eyes for a handful of sous. But there are few gentle smiles on offer. Just as he is about to turn into Rue de la Harpe, he is almost sent flying by a carriage hurtling past. Its rear wheel hits a filthy sump in the road, sending a cascade of mud across the busy street. Forced to stop, the carriage is surrounded, the driver hauled to the ground and beaten by the crowd. William's neck prickles with the memory of London's anti-Catholic horrors. What is it with people today? Always on the verge of erupting into madness.

Another shock is in store at Le Bas' studio. It is the wizened shell of his old Master who opens the door. He ushers him past his apprentices to the back room. Despite the warmth of the spring day, Le Bas is wrapped in a heavy shawl. He settles into his seat beside the stove, as if that is now his favoured refuge from a sharp world.

'So, William, you come to pay respects to my shadow. When Lizabeth passed , she took the best part of me.'

'No Maitre.'

'*Si. Si.* She did, she left too soon... too soon.'

'Your hair, Maitre, is still without comparison.'

For a moment Le Bas loosens his grasp on the shawl. A bony finger pushes back one strand of grey-white hair. 'My father, you know...'

'... Yes, I know. He taught you well. As you did me.'

'You are still the King's Engraver?'

'I am. The pension is most welcome, though I have done little recently to deserve the title.'

'You no longer work your lines?'

William feels the rebuke. 'Oh, I have plates in hand. History subjects. But my venture is more in the selling of others' prints.'

'Ah yes, and there you English now show us the way.'

'We learned our lessons.'

Le Bas lets out a sigh. 'If only I could say the same of our leaders. They piss away our wealth on foreign wars and invasion threats that come to nought.'

'I saw the consequence...the streets are not what they were.'

'A sorry sight. I keep myself to myself.' The old man's eyes close for moment. The two friends contemplate time passing away between them.

Then, through the open doorway, William's attention is caught by movement in the studio room. The engravers are at work. A young woman, ebony black hair tied in a blue kerchief, turns to address her colleague. As she does so, her eyes catch William looking at her. A moment of recognition that startles her and him in equal measure. He turns back to Le Bas, who has nodded off.

'Maître...Maître?'

'Eh? No need to shout.' His rheumy eyes flicker apart. 'Ah, William. Just like the old times eh? Though without Lizabeth to fret us.' He smiles as a tear blossoms. 'The wind?'

'Maitre, there is a young woman among the engravers?'

'Ahh.'

'She is the image of her mother... Gabrielle.'

'*Eh oui*, that she is.'

William feels his blood rising. 'You didn't tell me.'

'We.. we thought it best...'

'After Gabrielle, passed, what happened then?'

Le Bas is silent, his eyes on the ancient coffee pot, steaming on its stand. He takes a slow, deep breath as if inhaling its fumes will give him the vitality to respond. 'We raised her as our own. Constance. Her name is Constance. You do remember?'

'She never asked..?'

'...About you. Oh, many times... We said her father had left Paris because of the war.'

William peers again through the gap in the doorway, but Constance is no longer visible. She must have moved to another desk. The blood is now thumping at his temples. She is just older than his daughter, Mary-Anne. What would the girls say if they knew? Should he stay? Look after her... ?

The dark memory of another bitter choice comes rushing back. It is so long ago, but why is there always so much at stake. Even now he could seek to make his fortune here, do right by her and his daughters, leave something for those who he must one day leave behind.

Le Bas is watching him.

'It is time you met.'

He reaches out for his stick. William helps him up. But when they enter the studio, there is no sign of Constance.

After the encounter at Le Bas' studio, William searches in vain for his daughter. None of her fellow engravers can help. The concierge at her residence is no more forthcoming. Though William is certain she knows more than she is telling. Constance appears to have disappeared without trace. Then a message arrives from Le Bas.

'Constance has left Paris,' he explains. 'She has gone to Ermenonville. A day's journey north-east. As to why, I think it best that I let her explain.'

So, here he is, now sitting beside a lake in a grand garden on the outskirts of Ermenonville. On a small tree-lined island, just opposite him, is the tomb of Jean-Jacques Rousseau. He learned on the journey up from Paris, that the philosopher had spent his last months living in a small cottage nearby. William has never known a gentler setting. The sounds of life are all abundant yet peaceful. Woodpeckers above, squirrels in the undergrowth and moorhens marking territory. But William's guts are churning in anticipation of his meeting with Constance. His feet are twisted tight across each other. He makes a conscious effort to untangle them and rests for a moment, breathing calm and steady. He closes his eyes and recalls the hours spent atop the Lambeth Tower, looking out over London. This park has the same power to inspire. If Woll were here he would have his charcoal out, capturing the sharp poplars and the dipping willows.

After some moments of contemplation, other sounds attract William's attention. They are distant at first, a call, a double beat of wings. He opens his eyes and there up above is a pair of swans, gliding in to break the mirrored surface of the lake in front of him. They reach the island and settle on the shoreline, preening themselves. He smiles, recollecting that image of Boucher from so long ago - his Leda and the Swan.

Just at that moment a soft voice emerges from the trees behind him.

'Monsieur...'

He turns to see the young woman with the ebony hair. This time the kerchief is red and she wears an ochre country jacket. He stands to greet her, but Constance is not alone. She is accompanied by a young man, of similar age. He has a bright physicality about him. And a smile.

'Bonjour Maître.'

'Oh, you may both call me William.'

She nods and introduces her companion. '*Je vous presente Patrick Duvalier.*'

'*Enchanté.*' William replies.

'My husband.' Constance explains with pride.

William inclines his head in acknowledgement. '*Ah. Felicitations.* I didn't know.'

'Patrick was also an apprentice with Maitre Le Bas. Now he is working on miniatures nearby in Senlis.'

William feels the blood returning to his feet. He is all pins and needles. 'Yes. Well. That is good. At least you are not in competition.'

She senses his awkwardness. 'Patrick has some sketches to complete, perhaps we can walk on around the lake while he works?' She offers William her arm with the easy grace of her mother. They set off on their stroll and Constance points out the island. 'You know that is the Philosopher's tomb, just beyond the swans.'

'Yes. We met once.'

'No?'

'Just outside London. He came to visit schools there . He had much to say about English gardens.'

She smiles at the thought. 'And now he has found his own, to enjoy...For eternity.'

'Fortunate man.' says William.

They walk on, both searching for words that will open up a past that is shared but not yet known.

Eventually William breaks the silence. 'So where to begin?'

'The beginning would be good. You and maman in Paris.'

Step by step, as they circle the island, his story, their story unfolds. It is like rediscovering ripples across a lake that have long since disappeared. He finds the lines again, engraving them from memory. The explanation of why he left seems shallow now, but she does not appear to judge him. There is no edge to her queries. It seems she has not inherited her mother's anger, or perhaps it has long since dissipated.

By the time they have completed a first circuit, the light has shifted. Patrick now stands in silhouette at his easel. They wave but he is too absorbed in his own world to notice. So, they continue on a second time around. He wonders how much she has been told about those early days.

'Maman did tell me of that last night, about Leda and the Swan.'

'I have it still, the plate. I brought it out for my Exhibition. Though it made me feel my years. It was once my calling card in London. To show what I had learned in France and Italy.'

'We would dearly love to see Rome one day. It is a dream for now...'

William's memories are surging up from the dim past, from his own days of dreaming. The harsh call of a magpie brings him back to this reunion with Constance. 'And you, your engraving? Le Bas says many clients sing your praises.'

'Yes, we have had success at Court, and Patrick too. Though this war makes everything so uncertain.'

As they talk on, something settles in William. He feels at ease to tell her of Mary, of their home in London, of William his son. Then he reveals that Mary Charlotte and Mary-Anne are now both in France.

'One day perhaps you will meet them. Though I will need to prepare the way.'

On the instant, he senses this is a step too far. Constance bristles at the news that they are not far from Paris. So he lets it pass and she in turn asks him about life in London. It is another dream she holds with Patrick.

'You are travellers then. Not like Gabrielle. She would not follow me across the water...' William lets the observation linger.

'She could not do it?'

'No. She would not.' He is keen to make the point.

'Well perhaps one day...' Constance says, looking out over the lake to Rousseau's tomb.

'If I can help in any way... '

'In Gabrielle's honour?' she asks.

'Yes, in Gabrielle's honour.'

Once back in Paris, William's business with the print dealer Basan is swiftly completed. *Elouise on her deathbed* will be published in France, with a share of the proceeds going to build up some credit for William. But he is not inclined to spend long in the Hotel Serpente, now Basan's permanent base. There are too many memories. So, he is soon ready to make plans for a far happier reunion, with his daughters at the school where they teach. It is on the way back to Calais. Before he leaves, he makes several trips to the fashionable shops on the Rue St Honore. Mary has sent him a list and his daughters have added their own. As the packages accumulate at Le Bas studio, his old master is amused. 'The King's Engraver is much in demand, I see.'

'A blessing in disguise. I learn what is selling on the streets.'

William's dream of the Bloomsbury mansion has now grown to encompass a host of other people's dreams. If he can just make them come true, would he then have settled his debts? The parting with Le Bas is a sad affair. Both talk of future encounters, but they know this may be their last.

'Take care of Constance.' William embraces his frail Master. They hold each other longer than they might.

By the evening of the following day, William reaches Averand-sur-Lie, a short ride off the coaching road to Calais. Some cottages stand guard beside the bridge over a sluggish stream. The main village clusters higher up, around a steep hill, crowned by a stone mansion known as the Chateau. Even in its earliest days it was probably no more than a fortified Manor House. Today it is the Academie Averand, a school for girls from France, Italy and England.

'Papa, Papa ... '

Two young women in their early twenties come rushing down the grand steps to meet him.

'Oh my. I would not have recognised you. Such beauty, such elegance... '

'But you Papa, you have not changed a jot. Still in your black.'

He shrugs. 'A creature of habit, always have been. You will not shift me.'

'No and why should we? Come, come see our domain. Madeleine left some nine months back. So now we are the joint mistresses in charge.'

'There is so much to show you.'

They take his arm on either side and set off on an enthusiastic tour beginning with the walled garden. He can see Mary's Lambeth influence in the blossom-rich orchard, the purring hives and the well nurtured beds, laid out for all manner of vegetables. He makes mental notes, knowing that he will be interrogated on his return to London.

Inside, the house is a bright sequence of high-ceilinged rooms, painted in light reds, deep greens and even bright yellow. There is a comforting order about the place. A scent of lily of the valley. Some young girls are repeating their latin grammar out loud. They smirk and grin at the guest in black, who is introduced as Madame Ryland's Papa. His chest tightens with pride. This establishment is now his daughters' creation, their charge, as delicate as any precious endeavour. That evening a concert is arranged in his honour. Several girls perform on the harpsichord and flute. Charlotte sings unaccompanied, to everyone's delight. William presents them with the gifts he has brought from Paris, including packages of muslin, taffeta and brocade for their pupils. If he could just bottle their excitement and gratitude, Mary would be in heaven.

William puts back his planned departure for a couple more days. He still has questions to be answered. Do they intend to stay even after Peace is agreed? Are there reasons of the heart at play? On this they are discreet at first. But on the last evening, over a third glass of the local wine the truth emerges. They are both courted by local men. One is running for the post of mayor in a nearby town, the other is a master in charge of a similar school for boys.

'But there is nothing more than polite discourse.'

'No proposals?' William chides them with a grin. 'You know your mother half hopes I will return with you. She misses those summer days with you in Lambeth. But a wedding feast might finally tempt her over the water. Who knows?'

They both smile though whatever is understood between them is not shared with William. 'There is time. We shall see once Peace comes. At least it will make the journey easier.'

The other matter preying on William's mind is the state of their finances. The school survives on the substantial fees they extort from enlightened parents but that income is not guaranteed.

'We do have occasional trips to Paris but money is always tight .' Mary-Anne explains.

He promises to do what he can from London. There is a deal in the making he explains, which if he can carry it off...

'Not another trip to India?' Marie- Charlotte asks, the wine making her tone sharper than intended.

'No. I have learned my lesson. A little closer to home. Supplying Liverpool with water.'

So, buoyed up by the spirit of a new generation making their way, William sets off for Calais. His heart is now most resolute. He must make a fortune from the Water Company.

Chapter 31

On reaching London, William reassures Mary that all is well with their daughters. The cider vinegar has held all ills at bay. Though he keeps any mention of interested menfolk to a passing reference. 'They are in excellent company,' he says. 'Much valued by their pupils and their community. A credit to us, to you.'

Accustomed to his failure to understand the true nature of her concerns, Mary sets to with paper and ink. Another letter is despatched to inquire more deeply into the company her daughters keep.

William now returns to the coffee-fuelled dens by the Exchange. He lets it be known that he is raising even more capital to invest in the Liverpool Water Company. The price of his shares begins to rise in response. Such activity always brings unsavoury scavengers to the scene. Among these hyenas and most prominent is Hagglestone, the colleague of the absent American Mr Lydius.

One morning sitting at his customary table in Jonathans coffee-house, William lets his news sheet drop and discovers Hagglestone's grinning countenance immediately opposite him. 'You have business with me sir?'

Hagglestone leans forward as if they are already in cahoots together. 'The Liverpool Water... My master, our mutual friend, is minded to become more closely involved.'

'You speak for him?' William asks, weighing up the benefits of engaging further.

'I have that honour.'

William half smiles. The claim is entirely inappropriate for this oily devil. But he does carry the odour of lucre about him. 'In that case, pray tell your master that if he can assist me in raising money to invest I will be most willing to engage with him.'

Hagglestone persists. 'A loan perhaps, a paper loan?'

'That might suffice.'

The smooth-tongued trader reaches into an inner pocket and proffers a handful of bills. William looks askance at such a direct exchange. 'This is most irregular.'

'Take them if you will,' says Hagglestone. 'I am sure you will find them most helpful in your endeavours.'

William looks around at the huddles of traders filling the corridors of the Exchange. For all he knows they could all be carrying out far worse a folly than this. 'I must examine them and give you a receipt of trade. Where do you dwell?'

'In Margaret Street, below Cavendish Square. But you are the most trusted gentleman in London, Mr Ryland. My master is no fool and suffers none.' He waves a piece of paper he has retained. 'I have a list. I know what we have loaned. I do not think there will be any dispute but you may give me a receipt as soon as you are able. Good day to you sir.'

Somewhat stunned by this abrupt investment, William takes a quick glance through the bills. They are all drawn on the East India Company and vary from small amounts of a hundred pounds or so, to one or two in their thousands. They appear legitimate with many signatures of assignees. They have been discounted several times and are due for payment in a year's time. Folding them as tight as they allow, he slips them into his coat and walks out of the Exchange. He is keen to place them in his secure chest at home.

Distracted by these events he strays a few streets north of his usual path home and finds himself in Bloomsbury. The streets are full of white-stuccoed mansions. No doubt built by East India captains. He imagines meeting Mears of the Egmont stepping down from his carriage. Perhaps returning from his country house, newly built and decorated with the latest designs from the Adams workshop. The thought just spurs him on to multiply his own pile of paper guineas.

In July Mary takes her leave of him. It is the height of summer and to escape the heat, she will go to Lambeth to her brother's house and orchards. William insists he will stay in Knightsbridge. 'I have my history plate to complete.'

He adopts a strict discipline, combining early morning work on the plate with a regular constitutional at midday. When he is not visiting his bankers to exchange or discount more bills, he passes the afternoons in the Virginian with Gwynn. Nowadays the news is often of passings and departures.

'Ramsay is off this autumn to Italy. Says it's an art adventure with his son.' Gwynn's tone betrays a hint of jealousy. 'Since Margaret died he has little to hold him here.'

William recalls that day in Soho Square, when he first went to see Ramsay's portrait of the Prince of Wales. How he had admired the Scot's red chalk sketches of Rome, the portrait of Margaret, with her white rose. 'Ramsay is bold to travel so far. I heard he had broke his arm in a fall, just months back.'

Gwynn yawns. '*Tempus fugit* from us all, dear boy.'

When William returns to Knightsbridge that evening, he sees light flickering in his first floor windows. Has Mary returned early? It is not like her. Old Pinney would never leave a lit candle unattended. He opens the door and listens intently for a moment. After the riots no home feels entirely safe. At first there is nothing awry but as he makes his way upstairs he can hear the rumble of heavy breathing. The drawing room is ajar. And there through the gap, he can see Bailey, arms behind his head, lying flat out on the divan asleep. William coughs loudly.

'Whoa... Who's that?' His old friend lurches forward, eyes staring, as if not sure whether this is a dream.

William's laughter brings him quickly to his senses. 'So, did she finally tumble to your vices and throw you out? You could have asked I would have found you a bed...'

'Most amusing.'

'Forgive me.' William goes to the dresser and pulls out a bottle of brandy. 'Come let us find something to toast.'

'It is on your account I am here.' Bailey swings his feet to the floor and accepts a tot.

'Indeed, that is a relief. I thought I was become a refuge for unwanted husbands.' William raises his glass, prompting Bailey to explain his presence.

'I received a message that I could not forward to you.'

'Good news or bad?'

'In a way it is good...' Bailey pulls at his earlobe. '...if one considers life a circle, as I believe it is, with many endings and beginnings at play within...'

'Come, now, enough of your philosophy. The matter is..?'

'Your daughter...'

'They are sick? Tell me not. I did wonder if they might suffer an ague...'

'Constance.'

'Ah, Constance.' William's face drains of colour.

'She is come to London.'

'Oh, my.' William reaches behind for the table, to steady himself. 'I feel as if it is I who have just landed, after a rough crossing from Calais.'

'Sit yourself down, Master.'

'To London you say? She is hereabouts?'

'Yes. I received her message-'

'-Why you?' William shivers. It is chill indoors after the warmth of the July evening. 'It must be Le Bas' suggestion, perhaps he thought it more discreet. She is well?'

'They are both well.'

'Her husband is with her?'

'No. And there's the issue. He was stopped near Calais. His papers not being regular.'

'And yet she dared to come alone... but you said both were well?'

Bailey takes a sip of brandy. 'She is with child.'

'Oh my. I see... how far gone?'

'Perhaps three... four months...'

'And still she came alone?'

'She is sure her husband will follow.'

Bailey's reassurance is unconvincing. William has a head full of echos. 'You know the snake, the alchemist's snake, that eats it's own tail... and signifies Eternity. It goeth on for ever...'. He sees concern in Bailey's eyes. 'Forgive me, it is the brandy talking.'

'I took the liberty, Master...' Bailey is up now, pacing back and forth.

'Yes?'

'I took the liberty of finding her a place, with friends, near Leicester Fields.'

'You did well, as ever, dear Bailey. But what is to become of her?

'She says she is a 'graver and they are much in demand.'

'Well, well. What comes around eh? I will help of course, where I can.' William also rises to his feet and seizes his old friend firmly by the shoulder. 'All will be well. Liverpool will have its fresh water from the Bootle Springs and we will all dine out on silver ware. Will we not Bailey?'

'I am sure we will Master. Let me forage below for some food. We must settle this spirit and think this through in quiet and comfort.'

So, over some radishes and ham, they discuss the options. Whether it is the food or Bailey's calming presence, William's mood does shift. 'I have a thought,' he says. 'If Ramsay and son John are off to Italy, perhaps there will be rooms for renting. T'would be more discreet than on Woll and Gwynn's doorstep. What think you?'

The arrival of Constance also prompts William into a flurry of financial deals. At the end of July, he sets off for his bankers, Down and Pells, in Bartholomew Lane. He has with him several of the Bills lent to him by Hagglestone, on behalf of his master Lydius. There are no questions asked, the funds are made available. William is after all a most trustworthy customer. But his plan is to use only part for investing into Water shares, the rest he sets aside to provide for Constance.

William then heads to Soho Square, to Allan Ramsay's house. He is let into the painter's inner sanctum where their friendship began so many years before. Ramsay's injured arm, and his recent loss of Margaret, weigh heavily. The discussion is of family matters until, just before he is to depart, William finds himself revealing far more than he intended. It is his second confessional encounter in as many months.

His story of the affair with Gabrielle and the arrival of Constance brings tears to Ramsay's half shuttered eyes. The passion in William's voice reminds him of the days when he and Margaret eloped south from Edinburgh, driven to risk all by her parents' disapproval.

'I would do it again.'

'Ah, there you have it over me.' William says. 'I followed a different siren when I left Paris.'

'But you have made good surely? The King and Queen's Engraver, shareholder in the Wolfe engraving, print seller to the ....'

'Enough, dear fellow... I have a French daughter, will you give her a roof?'

'I will, as if she were my own. Constance may have the rooms here at the back. I may even find her work when I return. All my property is now in the safe hands of my son John. So, should anything befall me on our Southern journey you will have him to see you right. He is as discreet as a church mouse, have no fear.'

'Oh but you are far from the shadowlands yet.'

'The spirit yes, but the body, that is in decline and worsening by the hour, so, let us drink now before my other arm gives up the ghost.'

'Amen.'

And so it is settled. It is only right that he takes care of Constance. That does not trouble William. It is the double game he must play. Could he reveal all to Mary? How would it benefit her that she should know? A young French woman, with child... the daughter of an alliance he has never admitted... Perhaps once her husband is over here. Perhaps then.

At first William keeps his distance. Bailey is now the go-between. He sees Constance lodged in the back rooms off Soho Square. He makes sure she wants for nothing. Food, clothes, an introduction to a publisher looking for a graver. William receives regular reports and struggles to remain aloof. He has the notion that he would like to show his daughter, the city of his birth. But how to do this incognito?

With Mary still in Lambeth, he has many nights alone. So he explores the wardrobe his son left behind, when he went as Strutt's apprentice. He always sported a rainbow collection of coats and hose, in greens and reds and blues. A fine contrast to William's customary black. Combined with a full wig, which William also rarely wears, the disguise is complete. It is a risk but his ventures in the money markets have heightened his affection for such hazard.

So, in the long summer evenings he takes Constance on excursions. A stroll through St James' Park, a boat ride to Chelsea. He avoids the Strand and the Lambeth side of the Thames. He has no intention of crossing Mary's path.

These are gentle entertainments, she being with child, but there is much gaiety in all that they share. Constance has an artist's eye for detail...the white rat peeking out from the boatman's hat... the young girls at a shop window, giggling at a tussle between a tailor and his mannequin. Neither is oblivious to the shadows from the past that accompany them. He wonders often why she has come to London. To reclaim a father, to follow a journey her mother never made? He is never sure. Her bright confidence is sometimes punctured by tearful episodes. He assures her that Patrick will soon arrive. She hangs on every promise of a Peace with France. While William's response is to continue the masquerade and be generous to a fault.

At the end of August, when Mary returns to their house in High Row, Knightsbridge, she brings unwelcome news. 'The word is out that Boydell has just sold a cargo of prints in Bengal. They have the market with India.'

William feels it like a veteran's wound, a sharp burn in his hip, that holds him rigid as she continues. 'And we have still not cleared our guarantors. Not even James who is forever understanding. As for Linnell, we are forever cursed.'

'Are we still not paying them their hundred a year?' He asks, though both know he is well aware of the truth.

'No, not even.'

'Ah. I thought, with the Wolfe print doing so well...'

Mary rolls her eyes, and in a speech which he senses has been long in the preparation, she lays out the true nature of the shop's finances. There is value in the print and plate stock, but how will his bankers in Lombard Street view another failure?

'Trust me,' he says. 'There are other irons in the fire, my dear, which will deliver in good time.'

'And your creditors will not use them to brand you a liar and a thief ?'

'No, you must trust me, I am not sunk to such depths.'

The tears well in her tired eyes.

'Oh, Mary. It seems like all the world is crying today.'

William lurches forward to take her hand in his. 'Come!'

It is a clumsy move and she steps aside allowing him to fall across the cushions of the divan. 'Dance, William! Are you quite mad?'

'Why yes, Mary, yes I am. Though no more than the world at large. One has to be a trifle mad, to rise and smile away each passing day.

Shaking her head at his ramblings, she hauls him to his feet and as the sun slants through the leaded windows, William whispers Milton's lines into her ear: '*Come, and trip it as you go, On the light fantastic toe*'. Sensing her grip soften, he leads her into a rolling step, a little heavy footed, but with warmth and verve enough to restore their intimacy.

◆》· · ·◆· · ·《◆

Some six weeks later, William is at his desk. The candles are lit around him. He is preparing for a visit to Nightingales, Sir Charles Asgill's banking establishment on Lombard Street. There is a mound of paper before him that he must sort through before the morning. He intends to raise three thousand pounds. One of the bills catches his eye. It is for two hundred pounds drawn on the East India company and due for payment a year hence. William remembers buying it off another banker back in May. It prompts a smile when he finds that it was first remitted to Archie Campbell, dear Allan Ramsay's son in law. Since then it has passed through many hands and each has left a signature. Though none look too complex. How fragile is this paper money? For some, two hundred is a good yearly income, the line that separates a gentleman from the masses.... but to the mighty Company, it is a mere pittance... would they notice, if another drop was added to the ocean of bills that must swill in and out of their doors every day?

William reaches for his stack of paper. He looks for a sheet that is of a similar colour and thickness and sets to work. As the marks are made, he thinks of Le Bas, that honest man. What would he say now to these dishonest signatures? He might compliment the artistry but warn against the temptation of forgery. That is the line that William now confronts. Could he bring himself to dupe...Ha! The word is apt... a trusting employee, a trader like him in paper money? This is no longer the sale of prints, of money on the wall, this is fakery, fraudulent betrayal. His skin is goose-bumped and chill as he contemplates discovery and eternal shame.

So he takes up the paper, holds it to the candle as if he would burn it. But he cannot. It is as much a child to him as Abraham's infant Isaac. But too dangerous a child to have wandering the world. He pushes it back among his other bills.

The following morning he is careful to take only the bills that were loaned to him by Hagglestone and some of his own. He leaves behind the one he copied.

The guineas ease the passage into Autumn. But most of them flow back out to pay William's debts, to keep Constance in food and to fund the Water Company venture. He has had some news from his fellow-shareholder, Ignatius Valley, who is now in Bootle, negotiating with landowners. It is still not clear what rights John Jordan had to the precious springs beneath the town.

William's next encounter with the persistent Mr Hagglestone, comes early in November. The fellow is waiting outside the Exchange, stamping his feet against the early winter chill. An overlarge hat of beaver fur makes him look as if he has just come from the backwoods.

'A gift from my master, the Baron.' No doubt, thinks William. So, Lydius the dealer in Indian land is now a Baron is he? The title is entirely of his own making. The old rogue is still in Amsterdam and has no reason to be ennobled.

'I would be wary of wolves, you are a tempting morsel in that cap.' William declares, without considering the tenor of his words. Hagglestone tightens his eyes. Are they really yellow? William tries not to smile but there is something in this man which he cannot take for serious. This is another masquerade but play he must if he would have more of this paper money. So, he asks if the absentee Master, Mister Lydius, has more guineas to invest in the Liverpool venture. And it seems he has.

'Since he is a man of some sharp intellect,' Hagglestone expands upon his favourite theme. 'He knows an opportunity. In New England he was much admired by the natives. Most industrious protector of their lands.'

So William takes another sheaf of bills. He promises to convert them into fine old English pounds and invest them further into the Water Company.

On the fourth day of the month, William visits the bank of *Ransom, Hammersley and Morland* in Pall Mall. They are stout, be-whiskered gentlemen who know him well. He has discounted many bills for them and they have returned the favour. It is a relationship of transactions, calm, orderly and trusted. He has several bills to exchange for guineas, all called on the East India Company. They are due to expire in Spring, the following year.

During the winter months, William begins work on a new stipple engraving. He chooses Mortimer's *King John handing over Magna Carta to the barons*. A subject most appropriate to the time. The American colonists have shown once again there are limits to Royal authority. One may stand up to a King and hold one's ground. Mortimer who is no friend of monarchy, gives King John a proud, sardonic smile. As William traces out the early lines and begins to shape the story on his copper plate, he considers what it takes to reveal the signs of guilt, of wrong intent. For now, he loses no sleep over the dilemma. He still has high hopes in the Water company. There will be no second bankruptcy.

On Monday, 31st March, William is at home in High Row, when two messenger boys arrive in quick succession. The first is from Mary at the shop in the Strand. An official from Ransom and Hammersley has come calling for him. *An issue with East India Bills. Please attend offices in Lombard Street, at earliest convenience.*

The next is more urgent. It is from Gwynn. So concise it is almost in code. *Leave High Row Meet Golden Square. 2pm Bring clothes. Beware EIC.*

In a matter of minutes, his world is upside down. What issues can the Company have? Which bills? Is it the Hagglestone devil who has stung him? His mind churns through a host of panicked thoughts, as he pulls on his son's brown coat and breeches. If he is to be on the run, any disguise is useful. He throws more hose into his old satchel and adds his copper plate and a set of burins. A scribbled note for Mary tells her to keep safe. He loves her and will return.

He hails a carriage from two streets beyond High Row, his face covered with a kerchief, as if unwell. As they set off, he is cursing Hagglestone. Why did he trust that cockroach? Then just as they are turning up towards Piccadilly, a darker fear pierces through the panic. He shouts out that he has forgotten a package and must return. They hurry back and minutes later he is at his desk, pulling out bills, scattering them across the room. But he cannot find the one he seeks. The mockery of signatures, the copy of the two hundred pound bill. It is not there. Does the Company have it now? Is that their concern? Have his perfect lines confused them with a duplicate? For a moment, he is laughing but it is gallows humour. His neck is on the line.

That night he stays at Gwynn's off Leicester fields. Hagglestone is cast as the villain in the piece. William cannot tell all, even to his oldest friend. Bailey is summoned and briefed with a message for Mary, to reassure her. The next day William will not stay abed or hide indoors. He defies Gwynn's orders and flees out into the City, in his brown disguise, to search for Hagglestone. He goes first to Margaret Street, to the address the viper gave him, just by Cavendish Square. But if this was indeed his residence no one has heard of him. Next William tries all of the haunts about the Exchange, even calling out his name in desperation in the coffee-houses. There are some that recognise the

King's Engraver but today none seek to detain him. The hue and cry is not yet announced. But all that changes on the morrow.

All the Wednesday papers, from the Morning Chronicle to the Evening Post carry the Company's announcement. William Wynne Ryland is sought for fraudulent transactions. They describe the wanted man... *his common Countenance very grave, but whilst he speaks rather smiling, and shews his Teeth, and has great, great Affability in his Manner.* A reward is announced. William now has the sum of £300 pounds upon his head. The news runs riot through the traders, in Sweeting Alley, among the bankers along Lombard Street. William's fruitless search for Hagglestone is now too dangerous. Gwynn insists that he must be go into hiding.

It is already dark, with a bitter wind rising, when they set off east across the City, accompanied by a young man of Gwynn's acquaintance, named Lewis. William is now clad in a worsted nightcap, a green apron and an old brown coat. Gwynn warns him to keep his face away from the window, then laughs at the idea. 'If they recognise you in that garb, they deserve to have you hog-tied and delivered.'

'I am glad you find my predicament amusing. Tomorrow the whole of London will be after me. William Wynne Ryland the Forger.'

'True. So your name must change to match your garments. I shall call you Mr Jackson from now on.'

'So be it' William's mood is turning morose. 'And Mary, is she now Mrs Jackson?'

'Leave Mary to me. They will follow her if she tries to find you.'

'She will not betray me.'

'No, but she should stay in Lambeth, till this all calms down.'

William shrugs. 'That devil Hagglestone...They knew nothing of him in Margaret street. Every other trail is cold. Gone like a will-o-the-wisp. Damn him and damn the Company, a vindictive cancer on this world... I have been a fool...' He lapses into silence unable to confess the full extent of his own folly.

When they reach Whitechapel, Gwynn calls the carriage to a halt. They peer into the grim night. There is a slaughterhouse nearby. Oil lamps are flickering inside but all they can hear is the bellowing of oxen unsettled by the stench of death.

'Lewis here will see you to your lodgings, a mile further on, in Stepney. It is best that I am not there. You will be above a cobbler's, the Freemans. Stay close, do not wander. We have told them you are a gentleman down on your luck, looking for a quiet refuge for a month or two. Tell them no more.' With that Gwynn gives his friend a farewell embrace. With the aid of his long cane, he lurches out of the carriage on to the muddy road. He stands there waving as the wheels roll on eastwards.

The next week William spends in isolation, never leaving the rooms above the cobblers. They bring him food. He leaves the empty platters outside the door. But by the Friday, he is becoming restless. He is keen to walk a stretch. Surely there can be no harm in that. No-one will know him out here and the country air will do him good. But when he goes to put on his shoes, he remembers the left one is ripped at the heel. Well, no better place to be. So he asks the good woman, Mistress Freeman if they can see their way to ...

'Of course, Sir. Just leave it on the steps. My man will attend to it.'

In the early hours of the morning, he wakes as if by cannon shot. That shoe he has just left out, has his initials, Wm W R, sewn into the fixing strap. He eases himself out of bed, lights the oil lamp and lifts the latch on his door. Inching along the corridor, he peers down to the bottom of the stairs where he left the shoe the evening before. Damn. Gone already.

He can only pray that the Freeman family are not readers of the Morning Post or frequenters of the coffee house. Though news like this can travel, particularly with the promise of a fine reward. He returns to bed but does not sleep. Just before dawn, he hears the sound of a door open and slam and the click clack of wooden heels. Through the shutters he catches a glimpse of Mistress Freeman, setting off across the square at quite a pace. Perhaps she is off to the bakehouse. Who knows? His mind is in such torment these days. To calm himself, he takes up his burin and copper plate and loses himself among the rebel barons and King John.

Chapter 32

Tothill Bridewell - April 1783

All he had desired was a life of ease and plenty. And now here he lies in a fetid gaol, his throat slashed by his own hand, sliced and diced with his own burin. The wound burns with a ferocity that will not relent. Since that dreadful morning in Stepney, when the thief-takers burst in, his mind runs back and forth across one instant. Why did he not defend himself? Was it fear of harming his old friend, Bailey? Was it because all was lost? All hope, all honour, all expectation. William cannot bear to open his eyes. What purpose would it serve? To see the rusted bars across the slit window, the bucket of night soil, the walls etched with worn messages of despair. No, it were best he were blind to all of it.

While William suffers, it is Bailey who takes matters in hand. It is he who persuades Anne Hunter's husband, the surgeon, to attend. He is renowned for his nocturnal dissections. This grim reputation is matched by a brusque manner with his living patients.

'In other circumstances,' he remarks to the prone William,' I would have been proud of that slice myself. Indeed. Exposing, yet preserving the vital organs.'

William groans.

'No, of course this was not your intention, but such observations must be made, eh? Honour paid where honour due.'

Another groan.

'Now we must do what we can to remedy the matter. And we will. I may be best known for my work on cadavers but I am true to my Hippocratic oath. You may rest assured.'

William turns himself to the wall. He has cheated Death but he is not enjoying the reprieve.

Mary is another frequent visitor. She brings his favourite pickled herrings and fresh clothing. She tries to bolster his spirits with news of the girls in France. 'There is still hope of peace this Autumn, but it is a long time a-coming. Young Will is doing well in his apprenticeship.'

But in the gaps between her words of comfort William feels a weight of disbelief, of accusation even. He grips her hand and wonders if she knows more of his unspoken truth than she lets on. When she is gone, the guilt lies heavy on his chest. Then, one morning, she comes breathless to his side. 'The bailiffs have been at High Row. Your creditors have declared you bankrupt. Without waiting for a trial.'

They agree that it is best for her to take refuge with her brother, back among her beloved Lambeth orchards. Perhaps she will come less often. Bitter as it is, William cannot deny he finds relief in that.

His friends have not given up hope. Gwynn, Strutt, Burke, and even Woll, the King's History Engraver, as he likes to call himself, have formed a Committee of Support. They meet at the Virginia, where Benson, concerned as they, provides them with a room apart. It will become their meeting place over the coming weeks. For now,

Bailey is their conduit to William. They plead his case in private with officers of the East India Company and begin a campaign to publicise his innocence. A wider list of friends, who can vouch for his good character, is also compiled. It will be needed when and if this comes to court.

When May arrives, instead of buds and blossom, it brings William a bouquet of lawyers. He has to prepare for a first examination before Sir Sampson Wright, the Chief Magistrate. Unable to speak for himself, due to the wound in his throat, he agrees to a declaration. There is some confusion in the matter because the Company are citing multiple cases of false bills. He will state that an acquaintance, James Hagglestone, supplied him with these bills. He, William Wynne Ryland, has always been honest in his transactions.

On Monday, 5th May, he is accompanied by Gwynn and Bailey to Bow Street. The renowned Sir Sampson is a deal more genial than Gillray's cartoons suggest. Though his protrusion of a belly is entirely true to life. The deposition is made and duly recorded.

The examinant states he did publish to Mssr Down and Pells Bankers, in Bartholomew Lane on or about the 27th Day of July last, the Bill of Exchange now produced purporting to be the Bill of Exchange of the Governor and Council of Fort Marlboro for the Payment of four thousand and sixty-four pounds to Nathaniel Brown Esq or Order on the Directors of the Honourable United East India Company.

That the said Bill of Exchange nor any part thereof is not of this Examinant's handwriting. That this examinant did not know that the said bill or the Acceptance thereto were forged or counterfeit. That the said Bills of Exchange with the Acceptances was given to this Examinant in the Rotunda at the Bank or at the Bank Coffee house the day before he so published it to Mssrs Down and Pells, by James Hagglestone, who this examinant understood lived in Margaret Street, Cavendish Square. That this Examinant borrowed said Bills of Exchange of said Hagglestone in order to raise money and gave him two notes as a security for that sum...

The reader of the statement rambles on and the details soon wash over William. But when all is done Sir Sampson allows the deposition to stand without question. Gwynn is encouraged. 'Sampson is a man who will not be gainsaid by the Company. He is open to the possibility that the absent Mr Hagglestone is entirely to blame. Your reputation still stands.'

But the gravity of the matter demands a full trial. It is set for late July. Until then William must spend his days in Newgate Prison, now repaired after the riots three years earlier. He is grateful that both Ma and Pa have passed on. They will not suffer the indignity of a son in jail so close to home.

William finds consolation in his engraving. Through Gwynn's persuasive skills and a pocketful of coins he has the blessed benefit of oil lamps and candles to light his work. He has the Magna Carta plate and also a history painting by Angelica. It is one that first made her name some ten, twelve years back, when he was in the throes of his Indian misadventure. The story is an English tale of marriage and deceit. King Edgar sends his servant Athelwold to meet his intended bride. But Athelwood falls in love with her and marries her himself, convincing the King that she was not beautiful enough to be Queen. When Edgar discovers the truth, he kills Aetholwold and marries Elfrida.

Now William's burin marks out the radiant Elfrida, displaying her beauty to King Edgar. Was Angelica drawn to this tale by her own doomed marriage with the false Count de Horn. If so, who was her King Edgar? The thought lingers but it no longer serves any purpose. Angelica is long gone, now married and adding to her glorious reputation in Rome.

Instead, William considers his own legacy. At least he had the joy of seeing his own exhibition flourish before this disaster. His life's work laid up on Pollard's walls in Piccadilly for all to see. But now he has no illusions that his life is in the balance. Perhaps it will be an infection in his wounded throat or a judgement against him in July. In this world of paper money, there is no crime more bitterly condemned than forgery. So he must look to a future without him. These plates must be for his Mary, for the girls, young Will and, yes, for Constance...

It is Bailey who brings word that William has a grandson. 'Stephane. He was born last week. A Tuesday child.'

Full of grace, William thinks, but cannot say, his voice still mute from the wound. Instead he takes a stick of chalk and scribbles questions as to the health of Constance and the infant.

'They are both well. I found the doctor you recommended. He was discreet and all is fine. But he cautioned against a visit. The air here is pestilent.'

There are other reasons too, that are left unsaid between them. A young woman with new-born child in William's cell? T'would only feed the gossipmongers already hatching motives for his alleged crime. And what if word reached Mary?

So, that night the tears drip without cease on to his copper plate. Elfrida's features are awash. Her lines are tiny streams of salt water. They glisten by candlelight. But in the sadness, there is hope. For a future that William may not see but somehow he has created.

As the trial date approaches, the coffee-houses are full of rumour and suspicion.

'There is talk,' Gwynn reports, 'that the Company are not certain of their ground on all the bills. They may choose to train their guns on a single target. If they can prove guilt for one bill alone, that will be enough to persuade a jury.'

Some days later, Woll arrives with more worrying information. He has heard from his Maidstone family, that Company men have been making enquiries at Whatman's paper mill. But he has no details as to their intention.

With nothing more to go on, William's advocates stress that his defence must rest on three pillars. His previous good character, the absence of any motivation and the lack of opportunity to commit such a crime. Above all, they must present his financial position in a rosy hue. He must appear to have no desperate need for guineas.

It is decided that William is still too ill to plead his own case. A full statement of defence is assembled and pored over for many hours by the Committee of Support. One of the delicate issues is the attempt he made on his own life, to avoid capture.

'It flies a guilty flag and will not sit well with Judge Buller,' Gwynn warns. 'He is a brute, who believes he must lay down the law on what is manly. Only last year he declared that a husband has every right to beat his wife, provided he use a stick that is no thicker than his thumb.'

William shakes his head.

'Take heart.' says Gwynn. 'But we must beware the taint of a self-inflicted wound. The jury must not see it as guilt. Rather as a rash act, *in extremis*, after days of isolation and anxiety...'

The lawyers prepare the requisite words and present it to William the day before the trial. He acquiesces with a nod then continues on with his graving at the table beside them.

26th July, 1783

It is the noise which strikes William in the most brutal fashion. After so many weeks recovering in the silence of his cell, the hubbub of the King's Bench is overwhelming. He falters for a moment as he steps forward into this theatre of justice. Below him are the advocates, the black-gowned lawyers. Their table is covered with stacks of accounting papers, bills and statements. And behind these advocates is the wide curve of the Judges bench where Buller will soon take his seat beneath the Royal sceptre. All around is the chattering of onlookers, some kind, some hostile, all eager for the battle to begin. Scanning their faces, he sees many friends, Benson is there from the Virginia, Bailey of course, even John, his brother, who has been so distant since the strained days of his first bankruptcy.

But then, among the witnesses of the day, he sees a face that sets off the familiar sharp tightness in his back. It is James Whatman, the papermaker from Maidstone. So, Woll was right. But what can he have to say for the prosecution? Their eyes meet for a brief moment. William can read nothing into the exchange. He will have to wait. The months in prison have somewhat dulled his senses. If only the jury can be shown that he is an honest man, a gentleman of integrity.

The prosecution's case is laid before the court by a Mr Rous. He cuts a stout figure, waving his sheath of notes before him, but he is so forceful in his delivery that William finds it hard to conceive that he is talking about him - this villain who intended to defraud both the Honourable East India Company and the bankers to whom he offered a number of forged bills.

It is soon clear from Rous' declarations that there is one bill of exchange in particular that is their target. This is the bill for two hundred pounds, which was in William's possession between May and the nineteenth of September, in the year of our Lord 1782. It is the prosecution's contention that William then offered a falsified copy of this bill in November the same year to Mr Ransom's bank. The implication being that between May and September, William had the opportunity to fake this copy with all the signatures on it.

The accusation is not unexpected and William's lawyers are soon on their feet, challenging the details of the case, questioning the memory and reliability of the various witnesses from Company and bank. They lean heavily on William's reputation for fair dealing, in the bankers' game of discounting. He has played it for many years, without hint of misdeed or dishonesty. This sows confusion in the court. How could a man of such good standing be guilty? He is vouched for even by those who now claim to be his victims.

But then comes the moment when James Whatman, the paper maker is called upon by the Prosecution. William still cannot fathom what his contribution will be. He glances across at his friend Woll, who shrugs back. They are on unknown ground. Surely their old acquaintance from Maidstone has not come to wax on about the quality of his paper?

Prosecutor Rous presents Whatman with the two bills of exchange. The one which William passed on in September and the other in November.

'What are you by profession?' asks Rous.

'A paper maker.'

You have been a long time in that line of business.?

'Upwards of twenty years.'

Rous indicates the second bill of exchange, the alleged duplicate. 'From the knowledge you have of paper, and the making of it, can you tell us when that paper was made?'

Ahh! That is their game! William's concern is now at fever-pitch as Whatman pulls out a sheaf of papers from a portfolio beside him. He declares to the hushed court room that he is able to tell exactly when the paper was made. His method is ingenious. Each of the moulds he uses has unique though minuscule defects, which are passed on to the paper during its manufacture. If he can match these marks to the paper moulds, he can determine to the month the age of the paper. His conclusion is damning. He shows a sample sheet to the jury.

'On the 21st of January 1782, this sheet of paper was made at the mill, on that particular mould, it has a defect on it. The bill has the same defect. The sheet of paper on which the bill was written was made from that mould. And that paper was sent to London the 3rd of May, 1782'

The court erupts at this damning proof that the second bill must be a forgery. Its paper did not exist at the date it was allegedly first drawn in India, in October, 1780.

William's defence attempts to question Whatman's analysis. 'You have not two moulds alike?'

'I never saw one.' Whatman declares without hesitation. 'And on this particular occasion, I have taken uncommon pains, as you may suppose I would.'

The prosecution then reminds the jury of a further damning point. This paper was delivered to London, in May, 1782, just at the time that the original Bill was in the hands of the accused. There is a chorus of "Ah-ha", accompanied by knowing nods. All eyes are on William now. He feels them boring into him, as if they could ascertain his guilt in some physical fashion.

He remains steadfast. He listens as his advocates cast doubt on whether this bill before them is the same one that William submitted at Ransom's bank in November. Could it have become mistaken for another within the Company's arcane accounting systems? But the attempt does little more than confuse the jury. Their minds are still full of Whatman's paper proof.

Despite this, William remains confident that his statement of innocence will carry the day. But with his self-inflicted wound, he can still not utter a word. The Clerk of the Arraigns steps up to read it on his behalf. The court falls silent as his deep, sonorous voice fills the room. 'Poverty and knavery are the parents of forgery. Both my creditors and friends will bear the most ample testimony, that I am not connected with either.'

To show that he had no need to stoop to criminality, William's present status is billed as 'rich beyond temptation.' The paper value of his shares in the Liverpool Water Company is offered as proof of this. While his earlier bankruptcy is dismissed as a series of misfortunes.

The Clerk continues to read William's statement: 'There is no proof of my having knowingly uttered a forged bill. As the prosecutors have not proved it, you will not presume it. That the bill was in my possession, was my misfortune, which claims your pity not your vengeance.'

He explains his flight from justice as motivated only by fear, once he discovered that Hagglestone was nowhere to be found.

'When I had all the horrors of a prison in my view, in compliance with my own fears, in compliance with the tears, the entreaties and prayers of a beloved wife, I fled.'

William scans the jurors faces. They hang on every word. Surely they must see the truth in his exposition, as much as in his countenance. Does he have the face of a villain, the smile of a villain? He can no longer tell. They must decide his fate.

His statement ends with a heartfelt appeal.

'Into your hands I commit both my character and my life, you know the value of both, and will not blast the one, nor sacrifice the other, on vague presumptions and ill grounded suspicions.'

There is a flutter of fans along the crowded benches. The July heat is taking its toll but no-one will forego this spectacle. Next up are the witnesses of character: Benson, guardian of the Virginia coffee-house; Archie Paxton, William's long-patient Wine merchant, who has known him some fifteen years. Then bankers, brokers, solicitors, clerics, clerks and gentleman neighbours of Knightsbridge... Some twenty upstanding citizens, who state with confidence their belief and trust in him.

Some hours later, it comes to Judge Buller's summing up. He directs the Jury's attention to the principal questions that will determine William's innocence or guilt. *Is this second bill a forgery? If so, did William knowingly pass on a forged bill? However fair his character may have been, it cannot weigh against positive facts.*

William's advocates are aghast. There is no mention of the missing Hagglestone and his involvement in the exchange. There is no proof that William himself committed a forgery. Nor any certainty that he knew the bill was forged.

The jury withdraws.

The court clock ticks the minutes by. William sits impassive, resolute. His is an honest countenance, he tells himself. And rightly so. But the whisperers all around him dispute the call. Some guineas even pass from hand to hand between them. The answer when it comes, comes swift and clean.

After only thirty minutes deliberation, the jury foreman stands to face Judge Buller.

He declares William Wynne Ryland guilty of uttering the second bill knowing it to be forged.

The common penalty for such a crime is death by hanging.

That night the Committee of Support re-assemble in the Virginia. Gwynn is bent on an appeal for Royal clemency. They have a week before William returns to the King's bench for sentencing. 'If our King George was apt to pardon William's highwayman brother, surely his own Engraver deserves the nod.'

'It is the Queen who is the keeper of the Royal heart' says Woll. 'I hear she is ever fond of that engraving of her daughter,'

Strutt intervenes. 'We must proceed through official channels. The Lord Chancellor…'

'Ah, but he is aware of the bankrupt accounts.' Says Gwynn with a sigh. 'Since this Hagglestone affair, that loose-loined Linnell is pressing hard for all that he is owed, which colours all our claims of William's present fortunes.' Gwynn accepts a tot of brandy from their host, the long-faced Benson. 'I would that this spirit could erase the day. But I have tried before and its effect is momentary.'

Each man there resolves to do his utmost, to apply whatever influence he may have. Strutt assumes the role of Mary's comforter. He will prepare her for what is to come.

The following day, William hears the tap tap of Gwynn's cane on the flagstones outside his cell. He sets aside his burin and copper plate. There are matters to discuss. He has a scrap of paper ready, since he cannot utter anything above a whisper.

Gwynn holds nothing back. 'Time is short. A few weeks at most, if the pardon plea is not upheld.'

William pulls out the plates that he has just been working on. He scribbles a response.

Lost all faith in paper wealth. Loved ones' future lies in copper, as mine should have done. My old plates which Mary knows. These two works by Angelica and one of Mortimer's.

'Are they complete?'

Again the scratch of quill on paper. *The Edgar and the Vortigern, all but some details. The Magna Carta...*

'Signor Bartolozzi?'

William scowls and makes to shape a blasphemy. But then he stops. What choice does he have? He looks up at Gwynn and nods.

'An old rival, perhaps,' says Gwynn, 'but he has offered to assist and the plate is in a style he knows best.'

William shrugs. Who knows? If the King is not tractable, it is all out of his hands, anyway.

Bailey comes in the evening, after his day's work at Boydell's is over. 'The alderman's niece sends her regards and wishes you as much peace as you may be able to achieve. The great man will not associate himself with a criminal. He has his heart set on Lord Mayor. He will do nothing to sully his reputation.'

William tries to say the name that has been on his mind for days. The effort is worth the pain. 'Con..stance?'

'Ah. There we have happier news. Her man sends word that he is travelling to be with her and their child.'

William sits back against the dank wall and smiles. There is hope then.

'She will not come by, for fear of upsetting Mary.'

William nods.

'Mary will be here presently. She has asked to stay beside you a while.'

No doubt guineas have passed hands but that is not his concern. He attempts another whisper. 'For her sorrow... and my joy.'

Over the following days, William sits working in the light of the oil lamps which Mary tends. She has brought the ledgers from the Strand, so that she may make lists of those plates that are worth retaining. But much of the time she watches him or drifts off into an exhausted sleep.

In that stillness, he senses there is such deepening of dark sorrow. If only he had been content to stay within the confines of his art. Would it have been different? But that restless urgency, that impulsion to be out building castles, to stand a head taller than his Pa, to be more than he might have been. What could he have done with that?

In her waking moments, Mary talks much of Lambeth and Master Ravenet, of his bright studio, the orchards in blossom, the Tower and its winding steps. Each day William feels the regret drain out of him. And she gains strength, without bitterness, except on occasion when she recalls how his family scorned her at first. He watches her and sees the strength, the hope still growing.

Their daughters send messages of love but they are bound to their school in France.

He makes no mention of Constance.

When the news comes from the Court, it is Gwynn who delivers it. 'His Majesty does not consider that a man of your means should defraud the Company. He will not act on your behalf. In a land that lives by commerce, by paper credit, there is no darker crime than forgery.'

The Execution is set for the twentieth day in August.

The Newgate Ordinary, a pious, well-meaning man by the name of Villette visits each day. His attempts to introduce the Lord Almighty into William's future plans fall on stony ground. Though even now there are surprises in his human journey. On the morning of the nineteenth, a familiar voice echos through Newgate's corridors. William recognises the insistent tones of Annie Freeman, the cobbler's wife, who betrayed him to the Company. She demands entrance to his cell. She has a package, which she will not allow anyone else to inspect. She stands beside him with tears streaming down her thickly-rouged cheeks. He pulls open the elegant wrapping to reveal a pair of shoes, complete with shining silver buckles. Annie asks his forgiveness, which he grants without a murmur.

'We are now in Bath,' she says. 'My Richard 'as his shop. We are at ease and most grateful to the Company.'

In the evening, his family take their leave. William's son and Strutt visit to exchange last words of comfort, eliciting a mix of croaks and paper scratching. Mary holds her to him for a last tender moment. She will not witness the horror of the Tyburn tree. She will pray for him from Lambeth. Finally, Gwynn assures him he has made the necessary arrangements. 'You will be kept safe... Dr Hunter has assured us. No bodysnatchers. He has connections.'

William whispers. 'Let him keep his scalpel to himself.'

'Fear not... You will soon be with Ma and Pa, in Feltham's country peace.'

'Oh and Woll sends his dearest regards. He could not stomach a farewell, but he says he will mark it in his own fashion.'

That night after St Sepulchre's bell has tolled for the soon-to-be departed, there is a thunderous blast. A cannon shot. It comes from the direction of Ma and Pa's old house off Ludgate Hill. Among Newgate's sleepless inmates, only William guesses the origin. It is his old friend Woll, sending him on his way with a bucket of black powder.

The day dawns. He is alone as he dresses. Black hose, waistcoat and topcoat with white lace cuffs. The shoes with their fine silver buckles. He wonders who will have them by the end of the day.

Ordinary Villette comes to fetch him to the inner yard. Five fellow inmates are already gathered. They stand shivering as their shackles are hammered off them. It is a sight he might have engraved in former times. Or perhaps it is more in Hogarth's line. A sorry spectacle of broken men. Two Johns, a James and a Thomas all condemned for housebreaking or footpad robbery. And one John Edwards, who forged a sailor's will to cheat him out of prize money.

They will travel by cart. William has the gentleman's luxury of a carriage, which he must share with the Ordinary Villette and his prayer brook. Knowing the drunken antics of the crowd on Execution days he is grateful for this final indulgence. It is also a shelter from the elements. The air is heavy. Despite the hour he already has a sweat breaking out. Black-bulging clouds threaten to unleash themselves on this macabre ritual on London's streets. Though lightning and thunder would be a relief. A moment for Zeus to appear, not as a lascivious swan, but in his full force. Gabrielle would have applauded that.

The dismal convoy sets off and is soon surrounded by the street mob, swelling and surging along on either side. They must be in their thousands, all come to see how men die. As William's coach turns into Holborn, there are the blackened remains of Langdales gin factory, still in ruins after the anti-Popery riot. The fierce spirit is no longer on offer here, but the crowds are thick, forcing the carriage to slow down. He hears a shout from just below. It is Bailey. And there beside him is Constance. They are so close. Bailey is lifting a bundle up to him. A young babe. It is Constance's child. His grandchild. William reaches out to hold the dear infant against his face and chest. She smells of mother's milk. He feels the hand of the Ordinary on his shoulder. This is most irregular. But he is a man of compassion. He allows William one last embrace then helps him pass her gently down, this gift from God. They are not alone in blinking their tears away. William waves to Constance. Now is a time for smiles. Oh, to smile and smile and be an innocent fool.

Then on and on, along the Oxford Road, past the streets that have borne him so much grief and joy, the echoes of love and life, of dissipation and ambition. When at last the procession comes to a halt, he is at the centre of a grotesque spectacle. There are steep, sloping timber stands set up all around. Thousands have paid their guineas to see him hang. They cheer his arrival as if he and his fellow condemned are the season's favourite actors. He has heard they may be among the last to suffer this indignity. If so, he is determined to put on a mask of courage.

It is even darker now, over towards the Queen's palace. There is a flash across the sky above the park. Zeus is exacting vengeance on the Royal house for its lack of mercy. William sits quietly smiling as a heavy rain beats down. He feels for the others in the open carts. They huddle together in the deluge. Though he is struck that one or two have the mark of defiance about them. They scan the crowds, perhaps looking for family, friends, even a vain hope of escape.

Some minutes later, the rains stop, releasing a lighter, more uplifting air. But as William stretches his legs he feels that his hose is wet through. He glances at Villette and blames the rain. The Ordinary nods and gently says, 'I have seen worse.' Then he gives him the sign of the Cross and helps him down from the carriage.

The carts are brought to a halt beneath the Tyburn gallows. William steps on to the nearest one. His companions shuffle aside to make room for him. They each then bow their heads to receive the loops of rope and a rough hood to hide their eyes. Even within the fetid sheath, he can hear the crowd's intake of breath. As if they are all to enter the unknown together. Perhaps there are many out there he knows. Some he may have hurt. Some he may have ruined, in his pursuit of a life of ease and plenty. Maybe Hagglestone is there? Yellow-eyed and wolverine.

So is this atonement? Payment for those marks he made. However innocent.

The horses rattle their bridles, paw at the dirt. They are uneasy, knowing what they must do. The hangman barks his order. With a short jolt forward, the carts advance, leaving death dangling from the ropes behind them.

William's fall is sudden, sharp and clean. He drops into darkness and in darkness finds his rest. The masquerade is over.

Acknowledgements

With deepest thanks to all my family, friends, experts in their field and enthusiasts of all types, who have encouraged me along this creative, historical journey. They believed in the resonance of William's story and in me as an author. They know who they are. It has been a long road but worth every step. Thank you. All errors are the sole responsibility of the author.

Afterword

The King's Engraver is inspired by the life and adventures of William Wynne Ryland. It is based on intensive research into historical documents and contemporary accounts. It is a blend of this factual thread with an imagined fiction. The intention is to flesh out the gaps in the historical record, to bring to life the encounters, experiences and emotions which led William from his illustrious position to the ultimate sad end on the scaffold at Tyburn. In recounting this tale, the author has also brought to life many other historical characters, particularly from the world of art and engraving. All of them can be shown through research to have had a direct connection with William, while he was in France or England. Alongside these characters, there are also some, such as Gabrielle and her daughter, who are fictional. Though perhaps they have as much truth as any in the tale.

About the Author

Chris' debut historical novel emerges out of a lifetime of re-creating the past. First as a writer, producer, director of over 50 international TV documentaries and, more recently, in the creation of award-winning, immersive experiences in the UK and Europe.

Whatever the setting, he looks for personal stories, with emotional resonance, which will speak to the present.

If you loved this book

Please leave a review and check out my website www.thekingsengraver.com

Sign up for my newsletter for some behind-the-scenes updates on my next historical novel.

Printed in Great Britain
by Amazon

40492832R00216